The Princess and
the Slaymate

Other books in the Dobrenica series

THE PRINCESS AND THE SLAYMATE

Sherwood Smith

BOOK VIEW CAFE

Book View Café

THE PRINCESS AND THE SLAYMATE

ISBN: 978-1-63632-328-2

Production Team:
Cover designer and artist: Victoria Davies
Proofreader: Steven Popkes
Interior designter: Marissa Doyle

Book View Café
304 S. Jones Blvd, Suite #2906
Las Vegas NV 89107

www.bookviewcafe.com

ONE

RULI

My husband was about to marry again, because I'd been declared dead.

My death certificate was a finesse, but in the tiny country of Dobrenica, such declarations, made by either church, temple, or royal decree, had all the force of law. What else can they do when someone finds herself numbering among the undead?

My name is Aurelia von Mecklundburg, and I am a vampire.

The sun sinks late in the summers, twilight lingering over the mountains ringing the little country where I was born. Past childhood I'd never thought of it as home. Paris had been my heart's home until a vindictive, backstabbing family relation changed everything.

Once night had fallen, I walked up to the royal palace on the hill. Strange. Now that I was not imprisoned there by family duty, I could admire the Fischer von Erlach-style: refinement, you could say, with intent. Lit brilliantly by modern electricity.

I slipped past the Vigilzhi guards, made my way inside without unduly disturbing the servants, and sniffed the air for Alec's scent.

I don't mean the soap he uses, or the trace of cedarwood from the closet where his clothing is stored. I mean the scent of his blood. To me, now, the blood of a living being is as fresh a scent as that clean, soapy aroma that I used to like on a man.

The sound of his heartbeat reached me next, and I located him in the guest wing. When I opened the door, I discovered him seated in a chair beside the great carved bed that had once belonged to a famous queen, writing a letter with his fountain pen. He used as a lap desk a heavy silver-gilt tray flipped over.

My cousin Cerisette used to coo that he was as hot as he was rich, but I had always found black hair and blue eyes uninteresting. There were many in Dobrenica with that particular coloring, the blue eyes from the Swedish invaders, the silky black hair from long-ago plains-riding raiders. My tastes had been for the classical profile, the warm browns and thick curls of the Mediterranean.

But I was no longer bound to Alec by duty, nor he to me. After a brief glance from him to the still figure stretched out under the lightest of coverlets, I let him hear a single footfall.

He leaped up, eyes wide as he thrust himself between me and the woman on the bed, pen falling to the floor, tray held as a shield. "Ruli." He exhaled my name on a breath.

"Relax," I said, keeping my distance; the anti-vampire charm on his signet ring scraped at my nerves and buzzed in my ears. I could cross it, but it would be painful. The charm was simple enough, using captured sunlight, which is deadly to me. "I just came from Kim."

He cast a startled look at the still profile on the bed so very much like my own. Then he turned to me, brows knit. A vein beat in his temple. I consciously drew breath, partly so I could speak, but also to gain control over the little thrill of desire. Not for sex. More vital than that.

I said, "You told everyone she was sick? I did not expect to meet her in the Nasdrafus."

"The Nasdrafus," he repeated, the vein ticking faster as he squinted at me. I had learned since my transformation that that protective charm makes me appear as if I were seen through water.

"Object," I said, "of many of the stories we were bored by as kids. My brother, of course, always denied it existed, but it is there — think of it as an extra dimension, if you will. Or an alternate Earth. Or even as Purgatory, as some of our ancestors did. My point is, Kim in spirit form is wandering around there. She and...ah. Let us say that the situation appears to be complicated, but I thoroughly expect her to find her way back to her body sooner than later. Time being slippery. And while I don't owe *you* anything —"

He raised his fingers in the fencer's salute that used to irritate me. It was one of those things he shared with my brother

Karl-Anton. So superior they had been about their fencing and similar idiocy, as teens.

" — I do owe it to Kim, one of the few people in my family who respected me as a person, rather than regarding me as a piece on the royal chessboard." That much I had planned to say. It sounded less impressive out loud. I could just imagine my brother's commentary on how I still whined even past the grave.

"I apologize for my part in that," Alec said. And then, in a lower voice, "And I'm sorry about Marzio di Peretti."

Ah, Marzio, my soi-disant beloved.

From this side of death, I could see what everyone else had been so annoying about: that Marzio had lavished on me the flattery and attention that I had never had from my own family. He had given me the smiles, the affection, and the words that I craved so much that I was determined to believe them real.

"Marzio," I said, "was proof that you *can* buy love. I know you despised him, but at least you didn't murder him. Whereas my family? Uncle Jerzy did the deed, but I could have believed it of half of them."

Alec glanced at Kim's body, so still on the bed, the quilt barely rising and falling with her slow breaths. He stretched his hand over her forehead, slightly cupped in a brief, tender gesture I would have thought entirely uncharacteristic, then dropped his hand. "Shall we talk elsewhere? It feels wrong to chatter over her like this. When she cannot hear."

The raggedness had faded from his voice, and he had control of his heartbeat once again. He picked up pen and paper, set the tray aside, and we entered the hallway, at the other end of which were located the rooms where we had last seen one another, sharing what turned out to be a drugged drink.

A quick glance, and I knew he was remembering waking up on the snowy cliff where he had been thrown, the only living victim of an accident staged to make him out to be a murderer, whereas I? When next I opened my eyes, it was to look into the red-glowing eyes of a vampire.

"Tony never believed in magic or the Nasdrafus," Alec said. "But he always believed in the existence of the inimasang." He used the old-fashioned, Dobrenican term for vampire. "I thought I knew most secrets hidden by the Five Families, but your family's pact with them was..." He shook his head.

"Convenient?" I put in.

He gave me an almost-smile. "New. Kim said that your grandmother Rose is one?"

"I would have been drained dry and my body left to rot if she hadn't been."

He opened the door to the sitting room directly across from Kim's bedroom. "Kim told us that there was a conflict between *inimasang* — what do you call them? Armies? Groups?"

"Families," I said. "You'll appreciate the paradox."

He winced, whereas Anton would have laughed. But Anton had always been careless of others' feelings, and much as I had lumped my brother and Alec together when we were all teens, Alec never had. He paused in the act of turning on a lamp, and glanced over his shoulder. Sure enough. "Will the light disturb you?"

"Electricity is no threat," I said. "Sunlight is the problem."

He flicked on the light and sat down. I chose the armchair opposite him.

"I take it that the, ah, enemy vampires have been routed?"

"You need not worry about them," I said — though I was far less certain than I sounded.

"Rose von Mecklundburg is your leader?"

Our leader is far, far older than my grandmother, perhaps older than the kingdom. But even if I had wished to talk to Alec about Antonius Augustus, there was a compulsion on me that prevented it. Though I have been learning to master the abilities inherent in my new state, as well as guard against its dangers, I was not yet strong enough to resist such compulsion. "Rose watches over our house," I said, "in her way."

Alec's ironic smile (I had hated that, too) acknowledged how oblique my answer was. But he let it rest. "Thank you for telling me about Kim." He let his breath out slowly. "Beka found her collapsed in the street off Roskvit Square, and went to get Natalie and her doctor kit. They couldn't rouse her. At least it was they who found Kim, so no one else knows besides the Vigilzhi patrol who helped get her into a car and up here."

Beka had found her. I'd never liked Beka Ridotski while we were growing up, though she had done nothing to earn it. I finally figured out that she was a living reproach to my frivolity, and when I reflected on the fact that she didn't intend that, either, that she actually enjoyed studying and later teaching, I could pity her for crushing on duty-bound Alec — and then, more permanently, falling in love with my brother, wild as he is. Talk about attraction of opposites in every possible way.

Of course Beka would be the one to find Kim, just as she would find a way to get her safe. "And the Vigilzhi are under your command," I said. "You can thus order the truth hidden in favor of a public lie."

Alec lifted a shoulder. "Beka insisted that there was some kind of magical glamor over Kim. We didn't know if she might be the victim of some vile attack aimed at me, so it's been mostly a waiting game."

I thought over the long, tangled story Kim had told me. "I think it's best to leave explanations to her, but I can say this: she *is* being watched over, and by others with whom I have no influence. Kim's first thought was getting back to you. But she has something to do first."

"Thank you." He looked away from me, and down at his half-finished letter. "But what you have told me doesn't alter the lie I was in the midst of writing."

"Lie?" I asked, my tone implying, *Another?*

He turned his head, gazing at a second-rate eighteenth-century painting of a pair of Dsaret princesses dressed up as shepherdesses — as if shepherdesses had ever worn their blond hair high-piled with curls in rouleaus, and short skirts polonaised under brocaded bodices and frilly ribboned blouses. I don't think he noticed those unlikely rosy cheeks or the tiny feet in those pointed, red-heeled shoes; I wondered if his mind had homed back to Kim, lying so still on that bed, last of the once-numerous Dsaret family.

He said, "Kim had agreed to begin her official duties early. I was in the middle of concocting a tale to postpone her visit when you appeared."

He laid the fountain pen on the letter, his expression shuttered in the way I had hated while we were all growing up. His control had appeared innate — easy — making it easy to assume he had no messy emotions like mine. But I'd seen the cost of that control during our brief state marriage, measured by the amount of fine whisky poured through decorative and discreet decanters kept in every room.

He had gone silent, and although I didn't hear the surface of his thoughts, as some of the older, more powerful vampires could, I surmised he was remembering how much I had loathed politics, and how I had refused to do any more than the minimum required of a dutiful princess. The only duty events I had attended had been social, involving ancient porcelain, gold tableware, and wardrobe by Hermes and Balenciaga.

"Not a soiree?" I asked.

"A tour," he said. "Mines."

"Mines? Kim was really going to tour *mines?*"

"Problems up there. I think her mysterious illness will become a case of influenza—"

I had to laugh. He looked startled, probably because he saw my teeth. "You suspect my brother as the cause of those problems."

He did not deny it.

"Oh, well, then," I said. "You owe me the pleasure of at least telling me what it is."

"The general problem is the secret mines." Alec opened his hands. "This is aside from the, ah, ongoing discussion between your family and the government about taxes and how they are allocated. But that's a centuries-old problem. This wrinkle became current, recently."

"Go on," I said, aware of the habitual tug to light a cigarette. I can still smoke, I discovered, but in the physical world it is a laborious chore affording no pleasure, and a danger of fire unless one has recently fed. In the Nasdrafus, the act evokes remembered pleasure.

"There is at least one unregulated mine up there somewhere between Mt. Dsaretsenberg and Mt. Dhiavilyi apparently reopened. The evidence is partly an increase in the crimes subsidiary to smuggling and theft, and partly to a disturbing number of fresh graves, as if from a mine collapse whose victims were dug out too late."

"And you think my brother's behind it." I said, enjoying his muted surprise at the fact that I was listening.

"He does tend to take a laissez-faire attitude toward laws, but there is no excuse for perpetuating safety measures that were questionable in the sixteen hundreds. You know that if I make an official tour, I'll only see what they want me to see. All will be on their best behavior."

He was stating the obvious. I waited.

"But Kim was popular on her own account before she and I announced our plans to marry. The people like her. Though an official tour is still likely to shuffle her from one scrupulously clean and polished site to another, I thought it possible that ordinary miners might talk to her. A sympathetic question here or there about mine collapses, anything she could do for the families of the survivors, and—" He shrugged.

"And you sic Dmitros in his Jazd Komandant uniform on

the mine owners, and shepherd the rest within the protection of the law. I see. But why go to that trouble? I would be delighted to confront my brother. It is about time he got to know the new me."

TWO

RULI

I expected to resolve Alec's question speedily without his having to trouble his conscience over hiding Kim's helpless state, her body lying in a kind of coma while her mind wandered the Nasdrafus. Helping Alec made me feel virtuous, but far more enjoyable was the prospect of jolting my brother's arrogant complacence.

Karl-Anton is technically my half-brother, but as his wild father, the first duke, had died before Anton — *Tony* — was even born, Tony had grown regarding my father as his. Fa had done his best by us both, in his vague, kindly, ineffectual way. He probably would have been happiest as a monk.

My mother had utterly refused to use the name Tony preferred. No duke would be called Tony — so she insisted, with an elegant moue. It was a name for shoe shiners and lorry drivers. *Anton*, especially spoken with a Parisian accent, was suitable, so Maman said, and I had grown up in her shadow. Including preferring French over English, the language of the social elite in her circles.

Ever since she used my life as her gambling counter in her attempted coup, I've been trying to shed the worst of her affectations.

Tony has always been taller and stronger, not just in comparison to me, but to most of the cousins. Phaedra and Honoré had also inherited the family's fast reflexes, yet the only one who consistently stood up to Tony had been Alec, and all the time we were growing up, he'd exhibited the black eyes, scrapes, and bruises to prove it. Though as time went on and he gained his height and strength, he gave as well as he got.

I still had access to the family's houses, though so far, I had spared my family the onus of my presence.

I left the palace, and—avoiding the poisonous scent of hawthorn and the angry-wasp nerve-scraping buzz of charms—crossed town to the hill where the grand houses lay, each a little citadel within its garden.

Von Mecklundburg House was lit, which meant the family was in residence. I eased my way in through the back door, past the kitchens where the new cook, Kim's mother, ruled by day. Most of the servants were new, and believed me safely buried in the family vault in the cathedral.

No one saw me. I have been learning to draw shadows around me, and people's own defensive crystal (or diamond) charms, which discourage my kind from entering their personal space, also make it more difficult for them to see me. The single servant aware of me was upstairs in my mother's suite. I recognized her familiar heartbeat.

She alone knows that I regularly raid my old room for clothes. I leave wrinkled, dusty things behind, as I always had, and they appear back in the wardrobe clean and ready to wear. Her aunt had been bitten, and serves my grandmother now; that was their family secret, as ours is Grandmother Rose. And now me.

I paused on the landing, listening to the heartbeats and sifting the blood-fragrances to determine who was in the dining room. As I neared, I heard the clink of silver on china, and the ring of crystal wine glasses.

The entire family had gathered, my cousins chattering away. While I would have loved to talk to Percy again, I had no wish to encounter Cerisette. And it must be admitted I was afraid to distress Percy further, though he had been kind. But I had heard his heart's frantic beat. As for Cerisette? She would probably be jealous at my being thinner and more pale than I had been in life, even if I had to die to achieve it. Les priorités!

The sudden alteration of voices and the scrape of chairs indicated the meal had finished early. They no doubt had a concert or party to attend.

Tony emerged, talking to Percy about the Eyrie. I drew back into the shadows, thoroughly cloaking myself, but even so, Tony gave a quick look around. Either I was not yet as adept as I ought to be, or it was old habit on his part. He trusted the world as little as it trusted him.

They parted at the next landing, Percy to the guest wing where he had a permanent room, and Tony to the ducal suite. I shadowed him, slipping in behind as he headed for his dressing room.

He must have sensed my presence, for he whirled, wrist cocked, and hurled a knife.

I dislike having to shift speed. It still takes tremendous effort, which then contributes to my needing to feed the sooner, but I felt a demonstration on this our first meeting might be more effective than merely stepping aside so that the dagger would hit the door.

Ambient noise slowed to a distant rumble, and tiny dust motes froze in the air, which itself wavered in slow currents as if underwater. I brought my hand up slowly, for momentum can be lethally deceptive. The knife slid at a glacial pace through the air, the air current whirling in a wake after it. Gently I closed my fingers on the hilt, matching my movement to the speed of the knife, and shifted back.

What he saw was me plucking the knife out of the air.

His jaw sagged. The reaction lasted less than a heartbeat, and I tried not to spoil the effect by laughing.

"Ruli," he said on a speculative note, his black eyes narrowed as if to bring me into focus. Effect of the charm in his diamond earring, of course.

"Tony."

My amusement sharpened when I noted the same vein ticking in his forehead that I'd observed in Alec, his adrenaline sparking.

Delicious.

"You are here because…"

"I want to know," I said, "which of the untaxed family mines you let collapse on hapless miners."

"What?" There was nothing false or studied in his surprise. "What are you talking about?"

"Collapsed. Mine. The words are fairly simple, and I don't think these fangs of mine garbled them. I've been very careful about that."

He crossed his arms and leaned against the wall. Probably near another weapon. "What *I* want to know is if you've been helping those damned bloodsuckers we had to fight off last winter. Despite the pact."

"No!" I gazed at him in surprise. "Didn't you ask Beka about that? The Vrajhus people know who did what. Probably more than I know."

He flushed—a rarity. "I…can't ask her," he finished abruptly. "She won't talk to me. Not until after Kim Murray marries her Prince Charming."

I wondered what he'd done to piss Beka off that badly. Or if she was pulled in far too many directions, between her regular commitments to family and temple, her Vrajhus studies, and Tony. The last one being the most volatile.

"She's probably working long hours with the Vrajhus people to find a way to break Kim's…" How to explain? He didn't care about Vrajhus matters. Had denied that they even existed. "Here's what you need to know. Uncle Jerzy lied about everything."

"That's news?" He laughed. "Or are you going to explain which specific lies?"

"His mother also lied. But here's the crux. She wants— wanted—she's dead now—to open the Esplumoir gate between our world and that of the unseen for some really shady creatures, and no, I don't understand anything about that yet. The point is, she managed to pull a lot of the worst vampires, and vampire wannabees, here through one of the portals in her plot to take over this country and make herself queen. You and Kim closed that portal. Those vampires you make the pact with had nothing to do with her plotting. One of them even stood by and watched her get staked."

That was a memory I'd just as soon not have.

I finished, "She's gone. Not all her followers are. But I'm not one of them. Now. The mines."

He laughed, then held out his hand for the knife. I dropped it onto his palm; his brief proximity buzzed like angry bees in my ears, my skin prickling as if burned.

I stepped back at the same time he did. He said reflectively, "I don't think I have ever heard you mention the family mines. A lot more has changed than those." A flick of the knifepoint up at his own canines.

"Perhaps. You claim not to have heard about any mine collapses, then?"

"Ah. That is a different question." He laid the knife back in its place behind a marble bust of an ancestor. That childhood habit still obtained: he had weapons cached all over the house. The servants learned to clean around them. "I've heard rumors.

Nothing definite. You know, or should have known, or will discover, that the mountain clans are very jealous of their secrets."

Secrets that included relatives like me. I nodded.

"As I say, I've heard rumors, but I assure you, nothing on our mountain. What little I've heard is mostly about old mines in the valley beyond what the mountain people defend rather enthusiastically as our border. Third-hand rumor insists that enterprising bravos have reopened some of those."

"I thought abandoned mines were abandoned because the minerals had been tapped out. Or they were too dangerous to continue with."

"Yes, but modern tools can detect veins that our ancestors couldn't." His indifference was to be expected. He'd regard outlaw mining as Alec's and the Vigilzhi's problem.

"But?"

"But this week there was another rumor that these same bravos are not Dobreni."

"Russian?"

He shrugged, his pale blond hair the color of my own drifting across his brow, not quite hiding a sheen of sweat. "Likely Russian," he said. "They aren't ours. But they want what we've got."

"Of course you haven't told Alec."

Another shrug. If they were Russians trying to make inroads, Tony was far more likely to raise his followers on Devil's Mountain, who would love any excuse to grab rifles and swords and ride thundering down to the attack the age-old enemy. Due process be hanged.

I turned to leave.

"Are you going to tell me why you ask? And incidentally, tell me—"

I shut the door on his question.

"Ruli?" He opened the door again, but I pulled the shadows around me as I ran down the steps. The internal buzz of angry bees eased the farther I got from the charms in the crystal chandelier hanging at the top of the stairwell.

Tony laughed, mocking us both. He found me interesting for the first time in either of our lives, though he had always loathed vampires.

So had I.

THREE

RULI

Until I staked Uncle Jerzy, I was unaware of how angry I was.

The English novelist Anthony Powell observed in *A Question of Upbringing*, "…at that age I was not yet old enough to be aware of the immense rage that can be secreted in the human heart by cumulative minor irritation." In my case, a lifetime of enduring disinterested belittling. At first I was terrified at how very much I enjoyed watching his horrible death. My head reasoned that it was just, he having killed a number of relatives as well as other people, but my heart knew a deep, angry joy when my hand struck. And struck again, before the wood began sprouting through his body.

When you are physically weak, you dare not express anger. If it cannot escape, it turns inward; until I struck that first time, I had not truly understood that I was no longer physically weak.

Thence my introduction to irony. He, wary and distrustful, had not given me a second thought, even though he knew I was a vampire — even though I had just finished turning him, under Rose's direction.

Well, his mistake.

When I reached the palace, I found Alec in his office, having been replaced in Kim's bedside vigil by Kim's doctor friend Natalie. He was in the midst of dealing with a stack of reports, the remains of a hasty meal lying forgotten on a golden tray. He looked up.

I said, "I would like to take Kim's place on that official tour." And watched for his incredulity.

I got it. The year before, Kim had posed as me, not only abroad, but in Dobrenica. My family had not believed her guise for a second, of course, but the people had, and for the first time in my life I became a heroine, through no efforts of my own. Kim, in short, had been a better Aurelia von Mecklundburg than I ever had.

But would anyone think I could masquerade as Kim?

Alec must have seen my thoughts in my face, for he said quickly, "Ruli, this will be a daytime tour, of course. Isn't sunlight dangerous to you?"

I suspect that his first reaction had not been concern for my danger, but I gave him credit for the effort. Tony would not have bothered; danger, to him, was part of the fun, if not the whole point of any endeavor.

Cousin Cerisette would have rolled her eyes in disbelief that I would even try.

"I can get there before dawn," I said. "No one will see me until I want to be seen. Get someone trusted to drive up there in one of the cars with tinted windows, and pretend I'm in there."

Alec pawed through the stacks of papers and reports. "Ah." He picked up his half-finished letter, then turned my way. "You're certain?"

"You thought Kim could masquerade as me to the family and the city I grew up in, but you don't think I can masquerade as her to a group of miners?"

"I beg pardon," he said, as I heard a heartbeat approaching from down the hall. "That wasn't my thought at all. I'm trying to get used to your change. Not just these." He tapped his teeth. "But your motivation."

A knock at the door. He left the implied question, and turned off the overhead light, leaving only the lamp on the desk still lit. I withdrew into the shadows as he called, "Enter."

A young page came in with a new sheaf of papers. "His majesty wishes to know if you are attending the concert."

"Tell his majesty that I will meet him there. And could you find out if Captain Danilov has a moment?"

The door shut, and Alec let out his breath. "It seems Milo expects me to put in an appearance at this concert. One of us has to be seen." He gave another of those tight-lipped glances in the direction of Kim's chamber, then said, "Ruli, do you mind waiting here? I have to get into evening dress. If Phaedra is free, I'll send her to you."

A surprising idea occurred. "Phaedra is 'Captain Danilov'?"

Alec paused with his hand on the door latch. "She can explain."

There were only two Danilovs left, my cousins Morvil and Phaedra. She had always wanted to join, but until now the Vigilzhi had been limited to men, even though she was very nearly as fast as my brother in fencing, she was a better shot, and about equal in breakneck riding. They had all competed against each other to surpass the Vigilzhi physical standards by the time they reached sixteen.

A very short time later, there she was, tall and slender, muscled like a lynx. She was so stylish that she even made the stodgy Vigilzhi blue wool uniform look good. Though of course it was also tailored to a fare-thee-well, the brass buttons real gold, matching her hair.

"Ruli," she said, her voice still incongruously high for so tall a person. I barely came to her nose, and I am not short. "I'm glad to see you, but I feel I should say, if you bite, I fight."

"I won't bite you," I said.

"Good." She came in, stopped at a prudent distance, and shut the door. "Alec said Kim's...not here?" She flicked a hand to her forehead then outward.

I began to explain about the Nasdrafus, but she chopped her hand down. "I don't understand it. I don't want to understand it. Give me something that I can fight, otherwise just tell me she'll be back to normal."

"She will, but I don't know when. Soon, I hope. When did this happen?" I pointed to the uniform.

"It began when Kim insisted on a woman being part of her security team." She lifted a shoulder in a shrug. "The 'captain' is a courtesy title, due to my birth. I am not part of the chain of command. Yet. The older generation has their knickers in a twist. At best, they see me as an adjunct. But I hope to get past that someday."

"How does Kilber fit in?"

"They booted Kilber upstairs."

"Really? Why don't they just retire him? He has to be in his mid-eighties." Though we'd always thought him made of iron.

"Kilber? Retire? He heads Milo's security detail again. As when they were young. But since Milo seldom goes anywhere anymore, Kilber can take it easy while still being on the job."

We regarded each other. Out of all the cousins and near-cousins, Phaedra had been my favorite among the girls. She, like me, had had difficulty with reading until we were sent to boarding school in France, and our dyslexia was recognized for what it was.

For me, the solution turned out to be easy — a modified screen, and for reading the printed page in Dobrenica, where computers seldom functioned, green-tinted spectacles — but it had not been so simple for Phaedra. To get through school she developed a ferocious memory, as accurate as her rifle shooting. But the damage had been done. We both had grown up believing ourselves what the more predatory of the other cousins had called us: stupid.

Phaedra dropped into Alec's chair. "Tony won't tell me anything, now that I'm connected to the Vigilzhi. Alec says you got something out of him."

I told her the little that Tony had told me.

She nodded slowly. "There are vague rumors, but you know how clannish the mountain people are. I wouldn't have known anything, except a great-uncle of mine, not on the Danilov side, slipped me the word that Niklos has been nosing around in the valley."

"Everyone knows Niklos is Tony's drota'vos," I said. (The word is untranslatable, it's been used on Devil's Mountain for so long, though "drot" is maybe related to the German "Ritt" as in riding, or Rittmeister. But think of it somewhere between aide-de-camp in French and "commander of the guard" in English, partaking of both.)

"Exactly. The fact that he had to go scouting means the Devil's Mountain people are being shut out, and they have connections all over those valleys. It's got to be the Russians. Or some Russians," she amended quickly, as "the Russians" are anything but a monolith. "Whoever it is seems to be operating on the assumption that possession is nine tenths of the law. But we have to catch 'em at it."

"Would an official tour be the least use?" I asked.

"Maybe. Maybe not. Dmitros has people up there checking. And Tony's got Niklos, as I said. But you know how they can close ranks in those isolated valleys."

"I know, I know. The only time they'll sink ancient feuds and unite is when strangers nose about. But I'm curious why they haven't done that now, especially after a mine collapse?"

"As are we. Alec is right in that some valley miner might be more likely to talk to Kim than to anyone, if they won't talk as a group. Someone who might be seeking justice for some relative buried in that collapse, in spite of the fact that they have been probably ignoring the laws of the past seventy years."

"Which have changed roughly once a decade since World War II," I said.

Phaedra's lip curled. "My point."

I said, "What if I try my own masquerade. Will you help me?"

She flexed her long, slender fingers, then laced them and cracked her knuckles, a trick she'd learned from our extended family's studious recluse, Cousin Honoré. "Why, I'd like nothing better," she said.

Once I stopped swapping clothes with Cerisette and Phaedra when we were girls, I'd never looked inside someone else's wardrobe.

It is odd, this going through another's things. Here is all the evidence that makes them who they are — the outer person — yet there was a Kim-shaped hole in the center space.

Phaedra cleared all the servants away from what would soon be the newlyweds' suite there in the royal palace, so that we could examine the clothes. Kim favored California styles and scents, though she had demonstrated her usual enthusiasm in adopting Dobreni fashions. She'd even adopted the same dressmaker I'd once used, resulting in some clothes I would not be embarrassed to be seen in.

But when I selected a couple of outfits, frowning over the fact that muscular Kim is a size larger than I — I loathe ill-fitting clothes — Phaedra said, "No."

"What?"

She stood against the back wall, arms crossed. I could smell her adrenaline spike: a little fear, mostly excitement. Her heart rate had elevated. She thought I might attack if she crossed me, and she was ready for me, an attitude she shared with Tony. This was not the first time I reflected on how she ought to have been born his sister, and I Danilov's. Of all the cousins, Danilov was easily the most stylish.

Phaedra nicked her chin toward the outfits. "Those are what *you* might wear."

"Yes," I began.

"Kim picked them, but she's scarcely begun wearing our styles. Everyone still expects her to look like a foreigner. You want to go out there dressed like the foreigner they expect, so that no one looks at you and thinks Ruli."

"You're right." I chose one of Kim's summery California cotton print dresses and matching sandals, and fingered my hair up into a coronet. "Well?"

Phaedra tipped her hand back and forth. "Better." But she didn't look convinced as we went off to see Alec.

As soon as he saw me, I heard his heartbeat quicken, and smelled the shock of pain that infused his blood.

Oh, delicious.

I had taken care to feed well before facing any of them, so the hunger was easily resisted. But again I was surprised at its intensity, how emotions act upon the blood the way spices enhance food.

His expression shuttered in the way he had learnt to master when very small, and again it struck me what a burden it must have been, growing up in old Milo's shadow. Then he said, "Ruli, the same reasons your cousins were not fooled when Kim showed up as you, work the other way. You're moving like you, not like Kim."

Phaedra, standing in the background, gave a grunt. "That's what's wrong. I thought it was the bloodsucker thing."

"Please walk around the room," Alec asked, at his most inscrutably polite.

I wondered what I looked like to them—having fed recently, I ought to be healthily pink, and even closer to human temperature to touch—but then Alec narrowed his eyes and said, "Looser arms."

Phaedra gave a crack of laughter. "Yes. Californians use so much space. She grins a lot—no!" Phaedra flinched. "*Don't* smile."

"Please don't," Alec echoed on an exhaled breath. "Longer steps, shoulders back. She walks on the balls of her feet, like a dancer."

"Like a fencer." Phaedra cracked her knuckles.

Together they critiqued my walk, and I obliged them, until at last they pronounced themselves satisfied.

Alec said, "If Kim has not woken up by day after tomorrow, how do you want to handle this? You cannot risk sunlight getting in and out of the car, I gather."

"No. I will meet you at the designated place, if you can get a car there, and park it in a cave or somewhere out of the sun, without raising suspicion."

"We can use the excuse of the afternoon thundershowers to demand garages or shelter," Phaedra said. "We'll send one of the old cars with the darkened windows, so no one will see that it is empty. And I know whom to ask for from the Vigilzhi—either Honoré's Hirschmann cousin or one of the Trasyemova twins. They will never talk."

Alec turned from her to me. "I can't thank either of you enough."

Phaedra gave him Tony's grin. Not the arrogant one, the one anticipating action.

I said, "I'm doing it for Kim."

His brows lifted, and I saw his shift in attitude. Though I had spoken the truth, I could see—smell, really—the pressure of obligation fade from him.

A chime rang in the distance, and Alec's head came up. "The concert," he said. "I still have to dress."

He excused himself and opened the door to leave. I turned to ask Phaedra for a map of the mines to be toured, but I heard a couple of cadets in the hall saluting Alec, then approaching the door.

I stepped back into the corner, drawing the shadows around me. Phaedra blinked, her attention drawn to the two young men who came through the door, each carrying messages. Both wore charms that jangled at my senses.

I had something else to do. I could catch her later, when she was alone.

FOUR

RULI

When Grandmother Rose first took me through the city of Riev as a vampire, she said, "Some of us choose never to go away and never return, or in my situation, rarely, but of course you must do as you think best. Just do not lose sight of the fact that you are no longer who you were, in their eyes." She waved her cigarette holder at the peacefully slumbering city below.

"You mean I am now a predator."

She smiled, looking young and sweet and a little fey in her fragile Jeanne Lanvin gown, still her favorite. "*All* human beings are predators, my dear. It's a matter of degree."

Sometimes I thought about those degrees as I learned to navigate the city without notice. Aside from the issues of killing other creatures and dressing their flesh into civilized-looking slices and squares for our plates, there are the kinds of predation that do not involve rending flesh from bone. My mother was a predator, one who hunted and consumed power. She married twice, both times for rank and wealth — after she failed to seduce Milo into making her a queen. She only respected other powers, even when she made war on them, using her looks, her charm, and the rest of us as her weapons. But she didn't kill. Though I don't think she would have thought twice if she'd got others to do it for her.

My father, in contrast, had been a gentle, melancholy soul. He'd designed gardens, because they were peaceful and beautiful, and raised horses, because they were peaceful and beautiful. Also, plants and horses did not lie.

He and I got along comfortably because we largely co-existed in silence when I visited him. Tony had ignored me when it became clear at a young age that I had more interest in clothes than sports. And though Alec had not wanted to marry me anymore than I him, he'd given me the freedom of our childhood relationship during the marriage's short duration, scrupulously leaving it up to me to choose when we were going to settle the matter of an heir, though I was well aware of his feelings. In short, the men in my early life had ranged from disinterestedly benign to indifferent to kind.

So I had no idea why I began to prowl the streets, listening for women's pain.

The overwhelming majority were content in their lives, except for these three I encountered by chance. And returned to again and again, resolving that if their men threatened their lives, I would act first.

Sareska, living over a spice shop down on Prinz Karl-Rafael Street, was talking fast and nervous, tucking all kinds of little 'dear's and 'sweetling's into her sentences as she fixed a late supper. I could smell her fear all the way from the street, but her dialogue mixed in a sickening mélange of anxious love. She had married a drunken brute; the only reason why I didn't take him down, with pleasure, was because she adored him.

He wasn't actually hurting her right then, so I moved to the next, to discover that Lisi and her sarcastic, angry husband were out.

When I stopped outside Gretl's home down near where the open market sets up, I heard low, broken weeping. Anger flushed through me until I recognized the weeping as male. Had he beaten her to death, then? Was I too late?

I could not get past the hawthorn and crystals at each window, but I strained to listen, and caught a whispered dialogue, *I'm sorry, Gretlina, I'm sorry, I promise I won't do it again, it's the liquor* . . .

Then Gretl had left him. For good? I'd leave him to his deserved misery!

I made my way back up the hill to check if Phaedra had gone home. She was not there. I passed swiftly through the night, taking care to stay out of the pools of light from the streetlamps that Alec's father had reestablished. People were still jumpy after Jerzy had opened the country to the

Nasdrafus's bloodsuckers before Kim and Tony closed the portal to them.

At the palace, I found no trace of Phaedra. I took myself to the headquarters of the Vigilzhi, and smelled her blood on the air as I approached the building.

There were fewer protections around this long-established military headquarters, and no hawthorn trees. I found it relatively easy to follow a returning patrol into the mostly-dark back door, shadows wrapped around me.

I made my way to the second story office of Dmitros Trasyemova, Jazd Komandant, or titular head of the Vigilzhi. Unlike some of his ancestors, he was not satisfied merely to parade around as a duke and leave the actual police and security work to underlings. He really functioned as Jazd Komandant, as Alec functioned as head of state.

Dmitros, a few years older, had always been a romantic figure to us. Not just because he was well built and handsome, a strand of Nordic genes coming out in his sandy hair and light eyes, but he had early lost his father to the Russians during the bad old days, and so had come into his title as a boy. Though we hadn't been permitted to use Dobreni titles, or even the language back then: everything was Soviet-style Marxism, in Russian. But we all knew just the same.

Phaedra was with him in his office. Mindful of Rose's warning, I listened to the murmur of voices not quite muffled by the solid wood.

"...but that is the whole point," Dmitros was saying. "Ruli *is* dead. Whatever is using her body is not human."

"It's not that easy," Phaedra retorted. "*I* spoke with her. *Alec* spoke with her. She told us that Kim's soul is caught in the Nasdrafus. Ruli didn't have to come here to tell us that."

"'Soul.'" Dmitros sighed. "I trust Alec implicitly—except maybe when it comes to Kim. I'm afraid he'll believe anything that might bring her out of that coma. Has it occurred to either of you that in listening to this vampire and her nonsense about Nasdrafus, you make yourselves easy prey?"

I fought the impulse to light a cigarette as some of the old anxiety reawakened in me.

Phaedra said, "Look, Dmitros, I never said there was no such thing as the Nasdrafus, not like Tony. But you know, if we've got vampires running around, and we put charms up, and plant hawthorn trees, why can't there be a Nasdrafus? One makes as much sense as any of the others."

"I think of the hawthorn trees and the rest of it as tradition," he said, but enough of a note of question remained. He knew now, after last winter's trouble, that charms worked. And he didn't like the subject, but ah-h-h-h! I heard it in his heartbeat: he liked *her*.

She said, "And if the Nasdrafus really exists, and Kim is caught there in some form, then...can it be possible that vampires can have different motivations, and are not all mindless, ravening fiends?"

They fell silent, while I listened to their elevated heartbeats. The real reason Tony had to pass the Vigilzhi physical prowess test by sixteen? Because Dmitros had. I happen to think that Tony is dyslexic, too; it might explain his trouble at school. But no one dared call *him* stupid. They were too afraid of his ready fists. And he was unbeatable on the playing field, or out behind school buildings. After he passed that fitness test designed for fully grown men, then Honoré, Alec, and the Danilovs had to, too.

As I listened to Dmitros's elevated heartbeat, I wondered if there might be some anger alongside his passion. He did not sound angry. The Trasyemovas had always kept their family separate except in the realm of general social harmony, especially from us von Mecklundburgs. I had no clue to what he thought or felt personally about a woman in the all-male precinct of the Vigilzhi. All I was certain of was that Phaedra wanted to earn her rank. She would loathe gaining it because of a relationship.

He said slowly, "Milo made it clear that you are an adjunct —"

"To protect the weak women, I know," Phaedra said bitterly. "Alec wants me to go. Further, I know, if Kim were awake, she'd be right there beside me."

"Were she awake, we would not be having this conversation," he reminded her drily. "Blyat! Since Alec seems to want this to happen, I'll shut up. But I'll also work up secondary plans."

"Good," Phaedra said. "I doubt we'll need them, but it should make Alec feel better about it all, and," she added in a tone more dry than his, "annoy the hell out of Tony."

Dmitros laughed, and I sensed that their meeting was coming to an end. I slipped down the stairs and waited out of the pool of light in the street, where again I had to suppress the idle wish to smoke. Yet another irony: now that I was past being harmed by it, there was no pleasure, either, unless I took myself to the Nasdrafus, and willed it so. A long way to go for a smoke.

When Phaedra stepped out the front door, I released the shadows and approached her.

"Merde!" She recoiled, then uttered a breathy laugh. "*Don't*. Do that, Ruli. What do you want?"

"A list of the mines we're to inspect. I was going to ask earlier, but I figured you would not want your messengers seeing me."

"You figured right," she said, her heart rate still fast. "As it happens, I can tell you the list." And she did.

Before my wedding, I'd had my hair done at Carita in Paris.

I had been planning to return to Paris for the Christ-mas holiday to have my hair cut again when my conniving great-uncle destroyed my plans, and me very nearly with them. It still keeps its shape — the stylist was too good for it not to — and the unwanted length was useful now. Of course there was over a meter's difference between the length of mine and Kim's, but if I French-braided my hair into a coronet, no one would notice the difference.

I never understood physics before I encountered magic, so I cannot begin to explain the intersection between Vrajhus and energy. I have begun to learn certain things, such as I need to breathe to oxygenate the blood I take in, and that blood can get used up. It lasts longer if I am careful, rather like driving with a light foot to preserve petrol, but if I need to downshift into fourth, so to speak, I can. And will need to refuel the sooner.

Another thing I've learned is how the mountains are not only veined with those elements we value, but they are also veined with portals. I cannot explain how, or why, it works; Rose taught me how to step through and envision the precise portal I want to appear at, and she had no idea when I asked. The drawback is that I have to know, and depict precisely, my destination.

Those first days after my transformation, to accustom me to my new state of being, Rose — impossible to think of her as "grandmother" when she looks significantly younger than I — took me all over Devil's Mountain to teach me the portals. I found myself in new mines, old abandoned ones, and grottos of various sorts yet undiscovered, except by our kind and others who drift from place to place through the physical world. Yet the ones that connect to the Nasdrafus are rare.

Once I learned these portals, we ventured into Riev, and she showed me how to get in and out of our family home. Those charms the family had assumed formed an unbreakable barrier didn't, if you already had permission to cross the threshold. The same with the royal palace, as I've indicated.

When I gained more confidence, I ventured during the dangerous daylight hours to explore the depths of the big mountain, Dsaretsenberg, and when the sun was safely blocked, the ancient, tangled valley between it and Dhiavilyi, or Devil's Mountain, ruled by my family. Each mountain has its own distinctive character, something I had grown up knowing, but in my new form I experienced in a different way. It's more than just clans and dialect differences.

I mention this now both to dismiss the idea that I sleep away the day bedded in a coffin (does anyone actually do that?), and because it will be easier later on when I have to describe my movements.

At nine the morning of the tour, Phaedra rolled up in a royal parade centered around the Ysvorod cream-colored Pierce-Arrow limousine with the windows darkened, two cars of Vigilzhi before and after, flanked by motorcycle outriders: the princess entourage that I used to have as my right, and now had been transferred to Kim.

The Pierce-Arrow pulled into a massive cavern where donkey carts are usually kept, petrol being at a premium. I was waiting. In the process of the others parking and doing a general sweep of the environment, Phaedra opened the door to the limousine's back seat. I emerged from the shadows, slid into the car, slid across the seat and then exited the other side, with no shrouding shadows. I was now Kim.

Phaedra's expression changed from tension to relief and then back to tension as she took her place at my left shoulder. I noticed the fully armed Vigilzhi guards all looking my way. The expressions on the faces of Sasha and Ilya Trasyemova and Florent Hirschmann made it clear that these three knew who I was. And I suspected from the sharp elevation in heart rates that they were under strict orders from Dmitros to attack me if I so much as moved wrong.

In this armed truce Phaedra and I rounded the car and approached the entrance to the Svetski Mine, where the chief operations manager and his assistants stood awaiting us, wearing their Sunday-best instead of work clothes.

Those Sunday-best suits serve as a perfect metaphor for how realistic this inspection was. It was more of a parade. As I walked past these stiff figures who addressed me by Kim's name, I wondered how she had felt when masquerading as me. The irony is that, as we share a face, we also share a first name, though neither of us use it.

I never would have dreamed I'd take the least interest in any such thing, but by the time I was halfway through the first mine, I could not help but reflect that old Milo, Alec's father, had singlehandedly managed to bring these dangerous areas about a century forward in safety equipment since the time I was born. We were still very far from computerization and other such technology, as EM and Vrajhus do not get along well together, but these spaces were as clean as humanly possible, shored up, lit, with air shafted in.

Everybody was on their best behavior as I tromped through, listening to memorized speeches, and receiving thanks and greetings. Phaedra walked behind me and to the left in bodyguard position, her gaze always in motion, the guards behind us watching me more than anyone else, but their obvious tension radiated outward.

I could hear it in their breathing.

I could smell it in their blood.

While Phaedra and the others had slept through the remainder of that night, and worked through the day, I had plotted my arrival at each mine without ever having to risk sunlight.

The tour was half over, but already I knew that for Alec's purposes, it was a failure.

When Phaedra and I met once again by the car doors, I stepped close. Her lips thinned, and one hand went to her sword hilt, but she didn't step away. I said, "Sasha and Flo are glaring at me so much that I think it intimidates the miners."

"They're supposed to be looking for danger," she replied under her breath. "With the others."

"I realize that, which is why the pistols and the rifles." And the swords in case the gunpowder misfired. "But the twins're watching me more than they are the surroundings, and I think the miners sense threat."

Phaedra sighed. "What can I do? They're under Sasha's orders."

Oh for the day when little brothers and cousins trotted

obediently to heel, carrying the picnic baskets or sports equipment in order to be permitted to join the older siblings! But Sasha and his twin Ilya were now even taller than Dmitros, and they only listened to Dmitros, or Alec.

"I think I'm going to slip away," I said. "Distract them. Don't let them panic if they notice I'm missing. I promise I won't attack any villagers or Vigilzhi."

I sensed in her heartbeat how much she hated the idea, but she brought her chin down in a minute nod. "Do it." Another sigh. "I'll go on to the next. But you better catch up."

I suppressed the impulse to say *Or what?* and walked sedately in, my old training taking over as I smiled and nodded to each side. When we reached the first tunnel turning, I stepped into the shadows, wrapped them around me, and enjoyed the startled looks as the miners blinked around wondering where I'd gone. Phaedra stiffened, her hands tightening on her sword hilt and pistol holster, but she marched determinedly ahead, trailed by the guard. I stepped back and chose another tunnel, relinquished the shadows, and continued on as if nothing had happened.

The ruse was useless. I saw nothing out of the ordinary as I paced along past interested gazes, accepting best wishes for the upcoming wedding, and responded with social blandness to equally meaningless social questions. I paid more attention to keeping my teeth well retracted than to those stiffly formal words.

In good order we retreated to the cars and motorcycles, and so to the next, which was a repeat of that.

Anticipation turned to endurance. Touring mines was exactly as boring as I'd always believed. Nothing was going to happen. These people were determined that the soon-to-be princess see nothing that she ought not to. I would go through the last two only because I'd agreed to, I decided as the cars pulled up.

Then I caught sight of a hovering water boy who watched me not with that fixed smile of people in the first line of long parades, but with anxiety and question that had nothing to do with my true nature.

Water boys — occasionally girls, when sturdy enough — are ubiquitous in the mountain reaches where piping is yet to occur. They trudge back and forth from the nearest stream or waterfall to the work site, bringing drinking water that has not been muddied by whatever water is running through or alongside the site. I've heard it said that poor boys did this job until they reached eighteen or so, at which time they would have built up enough strength and endurance to be hired into any other sort of active labor they wished. Smaller children being apprenticed afternoons following morning school.

This boy could have lived three hundred years ago, in his homespun shirt and thick trousers patched at knees and seat — probably handed down through the family for several generations. Bare feet, a shock of black hair, and an unremarkable face, except for that expression: I would never have noticed him but for the way his gaze followed me, and his lips moved as if in prayer. Pleading. His heart a frantic patter.

The tour set out to be a replica of the foregoing, but my interest had heightened as I sought a way to get to that boy without being noticed. The bends and dips of the cave tunnel, and the fact that he was expected to stay in the background in case he and his bucket might be needed, were in my favor. I used the shadows and waited until he rounded a corner, and there I was, pretending to fix my sandal.

He gave a startled exclamation, then came up to me, bobbing his head. "You're the Dsaret princess?" His voice squeaked with excitement, but underneath I could smell terror. Yet I was not the cause. He smelled of a long-endured state of terror.

"What do you need?" I asked, avoiding a direct answer.

"I ran away. They have the others. You have to come. My sister sent me. *Please* come."

"Can you start at the beginning?" I asked. "Where am I to come to?"

"Novitski Valley. The schoolhouse. The men came in with guns. I was at the outhouse. I was going to go out, but you can see through a crack in the door, and I saw men sneaking up on the school. I stayed where I was. In the outhouse. With the flies. Until dark, and I got out, and ran home, and went in my window."

He stopped and swallowed, and I almost swooned at the smell of his young blood.

"Go on," I said, fighting the urge to extend my teeth.

"Mam and my sister sat at the table. Brosya. Mam was crying. Brosya saw me. She said, how did you get away — the Russian leader said they had you all captured. I told her. Mam wanted me to go to the attic and hide. I did, and they brought my supper, and I stayed there for days and nights. Then Brosya came to me after Mam slept, and said that the Dsaret princess is coming, and I must find you and get help. For Papa and the men. In the mines. Bad men are with them, with guns. If they say anything, the bad men will kill everybody in the school-house."

I looked around. "But this is not Novitski Valley mine."

He shook his head violently. "Brosya said I should go over the slope to the church to hide. Not our shul. Or church. The priest, he says his name is Lukas, said to act as water boy for the miners, and he would send a quiet message into the city, but it is a long way on a donkey, and I heard you were coming, and you got rid of the bad men holding the Eyrie, everyone knows that, and I thought, you could come to us?" The last came out in a rush. "But it has to be *quiet*. If they see any bluecoats they will kill all of us in the school." His drawn young face paled, and tears rimmed his lower lids. "Everybody. Even my little brother."

"You did the right thing. What is your name?"

"Jakov."

"Now I need you to tell me everything you can about these men."

"My sister said…"

There is no use in repeating his garbled narrative, which doubled back on itself, and skipped over other salient facts, as even much older people are prone to do. By the time he was finished, I could hear the footsteps and voices of the tour approaching. "Run back," I said to Jakov. "Leave the rest to us."

He bobbed again, his pail clattering, then scampered off, sending one last glance back, his round face expressive of relief and worry.

I wrapped shadows about myself once more, and slipped into the line when they rounded a rocky bend. Phaedra had been on the watch, and pursed her lips in relief. "Where were you?" she asked under her breath.

"I think I have it," I replied.

I related Jakov's tale, then said, "His parents are the bakers for the village, but the father was taken by the invaders to the mine."

"What mine? There is no mine in Novitski Valley," Phaedra said. "That's right behind that ridge, and I know my map."

"Was there one historically?"

Phaedra frowned, then faced me, eyes wide. "Yes. Closed down in the early 1900s because the ground is unstable, and the gold veins had been tapped out. It ran through the eastern slope, not far from the Dacia Mine, the one we just left."

"According to what Jakov's sister overheard while delivering bread, the invaders are mostly Russian hirelings, and they seem to think there's oil down deep."

"If there was, Alec would know," Phaedra said absently. "I remember when he went through there with some people who had sophisticated detecting apparatus. Of course all bets are off whether their machines worked well in the mountains. But..." She shrugged. "I'd take Alec's results over mercenary gossip..." She scowled into the distance. One hand tapped her the knee of her uniform trousers with their knife-sharp crease. "How many of these guys exactly?"

"Jakov wasn't certain. Two at the school at all times, sometimes three, and four pairs patrolling the village. The rest in the mine, forcing the men to work; he thinks anywhere from a dozen to twenty altogether."

"What else did he say?"

"Nothing much. He was kept in their attic the entire time, until the sister sent him. He did overhear that the men patrol in pairs. He overheard his sister and mother talking, after the sister delivers the bread. She thinks she heard other languages, but the commands are in Russian."

"How do they get food to the hostages inside the school?"

"It's left outside in baskets, and one or the other of the guards comes out to get it. Automatic weapon. Should I skip the next tour and run back to Riev?"

Phaedra's fingers drummed. "Wait. We have one more mine scheduled for today. Let them see you get into the car, then get out and wait for me. I'll send them on."

I complied as she hurried off to talk to the captain of the Vigilzhi, and then returned. "Sasha thinks I'm in the limo with you, and the others think I'm in the jeep. They'll figure it out pretty fast, but if we act now, we can wrap this up."

She grinned the way she used to when Tony issued one of his challenges, and went on, "We don't know where their lookouts are posted, but they have to be watching the roads, so if they spot a lot of vehicles maneuvering, they might act. Let's act first. Sounds like they are a small group."

"Twenty?"

"Small-ish." She shrugged, the metal on her shoulder tabs winking. "Ruli, wouldn't you like to take them down? Just us?"

"You're mad." I stared at her, stunned.

"We could do it. There's always the chance their weapons won't work. You know how mercury fulminate goes inert up this high."

I had grown up hearing, with utter indifference, about how old-fashioned gunpowder was more reliable that the accelerant used in automatic weapons. And even that wasn't always trustworthy, which had forced those who wanted to fight back to hand-to-hand. The irony is that now I could sense the flow of Vrajhus currents that caused EM and mercury fulminate and suchlike to go dead.

She went on, "You have skills—weapons—they are not prepared for. And I...oh, Ruli, I would very much like a chance to prove myself. And I think Dmitros would support me."

"No, he wouldn't. Not against twenty mercenaries. That's what they sound like, lawless marauders, perfectly willing to kill. Jakov says they shot one of the villagers to prove their threat, then walked over the body as if it meant nothing. Like you, I wonder who sent them. And why."

"If they *are* mercs, they usually don't plan much past the score," Phaedra pointed out. "Yes, there very well might be oil down there, and they might even have scavenged some old oil pumps, but I'll wager you anything you care to name they haven't thought at all about legalities such as sovereign rights. Because they are used to breaking, taking, and running. But you can't break and take oil."

I said, "They might not be that ignorant."

"Blyat! You're right. Perhaps they think our government is toothless. We are about to crown a very old king." Phaedra rubbed her hands. "I'd love to see them smack into the wall called Alec, but he's already proved himself. Many times. I see this as *my* chance. Come, Ruli, what say you?"

I could see the problem turning fast into a messy, bloody affair. But I could always walk away. Any responsibility was something I chose myself. To the rest of Dobrenica, I was dead.

I turned to Phaedra. "What do you have in mind?"

"First, we reconnoiter, you, your way, and me in mine..."

FIVE

RULI

I once read a biography of Lord Byron that attributed some of his cultivated gloom to the fact that though he was generally regarded as handsome by both men and women, once he came to man's estate, he still thought of himself as the chubby, awkward choirboy he'd been in his youth.

I make no claims to its veracity; the analogy I want to draw here is to me. That is, Phaedra and I both trying not to see the former weak, sedentary Ruli in my present form, and to believe in my newly acquired strength, speed, and maneuverability.

As the sun sank slowly behind the mountain, and shadows gathered, the two of us divided the area to assess, she within the last of the light, and I the buildings in the lee of the mountain ridge, where sunset arrived first.

Then we withdrew up a ways into the narrow valley created by the stream that furnished the tiny village's water. Here we compared what we'd learned, and once she laid out her plan, I realized that I could accomplish it. Not easily, but it was well within my abilities. What was I going to worry about, that someone might shoot or stab me? It would hurt, but I'd heal fast from such wounds.

My worry was Phaedra's safety. It seemed madness for only the two of us to go up against all these armed brigands. But she had something to prove, and she believed that surprise as well as a tight plan would even the odds.

"Let's go," she said. And did not look back.

The plan was simple: she took out the roamers and left the guards inside the schoolroom to me. I used the shadows to approach the schoolroom, which looked peaceful from the outside, except for the closed windows and shutters, a rarity this time of year.

The schoolroom was not charmed against entry of my kind, so it was easy to slip in. It was overly warm and stuffy. I didn't trouble to breathe, but relied on my last feed — knowing I would soon get another as I ghosted through. The teacher and children sat on the clean-swept wooden floor in circles, doing lessons in tight, high voices, hearts thrumming with fear. The old desks and chairs had been jumbled together below the windows, in preparation for a siege, I guess.

I caught one man just coming out of the privy. He didn't make a peep as I attacked, fed, and then dragged him inside the privy again, his breathing stertorous. His blood was full of alcohol. I had to concentrate on burning the effect, which seemed to take a long time, though it was probably no more than a minute.

The second man prowled back and forth in front of the windows. Using my newly-replenished strength, I stealthed in the suffocating gloom toward him as the teacher read to the children, who looked half-asleep. I waited until he turned, then dropped the shadows so that he came face to face with me, scarcely a hand's breadth between us. He stank of stale sweat, and the sausage he must have eaten for breakfast. I caught his startled gaze with my eyes and he stiffened, stilled, for just long enough for me to catch him, throw shadows around us both, and when I was done, ease him to the ground.

I did not see a third, but I heard a heartbeat that did not belong to the schoolchildren or their teacher. I withdrew without anyone being aware of me, and made for the steep stairs — and there, in a narrow attic, lay the third, snoring, an empty zhoumnyar bottle standing neatly beside the pile of old blankets and coats he slept on. Though I was already sated, I fed on him, too. Now all three were unconscious.

I left, arriving in time to catch the last of Phaedra's takedown of a pair of roamers in a lethal dance, every movement a lesson in strength and economy. But she had not had it easy; her coat was ripped in two places, and her cheek bled from what looked like a knife slice.

She looked up, saw me, relaxed, and grinned, flashing me two fingers, and pointing to the right.

There were two more pairs some fifty meters away, as yet unaware of that silent, furious battle; they ambled toward the shul, automatic weapons carried in slack hands. She motioned me toward the one on the right.

We ghosted up, each to our target. Her fight was short and vicious. Mine was even shorter, so she was spared having to see what I did to render my target unconscious for a good long while; I do not know or care if she disabled or killed her share of the invaders. My avoidance of death was for my own sake, not theirs. I knew that once I began killing, it would be easy to continue. Then I truly would become lost to those who had come to matter most.

We dealt with the last pair in the same manner, and it was time to enter the mine.

"How will we tell brigands from miners," I began, then answered my own question. "Right. The ones with the weapons are the enemy, the ones with pick-axes and baskets are not."

Though there were more guards in the mine, they had spread themselves out in order to have what Phaedra called a clear field of vision, or as much as possible in narrow, twisting tunnels. It was probably good tactics for preventing other humans coming up, but it was no proof against vampires. After I took down two, Phaedra gave me a wry wave, as in *go ahead!* And she withdrew, I assumed to do another check.

It was an easy task for me as they were not expecting me. It did not take long. Again, I left the miners at their task, rather than cause a stampede in that perilous place, and withdrew to the clearing outside — to discover Phaedra backed against a slab of stone, hands up.

I saw what must have happened. She had emerged, expecting a quiet village, just as a jeep drove up with four men in it, all armed. She and they brought their weapons to bear. Outgunned, she was forced to surrender, and you can imagine the gloating, grating comments about her looks and probable abilities as an unwilling lover, interspersed with questions.

A lifetime of memory froze me in fear, but that scarcely lasted a second or two. My awareness of my present state never faded entirely. I was at my peak strength, and consciousness flooded me as I glanced up to make sure of the sun. It had slid safely beyond the mountain, leaving twilight.

Shifting speed was still as arduous as trying to run uphill while carrying another person, but I had the energy to spare. I had to be very careful to dodge little bits of dirt in the air kicked up by the mercenaries' boots as they advanced on Phaedra. The faster I moved in relation to them, the more like bullets dust's impact would be, and while that would not kill me, it would hurt and I would have to take the time, and energy, to repair myself.

Two had solid grips on their weapons. I carefully slid my fingers over them and pulled, which felt a bit like pulling up a tree from the ground. The snap of breaking fingers made me shudder as I maneuvered the sluggish weapons, disarming them, and launching the ammunition up into the air to land on the rooftops.

Two automatic weapons, two rifles, one machete, and three belt knives had gone down the privy before I had to shift back. By then my energy was waning, and moving was like trying to swim in honey. But when I came out, the result was laughably satisfying, two howls and curses of rage over suddenly damaged hands, then Phaedra sprang into action. Kicks to knees, punches to throats and sternums, and the four lay in a heap, groaning and cursing.

Then they saw me. To be precise, they saw my fangs. They stilled, flight or fight shooting adrenaline through their bloodstreams, nearly making me lightheaded with desire, compounded by reaction from my exertions.

Phaedra and I had a moment to exchange silent expressions of triumph and relief—we'd actually done it—and I bent toward the nearest one to assuage my thirst when the growl of old, unmuffled engines approached from the narrow road, and two more jeeps full of mercenaries burst into view, spewing dust and smoke.

Weapons clatched and clicked, rising to cover us, but above the noise of idling engines rose the rumble of horse hooves, and horsemen thundered into the clearing to surround the two jeeps. As I'd figured, Tony was not far to seek whenever there was trouble.

Crossbolts loosed with a spang! And both jeeps' drivers shouted in pain and surprise, one twisting around with the force of the bolt ripping into his right shoulder, and the other slumping over the wheel, a bolt squarely in his back, having severed his spine—I sensed his life fleeing.

Then fighting broke out, far too quick for me to follow. To my untrained eyes it was chaos, but for the moment no one noticed me as I swayed before the tantalizing scent of the anger-torqued emotions of close combat.

Tony eyed me uncertainly, and I suspected that he could not see clearly through the smoke whether I was myself or Kim suddenly recovered and resuming the planned schedule. Then he was attacked from behind. In that moment I swooped on a groaning mercenary at my feet and fed, and, strengthened again, I drew shadows around me as I scanned.

The mercenaries still on their feet had regrouped. They gunned the jeeps and peeled out, Niklos leading half of Tony's riders to gallop after them into a cloud of dust boiling up. The jeeps had already outrun the horses. But they'd have to stay to the roads, narrow and treacherous as they were, whereas the riders knew all the trails. If you had nerves of steel, that is, as most of those trails were nearly vertical, mainly used by goats.

Tony went from one to another of the mercenaries. I could have told him that three were dead, and one left for dead. The rest had been tossed into the jeeps before they took off. Two of Tony's riders were hauling the wounded man ungently to a sitting position when once more the sound of jeep engines brought them all to the alert. This time it was Dmitros Trasyemova, with Alec in the front seat. They were the vanguard of a considerable contingent. Alec gave Dmitros a short nod, and Dmitros waved a hand.

At once his people efficiently surrounded the scene.

"Tony," Alec said.

"Keep your knickers on. We've a talker here."

Tony took no notice of the Vigilzhi as he watched his riders wrap the wounds on the mercenary, then force a bottle between his bluing lips. The man swallowed, and choked as the pungent odor of triple-distilled zhoumnyar eddied on the dusty, blood-sweet air.

The man flushed as the liquor roused him, and Tony crouched down on his heels to face him, a rifle across his bent knees. "Just tell us who sent you, and you can walk out of here," he said in Dobreni, and when the man looked blank, he repeated it in extremely idiomatic, curse-punctuated Russian.

Alec came up and stood behind Tony, watching in silence, hands clasped behind him. While the rough-and-ready field triage was taking place, Dmitros Trasyemova, as Jazd Commandant, had been issuing orders to the Vigilzhi who had followed him in. They divided off to gather the dead, and to see to and reassure the hostages, both those in the schoolhouse and the men forced to mine under the guns of the invaders. As they tended the villagers, Dmitros and Sasha joined the little group around the single surviving prisoner.

Who was staring up at me. In fear. Had he seen me feed during the chaos?

Tony grinned. "Start talking, comrade, or we'll give you to her."

That broke the dam, and he began blathering a mix of curses and protests of ignorance. Dmitros listened for a second or two, then turned to Phaedra to ask if she was all right. She lifted a shoulder, and he said, "Well done. Though I wish you'd waited."

"We had it under control," Phaedra said. And then ruined the effect by admitting, "Until their backup arrived. But Tony was right on their heels."

The mercenary's flow of words stuttered, and he slumped.

"Dead?" Tony addressed me over the man's slack face.

"No," I said, hearing the man's laboring heart. "But he's in shock."

"Take him to the medic," Alec said to a couple of blue coats, who carried the man off to one of the jeeps then took off.

Alec went off to confer with the village elders, and I decided that I was now superfluous. I was about to head for the nearest portal when Tony caught up with me in a few quick strides, unkempt blond hair flapping on his shoulders. "What did you get out of this?" he asked, taking in the mountains with a circular gesture on the word 'this.'

"You mean the mine tour? Or this supposed gold mine?"

"Any prat with half a brain could see there isn't oil down there. Or gold. Or anything else but unstable rock," he said.

"The world seems to be filled with half-brained prats, then," I said. "Who don't know anything about mines. I got ignorance out of that man's babble. He knows nothing, but was promised lots of loot for a few days' work, as he said. But why here, after so many years?"

"I think," he said, "someone tried to set us up. Me, to be specific."

"Everything being about you," I retorted.

Tony grinned wryly. "When did you get so mouthy?"

"About the time you could no longer shove me into a Sky Tower room to serve as another marker in your plots."

He flicked up his fingers acknowledging a hit. But he didn't leave the subject. "He was hired by some wanker he never saw, who talked a lot of bollocks about advanced technology, but from what I saw, their equipment was second-rate tat from the sixties. I think someone is making a run at us." He glared eastward, toward Russia.

"A last-ditch run," Alec said, coming up to join us. "My guess is: before the 2nd."

September 2nd being the traditional day to invoke the Blessing—which about half the country was increasingly skeptical about. My brother leading the pack.

Sure enough, he made a face as if acutely pained. "You're still banging on about that?"

"Says the knob who hands off his own blood in a special urn every December." Alec's retort was uttered in the same tone he'd used on Tony ever since we were all children. It was a rivalry, not an enmity. If someone had hired those incompetents to try to drive a wedge between the von Mecklundburgs and the Ysvorods through Tony and Alec, it had been too hasty, too ineffective.

Too desperate, one might even say.

But who? Not Maman. In the old days, she would have sent Jerzy to do her dirty work. These days, though she was no longer addicted to the opiates Jerzy had been feeding her, she seemed slower, more cautious. Still maneuvering, but strictly within the law.

My mental line of inquiry dissolved as Tony and Alec began arguing along familiar lines. Whenever there was rumor of villainy, Tony was always going to look first toward Russia, the known enemy, then toward vampires, the other known enemy. Whereas Alec had been taught by Milo to look everywhere, ten steps ahead.

It was completely dark by then. The Vigilzhi had brought out their torches, and beams of light cut this way and that. Before those two could draw me into their row, I said to Phaedra, "I believe I'm done," and shifted speed, wrapping shadows around myself. While both Alec and Tony stared one way, I left by another, laughing to myself at the change in our dynamics.

SIX

RULI

A day or two later I returned to Gretl's home near the market on my sporadic prowl. Her husband sat alone at the table over his dinner, staring into the distance. He was only a monster when drunk. He must have been given a choice, her or the monster, and he apparently couldn't resist the monster, so she had gone back to her mountain. I could not know if it was permanent, but at least she'd had the strength to leave him.

Lisi was home—alone. I saw her through her lit kitchen windows, humming as she went about cooking a meal. Her husband must be at shul, then, for evening prayers; I had seen that he did his drinking at home. She did not look at all apprehensive, and I wondered if the two of them had reconciled, or even got the Dobreni equivalent of couples' counseling, which in Dobrenica meant listening to their rabbi, or a priest, or guild master, or auntie quote from ancient wisdom before talking things out.

Soon after I became a vampire, I sensed her sorrow reaching me the length of a street. I followed her home from her shopping, where she'd walked into shouted wild accusations from a voice sloppy with drink. He slammed out shortly after reducing her to tears and begging and I did not know that I was going to confront him until I did it.

How intoxicating was my sense of power when he stared at me in fear! I hissed (hiding how difficult it was to speak past my extended canines), "Are you afraid? Yes? Ah, how ssssweet!

Almost as sssssweet as your wife's blood smells when you terrorize her, bawling at her like an ape in a tree." Then I'd shifted right up next to him, taking his arm in my grip strong enough to hurt. "Next time I smell her fear, it will be your lassssst night on earth." And I'd let him go.

I hoped my threat had made a difference, but I know from my own experience as a drinker that drunks are the world's most adept blame-shifters. A similar threat had certainly made no difference to Sareska's brute, when I confronted him on Karl-Rafael Street, slamming out of a tavern. This man was just mean, sober and drunk. Yet she loved him anyway. I could hear it. Smell it. I did not understand it.

I drifted up to Prinz Karl-Rafael Street, to discover her sister there with them at supper, easily visible in the bow window above the spice shop. Was the sister watching out for Sareska? The brute hunched over the newspaper as the two women chattered. With my sharp hearing I heard as well as saw Sareska rise to ask if he wanted anything more — and, unseen by both, the sister studied him with the unwinking gaze and crimped mouth of cold hatred. It seemed that this sister was addressing the vexed issue in her own way.

"Why do you trouble yourself over these fools?"

I turned to find my teenage grandmother Rose standing beside me, in spite of my shrouding shadows.

"I don't know," I said.

"Did any of these women ask you to watch them like this?" Rose lisped.

"They don't know that I'm here. Unless Lisi's husband confessed my threat."

Rose laughed lightly. "I see! Then it's as Augustus says: you are as a babe playing with your new power. You'll tire of this game soon enough."

Does anyone appreciate being told they are predictable? I know I don't. It throws me back to Cerisette's contempt back in our teen days. But I reminded myself that Cerisette has no power over me that I don't permit her to have: her contempt was in no way a reality, merely her symbolic stepping on me in order to assure her place above me in the teenage social striving. And she could do nothing to me now.

I said to Rose, "'Soon' seems to be relative to our existence. In any case, what does it matter to anyone how I amuse myself?"

She looked so fetching in her bewitching fashions of the

thirties, which are my ideal: simple yet so elegant in line. I realized that though she still watched over the family, a lot depends on how one defines "watch."

"Where do you suggest I go, if not walking these streets?" I asked. At the time I thought myself clever, that the distraction worked. That her attention was like a butterfly in a wind.

"Where else but Paris?" She switched to the French of her day.

"Which Paris?"

"Ours, but of course." Her tone was possessive, to a relishing degree.

I don't comprehend the Nasdrafus, though I had learned this much: it can be very dangerous to those rare humans who, while still alive, find their way to it. By being whatever they desire most, it can beguile them so thoroughly that they are tempted to remain until their physical being dwindles and dies. For inimasang, its liminality detaches time, and nullifies the threat of the sun.

I followed Rose, never averse to the Paris of art deco and jazz and painters in the Montmartre bistros, who now have the freedom to make all the art they desire, though that art never appears in the physical world unless as dream or inspiration. Here, everything is easier, including smoking. I could light up and draw in that heady heat that sharpened my thinking and cooled my nerves, even if the pleasure is actually an artifact of memory.

It was only a step to the Rue de Cambon, where we found Chanel's shop open, all the fashions on the models evening gowns evocative of 1933. I chose a beaded silk of delicate mauve cut on the bias, and trimmed with tiny seed pearls. I ran my fingertip over the tiny, exquisitely perfect silken stiches, aware that here, the silk was as real as the memories, the expectations, of uncounted thousands who had come through before me. I slid my feet into pretty little shoes with kitten heels, and then threw round the whole ensemble a silver fox fur wrap.

"Put it on my account," Rose said as we passed to the door, and Coco Chanel bowed and smiled, knowing that heads would turn, eyes following her fashions, and she retreated to her back room to create more.

We walked out to swank along the Golden Triangle, foot traffic giving way in deference to our kind. We slowed when we reached the Boulevard de Montparnasse. Rose was attracted to La Coupole, center of the arts in the twenties? No, it was those on the outside of the arts whom she smiled on, mostly tall men with slicked-back hair and auras of menace.

Then we moved on without looking inside; she seemed to go where there were handsomely dressed men, at this moment a set from the days when Worth's fashions dictated what the elite women wore to grand balls, and mustachioed men of title (or pretended title) flocked about them, elegant in black swallowtail coats and swinging swagger sticks. They knew her, and called her princess; I saw that she never tired of this flirting, and when we stopped for the fifth time to chat with a bloody-minded writer who had ended up as one of us, I stepped away, as the streets resolved into my own Paris.

Chanel's fashions never go out of style, and many were the admiring looks my way, but we do apparently project an aura of *Don't touch me lest I bite you,* and no one troubled me. I'd scarcely gone twenty steps toward the theatres of the Grands Boulevards, hoping to find a diverting play, when Rose caught up with me.

Before either of us could speak, the street fell in shadow, and here we were before the moon-pale glow of an androgynously perfect face, flanked by two sentinels. Rose smiled up at them, as at an expected meeting.

I had not distracted Rose. I had been fetched.

Rose pursed her lips in a cupid's bow moue. "We really ought to look out for our own. We could become a mighty house, with a little effort."

The thought appalled me. Imagine eternity with Cerisette! Even in the world of the undead she would never tire of parading how much thinner and paler she was. Or was Rose talking about something else entirely? "Effort in what sense?" I asked.

"An alliance of interests," Rose replied with mild surprise. "With the willing. Such as Jeremiel, here. It's like the study of the simple lever; you permit the superior power to apply the effort, sparing you the fatigue. But you share in the result."

She inclined her shingled head in a graceful nod at the tall figure drifting before us. Very tall—at least seven feet, maybe more. Jeremiel's long black hair blended into a night-black cloak. "Your appearances are similar." The quality of that voice was as deceptively angelic as the face, like crystal wind chimes ringing. "But the other one is so uncouth. She requires your guidance."

"You're speaking of Kim," I said, nearly stepping back and

away from that aura of power.

I could understand why some perceived them as divine. Isn't beauty divine? The invisible fist of awe struck behind my breastbone, and I had to consciously dismiss it. I don't know if angels exist as humans perceive them. I've never met one, to my knowledge. But I do know when beauty is being used as intimidation, if not as a weapon.

The last time I was wandering the Nasdrafus I'd seen Jeremiel streaking across the sky among others of this kind. Such glimpses are rarely random. It usually means, Rose had explained on first introducing me to the Nasdrafus, that we have some sort of connection, however ephemeral. Just as I find my Paris, and she walks in hers, but we can find each other.

At this moment, it seemed that the connection might be through Kim. She had mentioned seraphim, and I had dully cautioned her, without really understanding why she was in a seductively dangerous setting or who had brought her; my first assumption was that she was there in dream. Whatever had happened to her since then, it seemed she was still in their interest.

Jeremiel stood before me. What might at first be taken for a night-black cloak was in fact a pair of jet wings, the ends of which folded neatly over a sandaled foot. Likewise, the shadows stretched far above Jeremiel's head were a second pair of wings, and a third pair flicked outstretched, giving the impression of limitlessness from horizon to horizon. One companion had silver wings, the other the pale ivory-gold of a pure, rain-washed dawn.

"We are guardians of the Esplumoir. As a gesture of amity in our alliance, we invite you to bring Aurelia Kim Murray back to us," Jeremiel said. "Before the moon wanes."

In other words, I realized, before the first of September. Or rather, before September 2nd — AKA St. Xanpia's day. Also, the day of Kim's wedding, the traditional day to invoke Xanpia's Blessing, a legend my family scorned. And yet they had striven to complete their machinations well in advance of it, the year previous.

I was being given a choice. Or rather, I was to believe I was being offered a choice. But I had grown up among people who knew all the subtleties of threat, and used them to get obedience.

"I'll try," I said, my accustomed deflection, at the time just wanting distance, and Rose clapped her hands lightly, cooing with pleasure.

The seraphim dissolved into glimmering mist, and Rose and I headed for our own portal. I glanced back once, annoyed that I had not thought to ask why. But there it was, that old self-image, afraid to draw down wrath for my temerity in asking.

Ah, I don't care why, I decided. I was not going to do it anyway.

I make no claims to comprehending the Esplumoir any more than I do the Nasdrafus, except that it's a place, or non-place, that goes by many names, depending on where and when you were born and raised. As I understand it, there are three such in the world at present, one of those being in our valley. An Esplumoir is not limited to a specific spot so much as an area. I think of it being a bit like the vents of mountain caves.

There is a "vent", for example, in St. Xanpia's fountain, a wellspring that dates back to Roman times. Maybe long before. That wellspring is ancient, and an entity dwells there. I can feel it, like a piece of the sun deep in the waters.

I use the 'sun' simile advisedly, because that fountain is poison to inimasang. And yet poison is not the right word, for its connotations of destruction; I sense an ingathering there, an obliteration in light. But that's not right, either: when I was alive, it was just a fountain where people have come for water for centuries, and lingered to talk or play or sit and dream. City children splash in the lower fountain water on the rare hot days of summer. Though of course *we* were never permitted. It was common. Vulgar.

Part of my imperfect new knowledge was that the mirror that I'd seen all my life whenever I was up at the Eyrie was actually a portal to the Nasdrafus. Despite the overly ornate baroque "upgrade" one of my titled and tasteless ancestors added to it some four hundred years ago, that mirror of polished metal is far, far older than the Eyrie, as if the castle were built around it.

"It's our own door," Rose told me when she showed me how to use it. *Our*. She did not tell me if that "our" encompassed the von Mecklundburgs, or if — like the mirror — there was a far older story here, and we are mere late-comers. But the honorary title of that very ancient vampire, Antonius Augustus, and the way my brother's name has persisted over the centuries, hints that the answer might not be all that simple.

Here is final strange fact about the Nasdrafus: though I had shucked on Chanel's dressing room floor the black silk dress I had been wearing for my prowl through the streets of Riev, when I stepped through the mirror into the physical world, it was back on me, the Chanel gown gone. "It's the same for physical bodies of the living," Rose had said. "The rare ones who get to the Nasdrafus while conscious. Dreamers, of course, leave their bodies in bed."

"You mean, people Who choose to go there pile up in a coma before this mirror?" I pointed.

"No," was all she said, airy and careless. "One of the mysteries. As we are ourselves."

In descending the grand staircase, I had to bat my way past scaffolding of ladders, canvas, and lines of paint cans. My cousin Percy had been overseeing the repairs and restoration of the castle after the place was shot up the summer previous, when I was imprisoned in the Sky Tower to await my mother's and brother's respective coups. Both of which failed.

Tony didn't seem to mind bullet holes in the walls, but the rest of us did, and Percy, the family artist, had promised to oversee restoration as soon as the Opera House was finished. The smell of wet paint meant that Percy had to be in residence.

Percy, the youngest of us, and very left-handed, is another profoundly unwarlike spirit, though the older cousins made sure he could defend himself. He, like Tony, abjures the splendid dining chamber that my mother always insists on using while in residence, as does my Uncle Robert, descended from our great-great grandfather's third son. I can now smell how much Uncle Robert wishes Tony would meet with an accident so that he can assume the title. But Maman is equally determined that he not inherit. Equally so Percy, descended from the fourth son. Still less does she want the ducal title to pass to Cerisette, Robert's daughter.

Percy sat in the cubby off the kitchen, ancient papers spread before him, and paint dotting his waving red hair. That impressive chin that he'd inherited from a Habsburg princess who had married into his mother's family after the Napoleonic era nearly rested on his breast.

When he looked up, he started, but my hand was up in our old gesture of *pax*.

"Ruli," he breathed.

"Any news?" I asked, mostly to let him know that I was not in any way targeting him. He was the one who had offered last spring to do something to the charms to make it bearable for me to come and go in my own home. Though I'd always liked him,

I owed him for that gesture of trust.

"Did you know that Kim was in a coma?" he asked.

"Was?" I repeated, not answering.

Percy's smile broadened. "She woke up today."

Percy, left to himself, likes everybody. That included Kim, in spite of my mother's determination to make her out to be a bastard gold-digger.

"We weren't to know about the coma, but Phaedra told me about you taking Kim's place on that mine tour earlier this month."

"What is the date?"

"August 13ᵗʰ," he said with a mild air of question.

Full moon—worst time for inimasang. The strong moonlight was rather like a persistent sunburn. "Half a month before the wedding," I said, remembering Jeremiel's "offer."

I could linger here, but Rose seemed to be taking it upon herself to declare an alliance with Jeremiel, for what-ever reason. How many of the inimasang would agree with her, and thus take it upon themselves to make sure I obeyed that suggestion that was an order?

Then an idea occurred, the perfect wedding present for Alec and Kim: my absence.

I would go to the real Paris.

SEVEN

KIM

Between the time I woke from the Vrajhus-injected not-a-coma and my wedding, the days slipped by like a dream. It was non-stop preparation, broken only by my determination to get back into shape. For that, I had Phaedra Danilov to thank — she who I'd insisted on having as my future Kilber, if I had to have an equerry / aide-de-camp / bodyguard at all. She was very willing to keep fencing with me, as we had since winter, before that coma.

I've already written a bit about my wedding, but I can't resist adding a little more, beginning with climbing into that fabulous wedding gown with the mile-long train (really, what use are trains, except as ambulatory floor polishers?) and heading for the cathedral to be turned into a married woman.

And into a princess. Let's not forget that sideways hop into the surreal.

Physically, I was fine. Mentally, I was slowly coming out of the head-cloudy residue of that lengthy stay in someone else's life while my body lay pretty much like a sun-stoned vamp, except, you know, alive.

I think the last of the residue burned away during our wedding vows, as Alec's warm fingers gripped mine. I still see the light sifting down through the high cathedral windows as he slid the ring on my finger. I recollect the pungency of incense and candlewax from the altar. And feel the slight tremor in his warm, steady grip, that conveyed wordlessly how deeply his emotions had been stirred, though he was so much better at hiding them. A lifetime of training — with corresponding cost.

I've already described my flash from the past. It was during the coronation vows that I remembered there were actually three entities fusing in this ancient ritual: me, Alec, and Dobrenica. It was going to take some time to really get what that meant.

Before dawn we tossed a couple of suitcases into Alec's new Daimler — a gift from Milo — kissed our families, and took off, me with Beka Ridotski's murmured words echoing in my ears, "Remember the Salfmattas' warning: no slipping into history."

Look, but no touch, in other words. Grandma Ziglieri didn't think I ought to be even looking, without the limiting filter of my prism. It had become too easy to just let it happen, and I had been too ignorant to figure out how to flex that inner camera-filter, so to speak, to keep myself grounded in the now. The danger of my slipping into the past and getting stuck there was too great.

I noted how watchful Alec was as we drove down the narrow, winding roads out of Dobrenica, at its mellowest in the glorious colors of early autumn. We'd been driving for an hour or two, me wondering if we'd feel it when we crossed the border, when I ventured a question: "Do you think the Blessing worked?"

"Or is there such a thing outside of the archivists' imaginations?" He smiled my way.

"Okay, what's bugging me is this. If it's real, and you and I getting hitched is a big component of it, does that mean we shouldn't actually leave the country?"

He laughed. "A bit late to be thinking of that, isn't it?"

"Hey, I think I'm doing pretty good, considering we just pulled an all-nighter."

"True." Being the innately kind person he was, he didn't point out that he'd been right there beside me for that all-nighter, and *his* brain was still firing on all cylinders. "According to the private records of Jaska Dsaret, the Blessing worked, yet he was able to travel to Vienna to be part of the Vienna Congress. It was reading that," he admitted, "which convinced me years ago that there was no actual Blessing. That Dobrenica was just lucky that wretched weather, and the equally wretched state of Napoleon's Grand Army, was what kept them from discovering this valley. While I'm now on the fence about that, I do believe we should be all right."

Sure enough. There were no mysterious fogs, no warning figures floating out of the shadows. Eventually we reached civilization, and it was just the two of us, enclosed in our sphere of bliss.

During our leisurely drive over the next few days, I sensed our newly-married life beginning to purge Alec of the lingering emotional toxins of the alcoholic haze he'd used as desperate (and futile) escape from his first brief, obligatory marriage. Poor Ruli — shackled into duty as much as he had been, until she was betrayed altogether by a family connection. Jerzy von Mecklundburg doesn't deserve the term "family relation." And Ruli had not deserved that end.

I knew that Alec did not blame Ruli for that travesty of a marriage, short as it was. He'd respected her willingness to stay in Dobrenica, and to try to be a proper princess, though she had not wanted the marriage any more than he had. There'd been no honeymoon, by mutual agreement. But forced proximity with the wrong person rendered unbearable the otherwise innocent aspects of their life as a couple until they both started the day with several drinks between them and the rest of the world, as if the buffer of booze could mitigate the emotional anguish.

It had not.

I would have been content with a honeymoon at Ysvorod House, if not just holing up in the palace, but Alec's closest friends separately and collectively insisted that getting him entirely away would be the best thing for him. So I'd told Alec, "Surprise me with a cool destination!"

I'd wondered how he would do without servants. I ought to have figured out that though he was used to them, he wasn't helpless without them. We traded off driving. We grunted our own bags. As for laundry, I was willing to pig it, as that was what I'd done when living and traveling on my own (washing underthings out in the sink, and locating a laundromat for the big stuff) but he said, flipping his credit card between his fingers, "I picked hotels with laundry service. What's the use of having money if we don't use it?"

I have to say, I do like staying in nice hotels rather than down-and-out fleabags, if I can get them. Not the bland may-as-well-be-in-America mega-hotels. He opted for places that had history, and walking-distance access to great local food.

We made our way westward and south, still sheltered in

our happiness; the only intrusion of responsibility was his nightly cell phone call to one or another of his equerries, who traded off driving down the mountains into range of the nearest cell tower to report on governmental matters. Of course Milo, as king, was in charge of the country, and Prime Minister Ridotski backed him up, but Alec was the primary interface between the Council, the Vigilzhi, and the people. It was Milo who had (I think at my grandmother's request) backed up the suggestion that Alec get some actual vacation time.

I did not care where we were going. The journey — our time together — was everything.

But eventually anticipation gripped me: what destination had he chosen? What would it say about him? About what he thought I'd like?

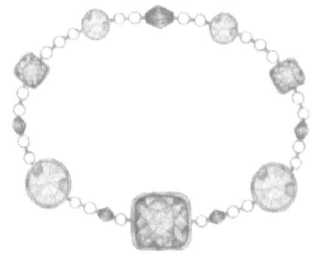

Eight

Ruli

As I said before, when in the Nasdrafus, one has a connection with others, wanted or not. That is, they can find you. The "they" in this situation being the seraphim. If I went to the Nasdrafus, they would probably confront me to ask when I was going to bring Kim to them.

Therefore, I had to travel to Paris the customary way.

Dobrenica has a small air strip at the bottom of the valley. When I was a child, all planes flew east into Russia, up past the Eyrie. My brother used to target them with his slingshot before he figured out size relative to distance. He must have been about twelve when he first attempted to shoot a helicopter down with a shotgun, and managed to ding the tail enough to send it into a spin. There were fewer helicopters buzzing the Eyrie after that.

Once the Russians left, Milo arranged for Dobrenica's solitary plane, a twin-engine type left over from World War II. Tony could tell you what make it is. All I knew about it was that it served to get me to Paris, a city which entranced me from my first visit.

The Dobreni plane flies once a day—assuming there are passengers enough to make the trip worthwhile—at times convenient for the passengers, who are usually from the Five Families. No one else could afford it, not that there's much demand outside of various business interests, and once in a while humanitarian causes. Those trips are invariably paid for by the crown.

Most who have occasion to leave Dobrenica either drive or take the train, which comes once a day, except during heavy snows. The plane, like the inkris and wagons and carts and the tiny fleet of taxis (which include horse-drawn buggies) all come under the Transportation Guild, but you can be sure Alec knows who flies in and who flies out.

I expect anyone wanting to understand the dynamics between the Families might be interested to discover that it was my mother who smuggled Uncle Jerzy in the previous Christmas, in the guise of a servant. Alec probably knew, but overlooked it on the grounds of family and holiday.

Maman, I knew, saw Jerzy first and last as a servant. We, the younger generation, accepted that; it never did to disagree even slightly with Maman. (*"The boys will be spending the summer in Dobrenica with Kilber, learning orienteering, or whatever they call it." "But where is Milo, Maman?" "How should I know? In prison or some such."* This while checking her lipstick in the hall mirror. *"Whatever trouble he might be in, he'll get out of it. He always does. My point is, you will be spending the summer in Switzerland, perfecting your French." "But Maman, we're in Paris! And my French is perfect!" "It's Parisian. You will learn pure French, Loire French. And you will learn better manners; it's impertinent, not to say unbecoming, to talk back to your elders. Phaedra will be going with you. Someone has to teach that horse of a girl how to enter a room without knocking into furniture. They might as well try to teach her to read, too — they're said to work miracles. As for the twins, Jerzy will find something suitable here in the city..."*)

Though I would never defend Jerzy, his actions might in some wise be understandable; it has to have been galling to always be reminded that he was part of the family only on sufferance. As an illegitimate son, he would never inherit, and his raison d'être was to see to all the tasks that mother needed an (unpaid) equerry for.

Of course he could have responded in any number of ways besides murder. But he's dead now. By my hand.

En enfin! The flight lists were now sent up the hill to the Vigilzhi to be checked before the plane could take off. Knowing this, I went directly to Phaedra, expecting that Dmitros would both be grateful to me for my help with the matter of the mines — and that he'd probably assent to my flying out, without even having to consult Alec. They would both be glad to see me go. Not out of animus. But I no longer fit comfortably within the thinking that there are humans, and there are inimasang.

And inimasang are the enemy.

As I expected, Phaedra came back to me, saying, "You're cleared to go; the other two passengers had no objection to leaving after supper tomorrow evening. I can drive you down to the airfield."

I thanked her, and we met again as soon as the sun set the next night. As we climbed into her racing Maserati, I said, "Was there any information from the surviving mercenaries?" I was thinking of the seraphs—though imagining a connection was probably mere fancy.

"As expected, they were just hirelings, told that a little work, a little bullying of ignorant mountain people, and they'd be rich. Alec dealt with them his usual way."

"Which is?"

I had never troubled myself over Alec's political affairs hereto, and Phaedra sent me a mocking look. But she only said, "Gets their pictures done. Shows them. Says that now their faces are posted, and if they dare to cross our border again, they will be shot on sight. And they get dumped at the border."

I thought of their long, mountainous walk ahead, and laughed.

She pulled up at the airfield, gave me a casual wave, and zoomed off. I had my passport in case going to shadow proved difficult, wore a scarf and dark glasses, and boarded the plane. I was ignored by the two men who shared the plane with me.

It usually lands at a small airfield on the Baltic, and sometimes at an outlying facility at Berlin Brandenburg. After landing, with several hours' cushion before dawn, I had many possible choices. Traveling this way was tedious and time-consuming, and the moon was full, but avoiding portals meant that the seraphim would not be able to track me, if they were so inclined, unless they entered the physical world. The fact that they hadn't suggested that they couldn't.

After a few days of arduous night-time travel, I reached Paris. I had no trouble entering our flat, but I heard the moment I got inside the three slow, slumbering heartbeats that meant Maman had indeed sent ahead staff to ready the flat for her arrival before the holidays.

I was tired, my energy nearly spent. I set out that very night, reveling in the familiar lights of Paris. I breathed in the air, a complexity of the Seine and rain-dampened falling leaves, with a trace of diesel lingering from the streets. It's at all times an enchanting city; even with inevitable shortcomings inescapable in modern civilization, it's still Paris.

One of those shortcomings, common the world over, was evident not long after I set out. It was late enough, with a thin drizzle falling, that the streets were fast emptying. I caught a whiff of fear-laced irritation, mingled with lusty intent, and there, across the street, I spotted a bus stop. A very young woman stood with her arms full of a bulky package. And next to her, far too close, a man talking to her. At her. Her rigid body radiated discomfort, though the other two men waiting for the bus paid no attention, one smoking in indifference.

The roar and hiss of the bus broke the moment; the woman's shoulders dropped an entire inch. The bus pulled up, the man made a reach for her package, and I heard him offer to help her. She turned away, repeating stiffly, "Pas de problème." And hurried onto the bus.

The man laughed and strolled away, looking around for…a new target? When we drew abreast of an alley, I struck, and left him sitting upright, dazed and very relaxed from loss of blood.

As I walked away it occurred to me for the first time that it was always men. I'd never yet taken blood from a woman. It wasn't as if there were no obnoxious women. There were plenty around—beginning with Cerisette. Predation, I thought. The thought of attacking women, who, like me, had been targets of predation in the physical world, was repugnant, whereas I rather liked preying on predators.

My initial pleasure was wearing off. The weather? I walked some more, until the rain began in earnest. I returned to the flat and quietly made myself a kind of hermit retreat in my commodious closet, counting on no one troubling me there.

As expected, the staff did not venture into the family wing. I went out again the following night. This time I took money with me; I knew where there was always a stash of euros. The weather had warmed, a perfect night. Everyone was out, strolling along the river, or in the parks still open, and of course the cafes were packed.

I was still brimming with energy after a day's rest, so I sat out on a sidewalk café, and ordered a coffee, sure that this familiar habit would bring me back to my old Paris pleasure. I tried to enjoy the night, the lights, the drifts of conversation around me as I sipped the coffee, but increasingly I was aware that I was pretending to be myself: human. Alive.

Was that it? The pretense, or the sense of isolation, me quite

alone in this sea of warm flesh and beating hearts? People who
could expect a future with romance in it. Maybe even children.
I had never thought about children, ever. This is maudlin, I
decided, and left, to walk about aimlessly once again. Perhaps I
ought to try a film, even a show. I'd always loved both.

I stopped at the nearest cinema. The billboard displayed
posters for a romantic comedy. I bought a ticket and went in.

My vampiric senses were at once aware of the breathings,
the heartbeats around me. And as the film commenced, I was
distracted by the changes in both, the evolution of mood and
emotion, though to me the soundtrack was mere sound, and the
story demanded scarce attention. I found myself more
interested in the subtleties of emotional heightening around
me, until the climactic sequence began, and the accumulated
intensity of passionate reaction made my fangs itch in my
mouth. I had to fight the urge to sink them into the lanky young
man next to me, who had pulled his companion up against him,
his fingers entwined with hers.

I walked out, nearly stumbling when I sensed one of my
kind intent on the hunt not far away. I hurried in the opposite
direction. Was that ferocity what I was like when I stalked mean
drunks?

I returned to the flat to discover the noise of laughter and
the clink of glasses. The staff were having a little gathering of
their own. That compounded my sense of utter isolation, and I
withdrew to my closet, thinking: is this it, then? An eternity of
this travesty of life?

Now I began to understand what Rose had said about those
who went mad, or sun-struck. She'd even said one night that
there was a rumor that those who starved themselves long
enough before taking that last walk into the sunlight were
sometimes so desiccated that they did not turn to stone, but
puffed into dust, to be carried away on the wind.

The temptation to do the same was there before me, stark
and plain. Could I have wept, I might have, for the tide of self-
pity splashed up against the backs of my eyeballs, figuratively
speaking. I had not yet found purpose in my life before. that life
was taken away. Rose was right to laugh at me and my abysmal
attempt at finding purpose by prowling Riev for women in
pain…

Except that I *had* actually accomplished something, though
Rose had despised me for it. The truth was, I *liked* roaming
around, looking for women who might need my strength, my

speed, and my very lethal powers.

All right, I could make one more try. I was here in Paris, where I'd always longed to be. I could go out hunting for the likes of Bus Stop Bully. I would see if that made a difference for me. It certainly might for the victims.

NINE

KIM

Signs began popping up on the roadways, and we ended up on the outskirts of Venice. I'd always wanted to visit Venice!

Venice + Alec = honeymoon: Best Idea Ever. I nearly had to staple my lips shut to keep from yammering, "Are we there yet? Are we there yet?"

The first surprise was: no cars allowed. We separated out a few days' light clothes, as the weather was warm, leaving most of our stuff locked in the Daimler—including stuff like his shaving kit, with his cobalt ring tucked into it, as we'd discovered during our more enthusiastic honeymooning that the carving on the signet sometimes caught a strand of my long hair.

As he tucked the ring away, leaving only his plain gold wedding band on his other hand, I smothered a laugh, wondering if those Regency rakes with their signet rings had had a similar problem when they were tomcat-ting all over London. Or maybe their ladies just stifled yelps and later demanded diamond necklaces as compensation.

With our much lighter overnight suitcases, we set out toward the briny breezes.

Was it Robert Benchley who sent a friend a cablegram, ARRIVED VENICE. STREETS FULL OF WATER. PLEASE ADVISE? I was enchanted from the moment we stepped aboard the vaporetto, the Venetian water-bus, then rolled our overnight cases along a narrow street lined with shops, and up and over two bridges before we reached our boutique hotel.

At first I found it disconcerting to hear the scolding of seagulls as they swooped and dived, for seagulls are a part of my childhood near the palisades in Santa Monica, California. But the brilliant sunlight and the pungent scents and the colors of the Rialto grounded me firmly, and I had to fight the instinct to let glimpses of its thousand-year-old history beguile me. Stay firmly in the present, Kim! My euphoric happiness helped a lot on that score.

Our first morning, after a breakfast of cornetti and café-au-lait, we took a gondola ride in order to see the main landmarks from the water, but the rest of the day we spent trying our best to get lost as we wandered randomly chosen passages and streets. You can't really get lost in Venice, though you can get turned around if you stick to the narrowest alleys, but inevitably you'll reach a plaza here called a campo, often with buildings jutting at fascinating angles, with stairs leading toward one of the many, many bridges — each with its own history.

Nighttime Venice is almost a different city than Venice in the day; the terracotta-colored roofs and the buildings of brick and stone, painted varying warm shades of gold, rose, pumpkin, and beige, give way to a uniform softness of shadow dominated by golden lights reflecting off the quiet waters. The gondolas, graceful as black swans during the day, become gliding shadows at night.

The next morning I woke to discover Alec already awake. He lay on his side, smiling a little, his blue eyes clear.

"Did I do something gross?" I asked, instantly alert. I was still getting used to waking next to someone else; though I'd infrequently dated, I'd always preferred to come home to sleep. And while my parents would not have cared if I'd brought someone with me, Gran would have. So I never did.

"I was enjoying the view," he said. "And the sound of your breathing."

"What?" I asked, and then after a horrible thought, "You're hinting delicately that I snore?"

"No." He shook with a tremor of laughter. "That was my attempt at being romantic."

That led to the inevitable tangle in a glissade of bliss, but afterward, I was beginning to perceive, was a more subtle reward: he was beginning to talk to me not just about history, and books, and music, as we'd been doing all along, but about himself. A rarity. "I never shared a room," he observed. "Even at school, I'd always had a private chamber, small as it had been."

"Not surprising we're alike in that. Was it because we were both only children?" I asked. "Anyway, if you can stand my morning dragon breath," I said, "seems to me you're not as picky as you think you are."

He took that as a challenge.

And after an agreeable interlude, he reminded me that after all, we were in Venice

"Why did my bones have to dissolve?" I moaned. "Here I am, sweating like a horse. How am I going to get to that bathroom? You can go first. While I make a supreme effort to stand up."

"How about," he whispered into the curve of my throat, "we go together?"

We soon sat facing one another in the enormous bathtub, naked as the day we entered the world. I had to laugh.

He said, "What are you thinking, your highness?"

"Ex-cuuuuse me, my *royal* highness. That still feels so, um, pompous? No, impostrous—if that's even a word. I mean, I used to dress up for the Renaissance Pleasure Faire and we my-lorded and your-ladyshipped each other with gleeful abandon, but we never quite reached the heights of highnesses." I shrugged, splashing my hands in the bath water. "And it was not real. It was street theater."

"But court protocol is the essence of theater," Alec said. "What else can it be? It's a play everyone agrees to act out, each knowing his or her part in our pretense as civilized beings."

"And somehow, human hierarchy seems to always end up with someone as king," I said. "I know. We've been through patterns of history, and I am not complaining. For one thing, the bennies are fantastic."

"A royal palace? Or are you referring to the chauffeured Kingmobile?"

I lifted a ballet-trained leg, and with the precision of a duelist twitched my toes on a part of his anatomy that soon provoked a tidal wave. "You."

When the water resettled at last, I observed, "You've had my looks under your eye for a year all told. What were you really thinking, before I woke?"

"Contemplating all the permutations of happiness," he said. "I could stop there, and I know you'd accept that. But I cannot resist this new pleasure, no, a rarity — a luxury — a *gift*, of being able to say what I am thinking. Without pondering risks and ramifications. "

I retorted, "Once you've heard enough of *my* inner monologue, you might change your mind."

"You know what I think?" he asked as we left the tub, and mopped up the floor.

"What do you think?"

"I think your cracks are the impulse of a nature raised to regard happiness as conditional at best."

Yeah, he had me there. I'd always believed that I'd had the most tranquil of childhoods, but I prowled warily round the concept of trust. Especially of men. I expect I learned that from Gran, though she didn't intend it.

And because I, too, could now say what I thought as I thought it, I presented my idea. "It's tenderness, isn't it? That makes the difference? I'm trying to understand it."

"We've got the time to figure it out," he observed.

"Hear me gloat!"

By now we'd toweled off, and assumed our trappings of civilization. And when we'd finished breakfast in the hotel's little pocket garden, he asked, "Where shall we go first?"

"Surprise me."

"I think I know what you'd like to see next. And if I remember right, it's not far from here."

We walked out into the dazzling light, and he struck out with the firmness of memory.

The water-limned beauty of Venice imbued every building and bridge with a sense of enigma and slowed time. Occasional sun shafts revealed windows and archways below the level of the canal waters. The jumble of tiny bridges and narrow, twisting alleys brought us from radiant, reflecting sunlight into sharp shadow — then before our eyes entirely adjusted, we'd step into luminescence again, spangles off the water an intense glare. Though the time of year was sliding toward mid-September, that brilliant sunlight shone with all the strength of midsummer, especially after the mist-softened, and tree-filtered hues of Dobrenica.

But I had grown up in LA, where blazing sun happened pretty much year round, so I dropped my gaze away when we stepped into sunlit patches, distracted by cornices and quoins, the many pitted gargoyles glaring down, or peering heavenward; perhaps it was my mood of happiness, but my eye fell most often on those carved by someone with a decided sense of humor, as though those odd fish-faces and pop-eyed gremlins had been caught in the midst of laughter.

Alec finally paused outside a shop burgeoning with tourist merch, looking around pensively. Getting his bearings? Rather than hassle him, I leafed idly through postcards, until I became aware of his eye on me. I glanced up, to catch him suppressing a smile of amusement. "What?" I barked suspiciously.

"Nothing. Nothing." He raised his hands. "Just recollecting the, ah, deep moral dilemma that faced poor Emilio—and myself, I have to admit—over some postcards you were writing last summer."

I had to laugh at that. Then winced.

His smile faded. "What is it?"

"Pulse of regret, remembering who I sent those cards to. The fencing team I fought with has moved on, but…yeah, I guess I'm still thinking about how Lisa Castillo dumped me."

I'm very certain I'd bored him with tales of my oldest friend, a neighbor, actually, whose numerous family had enfolded me during childhood. Whenever I'd wanted playmates my own age, I'd gone down the street to the Castillos'.

Lisa and I had grown up with utterly different tastes, eventually sharing only one activity, fencing. But she'd regarded it as an efficient exercise, involving aerobics, stretching, and mind-focus. I'd chosen it because of the romance of the old films.

I hadn't contacted Lisa after my return from Dobrenica that summer because I'd been far too hurt—and then I'd landed that job in Oklahoma. But last winter, after everything was resolved, I'd written her a long letter, explaining six months of silence and its happy ending, and even offered to fly her over to Dobrenica to meet everyone. She could be in my wedding!

I hadn't heard back for a week or two, but I hadn't worried too much at first—no Internet in Dobrenica, phones are untrustworthy, and mail to the outside is slow.

But it was four and a half months before I got a letter. It was brief.

Kim: I'm glad for your happy ending. It sounds like what you always wanted. But the fairy tale stops with you; I don't have the time to take from prepping for the Bar to go jetting all over the world. So unless you plan to retain me as your future Los Angeles lawyer (and I would be obliged to inform you that I'm not studying international law) let's end this on a high note and wish each other well.

I heard my own voice after I uttered the words *dumped me.* "Check that. It's whining. We didn't have anything in common anymore, and I was reluctant to acknowledge it mainly because of all the fun we'd had as kids. But the friendship had become a habit, not a real exchange — she never really understood why I felt I had to go to Europe for Gran's sake, instead of fencing in yet another university competition. I guess she actually did me a favor in such a tidy ending. Anyway. Enough of that. You stopped here why? I didn't think you were the souvenir type."

"And you're right. I stopped because I'm lost," he admitted apologetically, "I thought I knew the way. It was a little bookshop full of really old books. I ended up spending half a day there when I was here last, during a spring storm. It really was a short walk from the hotel, but I seem to have taken the wrong turning."

"I don't mind a bit," I said. "And while I do want to prowl that bookstore, everything is all new to me, and fascinating. In fact, I was just counting gargoyles."

"Gargoyles?" he repeated, glancing around. "I don't see any." He turned more slowly, peering past the nearby little bridge, down the canal. "I see just about every sort of window shape, some with iron balconies, and many with flower boxes, but no gargoyles at them. Or the roofs. Exception, the whitewashed gargoyle mask above the church door that we passed a few minutes ago."

I pointed at a sly gargoyle slanting its wicked smile out over the green waters. "Do you see that one?"

Alec blinked, then said with mild wonder, "I do not."

It was my turn to blink, and concentrate — and the gargoyle vanished, leaving a sill with a window box of geraniums. Then I blinked again, and there was the gargoyle.

Before I could speak, I was distracted by a shape drifting over the bridge. A pair of tourists, coming toward us from the other side, walked right through the misty glow without any reaction.

"A ghost," I said.

TEN

KIM

Judging by its blobby blur, it was an old one. I caught the impression of a long, somewhat ragged skirt, and a bodice over which a pair of braids hung. Her pale oval of a face seemed to turn toward me. "She's just a kid. I wonder what she wants?"

A ghost that Alec could not see. Though he seemed to be trying, but his gaze bent toward the near end of the bridge as the ghost drifted toward the far end. A ghost, whose history lay somewhere beyond a turn in the air: a history and a mystery, and I had to follow, and to know.

"Alec? I think...do you mind if I just follow her a bit?"

"Lead on," he said, taking my hand. "Tell me what you're seeing," he added after we crossed the bridge.

"It'll be faster if I show you," I said. Together we ran down a very narrow passage, right behind a pair of oblivious tourists, as I squinted at the ghost floating behind them. The strong Venetian sunlight defeated me when we entered the campo, but there was the ghost again, entering a narrow alley on the other side. It curved to the left.

There was an abrupt turn at the end of a building where it abutted another. Here, the ghost looked back wistfully and diffused into the plaster-peeling over brick. A careful scan showed that the brick was somewhat lighter in a long rectangle—a bricked-up window, probably to avoid an expensive window tax several centuries before. I halted at the wall, Alec at my shoulder. I'd been wishing I could look inside the buildings to see how they lived back then. Here was my chance! I laid my hand to the variegated bricks that unknown hands had laid centuries ago —

And there was Beka's voice whispering that warning in my ear. It would be so *easy* to let my mind drift with the ghost to her time…

Don't do it, I told myself. Use your prism, Kim!

I plunged my hand into my pocket, where the thing had been thumping against me daily. We stood in the curve of the passage near the intersection of three alleys, the sea breeze toying with our clothes and hair, as oblivious tourists crossed back and forth, many with cameras aiming high and low.

I shut them all out as I bent over the prism, shadowing it with the brim of my hat so that the sun wouldn't stab rainbow shards of light into my eyes, and moved slowly back and forth, turning it in my fingers.

I was getting much better at this; presently I caught a flash of color. I steadied the prism, to find it focused behind me — there was Alec, leaning against the goldenrod-painted plaster, his cell in one hand. He looked pensive, even a little tense.

The ghost forgotten, I turned to face him. His hand dropped, and he smiled.

I hesitated. When does sharing every thought become nagging? "Do you need to call?" I asked. "I totally get it if you do. Is there something going on?"

"Nothing," he said. "And I don't. Even if I did try calling Gavril, I won't get him. He has to be out of range, or driving down the mountain."

Concern or nagging? There was no one right answer. It was always going to depend on the person, and the moment. "I saw you in the prism," I said, wagging it in the air. "You looked worried. I just want you to know," I added quickly, "that even though I said, 'Surprise me,' I don't really expect you to be doing all the work entertaining me, while I have all the fun."

"I am having fun," he said, smiling. "Seeing Venice through your eyes. As for…give me a few minutes?" He glanced toward the intersection.

I did too, finding that response unexpected. But he'd asked for time, so I turned back to the prism. The ghost had vanished, and though I spent a few more minutes moving the prism with excruciating slowness, all I got was a glimpse through the window now bricked up, into a very plain little room with a canopied bed, a trunk, and a prie dieu in the corner. It could have been any time before electricity.

"It's nothing," I said, though there is always a story. But I wasn't going to find it now.

And we moved on, Alec once again taking the lead. This time he picked a wider bridge, which led to a street lined with shops. We'd passed several stores full of Carnevale masks and costumes, but the gargoyle over the door of this one had such a laughing grin on its dog-like muzzle that I paused, lingering at the window display. There were masks of all sizes and shapes, some very beautiful, promising more skillful art inside, cheek by jowl with others cheaply made, aimed at the tourist trade.

A gold and white cat mask embellished with arabesques, and a huge, sinister Dr. Plague mask caught my eye. These, like the gargoyle, glimmered subtly with Vrajhus—and it hit me then that the gargoyles that I saw and Alex didn't, and the masks, might be Venetian protections, worked in the shape of Carnevale masks. Perhaps they functioned like Dobrenican crystal decorations?

I was going to point this out to Alec, but his attention was not on the masks, so I decided to save it for later. The street was getting crowded anyway. This was not a spot for a lengthy discussion of history and the weird energies of the unseen world.

But then he slid his hand under my elbow and bent toward me, saying, "Let's take a look, shall we?"

The slight pressure of his fingers caused a tingle of urgency. Was he trying to convey some meaning? If he wanted to see the masks, we'd see the masks, though I wasn't going to buy one. The carnival season is celebrated differently in Dobrenica. And I wanted to buy masquerade masks from Dobreni artists.

We stepped down inside the shop just ahead of a cluster of Swedish tourists marveling at the sinister Dr. Plague masks. I waited for Alec to lead me to whatever had caught his eye, but to my surprise he steered me straight through the crowded little store without stopping, past stands and cabinets of masks staring sightlessly from every surface all the way to the ceiling. We entered a very narrow passageway to the back door, which stood open for air circulation. There was a short walkway shared by the row of stores belonging to this building.

Alec hailed a passing gondolier whose boat was empty, and we climbed down. I was surprised a little—the gondola rides are not cheap, and we'd already toured the canals twice—

but I reminded myself that I was not a cash-strapped student but a princess on my honeymoon. We could have three gondola rides. I wouldn't get tired of it if we had thirty.

We sat hip to hip on the plush seat for two, and I relaxed against him, ready to catch more detail than I'd missed previously, as Alec said to the gondolier in carefully enunciated Italian, "Take us to the Grand Canal, please?"

We were somewhere near the border between the Castello and the Cannaregio sestieri, with lots of charming canal curves affording paint-worthy views. The gondolier pushed off, and floated us into the middle of the canal as Alex glanced back over my shoulder. "Do any of those people around us look familiar to you?" he murmured, smiling.

Totally surprised, I began to turn but he whispered through barely moving lips, "Don't stare. Think back."

I did. Most of my attention had been divided between him and the gargoyles, as I've indicated, but I did remember some fellow tourists, glimpsed more than once. "Two older American women," I said, keeping my voice low—though we were speaking Dobreni. "And the guy with the denim jacket. I noticed him because I wondered if he was sweltering in that jacket, especially wearing a black tee beneath, which would soak up the sunlight even—" Then the clue bat struck at last. "Do you think we're being followed? By them?"

"Not the women," Alex whispered back. "The bloke in blue, yes—"

The gondola began edging around a curve, approaching one of the areas with steps leading right down into the water. Without warning Alec pulled me up, and said, "Jump."

It was only a meter or so. I jumped, landing right on the steps. Alec dropped a hundred-euro bill into the hand of the surprised, protesting gondolier, said something I didn't catch, and leaped after me.

He landed running, pulling me up the last step. Together we plunged between buildings into a passage so narrow that we almost couldn't sprint side by side. I matched my steps to his so we wouldn't bump one another into the wall, and we ran, slowing when the passage opened to an intersection of two calles.

All the while he was scanning as my brain caught up. Followed? Why? I knew that pickpockets preyed in Venice—you get those in any city—but I couldn't see what there was about us that marked us as deserving of a chase.

Alec's attention was everywhere as he scanned and navigated, so I kept my questions bottled up and concentrated on matching strides until we turned down a street with no one in sight, and he pulled me into the first open door. It smelled of expensive leather, a place selling handbags, backpacks, and the like.

We maneuvered behind a display stand that blocked us from view from the front. Between one shelf and the next there was an envelope-sized space through which he watched the window, a narrow strip of dim light painting him from eyebrows to cheekbones.

"There were four of them, three beside the point man in denim," Alec said softly, still speaking in Dobreni. "I thought they were tourists, too, randomly turning up along our path. Like the two Americans."

"How can you tell the difference?"

"When I stared at the two women, they stared back, both clearly affronted at my rudeness. I met the eyes of the bloke, or tried to, but each time he turned and pretended to be interested in the tourist tat."

My first thought? So much for my comfortable assumption that the two of us existed solely in our little honeymoon bubble. He was always on alert. You, me, and Dobrenica, I reminded myself. Here's where it gets real, I guess.

"It wasn't until I spotted the other three that I was sure," he finished.

I figured then that I can either bewail the situation, or try to match the mental trajectory as well as the physical. "Point guy being the one who tags our shadow, and the others to…"

"Close around us," Alec said.

"Purpose? You're not thinking princenapping? Assassination?" I gulped.

"Don't know, yet. Rather not find out." He smiled suddenly at me. "Shall we ditch them?"

"No party-poopers welcome on our parade," I said back, as casually as I could, though my body was now thrumming with nerves.

Then he brushed my cheek with his fingertips and whispered, "God, I love you so much." He took my hand as I murmured, "And me you," and we edged to the door.

Clear. We were off.

He stuck close to walls, and we used knots of tourists as cover. At first I wondered why until I caught him glancing up at every corner, then I remembered St. Mark's Campanile, the tallest tower in Venice, and the T Fondaco Dei Tedeschi rooftop. If I was a villain, of course I'd stash nosers on both summits to do some spotting from there.

We made it back to our hotel without incident, but while I was ready to throw myself on the bed and utter a sigh of relief, Alec stood inside the door, frowning down sightlessly at the floor in a way I was beginning to recognize. His mind was going a thousand miles an hour.

I knew I couldn't hope to keep up. I hadn't the experience he'd had growing up, sneaking in and out of the country and playing tag-you're-dead with the Russian occupiers, until the last of them finally loaded up the last of their loot and vamoosed.

"Do you think it's Tony who sent those guys?"

Alec uttered one of those huffing laughs before saying, "Your mind leaped straight to him?"

"He'd probably love ruining our fun," I sniped.

A real laugh, this time. "Maybe. But it's not him. Or I'd be surprised if it was. What would he get out of it? If I vanished today into one of those canals, it would cause a short-order uproar, but then everyone would line up even more firmly behind Milo. Whatever replacement he picked would not be a von Mecklundburg."

"Aside from that," I hazarded, "from what I know of him, he'd want to have the fun of the grab."

"That's more like it. But I still don't think he's behind them. What say we leave Venice? We can always come back one day. But I want a clear field of vision. See what our unknown party-pooper is willing to put up against us."

The words "party-pooper" in his precise accent made laughter bubble up behind my ribs. "Say the word. I can be packed up in five, thanks to your insisting we leave most of our stuff in the car."

"Let's. But we'll leave once it's dark, shall we? I'm glad they gave us a room overlooking the front. I want to watch for a while. Join me?"

"Don't mind if I do," I said. "I'll get us some water. Or do you want more coffee? I noticed they had some decent teas in the coffee service. I might as well get some for me while it's right there."

"Coffee and water, thanks. There is connectivity here," he said, checking his cell phone. "I'll report in while you do that.

Warn them that we might go incommunicado for a day or two."

I left him to leave a message for the Vigilzhi as I got us our beverages. Then we sat at either edge of the window so that it would be difficult to make us out from below, and talk rambled from coffee to tea to far-flung trade, and thence to the fact that Venice had once had the most powerful navy in the Mediterranean. I learned, obliquely, that Alec, coming from a landlocked country, was fascinated with the sea.

We checked out once the church bells had rung sunset, Alec letting the hotel people know that we were traveling to Florence, in case our shadows turned up to snout about our movements. Then we retraced our steps, walking—always with crowds—and taking the vaporetto to the train station, which was adjacent to our parking garage.

Though we'd seen no one suspicious in those three or four hours that we sat at the window and watched, Alec said we had to assume that whoever had been following us had already staked out our hotel. And we couldn't know if someone was watching for us behind all those blank windows. So, other than making sure we were always in the middle of a pack of sightseers, we didn't try any evasive action until we were in the car.

Alec pulled us onto the main road leading south toward Tuscany. Though I'd been honed as a driver by LA traffic, he was the one trained in spotting and ditching automotive followers.

I was tired and hungry by the time he was satisfied that we had no one on our tail. He had to be feeling the strain as well, so I said nothing. At a point when there were no headlights in either direction he exited the autostrada. We navigated along country lanes, the beautiful north Italian scenery reduced to hairpin turns in the darkness, and occasional forlorn lights in small villages, until we found a village large enough to have a lit alberghi, which meant they had someone on the night desk.

This being autumn, they were not full, and we got a room. There was one eatery open; Alec pointed out that in Italy, if you avoided restaurants aimed at tourist tastes, you rarely got a bad meal.

So it proved now. After a delicious dish of pasta e fagioli and some hearty red wine, we crashed. And in the morning, Alec and I ventured into the tiny city center, got a map, and began making our way via country lanes toward Slovenia.

Eleven

Ruli

The following night, I went out early, full of purpose that was made urgent by need.

I roamed familiar streets and struck out into new ones, exploring parts of the city I'd never ventured into. Everything was peaceful, for block after block, mocking my soi-disant vigilante purpose. Occasionally I sensed vampiric intent, and chose another direction.

The streets began emptying of cars, of buses, of pedestrians.

Ahead, I heard the tick of heels, and the harsh, tired breathings of two women hurrying as if their feet hurt. It was somewhere between eleven and twelve, which meant they were probably restaurant or bistro servers, on their way home after closing time. They were both Parisian, I saw at a glance. Even after an obviously long work session, and wearing cheap shoes and bargain clothes, they were put together in a way that is indefinably but unmistakably Parisian.

I heard one's muttered imprecation. Their steps sped up. I hastened to catch up when I saw two street toughs coming up an otherwise empty side-street toward them. They stank on the physical level of sweat and stale drink, but their lust for this new prey sparked my own lust.

They began taunting and whistling. The women ignored them in the usual way woman have for endless time, bending into the chilly wind and walking faster. The remarks got personal, the invitations punctuated with raucous laughter as the women headed grimly for the Metro. I could hear their heartbeats going from fast to angry, an inviting surge, but it was their harassers who were my prey.

The men caught up, each to the side of a woman. The younger one on the left shouted "Casse-toi!" and the other plunged her hand into her bag. Mace, no doubt.

The men took a step back, both eyeing the one with her hand in the bag, and the two women bolted across the street toward the well-lit Metro entrance. The lechers shouted insults after their escaping prey before they turned around — to find me waiting.

For a single heartbeat, they grinned, but then I grinned back.

Wider.

I left them lying woozily on the sidewalk. I walked on, burning the residual alcohol from their mingled blood. My energy sang once again. Oh, how good it felt! This was so very sweet. And dangerous, there was the inner whisper: *You've been given the form of a monster. Don't become the monster.*

My awareness spread — and here came three of my kind. All women.

"Very well done," one said, mocking but approving.

"But you are in our territory," the second pointed out.

"Eh! You are new-made, I'm thinking?" the third had a high, treble voice. She looked like a doll, with marcelled hair and dark red cupid's bow lipstick.

"Since winter," I said.

"You are not French," the first observed, though I know my accent is excellent.

"Dobrenica. In the east."

"Ah, the east," the second exclaimed with an airy wave, as if it were the Himalayas. "You are here because?"

"I love Paris," I said. "And right now, I've nowhere else to be."

'This is our territory," the second one said again, not unfriendly. "But you did not transgress our rules: you left no dead to bring trouble, and you used the predators as prey, not their victims. It is just! If you wish to continue your excursions in our territory, meet at Cimetière du Père-Lachaise tomorrow, midnight. Oscar Wilde's grave. Tonight we are roamers, and we must be going."

They drifted on.

The cemetery? Oscar Wilde's grave?

I recollected him from school, retaining an impression of a louche poseur, but Alec had insisted there was a lot more to the man. One night he'd read to me from "The Ballad of Reading Gaol" in an effort to convince me, but I was drinking heavily that night, and I'd ignored the poem's plea for prison reform, and dismissed the religious thread, annoyed by my assumption that Alec was aiming the much-quoted line, "For each man kills the thing he loves," somehow at Marzio and me. In retrospect that was merely liquor-logic.

At all events, since I was in Paris I was ready to be convinced there was a more interesting reason for an invitational gathering at a pretentiously touristic venue.

After the sun was well down, I slipped out. I had a long walk before me, and the cemetery is enormous. When I reached the twentieth arrondissement, I leaped the fence, landing with little grace. Perhaps I ought to practice that, I thought, though I did not expect to be leaping high walls as a habit. But then all my habits are changing, I reflected as I sped down the quiet aisles between well-tended tombs.

I spotted the occasional ghost. These, I had discovered, were seldom the revenants of the buried person, many of whom never gave in life a second thought to where their remains would lie, but were usually a loved one, perhaps in the habit of communing with the dead at the gravesite, and now clinging to the last vestiges of the known.

I perceived voices preceded by the quick hiss of conscious breathing; there was Oscar Wilde's grave. The pale stone gleamed softly, marred by dark spots that turned out to be lipstick kisses. But I already knew that many Parisians regard certain monuments as luck artifacts. This grave was one of those.

Above the base, the square, blocky wings of an angelic figure acted on me as an unpleasant reminder of the seraphim, though as unlike those vast and graceful wings as possible.

I could not count the chatting figures, many in silhouette or obscured entirely in shadow, whether from age or dulled energy, I was not certain. My senses were drawn to the indescribable sense of a portal. Here? But portals could be anywhere, and it was unmistakably made by us.

I recognized the three vampires who had approached me, and now I had time to take them in: all my age when I was turned, or younger. Chic clothing, one in twenties fringed silk, the other two more modern. On the other side of the monument, I spotted a statuesque woman wearing a belled skirt and an off-the-shoulder bodice, her high-piled hair indicating at least a century, more like two, since she had walked under the sun.

"Here's a new sister met last night," the first of my trio exclaimed, and the rest turned to take me in.

"Preyed on the mecs, and let the meufs be," said the high-voiced one in a tone of decided approval. "And without a warning!"

"Meuf," if you are unfamiliar with Verlan (a French play on words) is a little like "chick." It was uttered in a friendly, almost fond tone. I learned very soon that these vampires referred to all living women as meufs, looking upon them somewhat as a Côte d'Azur lifeguard regards the oblivious small-fry splashing among the combers. Men were mecs or gars.

They wanted to know my story — where I'd come from, how I was turned, and when. "Though it is not at all necessary to tell us, if you do not wish to," one of the three hastened to say.

"I don't mind," I said. "I was set up by a relation. I was supposed to die in a car wreck. But I was turned by my grandmother."

"Grandmother!"

"Actual grandmother, or a term of hierarchy?"

"Actual grandmother."

"That's a new one!"

"I used to attend school here in Paris, and came back as often as I could. My family knows about me, but I don't know how welcome I'd be at the family's Parisian flat, though I have been hiding there." I thought it would entail too much explanation to bring in the seraphim and why I was avoiding them, and finished, "I'm not the only one who has returned to Paris after being turned?"

"No, no, no!"

"Not at all!"

That inspired an explosion of commiserating welcome as well as advice.

They began introducing themselves, first Perrine, she of the twenties fringed silk gown and the marcelled hair.

From their explanations I began to discern that the vampires of Paris more or less observed territories loosely following the borders of the arrondissements, with exceptions. Within those, there were loose alliances, some created families—that is, turned by an older vampire or leader, and others banding together. And, just as they had territories, they had preferred terms for themselves. These women did not like the word *vampire*, and still less the French version of bloodsucker, which was apparently favored by the more aggressive predators. *Les mortes-vivantes*—with the feminine endings—was their preferred term for themselves: the living dead.

Not a single one had wanted to be turned. The stories I heard were uniformly sad ones.

The three I'd first encountered were part of a group whose self-appointed mission was to look out for women. So much for your assumptions, Rose, I thought: some of them were quite old, their passions still burning from flagrant injustices during their lives. In fact, their titular leader, I was told, was none other than Olympe de Gouges, the humanist butcher's daughter who wrote "The Declaration of the Rights of Women and the Female Citizen" during the Revolution, and who had championed for the rights of slaves and for the imprisoned king respectively.

"The mortes-vivantes of that day tried to save Charlotte Corday, but could not," high-voiced Perrine said. "They planned better for Olympe."

With vigor and passion, as if she'd been there personally to witness, Perrine described how Olympe de Gouges was turned before she was beheaded, primed with blood and charms so that her life was not completely extinguished in spite of the guillotine. There were those who saw to it she was put back together immediately, which enabled her to heal, and someone else was buried in her place.

"There were far too many to choose from," one of the shadows stated, in an accent I couldn't define. "Ah! That was a very bad year for women. In the political struggles, the factions were getting rid of women they considered too forward, after a pretense of acceptance."

"Madame Roland," the tall one in the eighteenth-century gown murmured. "She was not even an activist."

"But she was a Girondist," said the shadow.

"However, we have Olympe," stated a vivacious morte-vivante. "I've met her, me! The scar on her neck is still there!"

Perrine picked up the story, describing how Olympe de Gouges organized the mortes-vivantes as champions of women, especially the poor women of the city.

Perrine then turned to me. "If you tire of hiding at your former home, you could come with us tonight. We've a safe place in the Marais. And we can show you where to go, and what to avoid."

"Like the sewers," another said.

"The *rats* prey there," a teenage vampire said stridently, her 'r' the American *urrrrr*. Making it clear that she was not talking about the rodents with fur and long tails.

I thought of continuing to sneak in and out of the family flat and thanked them; if this was a recruitment, rather than a prospective friendship, I did not mind in the least.

Perrine and Noemi — a tall one in jeans and black knit jumper — led the way. This group had a secluded pied-a-terre in the St. Paul village not far from the river in the Marais, a very quiet part of Paris that still preserves many fifteenth and sixteenth century buildings, and even chunks of medieval Paris. We passed a section of the old wall, onto which newer flats had been built. We walked down a very narrow passage that was so old that the stone guards still abutted the buildings every few paces. These ankle-high stone protuberances had long ago forced carriage and cart wheels from squashing the pedestrians pressed to the wall.

Perrine whispered that the neighbors had no idea the place belonged to vampires, as there were a couple of live women in residence, who in lieu of rent dealt with occasional but necessary real-world affairs.

"The living world must be monitored," Noemi said from my other side. "And money earned, to pay for the plasma."

"Plasma?"

"We have an arrangement for a fresh supply."

That was something not possible in Dobrenica — or, not that I knew of, anyway. I wondered if I could bear drinking blood cold, then dismissed it: I'd wondered if I ever could drink blood at all, but when the fangs came out, the appetite yawned correspondingly.

Perrine was still talking. "…Marie-Benoîte, who lives with us, became part of the committee to keep the entire area from being destroyed, half a century ago. Instead, only the old, falling down buildings came out, and running water was brought in for the first time."

Fifty years ago? That could have been Dobrenica.

"The caretakers know about us, of course," Perrine

explained as she unlocked the heavy carriage door set in massive stone walls two stories high. "But we do not trouble them, and they do not trouble us; their rooms are at the east wing, and everything else is ours. We even have our own washer and dryer, as well as our own kitchen. The washer and dryer being things that Clèmence, who does miracles with our clothes, considers miracles in themselves."

Perrine explained this as we crossed a courtyard around whose perimeter grew potted plants. They were all night-blooming plants; the delicious aroma of jasmine hung heavy on the air. Also glimpsed: moonflower, Angel's Trumpet, and elegant Casablanca lilies.

Then Noemi opened a very old carved front door and we entered a lamp-lit hall. The lamps were soft-glow LED lights, set in a row down one wall covered with yellowed paper of an Edwardian pattern. The opposite wall, from which the wallpaper had been stripped and the plaster smoothed, was in the process of being painted its entire length.

This painting was like a scroll I'd seen in a museum display, depicting a walk along a river that gradually opened into the outskirts of a city. Slowly the scenery became more crowded with buildings and people going about their lives, each person differentiated from the next, no matter how small or how inconsequential the task: the dusty-footed old man driving an ox-pulled cart full of baskets of vegetables had sparse whiskers of gray and white, each meticulously painted, was as lovingly detailed as the young woman in the palanquin being carried by eight husky guys. She wore an elaborate gown of red and gold, with a golden headdress on her black hair, one eye — wide with anticipation — peeking out from behind a round, tasseled fan.

I stopped to take in the sheer detail. As I did, the painter, dressed in wrinkled, paint-splotched robes, stood up. She was tall and thin, with slow-blinking wide eyes and a mild expression. I took her for a woman until I saw the shadow under her larynx. A man?

"This is Maëlle," Perrine stated with obvious pride. "All the art in the house is hers." Woman, then.

To Maëlle, "Ruli is a newcomer from the far east."

Maëlle glanced at her painting, and I was going to say, "Not that far east!" but Perrine was already moving on, and Maëlle had turned back to her palette to mix colors.

I accepted that, as yet, I generated too little interest for corrections. Just as well. Perrine showed me through the vampires' kitchen, also lamp-lit. There was the sink with running water, the refrigerator full of blood plasma, and the washer and dryer. There was also a tiny stove, mute testimony to cooking being occasional, and next door to the kitchen a large and elegant bathroom — the single bathroom for all those inhabitants more silent proof that showering for our kind was an occasional pleasure rather than necessity.

As if her thoughts ran parallel, Perrine said, "We do sometimes make coffee. Tea as well. And the youngest of us still likes to eat." I thought about how much extra strength that took, to emulate the human life we would never actually have again. I understood a new vampire desperate to reclaim the life taken away; though for me, it had taken the form of staying in the Nasdrafus, and going to hair and nail salons — though of course everything physical reverted to the way it had been when we were first turned, once we reentered the physical world.

There were a lot of rooms, as the place was three story, not including the attic, with tiny rooms that once had been storage and servant quarters. The rooms at one end belonged to the human residents. They had a thick, well-fitted door between their hallway and the rest, so that no light would ever penetrate. The vampires had the L-shaped remainder, three floors' worth of rooms and the attic.

"Clémence and Agnès share that chamber," Perrine said, and, lower, "Agnès stays longer and longer in the other world, only coming out for sustenance. Clémence comes out more often, and does up our laundry perfectly. She was a laundress, before the troubles in 1830. She says that doing up our clothes makes her feel useful. They rarely leave the house anymore."

And then, "That's Lotte's chamber. She is out roaming. She's our most assiduous roamer. She is training Lya, our newest."

"Is it permitted to ask Lotte's story?" I ventured.

"We do not ask, as a rule, until someone offers. As it happens, she will not mind your knowing: she was attacked by a German soldier when Paris was occupied. She had just sent off her son, who was part of the Resistance, but the Germans did not know that. She was attacked because she was there, and she had a pretty face, and she said no. He left her for dead, but she wasn't. And one of our kind came by. He thought it a shame for so beautiful a woman to die. Ah! You know Frenchmen," Perrine said, with a lift of her shoulder. "And so she survived —

and her son never came back. Her husband had already died. She is indefatigable," Perrine finished.

"I am next to Lotte," Noemi said, turning to a beautiful stairwell, old and finely made. "And Perrine next to her. Up this staircase, Lya, and the guestroom. Marie-Benoîte has the library, and Maëlle the far room."

So saying, Perrine opened the door to the guestroom, and I used my night vision to look around at the stolid old furnishings from early in the twentieth century. The bed was canopied. The tall windows had shutters neatly fit in; behind them, curtains and behind those, glass. The house would look like any other house from outside. "Linens at the end of the hall," Perrine said.

The next night, I emerged after dusk to find many of the others gathered downstairs in a very nice salon, redone in the thirties, judging by the art deco décor.

Among these were Lotte, a very beautiful woman with sad brown eyes, appearing about forty, slim and neat, with a teenage girl I'd noted before. Lya, I remembered. At first glance Lya was a vampire cliché, dressed in Goth black, with knee-high boots covered in buckles. She wore black lipstick and eyeliner, and her hair was dyed an uncompromising black that had very likely badly suited her complexion when alive. Cerisette would no doubt admire that corpse-like paleness now. Her inner forearms were covered with the evidence of a heroin addiction. Snail trails, the girls at the boarding school had called them, with knowing condescension.

This girl had an angry mouth under that black lipstick, and the general demeanor of a cat a heartbeat from springing to claw your face. "They brought you back here?" she asked, her French heavily accented with American vowels and consonants, bringing Kim unexpectedly to mind. "How'd you end up vamped?" she said in English, then repeated it more consciously in French.

Perrine said, not to chide, but more like coaxing, "Lya, chérie, we do let people speak of their past experiences when they are ready."

That coaxing voice, the way the others all stood facing Lya made me realize that this Lya was their poppet, their mascot. Further, that my being accepted might even be contingent upon Lya's acceptance of me.

"I don't mind telling it," I said in English.

"Oooh, you've got that snobby English accent."

I could have retorted about snot accents, but engaging with a teen, however obnoxious, would achieve nothing. I ignored the remark and gave her the same account that I'd given the others. (She'd been there, I distinctly remembered. But clearly not listening. Either that or she wanted me to know she had not been listening.) Then I waited, ready to depart at the first sign of trouble. When I was growing up, I'd had to swallow the gnat-stings of derision, but I did not have to now. At least I'd brought nothing with me.

But Lya said, "Wow. Your uncle? Wow, wow, wow. That sucks bigtime! Even my dumpster fire family wouldn't go *that* far. But I bet they would if they weren't chicken about ending up in jail," she remarked.

This seemed to be conditional approval. At least the others reacted as if I had crossed an invisible line, and I tagged along as Lotte and Noemi took Lya for an instructional hunting lesson.

There were things they could teach me about taking down the target, and that night, and over the next few, I learned useful things about other vampire families, clans, gangs, in Paris. Who was an ally, and whom to avoid.

I brought over armloads of my darkest clothes to my new room (one of the other empties was now designated the guestroom). I had to find a way to contribute toward the plasma supply, but that was easy enough, through my accounts still not closed out. Maman would eventually know, of course, but she would not deny me anymore than she did Rose. As long as I stayed away from her.

In short, I had chanced into as accommodating a situation as I ever could have hoped for. But it was not perfect, for there was the teenaged Lya.

By the fourth day or so, I realized that Lya was as jealous of anyone drawing attention from her newfound coven of pet aunties as she was determined to personally hunt down every rapist, bag snatcher, and pickpocket, in Paris. But I was adept at keeping myself in the background when dominating personalities got aggressive, and Lya gradually accepted me as yet another pair of ears to listen to her opinions as we drifted through the Paris nights.

Dépaysement is a French term that can connote the sense of being out of place in your own country. To the mortes-vivantes, it meant the existence that is no true life. The quiet, four-hundred-year-old house had beautiful art both framed and slowly emerging on the walls every time Maëlle returned from one of her Nasdrafus wanders, and it had comfortable furnishings. It had companionship and there was a sense of belonging, even purpose. At the same time there was in the boarded and blocked windows, the weak light that was mostly for atmosphere, and in the lack of a pantry and a dining area, that mutual awareness that there was no possible marriage in the real sense. There would never be babies born, no schoolkids bringing home the fresh possibilities of the future. No shared strolls in the Tuileries Garden in spring sunlight.

But we did have purpose.

Twelve

Kim

On that dash through Slovenia, I learned that Alec had two modes of travel: the prince mode, i.e. comfortable (the most comfortable being with a couple of equerries along to handle all the exasperating logistics, nice hotels, great car, as we had on our summer masquerade down the Adriatic coast last summer) and what I think of as "on the run" mode.

I knew he'd been raised to zip in and out of Dobrenica. He mentioned once his first solo trip was as a young teen. Teen! I tried to imagine myself in junior high successfully getting past the border of the Iron Curtain. Not likely. I guess it all comes down to what you grow up thinking part of normal life.

At least we had the comfortable car, though I hated to think what those rutted, potholed roads were doing to the finely-tuned suspension of the Daimler, even as slow as we were forced to go. A jeep would have been faster, though it probably would have jolted us even worse.

We never stayed in one place past a night. We found cheap places to stay, which usually meant sharing the WC with everyone else on that floor, and ancient bathtubs instead of showers. No bathroom heating, of course. Seldom amenities like hair dryers, not that I used one with long hair. But Alec never seemed to mind leaving with a wet head.

I learned that travel with someone congenial takes a lot of the irritation out of all the little discomforts of finding yourself in strange territory, nothing you expect ready to hand. At first we Alphonse-and-Gastoned each other with determined politesse, "No, whatever *you* want," back and forth, until I figured that I was going to have to be the one to speak up. He was at a disadvantage for reasons I was only beginning to understand.

My mom is not one for handing out advice, but she did take me out to lunch a few days before the wedding. She filled me in on a lot of the von Mecklundburg dynamics, and we laughed about human foibles, including our own, as there's a lot of the wicked Count Armandros in us both. Then, before I headed back to the palace that still smelled strongly of paint, she fluffed her brightly hennaed hair and said, "I think you and Alec have a great thing going. You're a lot alike in the best ways, but also in some ways that might mean you'll need to be the one to take the first step. Milo's wired him too tightly into polite mode. The only time he knows he can really cut loose is when he's up there somewhere battling Russkies." She'd waved toward the mountains. "So let me tell you this, then butt out: never go to bed angry. Talk it out."

Though I'd never had sibs, I had had friends among neighbors and schoolmates, and I'd learned that "talking things out" could turn into bickering at the first angry, fretful, or *why?* accusation when the other cared enough to feel obliged to defend.

I could say, "Wow, this sucks," and if it sounded accusing, Alec would retreat behind the polite façade, while exerting every nerve to make me comfortable, even if he wasn't. As Mom said (and I'd already discovered) he had to fix things.

But if I said, "Wow, this sucks," with a laugh, or a tone of discovery, it left the way clear for him to agree, and for us to figure a way to fix it together.

It could get trying, living on the run like that; he woke at every noise, was constantly aware of the environment, and ceaselessly observed comings and goings, even sudden bursts of birds from roadside foliage. But I did my utmost to roll with it, striving to make it fun. In fact, sometimes I test-drove some imaginary voice-over commentary, to be used in relating our journey to my doctor friend Natalie later, and I marked it as a score if I could get him to laugh.

In-jokes and code words evolved. Like, after a spectacularly bad night in an especially egregious offense against the guest house industry, named Smrekar Lux (which had no vestige of Lux about it—probably hadn't since the local tribes hooked their wagon to King Samo in the 600s), "Smrekar" became our private term for "nuclear trash fire."

Once he stopped worrying about how I was taking every little setback, Alec settled into run mode, which intensified our companionship. And even if we had to try to sleep on a sagging mattress that felt like it had seen service during the Thirty Years War, we ate well, always locally.

Alec never complained about having to toss his plans to the winds. The only acknowledgement he made was that continual watchfulness, and he suggested on our second morning that we began the day by a set of pushups and stretches, then some light sparring. Always light, as we had no protective gear, and we were both wearing rings—he'd put the signet back on as it was too easy to lose small stuff while living on the run.

Phaedra had told me once that Alec liked being read to while doing workouts with the Vigilzhi, if he had no one there giving reports or debating Council stuff. It didn't surprise me (much) therefore, when our first morning, as we faced each other, me in my yoga slops and he in workout duds, he started quoting from Seneca while getting through the tedium of pushups and the like.

Instead of counting off reps, as I did ballet and he did the Dobreni martial warmups, he tested his (he said) rusty Latin by quoting from *Apocolocyntosis divi Claudii*—which, it turned out to my delight, roughly translated means, "The Pumpkinification of the Divine Claudius."

Seneca, I knew of, though my history studies had begun later. My Latin was minimal, mostly taught me by my dad, the afficionado of Ancient Rome. I knew that Seneca had tried to introduce some humanity into Rome between the monsters Caligula and Nero before he was told to drink poison, but I'd assumed that his surviving work was lugubriously tedious. Well, his dramas are, actually. But this one is satire, and Alec had me laughing by the time we were ready to try sparring.

"After all," he said, as we did some feints and jabs, "human nature is human nature."

"And some bozo is always going to want to make himself king," I sniped.

"And someone always thinks he has to be king," Alec said—a man who sees his job as stewardship more than leadership. "Though history might call him a bozo."

As the days slipped by, we got more serious about those early morning sessions. He picked up from where Phaedra had left off in teaching me. Alec was slowly coming to trust that I was not going to say everything was fine, then complain about his choices afterward — the worst sort of travel companion. We were buddies in this situation, rather than him having to watch for the two of us.

This really drove home the realization that this relationship was an ongoing conversation as well as companionship.

Neither of us expected me to be much backup if the worst happened and we ended up in a real fight. The sparring was for stamina, and helped us learn the other's rhythms. We'd need a third to work out how fight as a pair, but I, with my years of dance, and he with years of martial arts, began to sense how a glance, a breath, a shift of hip or a turn of wrist, projected a movement the other correctly interpreted. That in itself was a defensive technique, for me a lot more practical than the prospect of a mano-a-mano slugfest.

One morning, I loaded the car with our stuff while he paid, and I took the time to snoop more thoroughly through the Daimler's trunk. It was, as I'd joked, an arsenal, but there was also a first aid kit, a pair of blankets rolled into sausages, flashlights (full batteries), and even some German army ration packs.

When I pointed at those, Alec grinned briefly. "Kilber oversaw the prep on the car. He sampled rations from various countries. He likes these best."

I eyed the weapons case. "Did he understand that we were on a honeymoon, which is not a time one expects to defend a hilltop gun emplacement?"

"Be ready for anything, is Kilber's motto. Still, I don't plan to be opening that case."

"Good," I muttered.

We wound our way along scenic cow paths (roads only by courtesy) at a breathtaking top speed of about thirty MPH, with exasperatingly frequent stops and detours. But if we were being shadowed, it had to be just as frustrating for them. The only other traffic we saw was tractors, and big wagons, some pulled by teams of heavy horses, as bearded barley, hops, maize, and wheat were brought in, leaving stubbled fields with dust rising lazily, and birds circling around for gleanings.

We made it unhassled through Slovenia. Once we crossed the Austrian border, I breathed a sigh of relief; we were now only hours from Vienna. A city of safety. We could lose ourselves in Vienna.

Alec was on the same wavelength. "I think we can risk the Autobahn."

"I think the suspension on this ride will be as relieved as we are," I said, and mentally wished farewell to the ruts and bumps of those little lanes, many of them entirely unpaved.

He flexed his hands, then said, "Do you want to take this leg or shall I?"

"You're asking because…"

"Because if for some reason we haven't shaken off our tail, it might require fast driving."

Fast, on the Autobahn, could be very fast. Way past the California speed limits I was used to. "Over to you," I said.

He flexed his hands once more, then chucked his signet into the shaving kit again. I saw that, and knew that yeah, he meant *very* fast if necessary, if he didn't want the very minor distraction of a ring with a raised stone on his hands; the plain band of the wedding ring didn't seem to trouble him. Or maybe he refused to take that off. I hoped that we wouldn't have to test the Daimler's max mph.

We crossed the border as the sun rimmed the east. Very little traffic — and no bad guys. Buuuuut about an hour and a half into our beautifully smooth drive, he uttered an unheated Russian expletive.

"They're back?" I exclaimed.

"Two of them," he said. "Hang on. Let's see what we can do about that."

THIRTEEN

KIM

As I grew up in LA, my dad made sure I knew how to drive defensively before I got my license. Driving defensively is a skill. Driving to shake a tail is another skill altogether.

There is a difference between shaking a tail and driving like an insane jerk, endangering everyone on the road. Alec never tailgates. Nor does he cut people off. The nearest I can come to describing his high-speed chase style is a kind of physical-world calculus, in which all the cars are moving in ballistic trajectories, and he's calculating velocities several seconds ahead, plotting the smoothest and the tightest way to thread through them. The tight part being the diciest, as he was watching not only forward but back, gauging where he could change lanes yet the traffic we passed would reform so as to block our followers for a few precious seconds. And those seconds add up.

I didn't dare speak until, just past Wiener Neustadt, he said with satisfaction, "That did it."

All I'd seen was something to do with two trucks, one passing the other, and us slipping between, a minnow between whales.

"There must be an army out there. How else would they spot us?"

"Probably guessed we'd head for home rather than Florence," he said, his blue eyes intent, moving fractionally as he guided us successfully through the gradually thickening traffic. "And all it would take is two, maybe three cars on the other side taking it in turns, scanning for a green Daimler. Alas, rare. We're going to have to chuck the car."

"Not completely," I exclaimed in horror, before remembering that rich people see ownership differently.

Though not all that differently; Alec laughed. "I'll tuck it in a garage, and send someone to fetch it. At least we're nearly in Vienna, home turf so to speak."

He maneuvered us through the Sunday traffic. It was both strange and delightful to be in Vienna again—where my adventures had truly begun. Though I'd had two weeks in Paris, first.

Here and there I recognized buildings: St. Stephen's tower, the Karlskirche. When I glimpsed the white and gold grandeur of the Secession—a style close to the Art Nouveau style that I love—I placed our location. I was in time to realize we'd reached the grand buildings along the Vienna Wienzeile when, after first peering around, Alec drove us into a private parking garage, and when the guy behind the glass window peered at us, Alec rolled down the window and said, "Von Mecklundburg," and a series of numbers.

We were promptly passed through, and I held back the questions thumping behind my eyelids like bats until he pulled into a space next to a classic Porsche 911T, candy-apple red, parked next to a very new Bugatti Veyron. Also candy-apple red. Both cars the male equivalent of crimson, stiletto heeled Louboutins. Then we got out, and Alec flexed his hands.

"Oh, please say we're going to take that." I ran my hand over the curve of the Porsche's roof.

Alec laughed soundlessly. "Then we might as well stick with the Daimler. More comfortable."

"Noooo."

"It's an eye magnet," he pointed out reasonably. "Whoever is sticking to our asses so assiduously would have to be blind to miss us in that. If you want a Porsche or a Bugatti..."

"I don't want either of them," I said. "What I want is to pinch whatever would annoy Tony the most. Somehow, I don't see Aunt Sisi driving a super-powered wumblum like either of these."

"Wumblum." Alec's laugh rang through the stone-and-cement garage. "If you pinch these cars, Tony wouldn't blink. Cars are just machines for speed to him. Try riding his favorite horse if you want to take the piss out of him."

"I'll keep that in mind," I said—though it was just hot air. I can barely keep myself on the back of a placid old pony. Then the usual patented Kim Murray belated thought: "Uh, you did say this is the von M. Vienna lair? What if it turns out this is the bad guys' HQ?"

"We'll talk fast," Alec said, and then, seeing my expression, he added dulcetly, "Don't you have questions? I know I do." And relented. "But I strongly suspect the place is empty."

He was right.

The first sign that we were in the clear was a very dusty key on top of the storage cabinets. Nobody had touched that key for at least a year. As expected, he explained as we trod up a flight of stairs. The previous summer, when he was searching through Vienna for Ruli, nobody had been there. And he hadn't wanted to advertise his presence by letting himself in if someone did turn up, so he'd decided to make it a one-day run, with Kilber and Emilio helping to check all Ruli's old haunts. And when Emilio spotted me following a ghost, they'd gone to a hotel.

We entered a huge flat with still, dusty air. It was clear that no one was expected: furniture all covered, nothing whatsoever in the fridge. But they did have a laundry room, so we humped our big suitcases in, and while I started loads of wash, Alec snooped through the freezer and the pantry. Unsuccessfully.

"If we want to eat, we're going to have to risk going out," he finally said. "But it is Sunday, and the Naschmarkt will be crowded. Good cover. And plenty to choose from."

"Oh, let's! We can grab some fresh food and bring it straight back here. As for any possible bad guys catching up, though I don't see how, why don't we change our profiles? Just in case. I saw a pair of mirrorshades on the dash of the Porsche. You'd never wear those." And when he made a corroborative grimace of distaste, "Maybe there's a hat of some sort. For me, I remember I accidentally stumbled over Ruli's favorite dress store—"

"One of, oh, forty favorites," Alec cut in. "We boys used to have to accompany the girls at Aunt Sisi's insistence, and Ruli would make us carry all their bags."

"Which means that Ruli has to have her own bedroom here. And closet. I take it you did stay here, before Aunt Sisi any Tony tried to double-team you with their coup?"

"Long before. When young. Milo insisted I learn German, as pretty much all our governmental papers had been in

German for the past several centuries. Aunt Sisi was not going to leave her two behind in anything that had to do with governing. As for Vienna, historically our contacts here were with the Hapsburgs."

We separated to raid closets. I suspected that Ruli wouldn't mind my helping myself to her wardrobe. Since I'd packed mostly jeans and comfortable tops, I'd opt for something dressy, assuming I could fit into it, as she was lighter in build than I, and she preferred her clothes fitted.

But I found a nice wrap-around skirt with a loose top to match, and as her shoes would be way too small, I dug my nicer pair of sandals out. I wrapped my hair in a scarf to match.

I met Alec in the main room and smothered a grin when I saw him wearing a Y2K-styled leather jacket and cargo pants. "Let me guess. Percy's?"

"Got it in one," Alec said, and hitched up the pants; Percy, though a bit younger, was more husky. Alec and Tony were both built like greyhounds, Alec slimmer, which meant he could probably fit any clothes Tony had left. But Tony's usual style wasn't all that much different from Alec's casual clothes: jeans, tee, and a shirt over it. Whereas Percy's boy-band style was effective as a disguise, at least from the back.

Alec plopped a French beret on his black hair, grabbed the keys and his wallet, and we ran hand in hand down the curving stairway, then out of the beautifully decorated building.

We decided to start at the upper end of the market, toward the inner Ring. But scarcely had we begun scanning the choices of outdoor seating for coffee and tea when once again Alec let out one of his Russian swear words, this time heated. "Don't move, don't turn. Coming from behind."

We both started toward the long rows of market stalls; at the same moment we moved slightly apart, so we weren't so obviously a couple. Out of the side of my eye I caught two big Fords with tinted windows—cliché bad guy cars, though I supposed they are the most practical if you're a villain shopping for a durable pursuit vehicle into which you can stuff a bunch of burly minions.

Linke Wienzeile is a one-way street; at the extreme edge of my vision, as I paused to eye some fruits in boxes, I saw one of the cars pull over, and ignoring the traffic around it, slide open the back door so that burly guys could jump out. Empty hands, but they looked menacing as the spread out in line-of-sight, scanning the oblivious crowd.

"See that?" I murmured.

"They're looking for a pair," Alec said. "Behind me."

My adrenaline spiked. What now? We didn't even have access to the Daimler's arsenal! But Alec was already weaving through the crowd, smooth as an inline-skater.

I stayed maybe ten feet behind as he eeled through the strollers and shoppers. He passed the row of eateries, heading for the thickly crowded row of vendors selling all kinds of goods, from food to spices to clothes and hats, with plenty of room for stuff like porcelain and umbrellas.

First to go was the beret, laid on an unoccupied chair. Alec had wallet in hand; he dipped around a family clustered around a display, and on the other side emerged wearing a Tyrolean hat. I was just in time to see him stuff a large Euro bill in the hat's place on a rack.

Next to go was the leather jacket, and half a minute later he reappeared wearing a long, loose brown silk shirt, again after leaving money in its place. I just followed; I had no cash, and anyway Alec was the target. I just had to make sure I kept him in view.

I dared not look back. I knew the nasty, crawling sensation between my shoulder blades was my imagination. I kept going, flick, flick, flick, quick glances to either side without moving my head. This was a very long market, but not infinite. What was going to happen when we ran out of vendors?

Not five seconds after that thought, I completely lost sight of him.

Worry spiked but I gritted my teeth and kept on at the same pace, forcing myself not to whirl around looking everywhere — thereby drawing attention.

Two, three seconds went by, and suddenly there he was, emerging from between two racks of gauzy, striped skirts. He clasped my hand and drew me past the racks, around the side of the booth. He chucked the Tyrolean hat onto a folding chair next to a display case full of Mozartkugeln, and ducked through strings of hanging beads in the door of a tent behind a row of vendors.

He stopped two feet inside, turning apologetically toward a startled older woman in the process of shifting embroidered aprons into a box, saying in German, "Excuse me, very sorry, but my wife twisted her ankle."

I promptly sank to the tent floor, wrapping my hands around my "twisted" ankle and let out a moan.

The woman kindly tsked and offered a chair, water, should she send for the Polizei, there's a first aid station, and while Alec thanked her repeatedly and said that he'd help me to the first aid if I could just rest a moment, she turned to a teenager reading comics further inside the tent, and in broad Wiener Dialekt, told him that he could stop lazing around and go to fetch the medic, which of course provoked a typical teen response.

While they were talking, Alec crouched down. "You have your prism?"

"Always," I said, clapping my hand to my stomach, where it rested on its chain inside Ruli's top.

"Can you extend whatever protection is on it over us both?"

Totally taken aback, I said, "If you touch me, I think so..."

He took my hand, and watched intently through the beads as I said, loud enough for the others to hear, "I think I can walk."

"Going back the other way," he said whispered, so I took my time rising to both feet and taking an experimental step in place.

"See? The lady is fine," the kid said.

"Are you sure?" the woman asked, hovering in kindly-meant concern.

"She said she's fine, so I don't need to go anywhere," the kid put in, which distracted his mother, who used the opportunity to scold him for his lack of politeness.

All this bought us a few extra seconds. Then Alec gave me a short nod: all clear. We both thanked them profusely—more time wasted—then we slipped out, me limping until we were out of sight of the tent.

That began a nerve-wracking jolt-and-jog from relative shelter to relative shelter as we watched for pursuit, Alec ahead, and me behind. Along the way we did manage to collect some eats—fresh fruit, mostly, some bratwurst, cheese, bread. When at last we reached the von Mecklundburg flat, Alec went straightaway to his big suitcase, and retrieved his cobalt signet from the shaving case and put it on.

I said as I began washing the fruit, "I thought vampires weren't political." I remembered their siege of the Dobreni Council—but that had been sparked by Jerzy's plot. "But we don't know who sent them."

"It's only a guess," Alec went on. "Both times they came at

us, I didn't have my ring on." He lifted his hand, spreading his fingers as the cobalt stone flashed blue — loaded with protective charms.

"When did you talk to your Vigilzhi guys last?" I asked, nodding at his cell phone, which he'd laid on the table next to his wallet.

"It's been a few days," he said. "I tried last night, but we were still too far out of range." As he spoke, he fired the phone up. "Needs charging," he muttered, and went to get a charger out of his suitcase.

Mechanically, I was chopping and peeling, then I plated the fruit, added a wurst for each of us, and set it on the table as he came back in, speaking in the quick voice people use when leaving a message. He went to plug the phone in to charge it, and I thought I might as well switch the laundry over. It could dry while we strategized.

"Not surprising, no answer. When whoever's on duty today is in range, we'll have backup within hours." He toyed with an apple slice.

"But you don't look any too sure," I said.

Alec's response surprised me. "Didn't you once say there might be one of those mysterious portals in this city?"

"At the Kaisergruft — but that was in the Nasdrafus. I don't know if there's one...here."

"I don't know anything about portals," he said. "In any case, I suspect I was merely the vector." He held up his signet, which glittered in the air. "Both times they turned up, I wasn't wearing this ring, which meant I was unprotected charm-wise. Which has never mattered before," he added slowly. "I'm beginning to believe they have no interest in me, except to get past me."

It felt like a mule had drop-kicked me right in the ribs. "To..."

"You."

FOURTEEN

RULI

I was just beginning to fall into the mortes-vivantes' pattern of roaming certain portions of Paris that was all the more agreeable because it was completely self-directed. The mortes-vivantes sisters were entirely self-reliant, save only for their watchful guidance of Lya, whom they watched over protectively.

Vampire on vampire violence is extremely fast and furious. I witnessed a single attack on a night out with Perrine and Noemi, and discovered that to survive it, no matter how much energy I had or lacked, I must shift into speed mode, or be obliterated. They want your life force. The violent manner in which they get it is a pleasurable side-benefit.

But Noemi—the only one besides Maëlle whose background story I did not know—turned out to be a super-lative fighter. While I had no interest in accruing power, I had a strong interest in avoiding the predators. I could learn defense from her.

The evening I decided to ask if I might go with her when she trained Lya, I woke from the reverie that is our sleep, startled by a crack of thunder directly overhead. The sun's thermal plasma is deadly to us; lightning's flash is not harmful, but no one, human or vampire wants to risk being struck by lightning.

I had gradually laid aside my human habit of changing my clothes two or three times a day. Because our flesh is more lizard-like in its lack of oils or sweat (or warmth) there's no need, unless an outside source makes us dirty. Some of the others wore theirs months at a time. Perhaps longer.

At this point, a week was customary for me, my most frequent outfit being a black silk shirt and black silk palazzo pants. If we were to go out despite the weather, I'd wear practical flats. I did not like to prowl all night in my beloved Louboutins or Jimmy Choos.

As I entered the hall, I heard Lya's voice echoing along the hallways, "I don't mind lightning!"

"But I do. I saw one of us struck by lightning once—he seemed to think he'd found a way to draw in the power of the bolt. He was wrong. He became a torch. Why don't you look at the television we got for you?"

"I'm *bored* of TV…"

"Bored *with*," Noemi cut into Lya's whine. "Or *by*. Have English prepositions changed that much?"

"*Everyone* says bored *of*," Lya began arguing.

I shut her out and glanced into the hall mirror that I was passing, since my room had no mirror. To my astonishment, the image blurred. An effect of the storm? Impossible. I blinked, to discover that the image was double, except my blond hair was piled up on my head—

"Kim?" I was not aware of speaking, I was so startled.

Her image blurred and blinked, her mouth opening and closing. Belatedly I touched the mirror, and caught her voice: "…you hear me? I see you. I think. Though it's really dark."

I touched my fingers to the mirror, and the vision sharpened to glare bright: there was Kim, behind her Alec, looking his most remote.

Kim said, "Ruli, do you know if there is a portal in the physical Vienna, and where it goes, and if there's some way for us to use it?"

"Why?" I asked, taken aback by all three questions.

"Because someone is trying to grab us," she said, as thunder rumbled sinisterly.

"If it's Tony—"

Kim shook her head. "We don't think so. There's Vrajhus involved. We're pretty sure." She held up a prism, but in the mirror, its charms had no effect on me. "As well as a pursuit."

That was the moment that I recognized the background behind Alec. They were in the family room in my family's flat in Vienna, all the lamps lit. That ruled out Tony and his games, as he'd very likely use the flat as the base of operations if he were there.

She went on, "In the Nasdrafus, there's a portal behind Maria Theresia's tomb in the Kaisergruft. There was another at the Nasdrafus's version of St. Stephen's Cathedral. And one at Notre Dame, in Paris—"

It was my turn to interrupt. "Which is where I am now. Paris, that is."

Kim nodded. "Alec said you might be. My hope was, if there's some way without danger to either you or us to get us from one locale to another so that we can get home again, as fast as we can. Even if we can't get all the way to Dobrenica, we need to at least get out of the search area of those guys."

I said, "If you're trying to avoid someone powerful, the portals might not be safe, in that whoever it is chasing after you could plant watchers at any portal they expect you to use. Has Beka or her Salfmattas taught you how to use portals?"

She gave her head a shake. "I don't think Beka knows how to do that. I suspect I'm the only person in modern times who's been in one. And both times someone else did the...whatever it is that makes it happen. They at least knew about portals two hundred years ago, but so much was lost in World War II, because all Vrajhus matters were passed down orally."

Rose had told me much the same, in her usual careless manner.

"Ruli?" My name, uttered with a French accent, brought me back to my surroundings.

Perrine stood by, looking curiously from me to the mirror that my hand lay against. "Your sister, eh? A meuf?"

I waited for another loud crack of thunder to die away. Then, "Cousin, of a sort, though we look alike, and yes, she's human, but she has the ability to talk this way." I nodded at the mirror. "She needs help."

Perrine's eyes widened. "From us? No. From you?"

I lifted my hand away, so that Kim could not hear me. "Do you know the portal at Notre Dame?"

"I know of it," Perrine said. "It is volatile, so I hear. Very volatile. I have had no occasion to test it."

Rose had said much the same when we stepped out of the Nasdrafus to the real Paris one night a few months before. "Volatile" translates to not being able to use a portal if there was a spirit connected to it which mislikes your intent. I'd wondered if that was akin to Honoré's reading of auras. She'd added that many sites some called sacred were similarly untrustworthy.

Noemi said, "I always use the portal at the Boatman Pillar under Cluny." Beneath Cluny was the much older Roman foundation, which had a portal that had been established by our own kind.

That gave me a trustworthy portal to leave for Vienna from—but where would I come out in Vienna, if I was to avoid churches? I had never ventured by portal outside of Dobrenica, except to the Nasdrafus—and I always used the mirror at the Eyrie.

Perrine's beautifully groomed eyebrows lifted, and I saw that the others had gathered, drawn by our voices. "You intend to exert yourself on behalf of this cousin? You trust her?"

Noemi said calmly, "My suggestion is, if Sister Ruli wishes to involve herself with humans, to do it once she has said a sad farewell to us."

"We protect human women," Clèmence spoke up, her county accent thick and quaint. "We don't muck with them."

"She and I...have a pact," I began to explain.

"But *we* don't," Lya said, looking from one to the next of the sisters. "Why should we help some meuf we don't even know?"

"*You* don't have to," I said, then crash! Why is it that a completely random weather pattern conveys, through its noise, an emphasis to one's words utterly unintended? "*I* must. I think," I raised my voice over the jagged boom of thunder. "The matter is sure to be important, perhaps affecting our government in my—"

Lya crossed her arms. "Why should some girl have anything to do with *governments?* Unless she's some president's daughter, or a princess—"

"Actually she happens to be a princess, yes," I said. "I can collect my things if the rest of you regard my situation troublesome—"

"A princess?" Lya burst in again, her attitude utterly changed. "I've never met a princess. Is she cool?"

"Few are cooler," I said, trying not to laugh at how Lya had transformed from a sulky teen to a semblance of a bouncy ten-year-old faster than a lightning flash. "You should ask her about fighting her way through my family's castle a year ago, using my great-great-grandfather's rapier."

"She sounds like a badass. Let's go get her!"

"Hush, mignonne," Marie-Benoîte murmured fondly. "Let

us reflect a little first."

I put my hand to the mirror, half-expecting Kim to have vanished. It testified to the urgency of her situation that she was still there, her expression sagging in relief when she saw me again

. "Tell me everything you can," I said, and added, "I am not alone here."

Kim had clearly thought out what to say. She told me the little she knew in five sentences, which I then relayed to Perrine exactly as spoken.

Then I lifted my hand away again as Noemi said to me, "What trouble did you leave behind, Ruli? I am beginning to think that these things might be related?" She indicated the mirror, then nodded at me.

I was not going to deny it. "Seraphs, seraphim."

Perrine's thin brows arched. "Real ones?"

"I believe they are more likely demons," I said. "That have assumed the semblance of three Biblical beings of the highest order—"

"Naturally the highest," Perrine commented. "Zut! Such arrogance!"

"—and to avoid their coercion, I left my home country and traveled overland, avoiding all portals in coming to Paris."

As I spoke the word coercion, I remembered my own malicious pleasure in threatening Lisi's husband. As a vampire. A demon, most would say. But I had regarded my actions as just. Would they regard their "offer" as just? I know my mother had considered her attempt to overthrow the government completely just—on the grounds that she, as the last king's only legitimate descendant, ought to inherit the throne.

"What do you mean? What does that mean, *démones*?" Lya demanded, scattering my thoughts. She switched back to English. "Aren't seraphs angels? I thought there was no such thing as angels and devils. Can we kick some demon ass?"

"The correct plural," Marie-Benoîte said, "Is seraph*im*. It comes from the Hebrew, meaning the fiery ones."

Perrine lifted one shoulder, and reverted to French, as most of the older sisters knew no English. "There are sundry names for those we meet in the spirit realm. Lya, you are much too fierce! Against such, whatever they call themselves, one must use a little wit."

"Wit begins with staying well out of someone else's trouble," Noemi said with a level gaze my way. Her English was perfect, with only the slightest French accent.

Lotte reverted to French as she stated in a low, fervent voice, "Whereas if I had ever had the chance to see, much less save, my son if he still lived, I would have done *anything*."

"Ruli told us she has no children."

"A twin—"

"She said cousin…"

The comments came quickly, and the stirred air brought the pungency of paint. Maëlle had already gone back downstairs to her river landscape.

Marie-Benoîte then said, "The winged demons I recollect as most dangerous only appear in this world at battlefields or in plague cities, though they prefer the former. They absorb the lives of the wounded and dying to increase their power. Even if we do nothing, it might be wise to discover, if we can, what they are about, and stay far from their field of endeavor."

"Put that way," Noemi said suddenly, "it becomes a matter of safety. With powers that immense, ignorance is never a defense. I will go to Notre Dame and see what I may see."

I put my hand on the mirror. "We'll discuss this further," I said to Kim—and she vanished.

"She will be in the mirror again?" Perrine asked, head askance.

"No. I'll go to Vienna to speak to her directly."

That seemed to satisfy them all. Perrine said to me, "Do. Take your steps as needed. Then you may, if you like, rejoin us when you have resolved your matters."

Lya had been looking from one of us to the other. "I want to go, too," she stated. "I want to meet this princess."

To my profound relief, Lotte spoke with a sad smile. "No, little one. It is too dangerous, and you are so very new."

"And a meuf princess is still merely a meuf," Noemi reminded her.

Lya looked mutinous, but remained silent.

My new state precluded having to ready myself in the ways I had when alive, something that both freed and unsettled me. Since I had not been told to leave permanently, I left my things where they were, and walked out.

When I saw the driving rain, droplets bouncing back up from the flagstones in a haze, I went back and fetched my hooded cloak—a garment I'd bought for a fancy dress affair years ago. I'd chosen one made of fabric that resisted water, as the weather had been unsettled then, resulting in the thing being very practical now. I pulled it around myself, raised the hood, then crossed to the carriage door, and out.

I had been thinking; in spite of the stygian darkness caused by the storm, it was still quiet early, scarcely an hour since sunset.

How to get to Vienna without using a portal? I knew that the reinvented Orient Express still left Paris every night, though its popularity was waning in favor of high-speed trains. Maman had preferred it, as one could arrange for a sleeper car, go to bed in Paris, and arrive in Vienna in time for breakfast. But these days more passengers wanted less transit time, and it seemed that the hundred-year-old train was probably doomed.

But that was not my problem, and the prospect of fewer passengers suited me, especially as at this time of year, its arrival in Vienna would be just before dawn. Very risky, especially if it was late—but I could always get off and go to ground if necessary.

The walk up the Beaumarchais was unpleasant, but at least it was relatively short. I turned my senses upward for possible lightning strikes, ducking under the shelter of eaves when I could. And when I reached the Gare de L'Est, I pulled shadows around me, shutting out the world and drifted aboard the waiting train, ghosting patiently along the passages until I reached an empty first-class cabin.

I did not make the mistake of entering it, and thus pinning myself there if a large party of humans turned up. I waited in the doorway, shadows deeply pulled around me, so that normal humans without protective charms would feel the cold and choose another cabin.

The storm no doubt aided me; by the time the train began to move, I had succeeded in securing the space to myself. I settled back, determined to conserve energy, but extended my senses…and there was the unmistakable awareness of another vampire. Was the train passing some random inimasang on the hunt there in Paris, or was this awareness moving in parallel, in other words on the train?

I waited. It did not move. It was definitely on the train. But not approaching me. Just as well, I thought gratefully.

The night passed uneventfully as the train made its way to Vienna, the storm apparently moving with it. When I, in Maman's company, had taken it before, I remember her complaining about arriving in the darkness, but the last miles I began to feel anxious. I could sense the poisonous weight of the sun pressing upwards in the east. At least the weather system that had drenched Paris seemed to be Europe-wide, or else there was a second wave, for the sky contained no stars nor moon, as far as I could see from the cabin window. Scarce protection, but every bit helped.

At last the train slowed toward Westbahnhof. The eastern sky was a deep indigo shade between the clouds slowly moving down the Danube. Very close to dawn. As soon as the train pulled in and the train personnel opened the doors, I wrapped my shadows about me and whirled off the train — to find myself in instant proximity to...

"Lya?" I gasped, as the few passengers bent to avoid the wet, cold wind, and hurried past.

She stood on the platform, her arms crossed tightly. "I want to meet the princess," she stated with a hint of her usual bravado, but then spoiled the effect by looking around dazed and scared. "I forgot about languages," she added in a small voice. "I thought everybody spoke English, and if they didn't, they spoke French."

"Lya, you have to go right back to Paris," I said — but there was that hint of bluing in the east. "We've got to get you to a portal. You do know how to use portals, don't you?"

She flung her black hair back — still brushed assiduously, I noticed distractedly. "You're not the boss of me," she stated, then added, "And I know *all about* portals. I went *all the way to LA* only three days after I got bit, to see if my brother..." She stopped.

No wonder Perrine and Noemi were so protective!

My expression must have changed, for her chin came up, and I fully expected her to fire back with something like, "I'm very mature for my age" — until I recollected from my boarding school days that that was the sort of phrase used by girls in the early teens, but eighteen was about the turning point, after which it was no longer a thrill to be perceived as older than you were. "I can take care of myself," she stated, though it was tragically clear from her standing there before me, her thin arms scarred beneath her red-glowing eyes, how well she had taken care of herself.

I had never wanted children. My mother had told me since I was small that I would be expected to produce an heir if I married Alec, but my consolation had been that I would have an army of caretakers so that I would never have to deal with diapers or spit-up or wailing...I would not have to fret over the responsibility for the welfare of another human being.

And yet, here I was. Even if neither of us was human.

And I could feel the inexorable lightening of the sky. We had a very short time left to get up to Linke Wienzeile, or die.

"We'll have to run."

FIFTEEN

KIM

"You," Alec had said.

He thought the pursuit was after *me?*

There's no use in recording our merry-go-round of what-ifs and contingencies, until we got to my great idea. "If you think there might be vampires involved, or this might be another Tony plot, shouldn't we talk to Ruli?"

"Why?" Alec asked.

"She helped you out when I was zombified."

"She did help us out," Alec said somewhat wryly. "She and Phaedra between them pretty much accounted for that gang of mercs. Granted, some of these were drunk, and none expected a vampire, but...let's just say that even Tony was somewhat taken aback on his arrival at the incident site, to find the area strewn with her victims, and her eyes glowing like a couple of hell sparks."

"Did she kill them?"

"No," Alec admitted. "The deaths were all by conventional weapon. But the fact that Ruli and Phaedra were the last ones standing gave everyone a little jolt. Especially Tony."

"Oooh, all the better," I crooned. "I love the idea of Tony getting a serious hitch in his giddyap. And by the sister he always looked down on!"

"He didn't really look down on her. He could be protective of her, in his way, but he regarded her as a negligible element in the various strands of von Mecklundburg power dynamics,"

Alec said. "That said. Much as I enjoy stinging Tony whenever possible, I don't really know if I want to bring Ruli to do it. It seems too much like bringing a flame thrower to light your dinner candles."

"You don't trust her?"

"I…want to," Alec said slowly. "But Kim, how much of the human we knew is left in her, really?"

I thought back to that terrible night when she staked that rotter Jerzy von M. She had been absolutely serious about trying to stay human. That is, moral. Buuuuut…that meant there was a struggle.

"Okay, point taken," I said. "How about this. If we don't come up with answers by the end of the day, and if a regular phone call to their Paris flat doesn't reach her, I could try to contact her with my prism. That's not physical contact, so we're not putting temptation before her."

He agreed, and that put us right back on the merry-go-round of guessing.

When the sun went down, I sat by while he used the phone to call the von Mecklundburgs' Paris flat. The short conversation made it clear that Ruli was not there. I took out my prism, focused on her, and turned it in my hand. Frustratingly, I kept getting flashes of a young and very young Ruli right in that room. I concentrated harder, ignoring the past…

And nothing happened.

I kept trying, but it was beginning to look as if contacting her was out of the question altogether, until suddenly there she was, a vague shape in profound gloom. But the way her head moved made it clear that this was the present.

My subsequent chat was glitchy, possibly because it was my first time reaching for her (or anyone) that way, but before I lost her for good, she'd clearly said she was willing to discuss it further. "That has to mean she's going to run ideas by whoever she was with."

"Vampires," Alec said, his mouth twisted. "Who else would she be with? She's not home, and you said it was dark. She has to be in a nest of vampires."

His cell phone buzzed then. It was Gavril of the Vigilzhi. Alec's entire demeanor eased as he dug the phone out of his pocket and flipped it open.

The subsequent conversation was short. They were relieved to be back in contact, but there was zilch to report from Dobrenica that could connect up with the pursuit. Alec told

Gavril to get more personnel involved, including someone to sit tight where there was cell connection in order to relay orders back and forth.

It would take at least a day and a half to assemble a site. Then another day to get a team to Vienna, for Gavril had to drive back up into Dobrenica, report to Milo and Dmitros Trasyemova, then drive back down again with reinforcements before they could make arrangements to *get* to Vienna.

What to do while we waited? We did not really know how safe we were. It was no secret in Dobrenica that the von Mecklundburgs had a flat in Vienna. Depending on who was chasing us and why, their minions might right now be staking out the building to wait for us to emerge. All we could be sure of was that whoever it was seemed to stop short of crashing into the building to get at us, and drawing all kinds of attention.

"Which means," Alec said, "we can probably get some rest."

"Rest," I repeated, staring at Alec so intensely I'm surprised my eyeballs didn't pop out and sproing off his forehead. "In beds not competing for the Worst Mattress Olympics. In a place with real bathrooms. That have lots of hot water."

"My exact thought," he whispered.

The von M.s might be a gang of oddballs with a few downright nogoodnicks, but they did know how to furnish a guest room. We luxuriated in a king-sized bathroom, then we crawled between 1200-thread sheets, and slept like we'd been smacked with a mallet.

Which meant we were up bright and early, well before dawn.

We were in the middle of our daily sparring as we debated our next step when there was a tap at the door.

"Neighbor?" I whispered, though of course he didn't know.

A louder tap, then an impatient bang.

Alec's short "Wer is da?" was not inviting—but Ruli's familiar voice responded, in English, "There are two of us."

Alec opened the door to the dim hall—and two pairs of red glowing eyes.

"I take it you have the extra house key," Ruli said tightly.

Everyone stood there for a second or two, staring at each other. Then, despite the extreme tension, I had to smother a weird kind of laugh at the way Ruli's gaze strayed to her companion, her expression a cross between frustration and the sort of aghast that hits you when you discover half of an unwanted life form wiggling in your salad.

The object of her gaze seemed to be a teenaged girl dressed up as a vamp for a costume gig. Everything super goth, ultra-black. The teen raised an arm, shrinking back from Alec. "What *is* that? It *hurts*," she complained.

Ruli turned to us. "Your charms…" She turned on the kid — still speaking in English, I noticed. "Stay here. You'll be safe right outside the door."

The girl shot back, "Like I'm really going out to work on my tan?" Then, in a less confrontive tone, eyeing Yours T., "Is that the princess?"

"Yes," Ruli said crisply as she stepped inside the flat. Of course she could enter. This was her flat.

Ruli shut the door practically on the girl's nose, and faced us, wincing. "Kim, could you back up a few paces? You've got a really powerful charm there."

"Oh." My prism. I hesitated, then thought, either I trust her, or end this conversation. I knew Alec and Phaedra had survived amending their charms in order to allow Ruli proximity. And so I performed the Person (name) and Presence (concentrate on the individual vampire while saying their name) charm that I'd been taught.

At once Ruli's manner eased. "This is what I know, which isn't much, but it relates to you, Kim, so it might be relevant. The false seraphim you spoke of when we met in the Nasdrafus wanted me to take you there by the time of your wedding. I decided to go to Paris instead."

Alec turned to me, and though he said nothing, I saw in the slight lift to his brows that he was thinking the same thing that I was: he definitely wasn't the target, then.

But why *me?*

Ruli said, "That's all I know. And you?"

"Even less," I said, then gave her a more complete description of our experience in Venice and the morning previous, followed by our subsequent guesses.

Ruli said, "I didn't see anyone out there, but I didn't look hard, either. The sun was coming up and we were running. I can say this: no one tried to stop us. These seraphim don't seem to be able to come easily into the physical world. Though when they are, they're drawn to death."

As she spoke, I flashed on memory, how the seraphim had hung around Napoleon, and especially Fouché, the Butcher of

Lyon, in the real world—but that had been two hundred years ago.

Ruli went on, "One of the sisters where I'm staying in Paris might know more. In fact, a couple of the older ones are fairly certain to know more." Then she looked pained. "I guess I ought to ask you to amend your charms for Lya."

I said, "Who is she? A vamp, too, right? Kind of on the nose with the goth look."

"Aren't the teen years pretty much a walking cliché?" Ruli smiled ruefully. "I remember distinctly that I certainly was. As for Lya, the short version is, I did not want to bring her. She turned up because she wanted to meet a princess. I guess I'm at fault for not investigating the moment I sensed another vampire on the night train."

Alec said, "Can we trust her?"

"I don't know," Ruli said. It was a little distracting, how she'd hiss in a breathe before speaking. As Alec had said, how human was she? "I don't know much about her, except that she's been a vampire for no more than a month, if that."

I turned to Alec, who said, "If it comes to it, I can probably handle a new vamp, especially one that age." He grimaced slightly, and I knew he didn't like the prospect of staking a kid. Even a kid vamp.

I said to Ruli, "I'd rather not let things get there. Do you think she came along because she wants to snack on princess blood?"

"I can't say for sure. But I think it's mainly curiosity."

"Let's have her in." Alec opened the door.

Ruli said, "Come in."

The girl almost fell inside—she'd been pressed up against it, listening. "I'm not snacking on anybody unless it's a creep! I'm not a monster!" she yelped as she stumbled to a halt and winced, eyes downcast, one hand to her head.

Alec turned to me, as if to say *your call*. I said to Lya, "Will you warn us if you do get the urge to bite?"

Lya mumbled, "Whatever," sulkily, but she didn't sound angry, or sneaky. I took out my prism, mentally drawing her image in with her name, as I amended the charm, then fixed the charm on his signet.

"Oh! That's better." Lya then scowled at Ruli, but before she could start in with some snark, I distracted her by saying, "I have to admit that I've only been a princess for a few days."

That worked. "How's that possible?" she asked.

"Marriage. To a crown prince." My thumb jerked toward Alec.

Lya swerved to stare at him. "What country?"

"Dobrenica," he said.

"Never heard of it."

Alec shrugged slightly. "If you get a big enough map, you can check its bona fides."

"Huh." She turned back to me. "I'm Lya. Do I call you Princess Something?"

"Please don't. Titles get put on with my ball dresses and tiaras, which we left behind in Dobrenica. Call me Kim."

She eyed my tank top and shorts, my usual workout clothes, and grinned, then turned to Alec. "You? Or do you have a lot of names, like princes in history books?"

"I do," he said. "It's fairly traditional. You don't want to piss off the older relations by leaving anyone out. But for every day, I prefer Alec."

Lya had advanced into the room and began looking around. "Ruli said in Paris that some fake angels are after you guys. Why?"

"That's what we need to figure out. Preferably on home ground," Alec said.

Since our sparring practice was now pretty much over, I suggested we shower and eat breakfast before we got to the planning. "Or will the smell of food gross you out?"

Lya's scowl snapped back. "We're *not* monsters," she said again, though nobody else had brought up the M word. "I'm still myself. Only I don't have viral hep anymore, or leukemia." *Leukemia?* But she was so defensive I decided against questions. She said, chin up, "I *can* eat breakfast. I *love* breakfast."

"You're welcome to join us," Alec said.

Lya unbristled, and began nosing around the von Ms' living room, asking questions about Dobrenica.

I excused myself and took a fast shower. When I came out, Lya was pestering Alec about the prince biz, which he fielded with a slightly resigned ease that made me think he might have got that treatment before, probably during his boarding school days.

He excused himself to shower — there were plenty of bathrooms, but we both instinctively felt it was better for one of us to keep an eye on the vamps — and I led the way to the kitchen.

"He's hot. For an old guy. You scored," Lya said to me,

with a thumb jerked in Alec's direction, and I tried not to laugh at the idea of Alec being old. "Where can get I me a prince or two?"

"If there's an Acme Supply for princes, nobody has clued me in yet," I said.

She grinned, and I tried not to be obvious about looking away as I beat the eggs while the pan warmed. "Roadrunner reference!" Lya ticked the air with her chipped black fingernails. "You watched that in your day?"

"My day?" I repeated. "You make me sound like I'm fifty. Anyway, the coyote versus the roadrunner's been around longer than I've been alive." Her expression seemed to alternate between pouting and a little forlorn. I said, "Do you want to help, or are you not into cooking?"

"When I was stuck at home we always had people for that. Or ordered in," Lya said as she began snooping through cupboards. "I didn't think princesses cooked. Oh yeah, you said you weren't born one. But why do you sound like someone from LA?"

"Because I'm from LA," I said.

"Really? Where?"

"Santa Monica."

"Santa Monica? How could anybody from Santa Monica end up married to an actual prince?" Apparently she'd accepted him as the Real McCoy, even if she was still dubious about Dobrenica.

"A whole lot of flukes," I said, though I was lying like a rug.

Not even Alec knew yet what my grandmother had admitted to me the morning of the wedding — and which I was still trying to get my head around: that while she was in that coma last summer, she'd believed she was dreaming, but she'd actually been in the Nasdrafus.

There, she had found herself in Dobrenica again, living in her old wing of the royal castle. She sat at the piano in the garden wing, where she strove to atone for her mistakes by playing until she could achieve peace for the entire kingdom. Sunlight streamed through the windows in an endless day as she played everything she knew by Rachmaninoff, Brahms, Mozart, Chopin, etc., in her desire to repair the peace she had destroyed by her departure, until a presence manifested: a woman, outlined in the sunlight.

A ghost. Recognizable from the portrait in the gallery:

Queen Sofia.

Gran said to me, "I grieved because I could not seem to speak to Queen Sofia. She never spoke to me, either, and I accepted that as a judgment, though she listened to my playing with an attitude of infinite kindness and of pleasure. I tried to demonstrate through music my regret for how I'd not only ruined the possibility of peace but I'd cut off my daughter, and you, the innocents, from their birthright. How I longed to repair my terrible errors. And then, there you were, breaking into the dream and speaking to me in Dobreni, telling me of meeting a ghost, and of finding your ancestors. Mina insists that my soul had somehow slipped into the Nasdrafus, and I had been in danger of being forever lost there, to wander as another ghost. Until you called me back."

I hadn't yet told anyone about Gran's words because it was her story to tell, or not. My point is, if Gran's mind had slipped into the Nasdrafus and wandered to its version of Dobrenica, much the same way I'd got pulled into the Nasdrafus with Aurélie two centuries ago, then there was a pret-ty good chance that there was no fluke in my meeting the ghost of Queen Sofia in Vienna. She might have come looking for me, somehow. I don't know how — trying to figure out time loops and the motives of ghosts makes my brain hurt.

But as I looked from the curious teenage vampire to Ruli, pale and soignée as she leaned against the couch, staring at a sepia-toned photograph of a lot of blond people in 19th Century garb, I wondered if I might still be caught in the middle of that weird loop somehow.

It was beginning to feel like unfinished business.

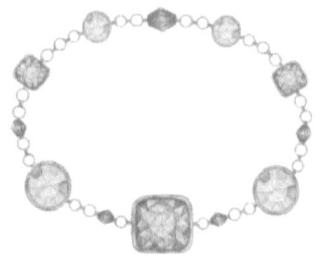

SIXTEEN

KIM

I said to Lya, "You might not know how to cook, but I bet you can slice bread. These semmerlbrots were fresh yesterday — if we toast the pieces, it'll be perfect."

Lya readily did so, slicing with such care it was clear that she had rarely been in a kitchen. I put the toast in the oven, as there was no toaster, and poured the eggs into the pan. Lya watched with an interest that leaned definitely toward the forlorn.

Alec reappeared just as the eggs were done, and we all sat down, Ruli with nothing before her. Lya made a bit of a business attacking her eggs with an appearance of appetite, as if she had to pass a test to prove she was still herself.

Alec said to Ruli, "What I'd like to do is get out of here and home as fast as possible. But there are only the two of us, no backup. I don't want to bring out weapons unless pushed to it. I suppose I could request police escort to the airport, but that has its own drawbacks publicity-wise."

Ruli said, "I didn't pay any attention when we got here. I was too anxious about the sun. But I was…listening, scanning, sensing just now, and there are three vampires in the vicinity. One that way, two…" She pointed first toward the market, then waved toward the rest of the flat. "Behind the building —"

"How do you know?" Lya broke in.

"I can sense them even if I can't see them. They aren't moving, of course."

"You didn't find me on the train—"

"I did, actually. Not your identity, but I knew another vampire was on the train. Since you stayed put, I did not want to pursue the matter."

"Can you teach me that?"

Ruli frowned slightly. "I don't know. It's just there, a...kind of sense. How do you explain smell, or sight? I assumed it was part of the change when I was turned."

Lya was shaking her head. "Nuh, uh. *I* sure can't tell. Perrine says talents sometimes come when you get turned. Sometimes you don't have to learn it, you just *have* it. Like me, with the portals! I mean, first I got inside a portal, easy-peasy, just thought about the beach where I used to hang out, and there happens to be a portal there, and I was only vamped for like two days! And when I came back from California, Olympe showed me the map and explained how you can get lost if you aren't careful. I didn't even know that but I did it right the first time! The sisters *all* said they can't do portals as easily as I can."

I noticed that she'd eaten half her eggs, and none of the toast, though she'd loaded jam onto it. Instead, she was giving us furtive stares, a bit too long, then away, and I was reminded of a dog licking his chops when he smells steak, but he knows he can't lunge at it. Then she pressed her lips together. Was she fighting against the fangs because of Alec's and my proximity?

A curl of atavistic fear burned along my nerves, pure instinct; I remembered how fast and strong vampires on the attack are, and here's me with no sword. At least I had my prism right there in my jeans pocket. But at the same time I was aware of a pulse of... sympathy? Respect? For her struggle against her own instinct, however new it was.

She said to Ruli, "The sisters don't have your radar, or why would we have to patrol looking for dirtbags? Did you tell the sisters about your radar? Seems to me you could just sniff out assholes so we can go straight at 'em."

"Except I can't tell identity, or if their motive is benign or predatory. I wouldn't want to 'go straight at' Olympe, for example."

Alec said to Ruli, "How far does your vampire-sense reach?"

"I don't know. Meters rather than miles, I suspect, but I have not tested it. And I have to concentrate. I can miss them if my mind is busy on other things. Like getting us here before the sun."

Alec said, "Will these three vampires you now sense outside the building know you two are here with us?"

"If they can sense, too," Ruli said.

Alec's eyes narrowed. "It seems to me that Kim and I'll have to get out of here while there's still daylight if we want to avoid meeting them. If those three are actually watching this building, and not just vampires who happen to exist locally."

He glanced at Ruli, who shook her head. "Impossible to tell."

I said, "Those twits we ditched yesterday might be lurking around, too."

"Right." Alec sat back. "We might head straight for one of the tourist areas, using the street traffic as cover, as we did in Venice. Get a cab to the airport. Fly to Berlin..." His voice drifted.

"And whoever is bossing them has more waiting at the other end?" I asked.

"I was just thinking that. I'm not used to tactical calculations that include Vrajhus." He smiled ruefully.

I turned to Ruli. "Do you know if there is a physical-world portal at either the Kaisergruft or St. Stephen's, and if so, how to work it? Can you get us through? Tonight," I added quickly, remembering that Ruli and Lya were not going anywhere while the sun was out.

"I don't know about the churches," Ruli said. "I've never had occasion to try. Rose said to avoid sacred spaces, but there is a portal used by our kind at Michaelerplatz, which in ancient times was a crossroads."

Alec leaned forward. "Can you get Kim and me through any kind of a portal?"

"I...assume so, since Kim has been in and out of the Nasdrafus, which is an order of magnitude beyond local portals. Though I've never heard of the living physically going to the Nasdrafus. We can try?"

Alec turned to me. "I've a diplomatic pass to the Hofburg's inner archive at Minoritenplatz, which I've never used. Once we get inside, we're effectively vanished, as the Hofburg has a hundred exits. Any pursuit would never know if we went straight through to one of them, or if we'd gone to earth inside. We can go to the Michaelerplatz when the sun is down. Meet there. Though we still haven't established whether or not you can show us how to use those portals?" Alec sounded tentative, as if he was still struggling with the idea.

"If she can't, *I* can," Lya declared. "I meant to say so, but we started talking about vampire radar. Portals are *easy*."

"How far do they reach?" I asked.

"Anywhere! That there's a portal, I mean. Local ones have, like, a local reach. Not beyond the curvature of the Earth. For longer distances you have to get there through the Nasdrafus."

Alec looked from her to Ruli. "Can you take us to Dobrenica that way?"

Ruli said, "Certainly, but I'm quite certain those seraphs will be camping in the Nasdrafus, waiting for us to turn up. They might even know our portal in the Eyrie."

"They do," I said, chill gripping me by the neck as I remembered my experience in the Nasdrafus, which I had no desire to repeat. "They lured us in through an old mirror at the Eyrie when I was with Aurélie. But that was two hundred years ago."

"The mirror is still there," Ruli said.

"Kim, if they asked Ruli to bring you, we can assume they have a welcome party waiting," Alec said. "Let's shake off our pursuit by going somewhere they don't expect, and travel the rest of the way conventionally."

Ruli said, "I know the Boatman Pillar portal in Paris —"

Lya bounced upright, her eyes crimson embers. "There's the one right there at Oscar Wild's grave! It's new, the sisters told me, only like a hundred years old, or eighty or something like that. They made it for him so he could visit his own grave."

"Oscar Wilde is a vampire?" I asked.

"Ghost. Perrine says that he talks with a lot of other writers at his grave in the Nasdrafus, which is different from the one here. Not all weather-beaten and gross. Doesn't have the kisses, either. He likes the kisses," Lya said, rolling her eyes — which still glowed a little, a very unsettling effect. "Lotte told me that. Ego, much?"

I thought it sounded a bit sad, but kept that to myself.

"Second thing," Alec said. "Can you get our things through?"

Both shook their heads. "If you mean your valises," Ruli said, "They will just stay behind. Things have to be next to your skin."

Alec turned to me. "Then let's put our passports and money inside our clothing. We can buy whatever we need on the other side. Shall we?" He tipped his head toward the door.

I wanted to be sure there wasn't a gang of slavering bad

guys waiting out there, but there wasn't any being sure.

"If this is as good as it gets, we'll deal with whatever comes at us from the other side," Alec said lightly, and I could see in the set of his face, his steady hands and alert posture the guy who had learned as a teen to deal with Russian toughs and whatever else he came up against.

I reminded myself that so far, the pursuit had stopped short of violence. And there were vampire stakes in the Daimler's trunk along with the more conventional weapons, which meant we could each stick a couple of them inside our clothes.

That was, as Alec said, as good as it gets. "Okay."

My heart was galloping as we descended to the parking garage. I put a stake up each of the sleeves of the shirt I'd changed into, which had buttons at the wrists. I decided against weapons. I didn't know how to handle a handgun, and wasn't sure I could shoot someone anyway. I said before Alec slammed the trunk, "If only Kilber had included a sword stick in that armory."

"We shall repair that omission for next time," Alec said, smiling. And I bet he would, too. I hadn't noticed what he'd chosen out of the hoard as I'd studied and dismissed each of the formidable choices; whatever he'd picked didn't show in his shirt or slacks.

We'd dressed up a bit, suitable for a private archive. We eased into the mellow sunshine from the parking garage door. My heart was really racing, but we saw no lurking figures, and so we headed out to the street to mix with people as we moved in the direction of the inner ring.

It took a while to get into the archive, partly because it turned out the building had been undergoing massive renovation, and things had been shifting around a lot as the building progressed. Then they had to check our credentials, and though everyone was polite, there was an air of "Why didn't you arrange ahead?" until the assistant assigned to us, a tall, weedy glasses-wearing librarian recognized fellow history nerds.

A lot of stuff was packed up due to renovation, but we professed ourselves happy to see whatever they had available. The result was a stack of imperial letters and papers of various sorts, all to be handled very carefully; Alec was intently interested in the inner workings of that peculiar patchwork that was the Holy Roman Empire, whereas I had more interest in individuals, and asked to see any letters by that delightfully outspoken princess Liselotte von der Pfalz, or letters from Maria Theresia to her children.

I scored examples from both, and hours slipped by as I pored over the difficult handwriting and, ah, creative spelling of the time, especially Liselotte's.

I hadn't even noticed the hours passing, or my stomach growling, until Alec reappeared, "They're closing up."

I'd gotten so involved in my nerd fest that it was a wrench to pull my mind out of the past that the letters evoked. Remembering chases and portals and vampires snapped me right back.

"Sooo…we're trusting Ruli, then?" I asked.

Alec's mouth tightened, then he turned to grip my shoulders. "I hate this situation. I'm fighting every instinct to use myself as deflection in order to push you through to safety—"

"Side by side means just that," I said, putting my hands over his, and running my thumb over his skin until his grip lost its tension. "Anyway, your importance to Dobrenica is far—"

"No." It was his turn to interrupt. "Never think that, never."

I kissed him. "Okay then. If we're going to get out of this Smrekar, let's look at what we've got as a plus. Starting with Ruli. She certainly didn't have to say she'd stick with us. And you said she proved useful up at that mine when I was a corpsicle. You know her. Can we continue to trust her?"

"We kind of have to. Also, as long as her eyes don't glow, and I notice they don't all the time, I almost forget she's not the Ruli I knew."

"She definitely seems more, I dunno, assertive."

"Assertive, yes," Alec said. "We'll trust her conditionally, how's that? But let's not forget that she isn't human."

I nodded agreement, but at the same time, I remembered reading a very old homemade Dobreni comic book about Xanpia as a girl, leading a group of supernatural kids. One of whom was a werewolf. If Xanpia had werewolf friends, why not vamps?

What it came down to, I realized as we started walking toward the exit, was the fact that I wanted to trust her. Not only to help us now, but behind that lay the burden of that promise I'd made Ruli, at her request: that if she turned into a monster, I'd shove her into the sunlight.

I didn't want to ever have to make that decision.

The sun had vanished beyond the buildings when we got outside. Two side-streets along the Volksgarten brought us to Michaelerplatz, which I remembered as the grand entrance to the Hofburg, across from excavations going back some 1500 years. Which I hadn't looked at because I had been distracted by Queen Sofia's ghost.

Night was closing in around the white-and-gold buildings. People strolled by. How were we supposed to do this without being seen? But I need not have worried. Ruli and Lya emerged out of the crowd, looking like an elegant woman and a girl both of whom liked wearing black. As they joined us, Ruli beckoned, and I blinked, hard. Suddenly the square blurred a bit, as if a kind of dry fog, made of shadow and not vapor, had sprung up. I remembered that bone-deep, icy chill, and shuddered as Ruli drew shadows around us.

She and Lya led us to the cordoned-off entrance to the excavation. No one seemed to see us as we vaulted over, then descended.

The two of them had apparently discussed how to manage because Lya reached for my hand. Hers was corpse cold, and I tried to squash a shudder, holding tightly to Alec on my other side. Ruli took his free hand as we approached one of the archways built by Romans centuries ago.

Then a kind of freezer-ice squeeze, as if between one step and another we'd gone from sea level to 11,000 feet, and then there was that glutinous, wading through jelly sensation, only far more intense than I remembered from when I'd bunged about in portals when I was attached in spirit to Aurélie.

Just before the intensity rose to painful we stumbled past some sort of blocky stone thing, into a crowd of shadowy figures, who turned as one. Eyes glowing red.

We were surrounded by vampires.

SEVENTEEN

RULI

I had forgotten Kim's and Alec's protective charms.

The salon of vampires who met regularly at Oscar Wilde's grave recoiled from Kim and Alec.

Lya pranced into the center of the circle as if the world revolved around her, piping, "Perrine! Did you see that? It was *me* who got us through! I *told* you I'm good at portals!"

I looked past the circle to Alec and Kim, who took up stances that reminded me of Tony and Danilov and Phaedra when they were poised for one of their mock duels. Though Alec wore a tight face, and I sensed sharp pain.

Then Noemi and Lotte confronted me. They were clearly unhappy with me already, and the sudden appearance of two uninvited humans boosted the tension; the vampires had backed away from the Kim and Alec, but those small sun charms would not prevent them from attacking if they chose to.

Noemi snapped her fingers in my face. "Why did you take Lya?"

"I did not take her," I said. "She followed me. I didn't discover her until the train reached Vienna, and the sun was coming up."

Lya elbowed between them as her voice rose shrilly, "I wanted to go. Ruli didn't even know I was there. I mean, she actually did know I was there, but not that it was me. She's got *radar*. And *I* have portal power. Crap. That sounds like porta-potty." She switched to her somewhat labored French. "Kim is a princess. I didn't know there were any left, other than the ones in England and Denmark and Sweden."

"Very well. I can see it was all accidental," Noemi said to me.

I looked past her, bracing against the very real threat of a mass attack on Kim and Alec. Sickly, I knew I would defend them. Or try.

Then I realized I could hear Alec speaking. Not shouting. He, like Milo, is adept at being heard without barking or yelling. It's merely training, though the opposite of what I had received; all my elocution lessons at boarding school and even after had focused on women being soft-spoken, poised, composed. Never loud.

At first I didn't understand what he was saying, except that it was rhythmic, then gradually the words assembled into sense.

> *And I and all the souls in pain,*
> *Who tramped the other ring,*
> *Forgot if we ourselves had done*
> *A great or little thing,*
> *And watched with gaze of dull amaze*
> *The man who had to swing...*

In the very short time since our arrival, while Noemi claimed my attention, he'd managed to capture their attention.

I keep forgetting how compelling he can be when he exerts himself. I even know how he does it, because he tried to teach me early in our brief marriage: "If you're faced by a mob, try to find common ground, and turn them into an audience."

> *For, right within, the sword of Sin*
> *Pierced to its poisoned hilt,*
> *And as molten lead were the tears we shed*
> *For the blood we had not spilt...*

He looked around. "Shall I stop there? It's the last poem he ever wrote."

Marie-Benoîte spoke into the sudden silence. "He has written more since, but only in the realm of the spirit—"

"That one actually sounds kinda cool," Lya interrupted, as if her passing thoughts prevailed over everything and everyone else. "I thought I hated poems, all flowers and clouds and *llllurrrrve.*"

And then, unexpectedly, Maëlle spoke in her pure Loire Valley accent, her mellow voice genderless, "He wrote that ballad in a similar spirit to Olympe de Gouges offering to defend the king, before she was killed."

"Exactly." Marie-Benoîte nodded approval. "Olympe despised the concept of kings, but separated that from Louis Capet the man. How many among you suffered for being regarded as part of this group or that, without being permitted to speak as an individual?"

It was mostly women who gathered there at Wilde's grave. Not poets and wits, as Wilde drew about him in the Nasdrafus, but women from many times and places. Most French, and from the working people, or merchants, or scholars. I could not tell you why they gathered at Wilde's grave, only that none of those women had finished out their lives peacefully.

Maëlle went on, "Olympe might wish us to permit the two humans to speak for themselves."

From the whispers and the thinning of the deep shadows, I began to perceive the mood shifting, but before anyone could speak further for or against the unwelcome human pair, another vampire emerged from the portal behind the monument, a short, square woman with a strong accent from the south of France. "Maëlle is entirely correct. She does not misstate me, as so many have!"

This had to be Olympe de Gouges herself—condemned and guillotined for daring to call for a referendum allowing the French people to choose what form of government they wanted, in the teeth of Robespierre and his Committee.

She raised a hand. "But this discussion, so important, must wait. There is trouble coming now, from Cluny."

My senses widened then, and I perceived this new threat as a kind of storm front, only moving fast, from the other side of the river. Perhaps six kilometers away, or less, depending.

Perrine said urgently to me, "I was going to tell you: the Boatman portal is being watched. This âme de boue must have followed you through the portal."

"Impossible," Olympe stated, smacking the back of her hand against her palm. "No one can follow through portals without touching. Unless they knew already where to look."

Noemi said to me, "Are you being pursued?"

"Not now, children. Take them away, little one, somewhere not expected," Olympe said to Lya, who drew up proudly.

"Easy-peasy," Lya declared in English, and then in French, "I know *just* where to go." She grabbed Kim by the hand again.

No one raised a voice to Olympe. Noemi said fiercely to me, "Bring her back safe."

I nodded, accepting the burden of responsibility. This was the cost of that quiet room in the Marais, and the steady supply of blood plasma.

Once again I closed my fingers around Alec's wrist, aware of the latent tension in his muscles and the thrum of his still-laboring heartbeat. My fangs pulsed, then subsided. I was getting better at suppressing the urge, like a hound learning not to drool.

The four of us plunged through the portal in a string, as before. I still didn't quite grasp how Lya accomplished this somewhat complicated maneuver. She was lightning-fast. Maybe talents did emerge on one's turning; I had to think about the simpler shift to and from the Nasdrafus. But Lya seemed to instinctively use the Nasdrafus as a mere conduit, which collapsed distance and time to meaninglessness. Unless the pursuit actually touched us, or stood waiting at exactly the right portal in the Nasdrafus to intercept us, it would be impossible to know where we went.

We emerged into air that smelled of brine. Nearby, the crash of ocean waves.

Lya turned to Kim, who squinted around, her gaze drawn toward dim lights haloed by salt-laden moisture. "Have you got some kind of magic thing with you? You're so easy to take, but Alec, you're *heavy*. It's like pulling someone through water."

Alec said nothing, but leaned against the sandy stone, his eyes shut. That sharp pain I'd sensed was exponentially worse.

"I don't have anything except my prism, but there isn't anything about portals charmed into it, or I would've been told," Kim said. "It kind of smells like home here, and I'd swear that's the Santa Monica Pier."

"That's because it is," Lya said. "I found this portal last time. When I came. To find my stupid brother. But I don't know what time it is, only that I picked night."

With an effort I could feel — and apparently Kim sensed as well, for she turned to look at him worriedly — Alec murmured, "Let's see the time." Moving with excruciating slowness, he flipped his cell open. "3:53 a.m. local time." He drew a breath. "We can go straight to the airport..." His hand had slid to his pocket. His trembling fingers scrabbled, then he turned to Kim.

"Your wallet?"

She smacked her hands to her pockets — both of them. She looked up at him, then to me. "My wallet's gone. But my prism is still there. And my stake. Did one of those vamps pickpocket me and leave the stake?"

Lya snickered.

I said, "I don't really understand portals, but I did tell you that you can't carry things. Apparently pockets are still carrying. The prism might be invisible to whatever it is that makes the portal."

"Then let's go back in and…" She hesitated, looking at Alec again.

"I'll bear it," he whispered softly, meant only for her ears. Though both Lya and I heard.

Then Lya said, surprisingly, "I think we better wait." Thoughts for someone else? Or just her with her own plans.

Kim nodded, running her hand over Alec's shoulder, as if that would lessen his pain. He leaned a little into her touch: maybe it did. "Dawn's not long from now," she said, glancing around again. "We can go to my house. It's about a mile inland from the pier."

Alec said, "I'm in favor, but if the pursuit is after you, do you think your house might be watched?"

"Right. Didn't think of that. I know all the neighbors, except for apartment building across the street and a couple of lots down. I guess someone could be watching from the rooftop garden. But unless the bad guys have my entire house surrounded — in which case the neighbors would be 911-ing so fast their heads would spin — we can get in over our back fence. The neighbors behind us are a retired couple. They'll be sound asleep right now."

The portal was inside a crumbling fold in a palisade, not quite a cave. Despite the early hour, the strand was not completely deserted as Kim led us to a set of steep, sand-gritty stairs going up to the street level.

The older houses were unlike European dwellings, made of wood instead of stone, and with porches and broad windows whose shutters were purely decorative, signs of clement weather year-round. I studied these as I kept my senses alert. One unmoving vampire in the vicinity, and an indistinct sense of more farther inland.

A murmur of question and protest, Alec's firm, "I can do it," and we began to run at an easy jog.

Lya promptly glued herself to Kim, blabbing a stream—from the scarce words I could not prevent entering my awareness, as usual she was going on about her favorite subject, herself. Alec dropped back to jog silently beside me, his eyes constantly scanning, his breathing harsh. Kim's and Lya's voices were barely audible in the still early morning air that became noticeably dryer the farther we got from the sea.

The more modern, grander dwellings gave way to the older ones as we pressed inland. These smaller, square bungalows might have been taken for servants' outbuildings elsewhere, except many had large yards in front, with enormous jacarandas. These were in full bloom, a brilliant lavender. And here and there, the famous palm trees of Southern California. Non-native—a symbol, one of my boarding school instructors had said with deep disapproval, of how impossible was the existence of such an extravagantly large city in terrain with no water. The whole, swept by the warm, dry wind, seemed surreal.

We reached a quiet, deserted street. Kim led us up a driveway and into a large yard of a small, weathered-looking house, then she and Alec moved ahead, scanning for watchers. I could have told them I heard only two heartbeats inside the dwelling, both in the slow thump of slumber. But I sensed no danger, and I'd decided that the fewer reminders of my no-longer-human state, the better.

As expected, they returned immediately. We all vaulted a cement fence into another large yard, dominated by a large oak, still full of leaves, though this was the middle of September. Kim told us to wait while she went to fetch a key that she said they always kept outside in case someone forgot theirs.

She opened the door to a kitchen, and stood aside to invite Lya and me inside; Lya was still too new, or too self-centered, to perceive this act of trust, but I appreciated it.

The air was still, as expected in a place that had been locked up for a couple of months. We glanced about the moonlit room.

"Wow, this isn't schizo much?" Lya commented. "This part of the kitchen, with that old table and that radio and those chairs looks like something from the fifties, but on *that* side, the stove and that prep table is better than our kitchen in Bel Air. I mean, you've got *everything* state-of-the-art."

"My mother is a pastry chef," Kim said, stretching her hand toward the wall's light switch.

"No light," Alec murmured.

"Right." Kim dropped her hand, looked around as if bewildered to find herself there, then rubbed her hands down her skirt-covered thighs. "I guess I could make tea."

I said, "We will be needing someplace to avoid sunlight within an hour."

"Oh, we've got Dad's lair for that," Kim said. "California homes don't actually come with basements. Earthquakes are a thing here. But the owners before us put a bomb shelter below the foundation. Dad fixed it up so he could keep his Roman stuff and his clock stuff from taking over the house."

"*Clock* stuff?" Lya wrinkled her nose.

"My dad builds fancy clocks from scratch," Kim said. "You'll see. If no one wants anything in here, we can go downstairs right now. It shuts out the light completely. We can plan in there, and when it gets light, you two can crash and Alec and I can go upstairs and rustle up some dinner. Breakfast. Whatever. It feels like I've been awake for days."

So saying, she opened what I'd taken to be a mud closet just inside the kitchen door. This narrow door disclosed a wooden stair. Down we went. I took in the tidy space dominated by a huge table, a tool rack off to one side, and shelves of clocks and artifacts.

Then Kim shut the door and flipped on the lights.

"Okay. This is kinda cool, in a geeky way," Lya said, examining an elaborate chiming clock with a revolving moon cycle in enamel.

I don't know who looked more out of place in this space, Lya in her black, or Alec, elegant even with sand on his shoes as he looked slowly around. I expect I was equally out of place. I felt that way. And yet the house in itself was not unwelcoming, and I still appreciated how Kim had invited us in without a check. As if she had not thought about it, though I expect she had.

"What now?" Kim turned to me and Alec.

There were stools around the table. She perched on one, and Alec sat next to her as he said, "Lya. Since you were able to bring us this far, can you take us back to Europe, specifically Dobrenica, tonight?"

"Are you sure you can deal?" Kim asked softly.

"I'll deal. Our passports, ID, and money are gone. I can try to arrange a private plane through secondary contacts, but it will take time. I want to get home as fast as possible. One more trip isn't going to kill me."

Kim looked doubtful; I raised my hand, and the other three turned to me. This was unexpected. I could not remember a time when anyone had ever wanted to hear my opinion.

Ah, but that was at least half my own fault.

I said to Kim, "Since we are not going anywhere, what exactly happened with the seraphs? I remember what little you told me when we met in the Nasdrafus. What happened afterward?"

Kim said, "They pulled some dirty work, turning one of us into a tree in a really nasty way." To Lya, "This was two hundred years ago. Except I guess that doesn't matter in the Nasdrafus, something that still makes my brain hurt if I think about it too much."

Then back to me, "But we rescued her and got out anyway, and back to Dobrenica. I was still in spirit form. It seemed pretty clear that they were following Aurélie, not me. Or, technically, I think that they were after…" She hesitated. Then finished with a diffuse look, "Some charmed stones she was carrying. She gave those to me, and I kind of made them disappear, right before I returned to the real world."

"Sounds kind of Tolkien-y," Lya commented.

Kim gave her a delighted smile. "You've read *Lord of the Rings*?"

"One of my teachers was really into it. He was reading it to us before I got kicked out of that school. There were a lot of magical stones in it, is what I mean."

Alec turned to Kim. "Then they're after you for revenge? This pursuit seems a lot of effort for something so petty."

Kim shrugged again. "Maybe they've got nothing else to do?"

"Or our guesses are wide of the mark," he responded. "Let's get back to what we do know. Nothing happened while we were in Dobrenica. Not until we arrived in Venice, and I left off my ring with its wards against vampires and the like. To me that suggests we're being messed with by those with access to Vrajhus."

"But you've been wearing your signet ever since, and they still turned up in Vienna, right on our heels," Kim said.

He gave a slight nod. "I know. The more puzzling the situation, the more I want to face them on home ground."

"Where we can dump the Vrajhus questions into Beka's lap." Kim rubbed her hands, then smiled at Lya. "Soon as it's night, you can take us to Dobrenica?"

"Sure," she said. "As long as Ruli knows the door — the portal at the other end."

"I do."

Kim looked at Alec, then said, "Let's get us some tea, and maybe some breakfast, depending on what Dad left in the freezer. There's almost always a pack of bagels. Then you can take some aspirin, okay?"

He did not object, and turned to the stairs.

To avoid having to listen to more of Lya's bragging or complaining, I followed Kim and Alec up to the kitchen, where Kim began going through cupboards and the freezer, as Alec headed into the front room, a modest salon with an old-fashioned television in it. He sat in an armchair beside the closed curtains, which he slowly parted no more than the width of a fingernail.

They had exchanged no words since coming up the stairs, but each seemed to understand the other without speech, a closeness evolving between them that transcended mere sexual attraction. Kim seemed to know him better after scarcely a year than I had for a lifetime, but then I had not wanted to know him; he'd been part of the furniture of my life as a child, and as we aged, a duty.

I reasoned so, but when she carried tea and toast to him, the touch of their hands, the quick smiles that caught and blended their gazes, dealt me an unexpected pang. I had never had that kind of relationship with any of my boyfriends. I had not known it was even possible before the chance was entirely taken away.

The press on my mood altered to awareness of the press of sunlight on the horizon, and I retreated downstairs to safety where, to my relief, I found Lya asleep, taking up the entirety of the single, very shabby couch against the adjacent wall.

We had fed right after leaving the family flat in Vienna, having caught a pair of purse snatchers stalking some obviously lost Japanese tourists. We left them both sitting in a conspicuous place, their stash of wallets lined up beside each; Lya and I had not gone twenty steps beyond them when I heard footsteps and a gasp, and someone exclaiming in broad Vienna dialect, "What's this? What's this?" and we'd both gone into shadow.

I took a chair, leaned back, and let my mind drift into the vampire sleep, a kind of twilight of the mind.

Some inward sense prompts me when the sun is safely

past. I returned to consciousness to discover myself alone in the basement. Lya must have drawn shadows about her to pass without my noticing.

I consciously sped up the stairs, touching only three times between springs. I had seen Elena lift entirely into the air and vanish. I hoped that learning that skill was like learning to balance a bicycle. Perhaps it came with age, but I feared it was more likely that such a skill was open only to those with measureless power, gained by subsuming others' life force.

Kim and Alec started when I entered the kitchen. He said to me, "Two suspicious cars, every two or three hours. Drove by slowly without stopping."

Then the house was being watched, but not constantly. "Bringing us right back to the same question: Kim is the target, or a target, but why? What would they get out of such a lengthy pursuit?"

"Malice," Alec said. "That might not be their sole purpose, but it's likely a driving motive."

"The rest has to have something to do with Vrajhus. I *really* want to get back and corner Beka," Kim said.

"Where is Lya?" I asked.

EIGHTEEN

RULI

Surprise rounded both pairs of eyes, brown and blue, and I heard their heartrates tick up. "Isn't she down in the lair?" Kim asked. "We've been sitting here in the dark, but surely we would have seen her go by."

"Not if she knows how to use shadows," I said. "And you two have been up all day, am I correct?"

They exchanged glances, then Alec said, "I slept a couple hours around noon, while Kim watched for drive-bys."

Kim sighed. "Then we're truly stuck here?"

"As long as the watchers don't discover us, we can make our way back," Alec said. "But it'll take some time without ID."

Kim smacked the table. "She probably sneaked by while one of us was watching out front and the other in the bathroom. But I bet I know where she went, to find her brother."

"Why wouldn't she tell us?" Alec said, looking a little surprised—there was his sympathy for children, which he rarely revealed.

Kim rubbed her palms along her thighs above the knee, a gesture I'd seen first right before she asked me to drive her to the border, having decided (wrongly, but valiantly) that she was Dobrenica's biggest problem, and to help us by cutting herself out.

"I've only one day's impression to go by," she said slowly, "but that included a core dump while we were coming from the portal to the house here. I think Lya's worried about this brother, and mad at him at the same time."

"She's mentioned the brother once or twice," I said. "Said he was stupid. I thought she hated him."

"I think she hates…his circumstances, maybe, but not him," Kim said cautiously.

Alec's expression diffused. "I heard a lot about Beverly Hills, and bad film agents, and figured she was trying to impress Kim, so I left her to it."

Kim turned to him. "You're not wrong. But that swagger about their hotsy-totsy mansion in Bel Air and her crappy agent had *a lot* of bitterness in it. Isn't bitterness the crust over unhappiness? It all reminded me of some of the rich poor kids I met during my high school days hanging out in Westwood."

"Which is…?"

"West of UCLA. Mom said even in her day it was the hippest spot besides the Sunset Strip."

"Rich poor kids?" I repeated.

"Maybe it ought to be poor rich kids? Anyway, Lya bragged about how she used to score and scam on the Hollywood streets while her parents never noticed she was gone. That was before she collected viral hep, and leukemia, which she claimed she got from the treatment for the hepatitis. And when they said she was incurable, she flew to Paris. Where she got vamped."

Alec's expression of sympathy hardened to severity. "She wanted to become a vampire?"

"Nope. She says she came to Paris to die." Kim winced. "She'd just turned eighteen, and now had control of her trust fund, so she flew over without telling anyone. She'd had to learn French at one of those fancy Beverly Hills schools, before she got kicked out, but she seemed to think Paris was a cross between Disneyland and Heaven. She bought sleeping pills and booze, then threw her passport and wallet into the river so she couldn't back out. She wandered the Père-Lachaise cemetery, looking for the prettiest grave, and hid out. Her idea was to lurk till midnight, then down the pills and booze and let a sorrowing world find her on the perfect setting, dressed all in black."

"Teenage dramatics," I said. "Lethal."

Kim turned my way. "Anyway, her plan for the beautiful end flopped. She was already so sick that the pills made her hork, and I guess some roaming sleazebags who'd escaped notice by the cemetery guards heard her puking and moaning and decided that she was the night's plaything, and attacked her. She said she tried to fight back, but..." This time Kim's entire body flinched. "The death she was getting was anything but beautiful."

I understood then. "And a vampire came along?"

"Two. Both women. Attacked the thugs, and then vamped her before she bled out. Scolded her not to waste a second chance. Now she says she's some kind of paladin, rescuing women. Ruli, how much of that is true?"

"I know nothing about her life, or paladins, but there is a group of Parisian vampires, all women, who've adopted her. They have a blood plasma source, so when they go out, their intent is to make the streets safe for women."

"Okay, then it sounds like there's a lot of truth in her story," Kim said. "Poor little rich girl. Nah! That sounds so patronizing. My dad once said that financial success can breed emotional poverty just as well as having no cash does. She might be eighteen but emotionally she's still thirteen — and it sounded like the parents are about the same. As for the brother, there are a bunch of step-sibs and half-brothers and sisters, between Mom and Dad's various marriages and relationships, but she and this particular brother, Blayze-with-a-Y, only she calls him B, they were close. She took him to all the cool places she'd found on the streets in Hollywood, and he knew how to score before he was ten. She was actually proud of that, poor kid."

"Where are the parents in all this? Dead?" Alec asked.

"They're in the film biz, didn't I say? The mom acts — I've actually heard of her, and as you know I never really got into the TV habit. The dad wears a lot of hats — singer, songwriter, producer, director, you name it — but sounds like the one he wears least is Dad. Lya insisted the kids were pretty much raised by the servants, or their agents. Anyway, right before we got to the house, she said that B got sucked into some religious cult and they wouldn't let her in the door. But B is a regular on some show, and when she came to LA a few weeks ago, he was on location somewhere. Long story short: that house in Bel Air is where she headed, I'm pretty sure, to find Blayze." She spread her hands. "Now what? Sit tight and hope she comes back? Or...Ruli, can *you* get us to Dobrenica? Since Lya is the best at real world portals, which means she can get herself back to Paris okay, we don't have to wait on her, do we?"

We did if I ever wanted to return to that house in the Marais. However, that was my problem. "I don't know if I can get us safely to Dobrenica, without experimenting first," I said. "Here's my suggestion. You two get some sleep. I'll go out and explore. I sense roamers; if she runs afoul of them, I can help. If you give me a general direction, I'll try to find her. Is Beverly Hills far?"

"Nope. You could cut down PCH, about ten minutes' run if the lights go your way, then turn east on Santa Monica for..."

I barely had a chance to notice that Kim seemed to measure distance less by miles than by traffic time, when I sensed presence outside the kitchen door, and crossed the room in an instant.

It was Lya. Back and triumphant. "I found him! It's a night-for-night shoot on location, so the *Finneys* can't keep me from seeing him!" She spat the name Finney as a curse.

I was going to do my best to demand that she take us to Paris first, then she could return whenever she liked, however long she liked, but Alec forestalled me: "After you see him, can you take us to Dobrenica?"

"Sure," Lya said carelessly. "Soon's I see B."

Kim rubbed her hands. "Then let's all go."

After a fast check of the empty street behind the house, Kim led us to a bus stop. I had never been on a bus before. The Los Angeles night life was only beginning; a bus came along fairly rapidly, and was quite full.

Kim had scrounged up a few American dollars in her house, and paid for us to board. Lya took no notice of the route. She was watching the people and talking continually to Kim, who had clearly become her new audience. I noticed that Lya's bedraggled black barely got a glance from the other bus riders.

"What kind of religious cult?" Kim murmured.

"I don't know. Aren't they all the same?"

"Nope."

"Whatever." Lya jerked her shoulders up. "B met Radford Finney when he started middle school, when I first got sick. Next thing I knew, B was staying overnight with the Finneys, and they even got him a bunkbed in Rad's room," she said angrily. "When I escaped rehab the first time, the Finneys *said* I could see him any time I wanted, *surrrre*, but I had to be *clean*," Lya slapped her inner arm, "as if it was any of their business..."

I decided that Kim was right about Lya being mentally thirteen, the most abhorrent age. I shut out her whining and concentrated my surroundings. I could see immediately why there were so many vampires in Los Angeles. The night air had no vestige of the bite of impending winter, unlike Europe. And the streets were brightly lit, almost like day, but free of the sun's poison.

We got off at an intersection much like the others, and stepped into arid air, with short gusts of a hot wind blowing. Northwards rose hills defined by many lights, surprisingly full of lush green foliage of a wild assortment. Where did they get the water for so much greenery? We had not passed so much as a stream. Just cement, and more cement, and of course buildings.

Lya was still chattering as she and Kim set off up a side street. I sensed three vampires somewhere in the vicinity, two together and one farther off, amid the thousands of heartbeats.

We turned onto a somewhat narrower side street, which was blocked off at both ends by enormous trailers. A mass of cars and trucks crowded the adjacent street, and a swarm of people stood around in clusters, or moved briskly about carrying poles and lights and other equipment, as thick cables lay everywhere. I recognized some of the equipment from seeing film experiments by Gilles, Honoré's twin, before he got his first job in France. Some people held thick binders, others battered scripts.

"Definitely a location shoot," Kim said. "They're kind of fun — for about ten minutes. Though I'd guess it's a whole lot more fun if you know that you're making megabucks — "

A big, intimidating man confronted us. "This is a restricted area."

I was ready to go to shadow but Lya darted past him, shrieking, "Beeee!"

A blond kid just starting to get the gangling bones of a teen whipped around, his face lighting with surprise and joy. *"Lee?"* And to the security guy catching up with her, "Let her by. That's my sister!"

"They're with me," Lya said with airy self-importance, waving at us.

The security man said, "I'll have to get permission from the director. Stay here with Blayze." He faded back into the crowd, unnoticed except by Alec, who was tracking everyone, his mouth a thin line.

"Never mind that," Blayze said. "I'll make sure you can stay. There's already a million people hanging around." He waved in one direction; I could not tell who was supposed to be there and who not. It was chaos to my eyes.

Blayze made an awkward motion toward Lya, as if he was not certain he was to hug her or not. She crossed her arms tightly over her chest, and he blushed furiously. "Lee? Lyana? Where have you been? Why didn't you answer my calls?""

Lya said, "I'm Lya now. How are you, B?"

Blayze's voice was beginning the slide from the treble of a boy into the nasal twang of a teen in a growth spurt. "I tried to call on your birthday —"

"I went to Paris."

"Paris? Lake Perris? Or...do you mean, like Paris in *France?*"

"Yep."

"I guess that's cooler than coming over to the Finneys' for birthday cake. But we did have a cake for you. I helped bake it. Not out of a box, even. Chocolate all through, and double frosting."

"Those assholes don't want me," Lya said sulkily.

"They're not assholes, Lee — Lya —"

"Let's run through the scene," someone bawled through a loudspeaker.

"I gotta do this," Blayze said, agonized. "Stay here, okay? Don't go anywhere."

"I won't," Lya said.

"We really ought to leave," I said, sensing...focus.

Alec raised a hand. "I don't see any threats here. Let her have her say." There it was, his weakness for kids — siblings.

Blayze joined some other kids and teens, who stood near a cluster of burly men in dark-colored costumes designed to intimidate. They slipped on fright masks. Two wore long capes flagging in the warm desert-dry breeze. All moved into the street, under the brilliant lights.

On a shout from the loudspeaker they began a rehearsal — then were stopped. Started again. Stopped again. Restarted. I began to see what Kim had meant; this was nothing like watching a play.

"Which show is this?" Kim asked.

Lya eyed her in affront. "Don't you watch TV? *Kid from the Stars* is in its fourth season!"

"I'm a reader," Kim said. "And TVs don't work in Dobrenica, except with CDs."

"Ohmighod that sucks bigtime! I'd die if..." Lya faltered, then flipped her hair and uttered a mirthless laugh. "Yeah. Anyway, it's a family show, set right here in LA, where this kid inherits superpowers from a mysterious visitor that turns out to be his cousin, and he gets a magic hat for his bestie —"

"QUIET ON SET!"

This time, the sequence was conducted at running speed — the kids yelling their dialogue, and then the fight, using obviously fake weapons that clacked plastically, with much posturing and grunting — and just as they got going, the loudspeaker blared, "CUT!" and everyone stopped.

"It looks ridiculously fake," I commented to Kim, as a swarm of people rushed out and started fussing around the actors, combing hair and so forth.

"My guess is, this thing is low budget, four seasons or not," Kim said, looking around. "But you have to admit it's a great location — on that side of the street, the houses, the cars, trash cans, bikes on lawns. Everything like today. Then right across the street, that fake-medieval library and the garden. All they have to do is hide the fire hydrant and the modern sign and the lights with all those flags and stuff, the kids run across, they add fireworks in special effects, and it looks like they burst through a portal between worlds. No blue screen needed."

I ignored the comment about blue screens. "Portals have no fire. Flames would burn anyone going through!"

Kim grinned. "That's because the portals you're talking about are really real. TV portals have to have a lot of razzle-dazzle, or viewers feel like it's fake. Like jet packs. None of us kids watching science fiction series ever thought about having booster fire burning your butt every time you took off. We just wanted to see the characters zooming around."

I said. "Actually, I meant that fighting. It looks so unconvincing."

"That's stage fighting. It'll look better jazzed up with special effects and sounds and quick intercuts at sharp angles."

"Stage fighting and weapons are more convincing."

"Still choreographed."

I had never thought about it, but it made sense. It had always looked so real on stage. I found myself a little interested. So were the neighbors, from the looks of faces in windows out of range of the cameras, and gathered on lawns to enjoy the free show.

"In stage fighting you hit one another's weapons. They work hard to avoid hitting each other. Wounds and stabs all get done in special closeup setups, then edited together."

"Did you do this before you came to Dobrenica?"

"Only in student films, for friends at UCLA's film school. I can't act, and my voice sounds to me like the squawk of a chicken. But I did a lot of action stuff for the price of a good dinner—all of us in fencing class did. That's where I discovered that stage fighting isn't like fencing. Then in Dobrenica, that's where I discovered that sport fencing isn't like real sword fighting—"

"QUIET ON SET!"

The actors returned to their spots, their hair was combed, then they went through the sequence again. This time they got maybe three seconds into it before the loud, "CUT!" And a couple of adults went to talk to one of the kids, whose shrill voice rose from a little girl, "Jaydin keeps waving his hat too close on my right!"

"Jaydin! Let's re-block the hat sequence…"

"Ten minutes!" someone bawled.

The words ricocheted through the crowd, setting everyone in motion.

Lya's brother elbowed through the crowd, his freckled face red from his efforts. "Come into the trailer? No, everyone else will be in there." He faced the adults clustered nearby, some staring from Lya to him. "Me and my sister would like some space, okay?"

The adults began to move away, though one said, "You've got about eight minutes left, Blayze."

Blayze said to Lya, "Lee, *of course* you're welcome. *Any* time. I was *there* when both Aunt Elizabeth and Uncle Ben invited you—"

"They aren't your aunt or uncle," Lya stated, arms still crossed.

The boy looked down, then up. "They're kinda my family now. But that doesn't change anything with *you*—Mom and Dad are still Mom and Dad, and you're still my sister. Same with Porsche and Nirvana. And Kaid and Declan are still my brothers. I have two families now. Half the kids in school have at least two families, Lee, you *know* that. The Finneys *said* you can come any time you want. You just can't be high."

"Which is my business," Lya snapped.

Blayze put his hands out. "Okay, okay, okay. But I hated seeing you looking so sick, is all. And I don't want you to end up like Kaid or Porsche."

Lya's gaze shifted at that.

"The Finneys are nice," Blayze added. "They're nice to all

Rad's friends. When you were in the hospital the first time, they gave me meals. Every day. They didn't have to do that."

"You could get that at home."

"Not if there was a party," Blayze said, his voice cracking. "And I got so tired of pizza. And nobody being there, except the help, and you know how they acted if we wanted something, if Mom and Dad weren't there, and if they *were* there, they were always partying. The Finneys have breakfast every day. Dinner, too. It's like living in this show, everybody around the table, but it's *real*. It's a real *family*."

"Except they're stuffing you with that religious stuff. When that woman told me to come back when I wasn't tweaking, the old one said she'd *pray* for me." Lya spat the word out. "Don't tell me Radford is into it, too!"

"I'm sorry about Nana Finney. She gets like that. But I *like* going to church with Rad and them. I mean, it can get boring, but I like the way I feel about myself when I'm not just thinking about me," Blayze said. "Okay, okay, I see you're about to hurl. But Lee—Lya, you can talk to me *whenever you want*. Send me text messages. I don't care how much it costs—I get plenty of allowance every month, you're always welcome—"

"Break's over!"

Lya grabbed him by the arms. "B. You'll accept me no matter what? Even if those Finneys say I'm damned?"

Blayze rolled his eyes. "They're not gonna say you're damned—"

"Blayze, on set."

He started backtracking. "Stay there, *don't* go anywhere."

Despite myself, I had become so absorbed in Lya's sibling drama that I'd ceased paying attention to the environment. I sensed two vampires somewhere in the vicinity. Closer than before? Neither was moving. Curious about how television shows work? I was here, watching, myself.

To be sure, I cut a glance at Alec, who, like my brother, was very good at scanning peripheries. He was alert, head moving minutely as he tracked the orderly chaos around the perimeter of the lit-up segment of the street. But the very fact that he wasn't urging us along meant that his sympathies still lay firmly with brother and sister reconnecting.

Before us, the actors rehearsed some more. This time it appeared to be a continuation of the same sequence from a different angle, now focused against the library that was decorated to look like a castle. There was some dialogue, followed by a battle before the kids escaped toward the darkness of the library.

Alec glanced toward Kim and me. "Is Lya ready?"

"They seem to be working something out," Kim murmured.

Alec gave a tight nod, then said, "I'm glad they're finding one another again, but I confess don't like this situation. Feels like Vienna all over again—"

"LET'S SEE THAT FROM THE TOP."

Once again, the stop-start rehearsal, this time with a complicated battle before the kids ran toward the library. The rehearsal was broken three times by milling figures readjusting actors, cameras, and that one light that no one seemed to agree on. Then apparently everything was ready. We onlookers had to crowd well to one side, Kim and I obscured by a hedgerow. Alec stood near Kim, but from a place that afforded a clear field of vision. He looked tense.

"Do you see something?" I asked past Kim.

"Not sure," Alec said.

Kim whispered, "Let's give Lya another minute. It's clearly important to her."

"A minute," Alec conceded. "She can always come back now that she has found him again."

The hairdressers finished combing and patting faces, the crowd whose purpose I couldn't guess huddled around one of the cameras and peered into the little monitor, which set off another flurry of noise about a couple of the lights—and once more the actors were given a water break.

The boy ran back, and confronted Lya, breathing hard. "What do you mean, damned? You never talked like that before. What did you *do?*"

"Nothing," Lya retorted, high and shrill, yet not loud, as she was drawing in shallower breaths by the moment. "*I* didn't do anything! I was *dying!* The chemo didn't work! I went to Paris to off myself, but even that was—"

"Blayze! They want to check the lighting on you!"

Lya's eyes glowed, and the boy stared appalled. Then she stepped closer to him, grabbed him by the arms, and hissed, "I'm a vampire. Okay? You still think I'm not damned?"

Her brother stepped back, and she let him go. But he didn't retreat. He pressed shaking fingers to his eyes, then mumbled, "Nobody's damned unless they want to be. It's what people do to themselves. They make their own hell, and push it onto other people. Or, that's the Finneys say, and I think so, too." When two more people called for him, he dropped his hands. "You're still you, right?" he pleaded.

"I'm still me," Lya said, her own voice trembling. "I'm still me, and you're always my little B. B and Lee, like always."

Only "always" had changed forever. I could see it in both faces. Kim looked on, her expression distraught. I have never liked kids at the best of times, and Lya was not the best of anything by any stretch of imagination, and yet Kim seemed to have an infinite capacity for empathizing with the least worthy.

Blayze whirled around and ran to join the others for yet more fussing and adjusting. When at last the lights were deemed satisfactory, everyone in place, the person with the little square came out and clacked the top piece onto the bottom square.

The actors performed their dialogue, then the kids and adults began their long, complicated battle sequence.

Then Alec's breath hissed in. "Three o'clock," he said, low yet sharp.

Kim stilled, poised and alert as a duelist. "Which—" She bit the word off as a burly man in black jeans and tee emerged past the lights and shoved between a couple of actors play-fighting, heading our way. "I see him."

Alec dashed across the street, paying no attention to the film zone. He snatched a lid off a dustbin and sent it spinning, to crash straight into the ribs of the man heading for Kim.

Who was not there. She'd stooped for a garden rake in front of one of the houses, and wielded it with both hands, driving away the two men who tried to advance on her.

"CUT! Cut! Cut!" came a bellow from the cluster around one of the cameras.

"No, keep it rolling," someone else called. "We might be able to use some of that."

The nature of the brawl had changed; it seemed that the burly actors took violent exception to the hired ruffians in anonymous dark colors shoving past them.

The sideliners were all hooting, shouting, and clapping now.

"Is this real? It almost looks real," someone commented shrilly.

"I dunno—can hardly wait to see it on TV!"

Someone was herding the children away as Alec sent the nearest attacker staggering by a hurled clay pot of geraniums.

Then he stuck the toe of his boot under a child's plastic sword, sending it spinning toward Kim.

She snatched it out of the air, and the two stood back to back.

The director bellowed, "Security!"

But the security people had already joined the fray, some trying to eject the attackers, others attempting to herd Alec and Kim off the street.

Then a woman Maman's age among the enthralled spectators pointed at Alec, saying, "Is he Remington Steele?"

That was when Kim's face turned toward me. "Fridge," she seemed to be saying —

But I ignored her, for from the deep shadows between those lights, the two vampires emerged, arrowing straight for Kim.

I left it to Lya to back me or not — I had no idea if she'd be help or hindrance, and Noemi's exhortation still rang in my mind. I was not about to lead her into a fight if she did not know what to do. But she uttered a pungent curse, and shadowed herself and charged the first of the vampires, a tall woman with long, streaming hair, and madly glowing eyes.

"Stake," I said to Kim. "Throw it."

Her eyes widened. "But it'll hurt you —"

"*Throw it!*"

By then Lya had attacked, shrill and angry. But the vampire was faster, and Lya barely ducked her a strike with nails like talons. Lya skidded back as Kim hurled her stake toward the woman. Kim's throw did not match Tony's expertise, but that wasn't necessary, because I shifted into speed, and gave the thing a butt with the heel of my hand, accelerating it straight into the woman's throat —

I was not prepared for the immediate flash of transformation; the vampire recoiled into the shrubbery, her long hair whipping like snakes before it hardened, and suddenly there was a young hawthorn tree amid the tangle of other greenery.

The other saw me coming, and ran, but I was already in speed, my hand throbbing with excruciating slowness from its contact with the hawthorn stake. I caught up on the far side of the building. He was thin, a counterpart to Lya. Maybe even younger.

"Who sent you?" I hissed, pinning him against the building.

He stared uncomprehending, then his eyes narrowed with effort, and he threw all his strength into hurling me off. I staggered — the transition between speed and real time was like balancing on an unsteady boat. He faded into shadow; I could have pursued but I suspected I already knew who'd sent him. We still did not know why, but that kid was not likely to know either. And I had other responsibilities.

When I returned, three of the attackers lay in the street with a combination of security and actors on them, everyone yelling. Along the periphery, the watchers were clapping and commenting loudly and approvingly at the show — was it part of the show — where was Remington Steele? He's famous!

Kim and Alec were trying to fade through the crowd. I sought Lya, and found her beyond the hedge, where a ring of adults had sequestered the young ones.

"…take mine," Blayze said, pressing something into Lya's hands. "I can get another one by tomorrow. Call or text. Whenever you want. Doesn't matter about minutes." He ran back to the beckoning adults.

Lya clutched his cell phone to her scrawny chest, staring after him.

Kim and Alec turned up then. "Ready?" Alec said to Lya. "Closest portal?"

Lya jerked her head in a nod, and we eeled through the crowed, drawing shadows around us until we were free, and running hard.

Nineteen

Kim

"**Y**OWCH!" I yelped as the portal rammed us through.

There is a painfully obvious difference between ghosting between portals while in the Nasdrafus, and being yanked physically between portals that use the Nasdrafus as a kind of...I don't even know what to call it. Accelerant? Tesseract...thingy? Sandwich? For there's the physical portal, which connects to the Nasdrafus where there distance is entirely a mental exercise, then the next physical portal. When I'd experienced portals in spirit form it had felt like a sort of disorientation, which I thought of as trying to mentally wade through jelly.

The second one *hurts*. It wasn't so bad the first couple times – for me, that is – but this time, the longest one yet, spat us out staggering. I turned to Alec, who was distinctly greenish along the jaw, his lips compressed tightly as he breathed hard. "Can't do that again," he whispered into my hair as I held him steady.

"Agreed. That was *way* too rough," I croaked, shocked at the sight of his nose bleeding. He pinched his nostrils tight and tipped his head back.

Lya scowled as if I'd jabbed her – she and Ruli looked as if they'd merely passed from one room to another. I saw at once that Lya assumed I was blaming, so I said quickly, "Thank you so much, Lya. *You* were quick and smart. But portals don't seem to like squishy humans."

Her expression eased slightly. "I did it as fast as I could, so those dirtbags wouldn't get us."

"And you were awesome," I assured her, a droplet in her yawning gap of need. Not enough, I knew the moment the words left my lips.

"Thank you, Lya," Alec said a bit hoarsely as he swept the surroundings. Not that there was much to see in that tiny antechamber that had only an old, threadbare cushioned cabriole-legged bench from the 1700s and the gaudily ornate mirror that we'd come out of. He collapsed onto it as if his legs wouldn't hold him, still pinching his nose.

I knew he would hate fussing over him, so I turned to Lya to draw attention from him. "Did your brother's cell phone come through okay?"

Lya quickly, almost convulsively flipped open the phone, then clapped it shut without looking at it as she dipped her chin in a tiny nod. "I won't know his new number if he gets a new one," she muttered. "If those Finneys let him."

"It didn't sound to me as if he finds that a worry," I said, trying to find the right words to reach her, though it felt as if my brain was still back in LA. "When you get to Paris, you'll have to find a charger that works in Europe, since it's an American phone."

Lya's thin fingers ran over the phone, kind of caressing it, making me wonder what sort of catch-up her own mind—her new, vampire mind—might be doing. Her brother was back in her life, yay, but for how long? If she survived as a vampire, she would not age, though he would. What kind of relationship would they have? Love adapts, I thought. If you let it. But I didn't know her well enough to say it.

Ruli stepped to the mirror. "Let's get back to Paris while whoever is chasing Kim is still busy combing the portals of Los Angeles."

I knew it was unlikely I'd ever see Lya again, and I wouldn't miss her particularly; she reminded me a bit of holly, thorny but bright. The brightness was potential, a glimpse of who she might have been under very different circumstances — and yet, mess that she was, that love for her younger brother had come through as pure as gold.

I risked a touch, taking Lya's cold, skinny wrist in hand. I met her gaze, black except for a tiny smolder in each pupil — what exactly *was* that? Her flesh was so cold that glow couldn't be fire — and I said, "I think you'll figure it out. The main thing is, now you know you matter to your brother. A lot."

She jerked her shoulder up, but her lips betrayed a tiny smile.

Ruli took her firmly by the wrist I'd just let go of, and they plunged into the mirror. The glass bulged and surged in a way that caused an echo of nausea, and I turned quickly. "Let's go, before more vamps pop out of that thing."

Alec had stayed there on the bench as he fought for breath. But he got up and moved to the door to check beyond; between them, Ruli and Lya had brought us to the portal I'd been yanked through while I was Aurélie's duppy: in the Eyrie on Mt. Dhiavilyi, seat of the von Mecklundburgs.

I squashed the words *Are you okay?* I could see that he wasn't, but he was going to push on. His alert tension made it clear that he didn't trust this place, with its secret passages and history, any more than I did. After the weird experiences of the past…how many days? Or hours? I would not have been surprised if a howling, ululating mob of riders galloped up the marble stairs, waving swords as they streamed in and out of the weapons room. Real or ghostly.

"I think the bleeding's stopped," he murmured.

We passed the dark, silent ballroom, its high east windows showing the first dim hint of impending dawn. It had been early evening in Los Angeles, which meant we'd come out on the other side of the ten hours' difference. On the other side of the ballroom, we passed through the tall gilt doors into the cool hallways with its marble checkerboard floor.

We were alone.

I threw my arms around Alec, and he leaned briefly into me, his breath a sigh. Tired as I was, his warmth and his scent boosted my energies with far more fizz than any Vrajhus. "I want a bath and a bed," I mumbled into his neck.

"Bed," he whispered into the top of my frowzy head, and a tremor of laughter passed right through me, jacking the fizz to the max. "But not here."

Not here. Those two words dissolved the bubble of Just Us. I forced my own awareness outward, as I loosened my tentacles.

Alec had already stashed his now useless cell phone in his back pocket. Now that he was back, the responsible thing was to let the king, the Council, and the Vigilzhi know.

Moving stiffly, he headed past the state rooms for the more livable wing. "Ruli backed us more than I had let myself expect," he commented, sniffing at the scent of paint and paint thinner that hung in the chilly air.

"She did," I said. "Are you…"

"Glad she went back to Paris? Or wherever they've gone," he admitted. The bleeding had stopped, but eyes were horribly bloodshot. "I'm beginning to trust her more."

"But you still don't completely?"

"I think it's the jolt every time I catch her gaze, and there's that damn red glow. Do they actually grow a new membrane behind the retina, as some animals have?"

"It might explain how well they see at night," I said. "Does it creep you out, too?"

"I think it's more that the glow is an inescapable reminder that she is no longer the person I knew from childhood on —" He stopped, his footfalls abruptly going soundless, though his rapid walk didn't abate.

I shifted to a catwalk as well as I registered what he'd heard: voices echoing up the vast marble staircase from the floor below, which was a vast warren of kitchens, laundry, and service areas at least as large as those under major hotels.

Then I picked out a familiar voice and relaxed. Alec started down the stairs at a rapid clip. Tony had claimed once that the von M.s were cash-strapped, but every time I stepped into this castle, it seemed to be at night, and it was lit up like Las Vegas. Either they had their own source of electrical power or they were supporting an electric bill the size of a medium country's entire gross national product.

"Percy," Alec exclaimed.

Redhaired Parsifal von Mecklundburg stood at the foot of the stairs, talking to a man and a woman loaded down with paint cans, plaster, and other stuff. Percy, a genial giant with a hero's chin, grinned amiably at us both. "Alec? Kim! You're back! Did I know that?" His gaze narrowed when he took in Alec's pale complexion and bloodshot eyes, then said diffidently, "Did one of the cousins bring you up here?"

"We need a phone and a ride into Riev," Alec said, bypassing the questions. "And weapons, if you still have a vampire problem here."

Percy gave us a reassuring grin. "No, no, no. Everything inside is as it was. Whereas I wouldn't trust the outside, not till the sun comes out."

"As it was?" I said.

Percy's smile altered to a wince. "Protections. Uncle Jerzy'd undone some of the charms in the paintings. I think his mother must have taught him how. But I've been renewing them while repairing the last of the damage from last summer."

"The paintings do have charms?" I asked—I'd wondered if that was possible!

Percy blinked at me. "Didn't someone tell you? Alec knows. And so should you, now. Here." He set down the box of color samples he'd been holding, and charged up the staircase with us on his heels.

On my rampage down that staircase the summer before last, and on my brief visit during winter, I'd vaguely noticed the full-length portraits on the walls facing landings and along all the corridors, but without paying them much heed. I'd been busy with other things, like not getting shot or stabbed.

He stopped at the first landing, gazing across at the larger-than-life portrait of a slim guy sporting a late 19th Century military tunic with sashes and braid and epaulets. I recognized him at once from the portrait exactly like this one in the gallery at the palace: one of the Dsaret twins. Superficially they resembled Tony, with the same pale hair, but with light brown eyes instead of black. No hint of the crooked smile in that gentle, pensively eternal gaze.

"Is this the twin who died in the duel?" I asked. "I've seen his ghost upstairs—he carries a dueling pistol."

"Yes. Though actually," Percy said, somberly regarding that eternally young face, "I think the ghost is his brother, who mourned Pavel for the rest of his life. Rudolf kept that pistol as a warning to his children, and his grandchildren, of the stupidity and waste of duels. There should be stories about him in your family, Kim."

"How can you tell the difference between the two?" I asked.

"I can't for certain, for some of what I see might be painter's interpretation. But the ghost just looks more to me like Rudolf, over in the palace, and not as much like Pavel here." He blinked, shook his head slightly, then pointed with a long, freshly-scrubbed finger. "But. See the gilding in his epaulettes, in the tassels at his sabretache and boots, and in his hair? And the thin line framing the whole?"

The glint of gold within the soft, rich glow of oil paint glinted in the electric light. "I do."

"Think of all that gold as laser beams." Percy's grin was decidedly impish. "We put sun-charms in crystal, as always, then grind the crystal and blend it into the gold paint. Have to be careful painting with it, but gold holds the crystal quite well, and of course the crystal holds the charm, making the paintings like a laser maze. No vampire can pass along any hall, or on the stairs, without getting a dose of sun poison."

A lot more practical than charms in the eyes of the portraits, as I'd imagined.

Percy blinked at me, as if remembering that I was being trained in the arts of Vrajhus, then added, "Exception, we perform the Person and Presence charm. I did Ruli's myself, last winter."

He ran back downstairs, then pointed down a hallway. "You know where you are, Alec. I think the phone still works. It did the day before your wedding."

That was...how many days ago? It felt like years.

"Would you two like some breakfast while you wait for the sun?"

"I need to report in, and get someone to come fetch us," Alec said.

"Oh, Sig can take you to Riev. He has to go in anyway." Percy still hadn't asked where we'd turned up from. I realized as he led us to the kitchen that he either didn't notice who came and went — possible in a castle this large — or it simply didn't matter.

Alec thanked him and went to make his call as Percy went into the kitchen to speak to someone, then returned to take me to the tidy servants' dining room.

Instead of asking questions he certainly had a right to, what with us popping up totally unexpected or invited, he filled me in on all the repair and painting projects he'd been working on, and it hit me that he'd probably developed his own way of surviving in that family of wildly different personalities. One way would be to disassociate completely from caroming political goings-on.

Alec returned at the same time as breakfast appeared; he'd stopped in a bathroom somewhere along the way and washed the blood off.

Percy joined us, making me wonder if he forgot meals when in the midst of his projects, and we mostly listened to him chat about the mural he was planning until a guy Alec's age appeared, his sandy hair still wet. "Durchlaucht," he greeted Alec, then he performed a little bow when he saw me. "Princess."

I fought the urge to say "Call me Kim," and nodded, my face heating up. Alec, Phaedra, and even Gran had convinced me that I was going to have to get used to titles, or else initiate an awkward exchange over my insistence on American social exchanges every single time I met someone. After which Dobrenis were more likely to go right back to what they were used to—or avoid me altogether.

Sure enough. My acceptance of the bow and title went by unnoticed, and Sig asked, "Are there any bags to go?"

"None," Alec said.

Sig's sandy brow ridge twitched, but that was his only reaction as he said, "The jeep will be in the courtyard whenever you're ready."

Alec thanked him, and we finished the meal. Percy then went off to his day's labors as Alec and I trod down a corridor to the courtyard I would never forget as long as I lived. The sight of a jeep was a jolt—it might even be the same one that that horrible Reithermann had died beside. And I'd collapsed next to, a bullet in my shoulder...

My mind veered away, as it always did, and lit on our current situation.

Vampires.

"Alec, I can't help thinking that I ought to go somewhere and hide until we figure this out. Because those seraphs, and whoever else they're sending are after *me*. I don't want you, and everyone around me, to be collateral damage."

"No," Alec said, flat and emphatic.

"But that makes me a moving target, and that might bring danger you don't need, otherwise I wouldn't think of —"

"Good. Stay with me."

" —I *want* to, *however*, I think I should —"

"No," he said again, softly, but his forehead had tensed.

I bit back a retort, and stopped in the open archway to that courtyard. "I'm trying to think past myself here," I said in a low voice that I hoped didn't reach Sig and the other guys yakking on the other side of the jeep. I studied Alec, and took a breath. "...but I can see that my heroic sacrifice is only managing to piss you off."

He took my hands. "You never piss me off. The situation, yes. Not you. We'll find a way to protect you. And the country. But can you see, if you take off —"

I could have said I can look out for myself, but he already knew that. I also knew that I wasn't 100% good at dealing with vamps. Also, he was worried that his protections might not be 100% good, but he was doing his best to create a perimeter of safety for us both. And the country. I ought to contribute to that perimeter, not jet off on my own, creating two fronts in his mind.

"Okay," I said, breathing out the frustration building up. "I see we're going to have to figure this out a step at a time. There doesn't seem to be a roadmap for how to do a relationship while threatened by vampires and other mysterious nasties, on top of running a country."

He kissed me, then breathed, "Thank you." Then coughed wetly into his palm. His hand came away dotted with blood.

We stared at each other, I stricken witless. We said nothing more—I could see that talking took more effort—but held hands for the entire drive into Riev.

TWENTY

KIM

I wanted to take him straight to the hospital, but he whispered that he'd get faster treatment at the palace, reminding me that Milo's attendants had medical training.

As the jeep passed the line of gingko trees leading up from the marketplace through the older part of the city, I could easily imagine Queen Sofia pointing the area out for the planting. I could also imagine her fourth daughter, Princess Margit, arguing that these elegant, imported trees would be wasted on this unsightly part of the city, then the queen observing sardonically that the area would be a great deal less unsightly with the addition of the trees.

A cool breeze rustled through the foliage, filling the air with golden leaves; we had returned just in time for the dramatic leaf drop. Everywhere else brilliant leaves still hung on, or had entirely given up for winter, leaving bare branches etched against the sky.

My heart brimmed with emotions, my hand tightening on his.

"It's all right," he whispered. "Already I feel a lot better. I just need to breath the fresh air."

He didn't look better. I fought the worry spiral by concentrating on my surroundings. There was the route I'd skulked after leaving the marketplace after my sojourn with elderly Tante Mina, who had once been my grandmother's loyal governess, though barely a few years older than she was.

To the left, I thought I spotted the chimneys of the Waleska inn, a block away.

Along the cobbled streets, dilapidated cars putt-putted along, not much faster than the ox carts that hauled produce and bags of newly harvested and milled grains, to be stored against the coming winter. Crystals hung in windows, which once I'd thought mere decoration. Ditto the many hawthorn and yew trees, and here and there climbing roses.

Were they enough to keep out the vampires that might be coming for me? As the delightfully distinct houses slid past, some still with window boxes with last, lavender asters among other late blooms, and others winter-ready, I considered this silent testimony to the centuries-long balance between the night walkers and humanity. There was no purely linguistic difference between the word 'vampire' and the Dobreni 'inimasang,' and yet there was a connotational difference. In LA, vamps were rare in ratio to the population, and effectively invisible. Mostly lethal. Not here. Ruli was a reminder of that. And her grandmother Rose, twin sister to my own grandmother, and yet vampires were still the enemy to be wary of. Like wolves.

I could not think of Ruli as an enemy, as a fiend to be staked on sight.

Complicated, just like this wonderful city, which I was passing through for the first time as a married woman, really — I couldn't count that parade directly after the wedding, fun as it was. "Married woman" was a concept startling enough without considering the surreal-adjacent P-word.

Among the many people on the streets, there were those who looked with interest at the passing traffic, and fewer quick enough to recognize Alec, though he was only in a jeep instead of one of the princemobiles. He'd been leaning his head back against the headrest, but now he straightened up, reaching for that projected air of calm that Milo had inculcated into him. Some of those widened sets of eyes took me in, then came the slight head-nod of respect, or hands pressed to hearts in salute.

I glimpsed St. Xanpia's fountain in the distance as the jeep bucketed over the cobblestones around the outer circle, then up Laurel Street. There the falling leaves, crushed under the tires, whiffed a little of eucalyptus, throwing me back to California. It almost made me dizzy. My gaze drifted to the tops of another plantation of gingko trees that I knew lay beyond the Council building.

The Vigilzhi guards at the palace gates stood at attention as we rolled in and up the long drive. It still didn't feel like home yet. How long had it taken Queen Sofia to feel at home in a palace? But then she'd had a head start, having been born royalty.

"Thanks, Sig," Alec said when we stopped before the palace entrance.

"Durchlaucht," the guy said cheerily, touching his fingertips to his forehead, though he wore no uniform. "I suggest you go sleep it off." He zoomed away to his errands, and we headed for the door, arms about each other. I was half-holding him up.

Servants appeared, and then Phaedra pushed her way through. "Let them pass," she said curtly, and the servants backed off, looking concerned, worried, one or two disapproving—and with a weird sense of panicky hilarity, I realized what we must look like, the two of us returning abruptly from our honeymoon scruffy, Alec red-eyed and staggering as if he'd been on a ten-day bender. There was no help for it—either I stopped everyone and explained everything, or shut up. At least Alec didn't seem to see them.

We got to our suite, where Alec dropped onto the bed, the fine skin of his forehead dotted with sweat. In came two doctors, one Milo's old and trusted GP. And a newer one from the hospital. With them was a small, frail old woman whom I instantly recognized: Salfmatta Mina Hajyos, Gran's governess. She had moved back to the palace to become Gran's companion.

"I'm sorry to trouble you," Alec murmured as Milo's physician bent to listen to his heart.

The doctor looked up. "There is strain in his heartbeat."

"Let me by," Tante Mina said, before the second doctor could speak. Because this was Dobrenica, the Salfmatta had precedence, and both men deferred. She sat beside the bed, one hand on her rosary, the other stretched over Alec without touching him. "Ah," she said. "I know what to do."

I had heard that there were Salfmattas who could heal. Not every disease responds to Vrajhus, or Dobrenis would all live past 100. But the portals were Vrajhus constructs, and apparently Vrajhus damage responded to her charms. A glisten, or shimmer, glowed about him as Tante Mina uttered Latin phrases in a calming singsong, and I remembered being taught that Vrajhus could be focused through words meaningful to the healer. For her, it was ancient Roman

Catholic litanies.

Gradually the glisten vanished, leaving Alec breathing far more normally. He opened his eyes, which had cleared remarkably. Then he sat up. "Much better. Much, much better. But I'm not doing that again any time soon."

The doctors then had to reassure themselves (for Milo, no doubt). The old one nodded judiciously after listening to Alec's heart. "Steady and strong."

The second one then checked his pupils and his blood pressure, asked some questions, then said, "You're sound, but the joint tenderness means your body wants you to slow down. Listen to it. Rest is the best medicine now."

"Thank you," Alec replied. "But I saw that line of messengers waiting. And the sooner I'm seen about my business, the faster rumor about my returning to my sot ways will die out." So he *had* seen it all as we passed.

The doctors cautioned, Tante Mina concurred, Alec and I thanked all three of them repeatedly, then they filed out.

I'd been about to reinforce their suggestion, but I could see that he was going to get up, regardless. *There are three in this marriage.* "Should we go wait on Milo and Gran first?" I asked.

"The Salfmatta will report to your grandmother. And I will no doubt see Milo at the Council," Alec said, giving my hand a last squeeze before letting go.

Honeymoon's over, I told myself, and kept my voice casual as I said, "See ya when I see ya." And as he walked out, Phaedra let herself in.

"You should have taken us," she said—meaning the Vigilzhi, as backup.

"It worked out." I shrugged, feeling suddenly very tired. "And Ruli wasn't bad backup."

"Ruli," Phaedra repeated. "I thought she went to Paris."

"Tell you what," I said. "So I'll only have to blab it all once, how about sending for Tania? And Beka, if she has time, though I expect she's up to her ears in her own alligators."

"Durchlaucht," Phaedra said with a nod—and I realized she had taken my suggestion as The Princess's Order. I suppressed the urge to bleat, "I didn't mean it like *that*," as she gestured to a young equerry, to whom she whispered a few words.

The kid galloped off after a duck of the head to me, and I said to Phaedra, "Now you're doing it."

"Doing what?"

"Durchlaucht," I repeated.

"It's what the Vigilzhi are permitted to call the heir," Phaedra retorted in her incongruously high kitten voice. "Which extends to his wife."

"But Sig, the driver who brought us, isn't Vigilzhi. At least, he was there at the Eyrie—and I'll get to how we ended up there."

"Sig?" Phaedra repeated. "Sigismund? Hair the color of a rock lizard? This tall?"

"That's the guy—I've never seen a blond unibrow before. Blondish. Both Percy and Alec just called him Sig."

"He grew up part of the mountain guard, though he wanted to join the Vigilzhi," Phaedra said. "But two years into the training, the old head of castle security died and Tony called Sig back to replace him, so Niklos could stay as captain of the guard. Didn't you see him when you were fighting Reithermann with Tony? He and Niklos led the resistance when Reithermann's mercenaries took the castle."

"I don't remember a lot from that day. Except getting shot," I admitted. "Is a castle steward a promotion or a demotion?"

She laughed. "Ask anyone in the Eyrie, and they will tell you it's a much-cherished promotion. No, just ask Magda, who he'll finally be able to marry this Christmas. As long as there isn't another vampire attack. Or another coronation. It's been postponed twice. Why?"

I snorted. "I was just wondering if there's any actual pay in this promotion. The way Aunt Sisi and Count Robert and even Tony moaned about being paupers."

Phaedra laughed again. "He told us the pay's about the same as a Vigilzhi captain, but the important thing is, they'll be part of the family. That means Magda Baker will move into the castle—no guard barracks for a steward. Any kids will be raised with our generation's kids. Just as it's been for generations. And of course he'll have a very short chain of command, with only Tony above him. He's equal to Niklos. Everyone else runs to their rein."

I was finally beginning to understand castle dynamics. Sort of. "So saying 'Durchlaucht' became a habit with him, though he's not Vigilzhi?"

"It's more that the others permit him to use it, because he was one of us for a while, in training. Everyone else uses the conventional titles. Except us." There was no mistaking the slightly self-conscious pride in that *us*. "Get used to it. Goes with the tiara, you might say. Speaking of, now that you're back—"

I held up a hand. "I know I have to start in with the patting babies on the head and visiting garden clubs, or whatever, but before my schedule gets filled with princess stuff, you'd better hear what happened."

On that note, I took a fast shower instead of the luxurious bath I'd longed for, and changed my clothes.

Fast as I was, I emerged as a civilized being again just as my guests arrived—or guest and my brand-new princess's secretary, Tania Waleska. From her earliest age, Tania had spoken with ghosts. Many hadn't believed her, just as they hadn't believed that some of the animals she befriended were ghosts. But she was one of the most truthful persons I'd ever known—and apparently she was regarded as a Talent by Beka's Great-Aunt Sarolta and the Salfmatta sorority.

I'd hired her as my "assistant" while I was still a free agent living at the Waleska Inn. Hiring her was a way of getting her out of an exasperating job she hadn't really wanted, so that she could help me with Vrajhus studies as she herself learned about how to detect Vrajhus resonance. Or, so I thought of it in English; the Dobreni words are untranslatable, but have to do with how refraction and resonance—light and sound—interact in crystalline structures. Specifically our prisms.

She arrived breathlessly, her long dark braids flapping on her skinny back as if she'd run the entire way. I was delighted to see that she still wore her favorite purple.

I had thoroughly expected Beka Ridotski to send a "when I can" message because I knew how busy she was, but much to my surprise she turned up not long after Tania, her face serious.

"Beka, I'm sorry to break into your day."

"It's all right. School just let out, and Council is still over there arguing. Milo released another segment of the treasury, as he and Alec and my father agreed. Of course it's loosed the customary brangles."

"Let me guess. Led by Aunt Sisi."

Beka's smile was sardonic. "The duchess has done her best to rouse the secondary families, but I expect you will get a much better report from Alec when he returns."

While she spoke, silent servants appeared, bearing a tray of roasted potatoes with wine-braised fish and fresh veggies, and for dessert, a kind of apple pie tart thing with a cream sauce that I loved.

"Help yourselves," I said. "Or not — I'm still catching up on missed meals."

Beka stuck to coffee, as usual — she kept strict kosher — but Phaedra and Tania, I was glad to see, did justice to the palace cooking. I loaded my plate, took two deliciously savory bites of everything, then launched into my tale.

The food had nearly gone cold when I finished up, and the slanting rays of the soft Dobreni sun were turning ochre, but I'd gotten it all out. "There. That's what happened. Now, tell me what it all means." And I attacked my food.

Phaedra said, "I really wish I'd gone along with you. I'd like to find out who's behind that pursuit." She smacked her fist into her palm.

Tania said nothing, but gazed from one of us to the other.

Beka stared down into her gilt-edged porcelain cup of coffee for a time. She said, finally, "*I* wish Ruli would come to me, but she never trusted me even when we were children. Though I don't know why. I tried to never let her cousins draw me into their squabbles." Then she looked up. "You told me something of what happened to you when you were taken in spirit during summer. Can you go over it again? This time, though, focus on the necklace that Queen Aurelia was given as a child in Jamaica. Everything you remember."

"The necklace? Why? It's gone. Two centuries ago."

"From what you said when you first came out of the coma, it seemed so, but I'd like you to think back, and this time be as exact as you can."

The afternoon light waned, and more coffee and tea was brought in, for I was rubbing my eyes hard by then. But the chance of getting at least some questions answered kept me going.

"…and Aurélie kept the necklace strictly hidden until the night Napoleon took Josephine and the household to an opera at the Tuileries. Aurélie wore it that night because she thought she was safe from theft, seeing as how she was surrounded by the Bonaparte family, who were all loaded with gold and jewels. Ditto the rest of Napoleon's court…"

Beka leaned close, gazing at me unblinking when I described the appearance of the seraphs that night.

"…it was hidden again until Aurélie wore it for the ball at the Eyrie. Following which the seraphs appeared, and suckered us into the Nasdrafus. It was then that Elisheva Barta told Aurélie to hide the necklace. She said…she said, 'That's what's drawing them.' Aurélie hid it, we finally freed Elisheva, and got away — and later she handed the necklace to me when we closed the Esplumoir. And it vanished, so it ceased to be an issue two centuries ago."

Beka sighed. "I don't think it's that simple. You're not going to like what I'm going to say next…"

"Try me," I said.

"You both failed the Salfmatta you called Nanny Hiasinte, who exhorted you and Queen Aurelia to keep the necklace secret."

"But we *did* keep it secret."

"Except that Queen Aurelia wore it, and you sanctioned that."

"We believed that the necklace had to be hidden from *thieves*. She was just one among many wearing jewels, that night. Both nights."

"I see. Now I'm beginning to wonder if Nanny Hiasinte did not know about the Esplumoir, only that the necklace had to leave her island," Beka mused. "*How* I wish that the Salfmattas of those days had left written records! So much was lost…but complaining changes nothing."

I said, "As for keeping its provenance secret, Aurélie did, until she met Queen Sofia. At that point, revealing the truth seemed to be important. And you can't convince me that telling the queen, or Jaska, afterwards, somehow brought on the seraphs. We saw them in Paris first. Also, it had become a matter of trust not to keep secrets from Jaska, who by then was her fiancé."

"I'm not trying to find fault," Beka said hastily. "Only explanation. The two of you did nothing wrong, or careless, according to what you knew." Beka thumbed her eyelids. She was clearly tired, too.

Then the import of Beka's words finally hit me.

"You say you're not trying to find fault, but actually it *is* my fault," I said, chill prickling up my back. "Except I didn't know what it was for. If I'd been told that it was key to closing the Esplumoir…"

"As I said, Nanny Hiasinte might not have known what the Esplumoir was, much less this intended purpose. Tell me again exactly what she said about the necklace, if you can."

"It was called the Navaratna," I began.

"Which is a type of necklace. I believe the name is Sanskrit," Beka said. "The true Navaratna is a powerful constellation of protections, though nine-stone necklaces are common in some parts of the world — you can buy them as luck jewelry in tourist shops."

I closed my eyes, bringing up that vivid memory. "Her words were, *Here is the truth that was said in the Sanskrit: this ruby represents the sun. It is your center. Red Coral for Mangala, the red star, an emerald for Buddha, the green star, son of the moon, a yellow sapphire for Deva-guru, father-star, a diamond for Shukra, the white star, a blue sapphire for Shani, the ring-star, Gomedaka for Rahu, when the moon is on the rise, and a Cat's Eye for Ketu, when the moon is descending.*" Elisheva, who was studying to become a Salfmatta two hundred years ago, said that in Dobrenica, there was a different legend."

"Most of which is regarded as peasant superstition nowadays," Phaedra put in. "I inherited one from my Danilov grandmother. The duchess refused to let me wear it to the New Year's Ball when I turned sixteen, not because it has any special significance except for the worth of the stones. She insisted I'd lose it."

"Do you still have it?" Beka asked.

"I do."

"I'd like to see it, if I may."

"You can, though I'm sure it only has the usual charm on the diamond. The note in the jewelry box said that Grandma Danilov's grandmother had had it made."

Beka nodded slowly. "I would love to know why she chose that form — but then the Danilovs originally came from…"

"The mountains in the south of Siberia," Phaedra said.

"Likely a simple luck piece, then," Beka said. "With charms from that region of the world, often included in dowries. Thank you."

"Elisheva used different words about it." I began to recite the words seared on my memory: "*There is the stone of Reuben Odem that protects families, Shimon Pitda that protects animals, Levi Bareket that protects children, Yehuda Nofech that gives the power to overcome evil intent, Yisschar Saphir that heals and protects vision, Zevulon Yahalom that protects the sleeper and guides dreams on the righteous path, Gad Leshem that grants true sight, Dan Shevo that protects the home, Naftali Ahlamah that prevents sudden death, Asher Tashish that protects the growing things, Yosef Shoam that protects the seasons, and Binyamin Yashfeh that wards the evil blood drinkers.* Calling it a constellation actually seems right," I ended. "Anyway, it's beginning to sound like the Navaratna was loaded with charms meant to do good, but I'm guessing you don't pack in that much firepower without a danger of it backfiring."

"Backfiring?" Phaedra's finely plucked brows arched.

"Aurélie had some pret-ty stiff nightmares about women who'd had the necklace in the past. I mean, way, *way* back. Some of that was assorted demons and evils trying to capture the necklace. Also, I think she was getting visions from the past of women who'd had the necklace and who might have gotten tempted to mess around with all that potential power, and it didn't end well. In any case, Nanny Hiasinte said that the necklace was supposed to magnet in some protection spirits to watch over the holder who stayed pure in heart. I can't tell you how a necklace defines 'pure in heart', but the poster child for that would be Aurélie, for she was never mean to anyone. Or anything."

I poured more tea, though it was beginning to feel as if my eyeballs were floating. Not even caffeine was working against the tiredness closing in.

Beka eyed me intently. "Did the necklace disappear *before* she brought you, or did it vanish when you went through the portal?"

I blinked. "They were nearly instantaneous. I had it in my hand, everyone sang the charm, then I found myself standing on the hillside with Xanpia. And no necklace."

"And you didn't think to ask her about any of this?"

"Why? The necklace was gone, the Esplumoir was presumably closed, and at that point I just wanted to get back here, as fast as I could hustle. From my perspective it had been *years.*"

Beka the scholar compressed her lips as if she wanted to unload a string of curses on my head for not grilling Xanpia while I had her. But then she relented. "I can see that. Especially as you only carried it yourself for about a minute."

"Right," I said.

Beka sighed. "I have to report to the elders everything you said. Also, it's getting late. We all have matters waiting for us. But I'll leave you with this thought: there's a good chance that the necklace is not gone. It's still there."

"Where?"

"The Place Between. And the false seraphim have been waiting for two centuries to get you, the last to hold it, to bring it back."

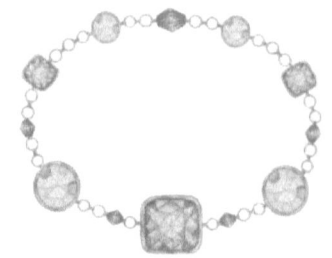

TWENTY-ONE

KIM

My dad left for the south of Italy the day after Alec and I headed off on our honeymoon. Through his long-time correspondence with other Ancient Rome nerds, Dad wangled an invitation to visit Pompeii and Herculaneum, where a new site had been opened. So it was just Mom who came over from Ysvorod House to join Gran, Milo, Alec and me for dinner.

Alec really did seem profoundly better that evening, though not his best self. At least he'd managed to shower and change sometime during his long day, before turning up in time for dinner. Milo, like Gran, was not pompous or even punctilious, but both had been raised to think a certain level of formality was to be expected at meals. Even Mom went so far as to brush her usually-neglected cloud of hair, and to exchange her habitual kaftan for a long, flowy gown that had a belt.

Nice clothes, fine tablecloth, porcelain and real silver — and all vexing subjects banned until after the meal. So, after hugs of "Welcome home!" all around, the subject went from my impressions of Venice straight to the music school's fall schedule for the new opera house, about which my mom, the opera lover of the family, waxed enthusiastic until the coffee and tea was served.

The only acknowledgment of the severely curtailed honeymoon and our unplanned reappearance looking like the leavings of a thousand prunebirds, was Gran's kindly, "Alexander, you will want an early night, I expect. Kimli, why don't you join me for breakfast tomorrow?"

And we were free.

"Was it bad?" my voice clashed with Alec's "What did Beka say?"

We laughed, Alec somewhat painfully. "What I'm grateful for, though I don't understand it, is that you don't seem to be feeling the effects of being dragged through that portal. I've still got a pounding headache, and every joint aches," he admitted. "What did Beka have to say?"

"Not much. She mainly wanted to know about the necklace."

"What necklace?"

"The one I had for about ten seconds before Xanpia brought me back."

He frowned. "I'd forgotten that bit of your adventures. My mind's mostly been taken up with your seraphs. Specifically, how to get rid of them, if they are the ones who put that pursuit on us."

"We can go into it when I learn more. After Beka learns more. What about the Council? Was Tante Sisi riding her broomstick and cackling as usual about the latest chunk of the Dsaret Treasure?"

He laughed softly, then grunted as he began to unbutton his shirt. I took over, and he sighed with relief, letting me ease him out of his clothes, after which he climbed wincing into our bed. He wasn't kidding about his joints. Elbows, knees, ribs, shoulders, were a deep, blotchy red that was going to be purple by morning. I shivered in sympathy, trying not to imagine what he'd have looked like before Tante Mina did her Vrajhus healing over him.

There was obviously not going to be any first-night-in-our-new-digs honeymooning that night. I sat up against the headboard, and lifted his head to my lap. I began massaging his temples. He sighed, relaxing into my touch, then spoke in a low, tired voice, "Milo and the Prime Minister have pretty well routed the duchess. As well as Count Robert's attempt to bully us into footing the bill for another grand building project. The key issues are still the solar panels up on the south-facing slopes, and wind farms in the valleys."

"I remember. But the mountain people don't want to give up their lamps and candles."

"The lamps and candles ceased to be a sticking point when Milo said we ought to approach it from the perspective of warmth, rather than light. Many of the mountain villagers might think electricity a useless luxury for light, but electric stoves is another issue, not only for cooking, but for warmth in winter." He grinned ruefully. "The tipping point, however, seems to be some bright soul in one of the Domitrian valleys having spread it about that solar panels function more like crystal than glass."

"They're not wrong, if you look at it a certain way."

"Precisely. And everyone knows that bigger is always better—"

I snickered. "Let me guess. They think if the solar panels are charmed against bloodsuckers, they'll get extra protection?"

"Something very like."

"Is it true?"

"You'd have to ask the experts about that. Though right now, I freely admit I'm too stupid with fatigue to comprehend any answer."

I fought a violent yawn. Though I seemed to have escaped the terrible bruises, my limbs felt as heavy as stone. "On that note…"

He was already asleep.

Despite being aware of the Sword of Damocles a-swinging over my head, i.e. waiting for Beka to get back to me, I managed to sleep like a rock.

When I woke, Alec was already gone. I got that long, blissful soak in a bath, which eased my small bruises. I wondered how much Alec had really recovered, but he was too much like Old Milo: if duty called, he'd crawl out of the grave if he could.

Finally the clock nagged me to get the day going. I dressed and went to have breakfast with Gran.

While she's firm about mealtimes being pleasant and civilized, when she feels it's time to get down to business, she's no slouch. And mornings are for work.

Gran nodded pleasantly to the servants who oversaw the serving of our breakfast, then dismissed them with an ease that revealed long habit in early years. To see her ease of command you'd never know that I grew up with her making my breakfast and packing my school lunches on the days my parents both worked, then washing the dishes afterward until I got old enough to take over that job myself. Whereas I still felt guilty for making trouble when servants waited on me. And I still felt I had to give a reason when I dismissed them.

"You look much more rested, Kimli," Gran said in Dobreni. "I'm sorry that your honeymoon was curtailed, and we will get to that presently."

While she spoke, I dashed some milk into my Assam, and lifted the beautiful celadon cup to my lips.

Gran switched to French. "Have you and Milo's boy discussed having an heir?"

I snorted the gulp of tea I'd just taken aboard and choked, coughing.

"Maouste!" Gran exclaimed. "Do not chug your tea, mignonne. We are not at a race," and waited patiently for my symphony of sneezes to end.

When I'd mopped my eyes and said a little huskily, "Not really," she went on, "You are young, so you have time — you've at least a year, more like two or three, before people begin speculating. But it will happen." She raised a hand when I was about to protest. "Yes, I know that in these modern days a couple has a right to make such decisions for themselves. But you're not just a couple."

"The fishbowl of monarchy," I said, more than a little petulantly. "Which is an absurd type of government, even Alec thinks so."

"A very bitter argument I had with my father when I was sixteen, to which he retorted that all forms of human power are absurd, but better to be a figure of absurdity than terror." Gran smiled thinly as she helped herself to shirred eggs. "That said, people like continuity, if they can get it. And by the way, I'm very sure that those self-righteous old men on that Council are pestering Alexander with the same question, for his own good. Though he probably won't tell you."

"That was once true, but now he tells me everything," I said.

"Does he," Gran replied, with an air of question.

"Of course," I said a bit defensively, as if I'd been challenged. No, more like I'd somehow fallen down on the job. At any rate, once it was clear we were in it for the long haul, I'd made sure to get myself on birth control. His acceptance of my taking responsibility had been all we'd said on the subject of future kids. As if there was even time, with everything else going on!

"Also," Gran went on—uninvited by me—"and this is purely personal, it would comfort Milo to see his line continued before he gets very much older. He asks for so very little."

Still, none of his beeswax, I wanted to say. But didn't. Longing for grandchildren wasn't confined to kings. And Milo had had a particularly tough life, all of it dedicated to Dobrenica. Which had left him somewhat frail.

"One last point before we leave the subject: there's a very good chance that you'll have twins."

"Twins!" I yelped—or tried to. What came out was a choked gargle. At least I'd taken a cautious sip this time.

Gran gave a tiny nod. "Twins regularly turn up in my line, usually every second or third generation. You would constitute the third." She then added very seriously, "You will have a great deal of help, naturally. But if it does happen, and I am granted the time, I would very much like to oversee certain aspects of their upbringing. I think it fair to say that matters might have fallen out differently if my own sister and I had been raised to regard us as one another's ally rather than rival."

Oof. That vividly brought to mind her sister Rose, the vampire who looked seventeen years old. The specific image was the smiling soignée Rose, who had faced off with Gran that horrible day when Jerzy von Mecklundburg had come gunning for Gran—and Rose was there, supposedly to watch.

"Does she…talk to you at all?" I asked tentatively.

"No. But I know she is out there. I hope one day to clear matters between us. If we can. But that is my concern. Now. To your ruined honeymoon. What exactly happened?"

I was getting pretty good at summarizing. She listened all the way through without too much comment, then said, "I am utterly ignorant about Vrajhus matters. But I trust you to keep me posted."

She went on to discuss some of the princess duties I was expected to execute. Breakfast soon ended, and I left, to find Phaedra waiting outside the door. "If there isn't anything urgent, I really need a workout," I said.

She grinned. "As it happens, my brother is at liberty right now…"

After two hours of fencing that left me feeling like a puppet with cut strings, I leaned into my Princess Prerogative and took another bath, this one with more bruise-easing bath herbs. As I lay there, I gazed down at my stomach, muscular from years of ballet and fencing, then put my hand on it. The idea of an actual human cooking inside me seemed as astonishing as anything I'd learned about charms, ancient necklaces — and vampires. Much less two tiny humans. But this was a subject to discuss sometime way in the future. Like, when I wasn't being chased by mysterious nogoodniks.

It was then that I remembered that I had left my birth controls pills with my luggage when we'd gone through the portal. That was a jolt — then it came to me that we'd been too tired, and too hurried, for honeymooning over the last day, so that would be all right, wouldn't it?

I surged out of the water, reached for towel and clothes, and went out to put in a call to Natalie Miller for an emergency resupply. Afterward, I had to face the first of my real Princess Duties, which was "chairing" a committee to pick the flower arrangers for the Dance at the Fountain, the traditional harvest festival in late September.

I actually kind of liked the idea of getting a chance not only to practice my Dobreni, but also to get to know individuals. I'd already begun getting acquainted with ordinary Dobreni when I was staying at the Waleskas' homey inn on the other side of town. The more people I got to know, the less I'd be depending on generalities about what people thought, spoken through others' filters. So even if the specific activities might be pretty frivolous — flower arranging committees — I thought that the opportunity to interact with people would be invaluable.

But I'd reckoned without the etiquette of princessing. While I'd been a free agent, it had been easy to wander over the city, practicing my stumbling Dobreni on ordinary citizens. Now, I seemed surrounded by an invisible barrier of Proper Princess Behavior. Since I know zip about the aesthetics of flower arranging, my post as honorary chair meant mainly smiling and praising all the entries. At least I had Phaedra and Tania with me, Phaedra constantly vigilant, and Tania diligently learning the intricacies of being a princess's secretary besides her own training, and our prism work.

I praised. I smiled until my face ached, and when it was all over and we crossed back to the palace, Phaedra said to my *How did I do?*, "Good enough, for a stuffed mannequin."

"But that's what they seemed to expect. At least, whenever I tried to ask an ordinary question, all I got was looks of alarm and mad assurances in polite-speak."

Phaedra grunted assent. "Some of that is the result of years of Duchess Sisi acting like uncrowned queen. Remember, she's been presiding until you and your grandmother arrived. You'll figure out a middle road."

After that we began to settle into a routine, as that sword swung over my head, invisible but oh so tangible, at least to me.

A few days passed, then a week. No Beka. No message.

I didn't get to see Alec except in glimpses through the day. Nights were ours, and though we still talked out our thoughts, I didn't bring up the baby Q. Neither did he; I wondered if he might be waiting on me, as most the work of popping them out was going to be done by me. I just was not ready.

Alas, there was no more sparring with him, as his schedule started very early. And I was reluctant to intrude into the sanctity of the Vigilzhi gym, which was heavy on the regimented warmups before hand-to-hand and other forms of combat. Instead, Phaedra and I joined her brother and cousins for fencing practice—before which I warmed up with ballet, something I was too self-conscious to do with a bunch of Vigilzhi guys around.

Honoré also came, and because of his still-healing leg, he was now a suitable partner for me. Not that I'm bad. I'm pretty good, largely because my reflexes are so fast. But the others have been fencing nearly every day since childhood, and are world class. Especially Phaedra's brother Danilov.

At the end of that week Tony showed up, mostly to fight with Danilov and Phaedra. It was always a lesson to watch them. He scarcely spoke to me until the session was over, and we were all drinking the tea and coffee Danilov's people brought in. Then he ranged up alongside the table where I was sitting. "I hear you saw Ruli while you were in Italy. Or was it Paris?"

I was going to ask "Heard from whom?" but I knew by now that if he didn't say, he probably wouldn't. So I confined myself to, "Wrong. She caught up with us in Vienna."

"Vienna? My mother mentioned that someone was at the flat. That was the two of you? Why?"

"We were being chased. Why and by whom, anyone's guess." I was giving him major side-eye while I spoke, but his surprise seemed real. Even disappointed, as in a missed opportunity for entertainment. "I did want to pinch your Porsche for the getaway."

Tony grinned. "If you're making a getaway in future, feel free."

I retorted, "But your permission takes away all the fun."

"And there's the cousinly zing. I'm glad to see that marriage hasn't ruined the snark."

I could have come back with, *Yes I can see how worried you were*, but I bit that back, sensing that verbal sparring was teetering on the edge of sniping. There was energy between us — still. But I'd found the borderline, and though his radar was set on permanent *yes* I will say this for him, he understood when *no* meant *no*. Besides, I had seen the look in his face when he lay on a hospital bed on the verge of death, his gaze locked on Beka. What vestige of a constant heart he had was hers. But impossible to say whether two such radically different people could find their way between the shoals of duty and expectation to a happy ending.

I just shot him an exaggerated eyeroll, he laughed, gave me a casual salute, and sauntered out.

The week after that brought the festival, and I still had not received a visit or even a message from Beka. "Salfmatta Sarolta thinks that someone has gone into the mountains to consult the elders," Tania said.

So I waited. It wasn't like there wasn't plenty to do.

I really looked forward to the festival, and it didn't disappoint. The city people gathered around makeshift picnic tables or blankets on the ground in the circle around the fountain. It had rained the day before, but the weather held off for the harvest festival. I got to enjoy watching everybody from little kids to oldsters come out in their embroidered waistcoats and pants and caps for guys, and equally decorated blouses under tight bodices, and ribbon-decorated broad skirts for the gals.

Phaedra preferred staying on duty, watchful as always, but I insisted on Tania joining the young people. It was good to see her dancing, at first only with her sisters. Though she sat with a group of twenty-year-olds of both sexes, plenty of covert and blatant flirting going on. Most of the time Tania looks rather like Wednesday Addams with a fondness for lavender and sky blue, but sitting with her old school friends, her sisters, and all their mutual friends (and flirts) brought color to her cheeks and rare but sweet smiles.

After the dancing, lamps were lit and everyone settled down to begin the feasting. But that was the signal for me to leave, because it was time to get ready for the Prime Minister's ball.

The guest list was of course the nosebleed league, so it was an excuse to break out the fancy ball dresses—and to see Alec in the Dobreni version of a tux, which is a long, tailored frock coat over a white shirt with high Mandarin collar, and a silk waistcoat of muted silver. I liked that silver so much that I'd had a dress made to match, and I now had an expert hairdresser on tap who did my mane up in loops and swirls, secured by a tiara. For the first time, I understood tiaras in practical terms— they are sparkly and pretty, but solid enough to anchor one's hair enough for fast waltzing.

We took a few seconds to admire each other, then I grabbed my satin gloves and the two of us joined Milo and Gran in the kingmobile for the short ride to the opera house.

The Ridotskis' mansion is relatively modest. Like, most of the ground floor is not the waste space of a vast ballroom. Many of the nobles, if entertaining on this scale, rent the opera house, and this time was no different. Mrs. Prime Minister had it beautifully decorated in autumnal colors. Beka was there at the main door with her family to welcome us.

Before we passed on, I caught Beka's gaze on me, and she mouthed the word, "Later."

I nodded, a bit surprised at this surreptitiousness at a ball, and moved into the ballroom on Alec's arm.

Once the king arrived, of course, the ball was officially begun, whether every invitee was there or not. All knew that Milo didn't dance (I wondered if he ever had), so Alec held out his arm to the Prime Minister's wife. The Prime Minister went to Gran, who declined graciously, then he came to me as next woman of rank, as Gran accompanied Milo to the throne-like chairs that everyone else steered clear of.

The Prime Minister, a pleasant man with an equable temper that hid a very shrewd mind, was an excellent though unflashy dancer. His chief hobby was orchids, I remembered, and I dutifully asked about these as other dancers surrounded us.

He laughed, then said, "As I have been warned that to speak more than ten words about my beloved Phalaenopsis will earn me a night in the lumber room, I will confine myself to thanking you for asking. And how did you find Venice?"

We chatted amicably until the dance ended, then we switched partners, and I got to dance once with Alec before the rest of the Council turned up for duty dances.

Even though there was no tango—the senior Ridotskis were far too staid for that—I never get tired of dancing; once the duties are over, the partners my age turned up, which was more fun.

Tony actually appeared, a surprise; I caught myself sweeping the exits to see if Niklos and a gang of mountain riders was ready to burst in and round us all up in some mad plot. I bet I wasn't the only one. But he only went over to Beka, hand out expectantly. Beka Ridotski's hobby was ballroom dancing. She's always good, but when she's with Tony, their chemistry crackles.

Since I was safely with Alec, I whispered in English, which most there didn't speak, "Is there ever going to be a happy ending there?"

"Do you think marriage for those two would be a happy ending?" Alec retorted in a low murmur.

I thought of Tony's roving eye, and Beka's dedication, which included religion. I could not see her living among the von Mecklundburgs, much less raising a kid in their style. "I hope they find one, however they define it," I muttered, holding Alec tighter.

When her "later" finally happened, it was adroitly done; Percy asked for a dance. He was not tipsy, though on the dance floor you'd never know it, as he had trouble with left and right at such times. But I was prepared for that, dancing with my toes turned out as he counted under his breath, and we got through it with no mishaps.

Then he said, "Phew! I need a drink. How about it?"

"Sure," I responded, and we strolled toward the alcove with the refreshments.

Where Beka lay in wait.

Screened by potted red twig dogwoods, behind knots of guests chatting over their cups and little plates of dainties, she motioned me to a small round table in a corner. Percy wandered away to fetch us comestibles, and I said, "I know that those who deal with Vrajhus prefer to keep things on the down-low, but aren't we being extra secretive right now?"

"I'll explain everything. Soon. But it's important for you to...live publicly, as much as you can, within a perimeter of safety. I'm trying not to draw attention because I don't know who might be serving as a window to other eyes."

What did that even mean? "This is about the fake seraphs?"

"Yes. Do I remember rightly that Ruli knew something of them?"

"She warned me about them when I encountered her in the

Nasdrafus—I know I told you all about that. Also, Ruli told us when she turned up in Vienna, that the seraphs told her to bring me to them in the Nasdrafus. That's why she went to Paris, actually."

"*Really*," Beka breathed. "I don't think you did tell me that."

"Didn't I? I thought I had. I guess I went on all about my end of things, and not so much Ruli's."

"Is it possible you could use your prism to contact her, and find out exactly what they said? Not now, of course, but when you've the time?"

Chill gripped my nerves. "I can try," I promised.

Percy reappeared with a tray of drinks and tiny cakes. I tried to get some of it down, though my stomach had a serious case of butterflies, and then Percy escorted me back to the ballroom, where I magnetted to Alec's side and stayed there until we left.

TWENTY-TWO

RULI

The night we returned from leaving Kim and Alec in Dobrenica, Lotte resumed training Lya, which enabled me to avoid the girl with minimal effort. The rest of the time, she was either rewatching her brother's television show over and over, or else exchanging text messages on the cell phone Blayze had given her.

For a few days, I thought she would return to Los Angeles altogether, now that she had repaired whatever rift she'd created with the boy, but unexpectedly, she said one day after we'd been bombarded with the inane dialogue in that stupid show nonstop, "There's no getting round it. I'm a vamp. He says it's okay, but what about next year? What about when he gets older than me? That would be weird. What if he gets *married?* That would be even weirder. Especially if I hated her."

Which was—for Lya—unexpectedly insightful.

Other than avoiding her TV show as much as I could— Marie-Benoîte and I visited the theatre quite a bit—I found that life (oh, that word) with the sisters was interesting and purposeful. There was the patrolling, during which I learned quite a bit by merely observing Noemi. Whatever her background was, it must have included martial skills. I began not just to realize but to internalize the fact that my brother had not inherited all the strength, speed, and coordination. But my awareness of my own possibilities had somehow been thoroughly eradicated when I was very young. I was to have poise, not brawn.

I made up for it now. It gave me pleasure to be faster than most of the others, even Noemi, if I exerted myself. Strong, as well. My need to feed increased correspondingly, but the hunting took largely took care of that, and when it didn't, I was contributing a princely sum each month for the plasma.

I tried to find the old enchantment that had made me long to live in Paris in the first place. But as autumn's warmth and color slowly waned with the month of September, I began to realize that so much of that allure had been inextricably bound up with friends and romance. There would be no more walks through the parks on sunshiny days, or lingering over delectable meals.

I had to find different pursuits.

Television was there, of course — I brought mine over from the Paris flat. Then I returned to sort through the boxes of old favorites stored in my closet. Many I brought over, then I came to *Buffy the Vampire Slayer*.

This show had amused me greatly once. When young, I'd been terrified of the shadowy inimasang whom my brother had met each winter solstice, in order to offer his blood to extend the old pact. Buffy's vampires had been so easy to kill, the hell-mouths absurd. Their inner lives so...paper thin. And I'd longed for a life like hers, surrounded by friends, and living an easy freedom while having the strength to thrive when life wasn't easy.

Now I had the freedom, but I'd become the enemy. In a way, I was now Buffy the Vampire.

Convulsively I nearly tossed out the entire collection, but decided to offer my CDs to Lya — who promptly annexed them. "I *love* this show!" She found it even funnier now. That kept her busy (and quiet) in the house, when the weather turned too foul even for purse snatchers.

I began attending the theatre again, with others and without. I also discovered the soothing effect of recorded books, when read well by voice actors. This spared me the effort of reading, and I could lie in the reverie that was not quite sleep, absorbing literature that once I'd been oblivious to, as outside, the killing sun pursued its relentless course across the sky.

My most frequent theatre companion, as I said, was Marie-Benoîte, who preferred the wit and style of her own time. The latest playwrights who interested her were the Romantics; after a restaging of *Chantecler*, she declared, "These moderns, phfft!

No ten of them are worth Edmond Rostand. Or Georges Feydeau. So many think vulgarity replaces wit. But what do you expect, when the imbéciles were so busy killing off all the finest minds in not one, but two vast wars, over the last hundred years, eh? Do we see *Phèdre* or Beaumarchais's *Figaro* often here? Much too rarely."

We both enjoyed dressing up. For the theatre, she brought out elegant Vionnet silk, new when she got it, whereas I'd paid ten times that much for vintage Chanel, which I wore with my strappy red Manolo Blahniks. When I walked in those, no one was searching my face for vampiric pallor or giveaway eye glow — they were looking at my tout ensemble; that school in Switzerland might not have imparted much knowledge, but I knew how to walk well in good shoes.

After the play ended, we crossed the street to a little café that made excellent hot chocolate, which she loved. I had liked it as a child, and ordered some, discovering that chocolate in this form is easy to metabolize. It was even mildly stimulating.

"Have you seen either play done in the Nasdrafus?" I asked one evening.

"Naturally! You can find all the greats staged there. And Molière wrote many new plays, but I find that these are much alike."

"What about Rostand? Is he in the Nasdrafus?" I asked as she sipped her chocolate, and sighed.

"No. And I looked, ah me! If there is a heaven, he was snatched up to write for the angels, of course."

Around the twentieth, someone among the salonistes who met up at Wilde's tomb decided to get up a party to travel to the Loire Valley for the Journées du Patrimoine. "It's always interesting, including attracting the criminal element that preys on tourists. We prey on them," Noeme said with satisfaction.

I declined to go; I have always loathed crowds. Though I enjoy historical sites in small doses, I've relied on personal tours in the past. I guess that is a preference my mother taught me.

Lya bounced around, bragging about her portal skills. I accompanied our part of the general party, reflecting on how quiet the house would be with Lya gone.

My going was meant as a gesture of politesse, but when we arrived in the cemetery, and found Olympe de Gouges among those gathered, once the party departed, I used the opportunity to approach Olympe. She was still vigorous, the skin bumpy around her neck where the skin had been sewn into place, stark evidence that we could heal after a fashion.

"I am not as new as Lya, but I'm new enough not to really understand portals as well as I ought," I said.

She stumped along beside me at a vigorous walk. "Talk, my friend! You talk, I teach." Her thick southern accent had to be an artifact of the south of France two centuries previous.

I explained what had happened, then she let out an exclamation. "What? Your humans, they ought to be dead! The child could not know—we seldom have to do with the living. Unless they had very powerful protections?"

"I don't think so." I thought back to finding Kim in the Nasdrafus, but she had been in spirit form. As had her companions. Hadn't there been something...? No, I could not remember.

Olympe shook her head. "To take the living body to the world of the dead, sapristi! It is not done, without very powerful protection."

I then explained about the seraphs, she agreed that they could have been waiting—might be even now—and that I was wise to avoid the Nasdrafus altogether. "If the child led, then they would likely not have seen you. Especially if you were in and out at speed. But avoid such, if you can! They will consume you in the blink of an eye." She clapped her hands.

"What is the truth of portals being volatile in churches? I don't understand such matters. My father was devout, but my mother taught us that religion is a tool to control the credulous."

"Is anything ever so simple?" Olympe asked with a wry look. "Tchah! Churches—temples of all sorts—many are built upon the very ancient sacred places, where indwelling spirits see into the hearts of those who would gain entry, and will not let evil pass into the world. I venture to say that if you are not bent on destruction, you will likely pass unremarked; I have come to see that many of those they used to call saints are far more merciful than those who worship them."

I thanked her, and we soon parted.

A succession of rainstorms moved in, giving us a taste of winter, I thought longingly of my plan to try to slip into the Nasdrafus to stay until winter ended, but that plan must be given up. As well. Perrine and the others expected me to help them roam Paris while the excursion took place. "The shop girls who can't afford vacations won't get a break," Perrine had said unanswerably.

At least I was left with Marie-Benoîte and Maëlle, both of whom had come from the Loire Valley during the centuries considered rustic and romantic now. As the former said, dryly, "To us, those site are too much like the homes we left, only turned into spectacles to be stared at."

Being left with these two (along with the elders, Agnès and Clèmence) was no misfortune. Maëlle was actually willing to put down her brush and join us patrolling. She was quite silent, distracted easily by a reflection of light on water, or a bit of graffiti done in the Ukiyo-e style, but when we discovered the beginnings of a gang circling a victim—in this instance a teenage boy—she turned out to be fast and utterly merciless. All in silence.

Later, while walking back from seeing an indifferent restaging of a play by Artaud, I said to Marie-Benoîte, "What is Maëlle's story? Or ought I not ask?"

"Don't ask her. She doesn't mind our telling the curious, as long as she doesn't need to hear it. She was born, ah, Noeme says the term in these days is intersex. Her family was very poor, already too large, and she was sold to a brothel at a young age. You can imagine the life. She was always sketching with the coal dust or wood ash, for which she was invariably punished. As soon as she had the strength, she ran, and ended up lured by an aristocrat who had…arcane tastes." A shrug. "That life ended when the aristo decided to expand his repertoire by seducing a vampire. He discovered, too late, what that meant, but did not survive to profit from the lesson. Maëlle was nearly ended, too, except this particular predator had a passion for fine arts, and saw in the cell where Maëlle had been locked up the drawings on the walls that displayed such potential. Maëlle's health was poor by then, so the vampire turned her, and sent her to Italy to study art."

"For amusement? Or was there a cost?"

"Purely for the sake of art, or so she was told. If there was a cost waiting, it was never paid, because Maëlle never saw her benefactor again. She ended up on a ship, due to some misadventures, took over the ship when she discovered that this supposed trader was a pirate, and left them in the Mediterranean. She discovered Persian art, and so began her wanderings east." Another shrug. "In a sense she has never left the art of the East. I believe she spent some years simply sorting stones at riversides in order to learn what shades would grind down to the best glaze for celadon."

We were crossing the courtyard then, and Marie-Benoîte lowered her voice. "When she discovered the Nasdrafus, she said she found pockets of pure art there, like wellsprings — those so passionate about their art that a single lifetime was not nearly enough. But art in the Nasdrafus is like a rainbow, gone unless someone who sees it comes to this side to paint it."

"She must think as do those who feel that art heals the ills of civilization."

"More correct, mirrors it," she murmured. "But yes, she seems to believe that art betters the world. But she is no mystic. Her early life was too hard for that. When she is presented with certain types of cruelty, out come the fangs."

So saying, Marie-Benoîte opened the front door. Maëlle was in the hallway, and demonstrated the sharpness of her hearing by saying in a voice devoid of passion, "It is not inapt as a philosophy. If one must have one." This without pausing the delicate strokes adding feathers to a headdress of a figure on horseback.

We sat in our salon as rain drummed on the roof, and though strictly speaking we don't need the warmth of a fire in the old fireplace, it provided an atavistic pleasure for all three of us, used as we were to the old ways of heating spaces.

Indeed, the smell of a fire unexpectedly brought Dobrenica to mind. I tried to dismiss such idle interruptions. I was doing exactly what I wanted to be doing. And yet the questions would come, centering around that memory of my elegant, eternally teenaged grandmother Rose smilingly introducing me to the seraphs.

To smother that subject, I said to Maëlle, "It seems that the many arts of Asia have drawn you. And yet you are here? In France — "

As I said the word "France" a flicker in the leaded glass globe on the lamp caught my eye. When I turned that way, I saw Kim's face in a reflective bit of the glass. I hadn't thought to glance in the mirror since our return to Paris. How long had she been trying to reach me?

"Excuse me," I said, and went to the hallway to gaze into the mirror. I was going to have to put a mirror in my room if Kim made a habit of this.

"Kim?" I laid my hand to the surface.

"Ruli, what exactly did the seraphs say to you about me?"

That was…unexpected. Yet it ought not to have been. Still, I tried to deflect her. "Why? Forget about them. You can avoid them if you don't go into the Nasdrafus."

"I can't forget about them," she said flatly. "I'm sorry to hassle you. Especially as you helped us out. I know you don't have to. Don't want to, and who can blame you? But I need to learn as much as I can if I'm to stay out of their reach."

And there again in memory, Rose lisped, *An alliance of interests. Our House.*

I gave up. "I'll come to you," I said, and lifted my hand away from the mirror, cursing as I returned to the salon. I'd go to Dobrenica, but first I was going to confront Rose.

Maëlle looked at me mildly. "I was about to say that France is my homeland. My blood spilled in its soil. Though right now my fascination lies with the arts expressed by other civilizations, I still come back here. My art must be French, for I will always see the world through the eyes of my ancestors."

In other words, *Go home if it is calling you.* I eyed her. "How much did you hear?"

A good question, as Kim's voice—I'd thought—was not aural, but internal.

"Never mind," I said. Or sighed, taking her point.

Once again I simply walked out, and left to hunt up a night train, since I could not trust any but local portals, which connect without resorting to the Nasdrafus. A transfer to Dobrenica from Paris required the Nasdrafus in between.

I changed trains going east until I found the one that goes to Dobrenica, which travels through the night, arriving at Riev in the early morning. All along its journey I wondered what might happen to me if the Blessing warded my kind. I had not asked Olympe, as she would know nothing of Xanpia or the Esplumoir. Would I dissolve into mist? Pop, like the goblins of the Nasdrafus?

What then?

As we slowly chugged into the mountains—some already dusted with snow at the crowns—I waited, but nothing happened; dangerously close to dawn I saw the outline of Mt. Dhiavilyi etched against the sky, and used shadows to leave the compartment. The train chugged so slowly that I merely had to leap into the air to shed most of its velocity, and land on the frosty ground.

I sensed other inimasang almost immediately, and I knew I was watched, probably by Elena's guard, as I sped upward

toward the Eyrie. But no one interfered—or offered me
shelter—and I barely made it. The tingling burn of impending
dawn had begun when I flung myself into one of the secret
passages, where I sat in the comforting darkness until I was able
to calm myself enough to rest until sunset.

When it was safe to emerge again, I commenced my search
for Rose, which I had assumed would be easy. I slipped from
portal to portal, but she was nowhere to be found, either on the
mountain, or anywhere in Riev. She had to be hiding in the
Nasdrafus.

I gave up, and since the evening was still early, chose a
portal that opened below Riev.

TWENTY-THREE

KIM

It took three days of intermittent tries with my prism, at night, until at last I snagged Ruli. Finally! I had my list of questions ready—just to find myself cut off, *I'll come to you.*

That sounded a little sinister, but that impression might largely have owed itself to the total gloom that reduced her to little more than a silhouette, except for two tiny red glows where the eye sockets ought to be.

I remembered that Ruli and Beka hadn't been the best of pals while growing up, before poor Ruli ended up vamped. But Beka had said she really wanted to speak to her, so much that I was to call her if she turned up.

Though I'd grown up with phones, in Dobrenica they were rare, and even in the huge palace I'd only seen two or three at most, all landlines, of course. Everyone sent messengers, who were usually kid apprentices serving their time before promotion.

Even though I was expecting her, it was shocking when Ruli just turned up in Alec's and my wing—once hers. She didn't rush or yell, but there was an impending-thunderstorm crackle around her that I felt more than saw. I jumped a foot or two, my hands inadvertently letting loose the sheaf of much-labored-over papers I'd been reading.

Alec handled her sudden appearance only slightly better than I did, and far less spectacularly. He glanced up sharply from his desk, where he was reading a lengthy snore about wind farms, only one hand suddenly held a stake that I hadn't even known he had stashed there.

I didn't blame Ruli for the unannounced arrival, once my blood pressure climbed down from the stratosphere: it wasn't as if she could go to the front door of the palace and wait for a page to announce her. I got up to retrieve the papers that I'd flung up into the air when I jumped.

Ruli, advancing into the room, said, "Sorry. I saw your light so I just walked in."

"Did you come by portal?" I asked. "The Eyrie? No, that's a long way away. Xanpia's fountain?"

"Train, then the Eyrie to a portal near the Old Market. There's one closer, below the ridge up here, actually, but that area is usually busy this early." As she spoke, she stooped to pick up a couple of errant sheets that had managed to nearly sail out the door. Then narrowed her eyes at the handwritten scrawl, somewhat smeared. "What's this?"

"Tania's sister Theresa writes stories," I said. "At home they'd be called superhero tales, with a dash of romance, though nobody wears a spandex suit or a cape. It's about the mountain heroes."

"Fyadar and Xanpia? Maman loathed those stories. Forbade us to sully our minds with such peasant trash. So of course we collected them when we were small. Percy used to draw comic books in secret, once he discovered the form. He shared them with us and his village friends on the mountain," Ruli said as she handed me the sheets.

I strongly suspected that this reminiscence was an indirect way to give us a few moments to recover from our panic, and I was grateful. As well as embarrassed. "Thank you for coming," I said, with maybe a little too much enthusiasm.

Alec smiled briefly, looked from me to her, then reached for the old-fashioned phone on his desk — practically futuristic in Dobrenica. "I'll call Beka."

While we were waiting for her, I sent an order for tea, coffee, and the little date-and-nut cakes common in this country for late night snacks, to signal a purely social evening to the staff. Tania, expecting Beka's appearance as much as we were, appeared, eager and curious.

Beka arrived shortly after Tania slipped in. She sat down, I served her some coffee, then gave her the gimlet eye. "*Now* you'll tell me what you meant by my needing to live publicly, and the rest of it?"

"Yes," Beka said, but turned to Ruli, her face calm. It was her teacher mode, and I remembered that among the four of us there were a surprising number of tangles: Beka and Alec had once dated, Ruli and Alec had married—reluctantly on both sides—and then there was me, the bull in the china shop crashing suddenly through their lives. (I refused to think of myself as a cow.)

But I wasn't about to make things weird by pointing out any of these thoughts, as Beka said very neutrally, "Ruli, Kim told us that you were approached by the demons with the purpose of drawing her to the Nasdrafus?"

"My grandmother Rose was the instigator," Ruli said. "I tried to corner her earlier, but she's gone. Probably hiding out in the Nasdrafus, and while I know I could find her, the demons would find me faster. They made it sound like a request. An offer of alliance. I don't know why they bothered, because it was clearly an order."

She paused, her pale, smooth skin taut, her pupils enormous, but they weren't glowing, at least—thanks to the brightly-lit room. "I probably ought to have asked why, but in retrospect it's just as well, as surely they would have told me what they wanted me to think. If not outright lied."

Beka rubbed her fingertips slowly together, and I wondered if this was her way of trying to shed tension. "There is a great deal we do not understand about how free will functions between the worlds seen and unseen, but I can say that free will is integral to our relations with those we regard as protectors."

"Like Xanpia?" I asked.

"Precisely. I told you before that I wished you'd asked her more about the necklace, and the nature of the Esplumoir—so many other things—but you very naturally wished to return home as quickly as possible, and she let you go."

I nodded. "I wouldn't have even known what to ask. Huh! As for free will, I gotta say, nobody asked me if I wanted to be yanked into the past right before my wedding."

"Would you have refused, had you known everything beforehand?"

"What?" I bleated weakly, then scowled at my unoffending tea as I struggled to get my brain to shift gears. "You definitely think now that the necklace was intended for the Esplumoir all along? So it's all tied together?"

"Yes. The necklace might even have served as a protection for the Esplumoir in the Himalayas for a time; the Eldest believe that such artifacts are used as reinforcement, or stopgaps when Esplumoir gates are breached by those who wish to force their way between worlds."

"But why me? Why not someone two hundred years ago?"

"Who would be an easier target. They wanted someone from the future, as a protection for them as well as for the Esplumoir. You are one of the few who seem able to slip into the past and back without being lost forever, though that will always be a danger. The Eldest of the Salfpatras pointed out that it has to have been a shared effort between many of the world's protectors, outside of time, to locate the right person and to protect that person as much as possible, while warding the demons."

"Whose MO is to cruise in and slurp up human life?" I asked.

"All forms of life," Beka said. "Humans are more efficient at killing one another, which draws them; though it pleases them to present an appearance of sanctity and beauty, they appear to mirror us at our worst. The other supposition is that the necklace had been hidden by other Esplumoir protectors, until Nanny Hiasinte received a message in her vision."

"From someone who sits outside of time?" Alec asked, a little dubiously.

"Perhaps. A lot of what I'm offering you right now is still conjecture."

"Go ahead," I urged, waving my hands. "It's such a relief to get *some* answers, even iffy ones, instead of the constant round of questions yammering in my head."

"Very well. To resume. The necklace had been hidden. It needed to stay hidden until it reached the Esplumoir to be set in place, where Nanny Hiasinte might have expected there to be someone to receive it. Only she likely did not know who, or even how, or she would have instructed you. All she knew for certain was that it must remain unseen. Even so, our Elders believe that the demons sensed it was coming before Elders of the past did."

"And Aurélie and I tipped off the demons by her wearing it in public?" I guessed.

Beka gave a nod. "We surmise that the demons sensed its movement, but were not certain who carried it, until it was revealed inadvertently by Queen Aurelia."

"So we blew it out of sheer ignorance. Except those fae near the Kittredge estate at Undertree sure knew what it was even though it was hidden, and tried to sucker us both."

Beka turned the coffee cup around in a slow circle. "The fae would be quick to sniff out precious stones that powerful, but from all I hear about them, their vagaries, and games, are local. They'd want to have it for themselves, not use it to loose floods of demons to gorge on the world's life, leaving destruction in their shadow. Though it's possible they might have traded it for something they considered of equivalent worth."

"Whoa." I sat back.

Alec said, "Sending it across war-torn Europe by a kid and a ghost to unknown recipients seems to me a lethally inefficient system, considering its importance."

"You must remember that this was occurring at a time when communication was far more difficult, not just over vast distances and different cultures and languages, but it required willingness to strive together to, ah maintain the world's balance. Which includes the sanctity of that veil between the seen and the unseen realms."

"Okay," I said. "And they were no doubt limited by whom they could trust to send. But! I find it difficult to believe that I was the only candidate for the guide part. There must have been princesses raised to do princessy stuff on the Vrajhus front all over. Including up and down the timeline, seeing as how I was yanked back two centuries."

Beka raised her palm. "I think you have it backwards, though again, it's a reasonable assumption. It wasn't princesses so much as specific talents they required. You could have easily — one might even have said preferably — been an embroiderer or goose girl. Human political arrangements are irrelevant, I suspect, to the non-human protectors. But you come from the Dsaret line, once known to be mystical. I guess it's inevitable that those with talent and skills beyond the everyday eventually end up in places of responsibility."

"So I was nabbed in spite of becoming a princess? But where does the Blessing come in? You know, marriage of the leaders, Five Families in harmony. All that."

Alec said slowly, "If Beka is right, it would be related. The importance appears to less in titles than in influence and intent. Working together. Symbols of harmony. That's the human part of the 'Blessing' bargain, am I right?"

Beka said, "I think that's as accurate as anything I've ever heard. Slippery slope here. We still don't have the vocabulary for a lot of the mysteries. But a royal marriage is a symbol if the people see it so. The more harmonious the shared intent, the stronger the protection, I think is the simplest way to put it. So individuals can choose to plot and scheme, lie and commit actions out of anger or a wish to destroy, but if most are united, then the protector..."

"Reciprocates?" Alec said.

"That's a way to put it." Beka turned from him to me. "Now to what we do know. Protections like that necklace also have to be made, and shared, by free will. You had not the time to be taught by the Elders two centuries ago, but you employed what you and Tony had learned from repairing the rift when Maritza's vampires were entering the country last winter. You chose to place the protection—you sang Xanpia's Wreath, did you not?"

"It was all of them," I said. "Singing together as Aurélie passed off the necklace to me. So you could say that there was definitely shared intent, freely chosen."

"And it worked. Though you did not specifically place the necklace, it found its place, I guess you could say. But it seems that the completion is yet. To come? That's the part impossible to know. Only to guess at."

"And so the demons want to grab it before the job is done, right? Meanwhile, it's out of sight. Is this kind of like the way Jaska's, Aurélie's, Mord's, and Elisheva's bodies went unseen until they got out of the Nasdrafus?"

Beka had been frowning as if groping for words, then her face cleared. "That's a good way to put it." Her frown returned. "The demons have waited for two centuries for you to return, as you were the last to have it. And when you did return, a few weeks before your wedding, they had to scramble to try to get to you so that you could be cajoled, or fooled, or enchanted into willingly giving the necklace to them."

"It'll backfire on them in some way if they jump me and grab it?"

"Essentially. But they can't get into the country anymore. You closed Maritza's rift last winter, so they couldn't use that to pry at the Esplumoir from this direction through their followers. They are limited to using their influence from the world of dreams."

"And that isn't creepy at all," I exclaimed, making a sour face. "I'd rather have a fight. If I can grab a sword."

"It's going to get worse," Beka retorted. "If they can't reach you, and it sounds like they tried, they will use those around you. Back to conjecture. We believe they found you again when Alec took his ring off — that is, they found you through your proximity to him. They first tried to lure you by dangling a ghost in front of you. Then they found easily influenced minds…"

"The goon squad who tried to corner us," I exclaimed. "But Alec never took his signet off again. And they still caught up with us outside Vienna."

Alec spoke up. "I'm guessing that my original supposition was right. By then they had expanded their numbers enough to have two or three cars on both sides of the Autobahn driving back and forth looking for the Daimler. It was an easy guess that we'd go the way we did. We ought to have stayed completely off the Autobahn, all the way to Vienna."

"Except they might have had someone watching in Graz, or other key points," I said. "What I want to know is, how did they catch up with us *in LA?* I had my prism on me, and Alec never took his signet off again." I looked doubtfully at Ruli. Was it *possible* —

"No," Ruli stated, the red glow flaring in her pupils. "I did nothing. And Lya's too stupid to see anything outside of herself and her issues."

"Not stupid," I muttered, my face burning. "Sorry, Ruli. You were great. Both of you. She's just young, and super messed up."

"They know your…aura by now," Beka said to me apologetically. "It probably took a little time to locate you. Your prism does help diffuse their focus, all the Elders insist."

"So, not precision nosing, like satellite images. But general direction nosing, effective enough, considering that they found us less than twenty-four hours after we hopped away from Vienna. All the way on the other side of North America," I muttered.

Oh, *great.*

Alec said quietly, "And the mine invasion several weeks ago?"

"I'm almost sure that was the demons, trying to drive a wedge between the various factions, in this case, Tony and you. Testing the waters, I guess you could say. Learning from failure."

That chill sensation worsened. "So what you're saying is, they're going to be trying to sneak more goons over the border to go after me?"

"What I'm trying to say…" Beka began.

Alec slid his hand over the top of mine. "They're already here."

"I was trying to find a less painful way to say so, but yes." Beka jerked her chin down. "It could be anyone. Anyone with a secret desire, a kernel of resentment or rage, a half-smothered ambition, that they can distort into motivation."

"But if they off me, then the seraphs don't get anything, right?"

"If your soul goes to the Nasdrafus, you will probably end up their prisoner for eternity. But it might not. Some of the Salfmattas believe they won't attempt to kill you unless as a last resort. They want you in the Nasdrafus where they can use whatever means to convince you to relinquish it to them."

"But they can't force me to hand it over, right? I mean, I don't even know how to get it back." But as I spoke, I strongly suspected that I did know how — all I had to do was go back up to that shrine between Dsaretsenberg and Dhiavilyi mountains, and let my time sense go loose until I reached into the air where I'd stood.

Beka then said, "Coercion will very likely act against their interests, depending upon what protections were laid on the necklace long ago."

"Free will," I repeated, rubbing my forehead. "You know, if Xanpia — or someone — had just taken the time to explain all of this to me before bunging me into the past, including the fact that I would only be gone a matter of a month max, I would've said, sure! Let's get it done."

"Then that decision would have been made for you," Beka said. "But discussion of the complexities of will are necessarily limited by our being human."

I shifted impatiently. I'd always loathed philosophical conundrums when no one can prove anything, really. "What I'm hearing is that slamming me back to the past and then leaving me to figure out the way forward was test as much as choice?"

"Excluding other circumstances, yes," Beka said. "The best plan, it seems, would be to find the most qualified person and hand the necklace off to do what's necessary. Then you will be able to return to your normal life."

There was no use in moaning and complaining. But that had never stopped me! "Until I do hand it off, it seems to me that what I've got to do is give everyone I don't know well the hairy eyeball, never go off with anyone alone without toting an arsenal, and…live like a spy in a Le Carré novel? I don't even like those novels! It's all tension all the time, no humor, and nobody wins!"

"You know whom you can trust," Beka said.

It was then that I added up the shifted glances and tight angles. "Who's the invisible elephant who just clomped into the room? *Tony.* Of course! You think it'll be Tony."

Alec said nothing, his air pensive. Listening. Tania looked scared, but she was tracking everything. Ruli sat motionless, poised and sophisticated in a way I never could be.

Beka let a long sigh trickle out. "I've been thinking about almost nothing else this past couple of days. And I really believe that in the main, you can trust Tony. He loathes arcane powers. Wants nothing to do with them. And he's smart enough to sense when someone is messing with him. I think that would include in his dreams."

"Then…" I asked, looking from her to Alec.

Ruli spoke up for the second time, her breath hissing in so she could speak, her tone just a bit dry, almost metallic. "They mean *us*, Kim."

TWENTY-FOUR

RULI

The swooping mood swings and bumps of accelerated pulses as Beka, Kim, and Alec spoke could have been a maddening temptation, except I was still exhilarated from my first vampiric kill.

It was entirely inadvertent. I'd used a portal that let me out at the bottom of Riev's hill, not far from the old marketplace, as the evening was still early and the streets still lively. To my left stretched the slope of the communal meadow that on Fridays turned into the parking place for the mountain wagons that brought goods to Friday-market. The poorer families used this meadow to feed their sheep and cows.

I heard footsteps, and smelled the mingled blood of youth and animal overlaid by the hot, metallic scent of inimasang on the hunt. No, this was a vampire in the old sense, long lost to whatever humanity it had once had.

With a flash of acidic heat the feral vampire veered from stalking them to attack me. One split second I looked into a ravening face of utter malice, framed by long hanks of wild hair, then the instincts I had been honing in Paris took over and I fought.

My reflexes are quick, and perhaps this feral had become lazy, after so much easy prey; we both shifted to speed, but I was faster, the edge of my practical flat going for the side of its knee. Spike heels would be even better, I thought as it stumbled. I caught hold of a handful of dirty hair and beard, stiffened by the blood of its victims and probably never washed, for dirt had caked thickly over the mats. I snapped its head to one side and buried my fangs in its leathery, filthy neck—

And lightning exploded through my vitals.

When shock flung me back into myself, I stood looking down at the corpse, power thrumming through me. The sound of two heartbeats drew my attention: the slow drub of the cow's, syncopated by the clean swish-whoosh of the boy's, now shuffling beyond a warehouse. I don't think he even saw the shadow-smothered fight, but some animal instinct warned him to get himself and his cow home.

Shock receded, as awareness caught up: I'd killed that feral, taking its life force in a single jolt, as if receiving a thousand kilowatts of electricity. It had been stalking the two innocents— it would have killed both, as the boy was too skinny to be much more than a snack. But I had not been defending boy or cow. Instinct had taken over, winning—and the reward was a single dose of all the power that vampire had hoarded.

So this was why vampire hunted other vampires.

I was still fighting the surreally powerful effects as I sat with healthy, life-brimming Kim, Beka, Tania Waleska, and Alec, their implied trust oddly ... sweet. With the addition of speed as well as surprise, I knew I could take them all. Such strength was slyly addictive because the temptation was there to use it. But I had to be my own leash.

All four heartbeats spiked when I said *us*. I think Kim and Alec had actually managed to forget me for a short time, though I wasn't so sure about the other two, as they listened to Beka's explanations; I wondered briefly what Honoré would make of Tania's aura, should they ever meet. Give that girl ten years, and she was going to make a formidable watcher between the worlds.

But that was the future.

"Inimasang," I said. "There are factions. Maritza's gang is not all gone." I was certain the mad vampire had been one of hers, lurking in the lower city to prey on lone individuals. "Elena is another matter."

"Who is Elena?" Beka asked, her gaze as serious as it had been in childhood. I'd mistaken that look for superiority, when it was more likely earnestness. The same earnestness one saw in Alec; they were a lot alike in many respects, and I remembered that they had once dated, however briefly. Had they seen the drive to duty mirrored in the other? They would make a terrible couple. Friendship was much better for that much single-minded determination.

Irrelevant.

How to explain the ancient vampires? I couldn't explain them. I could feel the proximity of the compulsion's brain fog. Elena, who had turned me during Jerzy's disastrous attempt at human sacrifice by the order of Antonius Augustus, the oldest of us all, had placed the compulsion on me.

But I could speak around it; I still did not know why I had been saved, though I suspected that the mysterious ancient had been warding Maritza from burrowing her way into the palace one bloodsucker at a time. In other words, Maritza was lurking below the spot where the car was driven off the road in order to get at both Alec and me, but Alec landed out of reach, and Elena got to me first. "Call Elena and her band the inimasang version of the Vigilzhi."

Nobody seemed comforted by this image. Nor should they have been.

Beka said, looking disturbed, "That implies a…hierarchy?"

Alec said with a hint of impatience, "Who else would Tony be making that damned pact with every winter? What's our strategy for protecting Kim, and thus, the country?" He turned to me as he got up and crossed the room. "Ruli, I'd really like to know why your grandmother thought it a good idea to hook up with these tools. Are the local inimasang working with the demons?"

"I plan to find out," I said. "Since she thought it a good idea to elbow me into the middle of it."

Alec reached into a wardrobe while I spoke, then brought out something long and narrow that had been wrapped in cloth. "Kim. This is as good a time as any to give you your belated wedding present from me."

"Present?" Kim said, looking hopeful. She took the thing, whipped away the cloth, then ran her fingers hungrily along the polished cherrywood of a very elegant cane.

Only… "Isn't that weighted more for a man?" I asked.

"Don't tell me. You really did it?" Kim's fingers gripped the handle, then worked over it, caressing the smooth carving and pressing. "Ah!"

A snick, and a spring released…the top few inches of a steel rapier. "This…is *awesome*," she breathed, ripping the sheath and blade apart. "My very own sword stick!"

"My suggestion is, you take a very public fall, and go about sporting an ankle brace for the foreseeable. The cane then goes everywhere with you," he said.

"That would work. Honoré goes everywhere with his cane, and no one even notices it anymore." A deep breath. "Don't tell me! Is his—"

"He gave me the name of his bladesmith." Alec was smiling broadly.

"Best. Wedding Present. *Ever*," Kim breathed, kissed him soundly, then hugging him as he winced slightly. She let go instantly, whispering, "Sorry! I forgot," and leaped to the other end of the room to whirl and stab experimentally. Alec's jolt of pain made me wonder anew how much our portal dash from Los Angeles had hurt him.

I knew better than to ask, unless it was relevant, and turned my attention to Kim. Her easy grace, the whistle of the steel, the flash of her blond hair flying, was not at all Dsaret, but thoroughly von Mecklundburg. Alec stood very still, his blue gaze riveted and his heart racing—which suggested a lot about relationship-dynamics. Not merely between him and Kim. Or for that matter, him and Tony, but reaching back for generations, between all the Five Families. Like our mountain border, it was a circle of interlocked energies.

Kim continued to figure away, then crowed, "I'll have to start working out with it so I get used to its feel…Boom! Pow!" A couple of innocent cushions spouted a few feathers. "Ooops. I'll have to sew up those holes myself. I don't want to shock the housekeeping staff, as well as make more work for them."

"Leave it," Alec said. "Repairing a small hole comes under the heading of housekeeping, and you'll discover that skewered bolsters is nothing new to them. But we'll get a lunging target up here tomorrow."

"I can hardly wait. Beka, thank you for coming over and giving us the skinny. But…can you stand one more question?"

"That's why I'm here," Beka said, looking amused.

With a covert glance Alec's way, Kim said, "The portals. I don't know how much you've been able to learn, but…we got through safely. Or rather, alive. However, for some reason it wasn't as tough on me, but it really hurt Alec. He's still got the bruises. He even coughed blood. Though only once, I'm glad to say, before Tante Mina, that is, Salfmatta Mina Hajyos, did some Vrajhus healing on him. Was it my prism that kept me from looking like I got kicked down thirty flights of stairs? Are its charms stronger than the ones on Alec's signet?"

"The charms on Alec's signet are as strong as we could make them," Beka said. "Much stronger than those on your prism. But that wasn't what made your portal journey easier to bear, I believe. That was due to the necklace's far superior charms."

"You mean, I'm protected by it though it's here, and we were practically on the other side of the world?"

"Yes. Humans are actually not made to cross beyond the veil with their physical selves still intact. Anything less than the protections of the necklace, would have killed the two of you. You're lucky to be alive. Especially you, Alec."

"And again, ignorance is no defense," Kim said, turning to Alec, her face distraught. "That is *so* scary."

"Now we know," Alec said. "Just as glad to never do that again."

"Don't." Beka rose. "I strongly suspect it would be harder to heal you a second time. The night is nearly gone, and I'm expected at shul by eight. I must go." She turned to me. "Ruli, I truly don't know what to say to you, except how sorry I am. I know how useless that is. If you…" She stopped herself. "I can't find the words. Good night."

She closed the door softly behind her, and Kim said to Tania, "It'll be morning pretty soon. Get some sleep, Tania. Tomorrow, report what you hear to Salfmatta Sarolta, then take the day off."

Tania softly wished everyone good night and departed even more quietly than Beka had.

Kim said to me, "Do you want a room? I don't think we have any without windows. We could fix you up in a bathroom. No, windows. Storeroom, maybe. That reminds me. Do you need a bathroom, by the way? Or is that a question that shouldn't be asked?"

I tried not to laugh. "My metabolism is different now. But I do still retain a digestive system, which would even work, were I to ingest a meal." I pointed to her tray of snacks. "I metabolize liquids—I recently rediscovered a taste for hot chocolate."

"That's…kind of cool, actually," she offered. "Got to taste better than blood." She shuddered.

I was not going to describe the sensation of hot, metallic blood, which has only a faint metallic taste if you don't swish it around in your mouth. The fangs bypass the tongue, which pulls back. "As for a room, no. There's nowhere in the palace that would be safe for me. None of the windows shut out sunlight to the extent that I need. But I have places to go. As for everything else, since the open questions involve my family, I plan to find out answers, if I can."

"Would you like a crystal? One that's not charmed," she amended hastily. "In case you want to contact us? Me?"

I suppressed another laugh at her attempt at delicacy, and said, "Crystals are awkward things at the best of times. I might begin carrying a purse mirror, since those appear to work well."

"A mirror! Is that how I get to you in my prism? I thought vamps couldn't see themselves."

"I expect that is left over from someone encountering one of us who uses the shadows to vanish in."

"Be alert," Alec said to me. "There have been reports of vampire attacks, several dead around the Old Market, and more around the old royal mines on Mt. Tanazca."

I hesitated from the well-trained habit to be silent. Deferential. Then said, "The killer at the Old Market is not a problem anymore—that vampire was tonight's dinner."

Alec's heartbeat spiked, but all he said was, "Thanks."

Before Elena helped herself to my blood, had I said anything that blunt in Maman's hearing, she would have given me days of the silent treatment.

Speaking of whom. I said, "If you're wondering if my mother might be the demons' next inspiration, why don't I encourage her to leave sooner than later? I could offer to move in with her here in Riev. That might send her off."

Alec gave me his rare grin, and Kim chortled, clapping her hands. "Though I bet my mom would be happy to be enlisted to keep an eye on her."

I turned to Kim, my gaze falling on the wrinkled papers she was carefully tidying—as if that was a rare, valuable ancient text, and not a schoolgirl's scrawl. "Speaking as past princess, you're not really required to read such stuff; if one of them gets encouragement, you might find yourself inundated by all the would-be poets' effusions."

"I don't mind," Kim said. "It's actually a really fun story. I mean, derivative, yeah, but what do you expect from a kid? But even that's kind of cool, as it shows what bits of story are transformative for kids now."

"More power to you," I said, and took my leave.

It was time to track down Rose. I'd go to von Mecklundburg House first, since it was closer, and if there was no sign of her, return to the Eyrie—and the vampires of the mountain.

I reached von Mecklundburg House and prowled around it. No sign of Rose. From the steady heartbeats inside, everyone was asleep except for one in the kitchen. I went around to the front entrance and upstairs to my room, intending to use this opportunity to change. As I rooted through my clothes for something that would do for the foreseeable, I considered what I'd said about moving in.

It had been meant as a jest, but what if I did? The household all knew I was alive. I looked at my windows. They could be blocked up, but my room was on a busy hall. Tony had the ducal chamber, its own wing of the house. If I could get him to trade—he had dosses at the Eyrie, and at Sedania, and who knows where else, not counting his various lovers—I could seal it off.

I'd finished and was putting my shoes back on when I heard the approach of a heartbeat.

I knew it was Maman. I was fairly certain that she'd been the one in the kitchen, below my room. Curious, I waited; if needed, I could speed past her before her eyes blinked.

She cautiously opened the door, then said sharply, though it did not hide the sweet scent of fear, "Aurelia Elisabet, is that you?"

"Yes," I said, though I wanted to deny both the queenly Aurelia and even more the name I shared with Maman. I hoped this would be the last time I heard that name.

"You didn't turn on a light."

"I don't need a light," I responded.

A pause, and I knew what was coming next: reasserting her authority. "What are you doing here?"

Hot resentment surged in me, like boiling acid—the byproduct of years of suppressed emotions flooding past my vampiric mental skin, bringing purely human turmoil. But I took the time to reassert that filter, very aware that I might have given in to the rage had I not encountered that ravening fiend of Maritza's earlier, who had been a furnace of resentment and malice. Giving in, however justified, might make the next time easier. And the next. That vampire had not been all that old, either in age or as a vampire.

She was my mother, and there was no undoing the past.

But I did not have to revert to our old dynamic.

I said, "Do you say the same to Rose, your mother? Or

don't you speak to her?"

A sharp intake of breath. The fear was back, intensified by horror.

"I came here looking for her," I continued. "I know she lurks around here a lot. She says she's watching over the household. I wonder how much of that is merely watching — and intended to ask her. Have you seen her?"

"No. Never," Maman whispered. "Go away. You are an abomination, wearing my daughter's form. Go. Get out. I'll have the bishop exorcise this house."

"This is the first time I've ever heard you mention the bishop, other than disparagingly," I said, a little relieved and mostly disappointed that this was the way she had decided to come to terms with my continued existence, now that I was no longer an extension of her will. "If Rose does turn up, you might tell her what I said."

This time I did speed past her, so what she would perceive was my sudden disappearance.

As I started for the portal that would take me to Devil's Mountain, I wondered if she'd be giving orders to have my room turned out and transformed to something else, even though she was leaving for the holidays. For she would not leave forever. She'd always have an ear bent toward Dobrenica, and the possibility of a return in triumph. She probably waited in hope to hear of Milo's death of old age, and Alec expiring in some accident; Marie Murray had been born outside wedlock, so she would never inherit, which was a large reason why Maman tolerated her. Marie Murray was truly a free spirit. Like her husband. Status was utterly irrelevant to them both.

I know that Maman did not, perhaps could not comprehend that. She truly believed she ought to inherit the crown, and that the old king's leaving the country to Milo was mere spite for Rose's having married against his will. That wasn't *her* fault. *She* was born within the legal bonds of marriage. This resentment for what she perceived as injustice, I believe, was her primary motivation.

I decided to leave word for Tony to keep my room intact. After all, von Mecklundburg House was his, not hers — it went with the title.

I used the cliffside portal to take me not to the Eyrie, for I doubted Rose would be there. I'd learned that she'd only visited there a few times; she had of course lived to age sixteen in the palace, and her brief married life had been lived at von

Mecklundburg House.

I needed to talk to the unseen inhabitants. And so I started up the ancient path, mostly paved in patches, rutted by countless cartwheels in places.

Each mountain has its own history. On Devil's Mountain, it mostly has to do with vampires. Such as the plot in my great-grandfather's day, before World War II, by Baron Bogdan Sigismund. Long fascinated by inimasang, he studied them, and finally made a pact with Elena. Once he survived being bitten, his first act was to go around one night, bite all his family, with the idea that he would raise a little vampire army and take the Eyrie, then the dukedom.

It failed, after a nasty battle whose sites still are anointed by candles and sprays of forget-me-nots to this day; the chief battle was not far from the gates to the Eyrie's main court.

That little half-circle of statues out at the edge of the Eyrie's garden, which the family calls somewhat grimly Bogdan's Coronet? That's what remains of Baron Bogdan Sigismund's little army—and his title. The only one who refused to join Bogdan's plot was Raoul, married the year previous, with a newborn son.

It's this son who is the grandfather of Lizard Sig, the Eyrie's security steward, and my first serious crush. Sig was baptized Raoul in honor of this ancestor, but he only heard the name at his baptism, and he would again at his marriage. He was Lizard as a boy, which turned into Lizard Sig during his teens, and finally just Sig when he joined the Vigilzhi.

No one called him Raoul, because Raoul Sigismund is still around.

The heavy perfume of roses drifted on the cold air, a poisonous drowsiness threatening me with distortions around the edge of my vision. I'd already reached a village named Dorike, halfway up the mountain. Most villages have hawthorn and yew plantations, but Dorike has an enormous, centuries-old rose tree.

This was the point at which I slowed down, not only so that whoever might be roaming could find me, but so I could extend my senses to catch roamers.

The first I came across was Raoul, pretty much as I expected. He was barely twenty-two when his own father bit him. He looks young and cheerful—his character a lot like Sig's. "Princess Aurelia," he greeted me, manifesting out of the shadows.

"Ruli will do," I said. "Is Rose up here by any chance?"

"*No.*"

That deep, icy drawl belonged to Elena, who had turned me, as she had Rose. Apparently, you can always locate those you turned. "Welcome back, Princess. Well done, catching up with that vermin of Maritza's."

So that news had already gotten about? I expected the body to be found before the sun turned it to dust, but not who had done it. Now that the ferocity of the exhilaration had died down, I had to consider whether or not I had broken my internal vow against killing. But a vampire is already dead — and that one had been utterly mad. Still. Was this the first step toward becoming a monster?

Elena is not the one to ask. It's a mistake to show any weakness before her, even when she is (supposedly) pleased with you. I said, "Rose is attempting to ally the House with the demons wearing the form of seraphim. Is this a directive from…"

There was the compulsion, keeping me from saying Antonius Augustus out loud.

I could not read her at all. The crimson glow was mainly a matter of angle, and ambient light, I knew, a little like the chatoyancy of cat eyes. Yet I was certain she knew whom I meant, and old as she was, a reminder of the most powerful was sure to evoke some reaction.

The fact that she did not immediately answer was interesting, if mostly inconclusive. Then she did speak. "Even the stupidest dog knows not to foul its own nest. Round up the rest of Maritza's vermin, then we will talk."

The shadows closed in, and she was gone.

T̸ẇ̸ENTY-FIVE

Alec enlisted the aid of Milo's doctor, a tight-lipped geez of the old school, who expertly wrapped my ankle. Riev first had to see me with crutches, then one crutch, before I could graduate to a cane.

Meanwhile I began working out with my sword cane. I decided to give it a name, so any eavesdropper would not accidentally hear "sword stick" or "sword cane." I considered names of many fictional swords, but settled on Sting, because Frodo and Sam, my favorite characters from *Lord of the Rings*, had both carried it.

It was lucky I'd already begun practicing at Danilov's, so nothing was out of the ordinary, save Phaedra's brother and Honoré being in on the secret. Honoré, who already saw auras and knew instantly if someone lied, would never fall prey to dream invasion. Nor would Danilov or Phaedra, without him knowing.

October first brought cold rain, the smell of hot cider on the air, and in the morning, the brilliance of piano music drifting the marble hallways, from the old conservatory where the grand piano lived. My grandmother was back to her old habit of playing each morning as the sun rose. Amazing, how the showers of sound seemed to waft tranquility and even warmth through the cold, drafty palace corridors.

Occasionally Alec slothfully remained to wake with me at dawn, thus we breakfasted together to the sounds of

Rachmaninoff and Chopin, which evoked such strong memories of childhood for me.

Dutifully, I looked warily into faces as I moved through my day. Phaedra was hyper-vigilant. Alec was, too. I knew this matter was another brick on the load he already carried.

Handing off the necklace to a Salfmatta or Salfpatra seemed the most sensible solution. To that end, I asked Beka to set me up with a Salfmatta or Salfpatra who knew most about Esplumoirs and suchlike.

"Ah, she said approvingly. "You would like to choose the best-qualified to hand the necklace off to. We have already begun making inquiries."

They did not keep me waiting. The next day, Phaedra drove me over to the temple, where I was introduced to Rabbi Viskaver, a giant of a man with a bushy, dark brown unibrow that made Sig's look mingy. But appearances could be deceiving, for it turned out that Rabbi Viskaver was an expert in calligraphy—that was his avocation, along with rabbinical duties.

I thanked him for taking time out of a busy schedule.

He raised a thick, strong hand, you'd think the hand of a builder, but he was the one who'd created the beautiful Hebrew calligraphy that I'd seen framed on a wall as we passed by. "He made that as a gift to the temple when he made his bar mitzvah," Beka had explained.

"My duty is to serve HaShem and also the king. When both duties are in harmony, it is a blessing indeed," he said, smiling. "How may I help your highness?"

I had to consciously ignore the title. Again. Imposter syndrome, the gift that keeps on giving! "What can you tell me about the Esplumoir, and how the necklace works with it?"

"That is a question both simple and complex. I am sure you've been told that much of what was known is still lost."

"Anything I can learn I'd be grateful for," I said.

He nodded gravely. "'Esplumoir' is a name given to the boundary between the world of the seen and the unseen. The name is nearly a thousand years old, arising out of what we might term the shared European myth of the island king."

"Arthur," I said. "Though isn't 'Esplumoir' Merlin's nest when he shape-changes to a bird?"

Beka nodded.

Rabbi Viskaver went on. "It probably had another name for a thousand years previous, and another before the Romans. Our

Esplumoir, we believe, might be the oldest. At least, ours is on more settled land, unlike the Esplumoir in the Himalayas, and the one outside the city named for a chief of an allied tribe to those who have guarded it for centuries."

"You mean Seattle?"

"That is correct."

His attitude was akin to someone referring to a lost colony on Mars, or something equally remote. Whereas Seattle, to me, was a wonderfully rainy but otherwise ordinary city north of Oregon and California.

"Both those gateways between the worlds are on volatile ground," he said, and I pictured the world map, specifically the middle of Asia, where the land torques upward into China from the southwest, and where the Pacific plate pushes against North America. "We do not know if the friction of active plates facilitates the creation of these boundaries between the worlds seen and unseen. But there exist those who protect the boundaries against harmful invasion."

"By such as the demons?" So far, nothing new, but I waited for him to tell it his way.

"Correct. There is also constant friction at the Esplumoirs; it is not merely tectonic energies, but the active attack by such as the demons who are drawn to the life in this world. We believe protections like the necklace serve as portable reinforcement when the boundaries are weakened."

"Do you know any of the protectors in Seattle and in the Himalayas?"

"Vrajhus is to the unseen world as air is to our world," Rabbi Viskaver said. "The guardian spirits seldom come to our world, and equally seldom do we go outside while still living. But there is communication, direct between human protectors, and indirect from the unseen world."

Through dreams and visions, that much I got. Which now made sense, if the Nasdrafus-side protectors aren't actually human.

"As for protectors in our world, the guardian clans outside of Seattle, and the temple in the Himalayas are like us: they hand down knowledge from one to another by teaching. Now, to you. We have had several volunteers, I am glad to report."

"More than we expected," Beka said.

"We have narrowed the candidates to three. All three are orphans, so there is no family depending on them, if the worst happens."

"In any case, a family would be cared for," Beka hastened to say.

"They are each well-versed in Vrajhus, and they know the potential danger here. You could choose any of the three to receive the necklace, and be assured that they are the best the country has to offer."

Until I walked in, picking a Vrajhus expert in training to hand the necklace off to had seemed the most practical solution. But that word "orphans" jolted me into seeing what I had managed to overlook: by unloading the necklace onto someone else, I'd be unloading the threat onto them, too.

In less palatable words, in order to make myself more comfortable, I had to willingly throw some no doubt perfectly nice person under the bus bound for hell.

The rabbi finished his CVs of the candidates, then he and Beka looked at me expectantly. I looked back. Of course their candidates were aware of the dangers. They might even understand them better than I did. They could hardly be more ignorant than I was!

But the fact remained, I'd still be putting another person into the line of fire. Arguments rose to my lips, to be squashed. I knew they would accept whatever I chose — including keeping my guardianship of the necklace. The person I had to convince was the one pushing the hardest for me to unload this unwanted burden: Marius Alexander Ysvorod of Domitrian, Crown Prince of Dobrenica.

I finally said, weak in my own ears, "Can I take a little time to consider?"

"Of course," I was assured.

I thanked them, and walked out, Sting tap-tapping with each step.

Who were my three potential hell-bus squishees? One woman, two guys. The woman was a personal friend of Beka's, a fellow teacher at the temple school. A teacher! One of the guys was in seminary, studying to become an Eastern Orthodox priest. The third guy was a farrier who had the healing touch.

As soon as I was alone, I let out a groan.

"Gut ache?" Phaedra asked, appearing out of the door of a café, from which she'd been able to see in all directions, but not be seen.

"Heart ache," I muttered. "No. No car, please. I'm…going to walk. I need to think."

"Durchlaucht," Phaedra said warningly.

"Please don't do that," I whimpered.

"I'm doing it to remind you that I'm not going to leave you alone. And why."

I heaved a martyred sigh. "I'm heading for Nat's place — we were supposed to have coffee anyway."

Phaedra gave a curt nod. "Go ahead and walk, if it helps you think. But I'll be driving right behind you."

I took the upper route, through quiet back streets with little traffic. Higher on the slope a line of beech trees flamed with color. Between a couple of houses so picturesque the Montmartre artists of the Nasdrafus would weep, three very small children squatted on the ground, playing a game with pebbles. A delivery girl bicycled by, her basket piled with oddments, including a pair of boots from which the smell of polish wafted. Usually these sights cheered me immensely, but my emotions roiled.

When I knocked, Nat came to the door herself, a woman somewhere between thirty and forty, with short brown curls and a curvy figure.

"I hoped to catch you," I said. "I'm sorry I didn't call ahead."

"You're in luck," she replied with a grin. "This is the season for the Christmas babies to pop out. Got a couple of buns still in the oven, but things are quiet today. Come on in. Grab a sitz."

I walked into Natalie's comfortably familiar digs, the front room crammed with bookshelves stuffed with medical texts cheek by jowl with history and literature. In and around these she'd pinned art from the USA, Europe, and Dobrenica. Crystals hung in the windows, opposite a fine stereo setup with a library of CDs.

She started as an emergency room surgeon before opting to become an ob/gyn, but the Dobreni believe she's just a really good midwife who happens to know something about doctoring. She's already my gyn. As I sat on the overstuffed couch, I looked through the open door to her surgery, which was also her one-pot kitchen and her jury-rigged shower-bath. My nerves jolted when I realized that when — if — I did decide to do the deed, she'd be the one monitoring my particular bun. Buns?

She came out with tea things, set them down, eyed me, then said, "You resumed your pills, right?"

"As soon as I got them, thanks."

"How's married life? You two started up the Snookums

and Sweetie-poo talk, with diabetes-inducing PDA?"

"PDA? Alec? Or me, I guess," I added, considering that for the first time; while I'd dated casually from the time I was midway through high school, casual it had stayed. Until I met Alec. "As for sweetheart and darling, neither of us grew up hearing that. At most, Mom might pop out with a chéri now and then, but those weren't confined to Dad. And...can you imagine Milo saying Snookums to *anyone*, even if Alec's mom had been around to hear it?"

"Milo!" Natalie rocked back on her seat, her eyes crescents of mirth. "No," she gasped. Then eyed me, still smiling. "I still think Alec was born by immaculate conception. As for Alec, I know from experience he's too hot to trot to resemble his old man in that department, but he's *way* too private about what matters deeply for public displays. Howsome*ever*...you cut the honeymoon short, and then that call for backup birth control pills on your return."

"It's totally not what you're thinking."

"Try me."

By now I'd summarized the mess enough times to get it out pretty fast. And that included the conversation I'd just had.

"Definitely not what I was thinking — which was less that you two had been a couple of monks than that Alec couldn't stay away from his desk, even for the prospect of unlimited humina-humina. Glad to be proved wrong, and there's hope for the boy yet."

I splurted tea, and she grinned unrepentantly, then sobered. "As for the missed pill, or pills, what with the stresses you were going through, and the usual stats, I think you're fine. It's too early to tell now, but we can check in a month if you're worried. As for the rest, I'm sorry about this demon threat. A teacher! An animal doctor who tends those who can't even tell you where it hurts! A priest! I can see you not wanting to throw them under the bus, like you said. But I feel obliged to remind you that you were assured all three are adults, aware of the dangers, and willing."

"True, all true. Generous, good people, probably better people than I am." I patted Sting. "Such good people I'm sure they won't go around with weapon in hand. But I saw those goons chasing us. Can you imagine putting a teacher out there to be hunted by thugs in it for the thrill, if not for the kill?"

"And probably a smacking good fee," Nat said. "Though they might get their blood money in one hand, and a blast in the ass as they go out the door, the way it works in mob movies." She grimaced. "However, their probable fate is not our problem."

"Right. What I'm getting at is, I'm probably the best protected person in the country right now. I don't say anything, but I know that Alec has doubled the outer perimeter watches. If I go out, there's a huge circle moving both obviously and invisibly around me. Phaedra's visible outside right now, but there's probably a couple of snipers on the rooftops of the buildings either side of us, and more lurking in the alleys. It's the kind of defense a prince can whistle up, and nobody makes a peep. Those candidates will have a patrol, but not to this extent. The Vigilzhi can't afford it — at least half of them are locking down the city in all the parts I might go."

Nat leaned her elbows on her knees. "Gotcha. And I take it Alec is antsy about you handing off that necklace thing?"

"*So* antsy. I bet anything you care to name, he put pressure on Beka, so that they found and vetted those three in record time."

"And yet you're still gonna tell him you changed your mind about the handoff?"

"I think I have to," I said, sighing yet again. "The more I argue in my head, the more I'm sure I can't hand it off. He's going to hate it. He's going to hate it so much it'll probably be our first fight. And the maddening thing is, if *he* was on the hot seat, no way would he let any innocent Dobreni face the danger for him. No way. But because it's me…"

"No argument here," Nat said with conviction. "I betcha he was even going to ask you to give the thing to him, except for old Milo. And the fact that he knows zilch about Vrajhus stuff. But he'll want *you* safe. So what are you going to do?"

"It seems to me the only thing to do, is either spend a lifetime dodging that sword swinging over my head, or find a way to take the fight to the enemy."

Nat gave a long, low whistle. "He's gonna go ballistic."

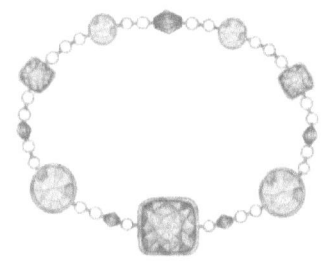

TWENTY-SIX

RULI

Habits are knots to unravel a thread at a time, I've found. You think you've cured yourself of one when you discover another that you've unconsciously performed unthinking. That goes for assumptions as well.

So it was with shoes.

I've always loved shoes. I must admit that the first idea that made my transformation bearable was the discovery that I would keep an elegant form forever; though I'd been critically regarded for every other aspect of my life, more frequently than not my mother would mitigate some criticism with something like, "At least you've a narrow foot and a delicate wrist. As long as you keep your figure, those will always be signs of good breeding."

And yet it took nearly a year before it occurred to me that, just as my body wouldn't age, my feet might no longer hurt in my beautiful shoes, which previously I'd only worn walking from house to car, and from car to house or venue.

Since it was quite late when I left the palace that night, I figured I had a better chance of finding my brother about to retire, hopefully alone. Both were true, and on hearing my request, he unsurprisingly said, "I wondered why this sudden order to drop everything and clear out your room. Most of your stuff is now in storage, waiting to be shipped off to Vienna."

"Vienna? Ah. So no one here will talk when my things get dumped into donation bins."

"I'll have it all put back. And I'll let them know at the other houses not to touch your things. But you have to do something for me: keep the rest of your bloodsuckers away from this house."

"That's supposed to be Rose's lookout," I said.

He snorted. "You, I trust conditionally. Her?" He lifted a shoulder.

I went down to the storage room in the basement, where I found everything neatly stacked. I located my Louboutins, slid my feet into them, savoring the perfect fit.

I set out for Mt. Tanazca. As I'd surmised, there was no pain in my feet. The heels gave me height. Poise. And weapons. I could not tango with Beka's whip-fast style, but I — along with the Cerisette and Phaedra — had taken all the same ballroom dance lessons, and I relished those lethal spikes under my heels as I descended to the portal below the ridge on which the great houses are located.

Elena was a law unto herself. I wasn't sure I trusted her even conditionally. She'd made Maritza, but had been perfectly willing to stand by and watch her staked. Now she wanted the same for Maritza's followers. I was quite willing, as Maritza had exerted herself to attract the worst thugs and outright criminals in her bid to build an army ruthless enough to take on the entire country, including inimasang unwilling to bend to her will. She'd kept her pack in line with her Vrajhus, but with her gone, the ones who'd escaped staking with her had gone feral. Maybe they were always feral.

When I studied the ever-flowing river of fashion, I learned early never to finesse the details. I applied that now: when I exited the portal below the old castle at Vezsar, I decided to take the time to explore Mt. Tanazca, which was largely unknown to me.

There were four inimasang within my range, and one at the extremity of it. Four roamers, terrorizing numerous villages by picking off the solitary man, woman, or child trying to go about their lives, to say nothing of their animals. I expect they enjoyed the terror they engendered. It made them feel more powerful — though why a sense of power is enticing might be debated. There could be no true communication within such a power imbalance, surely.

I also sensed regimented patterns of twos: elevated heartrates all. These would be Alec's Vigilzhi patrol, sent in pairs to protect the villagers as well as to investigate. But their human senses worked against them at night, and the daytime search, after tiring night patrols, would be difficult in such a wild tangle of forest, hidden crevasses and sudden waterfalls, the terrain honeycombed with ancient caves and mines. Despite doing due diligence, of course they had not managed to catch those creatures of the night.

I sensed the first roamer within an hour, judging by the descent of the new moon behind patchy clouds, a woman who appeared to be about thirty. She wore a village-style wedding dress, blue-and red embroidery on the tight bodice, and full skirts equally brightly embroidered, which did not quite obscure the bloodstains. The sickly-sweet metallic smell off one splash was fresh. This outfit was a lure. I found it obscene.

She eyed me, then smiled. "Sister," she cooed, her gaze raking down my black silk to my very red shoes. "Ooooo."

"You've been killing."

She looked sorrowful. "Just one," she said in a small voice. "It was an accident. And she was a wretch, a husband-stealer. It's all Octav and Gogu."

The wheedle was oily with long practice, each word edging her closer. Then she sprang.

She had just enough time to bare her teeth before Noeme's lessons gave me the vector and I was on her. The temptation to sink my teeth into her neck gripped me with frightful strength. But I had learned something from the earlier episode: you took their strength, but along with it you got that hunger for more of that seductive lightning-blast. The perfervid high bolstered by rage.

The very definition of a monster, no?

I broke her neck, pushed her blood-reeking corpse to where the sun would reduce it to dust as soon as it cleared the castle tower on the eastern ridge, and ran down the next prowler.

He wasn't far. This had to be either Gogu or Octav, a grizzled man whose sagging face was grooved with decades of cruelty.

That fight was tougher because brute force had been trained into his muscles, but I was just that much faster, and the final blow had been trained into *my* muscles: an extended gancho, a hard upthrust with spike heel to where it's most tender, even on a vampire. He recoiled, howling, and there was his neck. Breaking it instead of feeding left me dizzy with hunger, and though I had perhaps three hours of darkness left, I was going to have to retire purely to recover my equilibrium.

Before I did, I homed in on the cluster of heartbeats, and as expected, discovered the Vigilzhi outpost, which was little more than a box meant as an escape from bad weather. It had been hastily adapted as a headquarters.

I lurked outside until I recognized Sasha Trasyemova among the other Vigilzhi. "Sasha," I called out — to warn him of my presence, as I'd learned earlier from Kim's and Alec's surprise.

They all stilled, hearts racing as I moved slowly into the circle. "Just to let you know there's two left. I'll deal with them tomorrow."

Did they hear me? They still looked a heartbeat away from attack.

I slid into the shadows and ran.

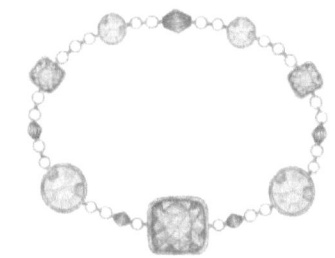

TWENTY-SEVEN

KIM

Theresa Waleska, Tania's younger sister, had two besties. Theresa and Katrin went to the cathedral school, and Miriam to the temple school. It was from these three that I found out about the "Swap," when all three begged me to attend.

The Swap is a typical Dobreni custom. It begins on St. Francis's Day. The kids of the temple school, the small Eastern Orthodox academy, and guild schools are all invited to bring pets for the Blessing of the Animals, after which a pot luck picnic is held.

A couple days later, on the first day of Sukkot, the cathedral school, Eastern Orthodox, and guild school kids would be invited to the temple school to visit the sukkah the students had made. In the sukkah, I was promised, the young scholars dressed up as Torah figures, and put on small plays to entertain the guests while feasting them, again pot luck.

With three hopeful pairs of eyes on me, there was no way I could say no. Doing stuff with kids hadn't been part of princess duties, but why not start now? I asked Tania to help me shift my schedule around so that I could get to the cathedral the morning of St Francis's Feast Day. As Tania is Theresa's sister, it was no surprise that she agreed promptly and enthusiastically.

I wanted to have Theresa's story read by the time I went over to the cathedral, because while she'd insisted she didn't expect me to read it all, and that I could keep it as long as I liked, I knew from my experience of much older students at UCLA's film school that creators are ever hopeful of audience, no matter what age.

Easier said than done.

I was still really slow at reading Dobreni handwriting, which had a lot in common with old German fraktur. My reading time was further constrained by my schedule, and by the lag that tight security required. And it was tight. While the small circle in the know waited for me to pick one of the candidates.

Alec gave me two days. Nights, really, as we barely saw the other during those two days. The third day was no different. We didn't meet up again until very late, when we both sat up in bed, papers on lap.

When I reached the last page of Theresa's manuscript, I laid it with virtuous pride on the stack. Then glanced over at him, and the pile still on his lap. A closer glance showed mostly numbers on top. "Is this going to be our thing, then?" I tried not to whine, but yup, I was whining. "Homework until our eyes won't stay open?"

"This is the busiest time of the year," he said. "Tax money comes in, and most of it goes right out again. It all has to be accounted for—that's part of Milo's insistence on transparent government."

I tidied Theresa's pages. "Got it."

"Pretty soon Council will recess until the holidays are over, except for a few leftover meetings like the never-ending print guild matter. Emergencies. There'll be a lot more free time between those. I still want to take you up to see the Ysvorod ruin before it's snowed in till spring. Perfect spot to camp out. It was a frequent hideout when I was young." He turned to face me. "But even if Council recessed tomorrow, we won't leave Riev until we know you don't have a target on your back."

"About that..."

"I realize you don't want to put someone else in the line of fire," he said with ready sympathy.

Oh, yes. He'd read me. No surprise there.

"But think how it's got to feel, waiting day after day for you to choose. They must be wondering if they are lacking in some way. Once you do pick one, the other two will be able to get back to their normal lives."

"Normal lives," I repeated. "Right now, I think I'm holding

back chiefly because *my* normal life includes protections that I don't think they'd get."

Alec looked puzzled. "Of course I'd assign a roving patrol to whoever you pick. Likewise at key places around their homes and work. And, being experienced with Vrajhus, they can take care of that end by nights."

"But they won't have Tania glued to their side, armed with a charmed prism. Or Phaedra, who I think is worth any two Vigilzhi. Maybe a squad. And they won't have Sting, because they're nice people, and I'm me—I feel better with a handy dandy sword nearby when I sniff danger. Also, being nice people, I don't think they'd give every strange guy the stink-eye the way I do. Though I try not to be too obvious."

"Go on," he invited. "Are you leading up to something?"

"Well, okay. It's this," I said—noticed his stillness, and chickened out for another round of hedging. "I've got the bastion of the palace, which the candidates won't have, and all my princess duties are right in the middle of the city. Oh, a bunch of determined attackers might be able to bull their way toward me, but they would never get past your outer ring closing in. Or past disgruntled citizens roused to defense on my behalf. Right now I seem to be popular. A tackle and takedown of the princess might have gone unnoticed in Vienna or LA, but it wouldn't go over well at a painting exhibition or a music quartet or a meeting of a good works committee here in Dobrenica. Am I right?"

"Yes."

"And these candidates just won't be the same as a princess, is what I'm saying. I think I'm the safest of all."

Alec's eyes narrowed. "You're not going to choose one?" he said in that remote polite voice that hid his reactions.

"It goes against everything that seems right. But I know it's a good idea. So I'm still wrestling inside…Look, let's get past the next few days—both of us have back-to-back obligations."

"As long as you keep talking to me. And," he said, his gaze steady, eye to eye, "you don't go running off to take the fight to the enemy."

I could not prevent a twitch. Had Nat blabbed? No. Nat didn't blab.

I busied myself tidying the already-tidy papers in order to hide my reaction, but he stretched out his hand to still my fussing fingers. "Kim, I think I know you pretty well. I wondered if you were contemplating such a *bloody terrible idea.*"

"No, no, no," I lied, because I could see beyond the veneer of humor that he was on the verge of being really upset.

He accepted that. Or seemed to. Then made a truly heroic effort to lighten things. "You seem to have finished reading the Waleska girl's opus. How was it?"

"It's a fun story," I blathered, way too quickly. "The part that tickled me most—and I'll never tell her this—is the kid's eye view of adults. Some of it's hilarious! Such as the villainous baron going into fits of helpless rage over our heroes lifting his judge's wig via a fishing pole from the gallery above his baron's throne. Do judges still wear wigs? And do barons have thrones?"

"The old castles still have thrones, yes. It's not just royal asses planted on thrones. The bishop has one. Thrones equate authority."

"Though I'd think the ones with bejeweled seats would be torture—which might make the baron crabby enough to hand down some pretty sharpish judgments. Do the dukes have thrones?"

Alec grinned. "Most do, yes, in the old halls."

"I can't imagine Tony lounging on a throne."

"He seems to prefer demonstrating his authority by riding at the front of his madmen. To finish with the wigs, again, in the mountains, where fashion changes about once every two or three centuries, a wig and a robe are part of the accoutrements of a legal court setting. Those wigs have been passed down through the ages, and possess monumental authority."

"As much as a king?"

'Sometimes more. Because the judge is there, and the king distant, a mere idea to the mountain villages. And it used to be weeks, sometimes months before someone in Riev reviewed decisions and either endorsed them, in which case no one heard about it again, or rescinded them, long after the fact. But I'm digressing unforgivably. Go on."

"Well, there's the romantic couple at the end of the climax having their huge wedding—it took three pages to describe her gown—then bride and groom go back to mom and dad at the end of the day, I guess to get a good night's sleep tucked up among brothers and sisters." I felt his chuckle resonate through me. "There seems to be a vague notion that once a kid comes along, they'll have their own castle, but no real thought as to how the kid gets there."

Ooops. Was he going to bring up The Subject of Heirs?

He hesitated, his eyes moving between mine as if trying to read me. Was he thinking about it? Ordinarily I'd ask right out. Like I'd proudly assured Gran, we were really good at talking, Alec and I. But somehow, this subject hadn't been one of the two million we'd canvassed so far, and I was hesitant to throw it out there now because I wasn't at all ready for a possible *Yes, toss the pills and let's get that bun in the oven!*

But that, surely, was me projecting. He had way too many annelids squirming in the tin to even thinking about kids. Right? What guy thinks that way? And if he *wanted* to get into it, *of course* he would have added it to the list of Princessly Duties we'd had before the wedding. Right? *Right?*

So I hustled past the hypothetical babies and patted the handwritten pages, wrinkled from having been shared from reader to reader. Eager readers, if loyal Katrin was to be believed. "Anyway, many of the cultural assumptions are lovely, mostly the mix of magic and real life being everyday wonders. But I think I'm missing the vital part of the story, which I suspect is her insertion of various classmates into the characters. Want to bet that's why her stories are so popular at her school? The kids are reading for signs of themselves."

He grunted. "Roman à clef has been an enduring trope for how many centuries?"

"I strongly suspect Hildegard von Bingen gave us word pictures of some of her fellow nuns, the way painters included their buddies in the background of historical paintings."

"Oh, farther back than that."

"Cave wall caricatures?"

"…And on that note, I give up for the night." He laid aside his lists, and held out his arms. I set aside the papers, turned the light out, and leaned into his warmth. He murmured into the top of my head, "Promise me you won't go charging off on your own, whatever you decide about the necklace candidates."

"Okay," I muttered, giving in, and hating it.

He knew how much I hated it, and his arms tightened around me, and my reward was not having to think at all, after which I dropped with a thud into dreamless sleep. No whiff of angel-faced demon — or anything else.

Morning arrived to the roar of rain against the windows. As usual, Alec was already gone, a ninja at sneaking out of bed without disturbing me. Whereas whenever I tried that, he was awake in an instant. I guess that was leftover habit from those "fun" days of camping in a ruin while Soviets roared by, when he was Theresa's age.

St. Francis's Day! At least the seraphs wouldn't be attacking through ankle-biters, I thought happily as I climbed into a warm outfit of navy blue. I still wore my sandals — it's tough for me to break the sandal habit until the temperatures get lower than we ever experienced in Southern California.

By the end of breakfast, the rain had stopped, leaving the sky the watery aquamarine that meant more rain on the way. The air was clean and clear, permitting me to walk the relatively short distance to the cathedral — all the exercise I expected to get in a day packed with obligations.

It was worth the effort, a respite from the Sword of Damocles. A wall of cheerful noise greeted me, treble voices, bleats, baaaas, barks, and over in the garden, under an awning, moos, and a whicker or two from three shaggy hill pones and one old and much-loved horse. Not all the kids got into the line to have the priests bless their animals; though most Dobreni at least nominally follow the religion of their ancestors, there are those of other faiths or no faith at all. But the Blessing has been a cultural catalyst for centuries, so there was no moral pressure. And there were plenty of kids who got into line twice, according to the philosophy that extra was always better.

Otherwise, the space was alive with the happy noise of petting, currying, patting, bragging, and showing of tricks.

Eventually parents or aunts or uncles came to take animals home, and the kids sat down to a sumptuous feast, as there was definitely showing off of various families' specialties.

The rain continued on and off through the day, unnoticed by me until sometime past four, when the kids had cleaned up the vast hall sufficiently for dismissal. My heart sank: the storm had moved in with a roar and apparently parked right overhead, which meant I would not be walking the relatively short distance back to the palace. I began to look for Phaedra (though I was sure she'd already have thought of getting a car) when the expected grilling zeroed in like dive bombers in the form of three eager young teens, Theresa Waleska — eager author — flanked by Katrin and Miriam.

TWENTY-EIGHT

RULI

The church bells rang over mountains and down valleys at the end of St. Francis's Day, the heavy rain bringing darkness early.

The last two of Maritza's ferals were waiting for me, one out as a lure, the other hiding. Neither sensed my approach — proof at last that "radar" did not come with the fangs and the need for blood.

I sprang the trap by taking out the concealed one first, thus catching the bait by surprise. I was starving by then, but did not want to attack any of Sasha's Vigilzhi, and the inhabitants of the Tanazca villages were all inside, worn by weeks of fear of the night. Two down. But there was another.

The lightning shock struck even stronger — but this time I detected a hint of nerve-malaise beneath, a feeling akin to an early experiment in eating nothing but sweets for a day or two. This malaise was not equivalent of sugar crash, but enough of an anomaly to serve as warning that a steady diet might build power but it came with the cost of taking on the other's madness.

I tracked the last, fairly certain that this was a watcher, not a killer, for its pattern had not been one of stalking but of observation.

I ran lightly — barely touching the ground was getting easier — to the top of a cliff overlooking the baronial castle, where I was surprised to see a diminutive form, its white hair ghostly under the rain-heavy clouds moving in fast by a howling wind. His brown cowl flapped, as did the hem of his aged, rough tunic, and the threadbare scapular. Around his middle, a cord with three knots.

"Konstantin?" I guessed.

Konstantin was the name of the legendary "Mad Monk" — attacked by marauding vampires from the east when he tried to defend the door of the monastery he'd been visiting more than five hundred years ago. In village stories, he protected sheep and cows from hungry wolves. Some said he preyed only on animals, never killing them. Other stories insisted he transformed to animal shapes to protect sheepherders and the like.

I had thought him merely another legend — myth, fiction — until last winter, when Rose airily mentioned that he had been the one to reveal Maritza's secret lair.

He looked at me through the heralding splats of the incoming storm. I said, "That is the last of Maritza's, at least on this mountain."

The old monk smiled, put his gnarled hands together, then dissolved into the shadows just as the rain bucketed down in a flood.

The Vigilzhi all had their weapons to bear when I turned up again at their outpost. When Sasha saw me, he raised his palm to halt them from closing in on me, but I could hear the terror in their heartbeats.

"Done," I said, and stepped aside into the shadows, drawing them around me as I shifted speed. Gratitude, I had not expected. Actual distrust was a surprise, at which I had to scorn myself. Why expect anything different?

I found my portal, and came out at the base of Mt. Dhiavilyi, whereupon I stretched out my now-strengthened senses for inimasang. I sensed someone a second or two before there was Elena herself, pale as flame, enormous pupils; if she'd ever had irises, they seemed to have been entirely swallowed in the black. Or that might be affect, for she used shadows in such a way that it was impossible to differentiate the drift of black hair from smoke or shadow. Rather in the style of the demon who styled itself Jeremiel.

"Was that haste to impress me?" she said.

I wondered if she knew about radar. I would assume so unless proven otherwise. I said ambiguously, "I wanted to get it done, the faster to resolve this entire matter. Where is Rose?"

"Where else? In the Nasdrafus, of course. Come along."

And to the familiar crevasse, but then there was a portal inside that I had never seen before. We went down into cold air that smelled of wet stone. Not quite dank — there was no rot or mold. "You've become more interesting than I expected," she said as she drifted ahead, leaving me to follow the shifting shadow. I could not tell if she wore a black gown, or if her hair reached nearly to her feet, or if she had learned to control shadow enough to use it as a cloak. Light and shadow seemed to be her preferred motif.

I made no response to that compliment. If it was one. Her timbreless voice was very hard to read for tone. It could have been a warning.

The silence produced the distant rush of water, or maybe that was the sough of air through stone chambers. I hadn't known about this tunnel, much less the grotto we entered suddenly.

There was a goldy-green glow, brighter than phosphorescence, but not fire, that churned within what appeared to be a glass sphere suspended motionless in the middle of the chamber. Delineating the chamber's rough hexagon, bands of agate glittered coldly, almost colorless in that weird light, throwing out a caustic network of curving refraction.

A slab of pale stone leaned against the far side. Cave paintings decorated it, bands of running creatures, horse-like, with hounds or panthers alongside. Below those, a string of ideographs of some sort, and then — below those — a sort of handprint. Painted? It looked like a cloven hoof stretched to finger length and attenuation. Not human or animal. My nerves tingled.

"You're potentially interesting, but your question is boring," she said.

"Not to me."

"What do you intend to learn from Rose when you do find her?"

"Why she pushed me at those demons in the form of seraphim. Or rather, what she thinks she will get out of an alliance with them. Alliance? I don't believe she's that stupid."

"She's not," Elena said, amused. "But you are if you believe that."

A new idea struck me, followed by the distinct impression that I'd fallen into the most obvious error.

"She's perfect to sit at their knees adoringly, isn't she?"

Elena added. "You could have done your part, solidifying us among them."

"But that would require..." I stopped before the word *betrayal*. Elena would only scoff. However, she did abide by some rules, even if I only perceived a part of the complexity of the really old powers. "...breaking a promise."

"To a human." She was of course dismissive.

I owed Elena nothing, and I was bone-tired of deference. Look where it had brought me. "I'm learning from Kim, though she's younger than I am."

"What could you possibly learn from her?"

"That altruism is possible. That, though I was raised to regard romantic love as childish, and community purely as hierarchy — my birth requiring me to exert myself to remain at the top — there is another meaning entirely." Surmounting those — though I did not trust her enough to say it — I had the previous night learned that joy arises out of the smallest, most innocent things. Because that was the emotion Kim had revealed when she collated that mass of schoolgirl scrawls: joy.

"What meaning? You're not making any more sense than the princess who replaced you."

I had expressed myself clumsily, but I refused to back down. "As I said, still learning."

Her mouth twisted in scorn. "You'll learn nothing from a human. Get rid of her, then come back. I usually wait for ten or twenty years — "

I will probably never find out if what was to come next was meant to be threat or not, because that familiar, neck-prickling ice burn of power silenced her, and we all stilled. "We" included the circle of inimasang that I'd been too focused on her to notice until now, waiting in the shadowy clefts.

A tense silence prevailed, then she uttered a short gloat. "Maybe we'll talk sooner than I thought. Out."

The compulsion gave me a brutal shove. Not physical so much as a compelling, nearly overwhelming sense of imminent danger, and I sped back down the tunnel and out, into lashing rain.

I could think again. Why would she gloat?

I considered the conversation, short as it had been. Talk sooner than...

Kim.

TWENTY-NINE

KIM

"Here is your story," I said, taking it from my satchel. Theresa took the manuscript, looking anxious. "Did you like it?"

"Of course I did! Thank you for sharing it with me."

"Did you *really?*"

I praised everything I'd liked — and, trained by film student friends, was ready for the inevitable next question, "What parts did you like the *best?*"

All three girls listened, then fell over each other discussing what had inspired this or that incident, and who X or Y really was ("The wicked goat girl is just like Xani, the nosiest girl in the school").

Finally, Theresa said wistfully, "I'm *so* glad you liked it. Uncle Adrian, you know, I told you, the one who first gave me Fyadar stories he'd had when he was a boy, well, he really only read a few pages, though he said he read more. I could tell."

"I don't care if he's a bookseller's assistant. He doesn't know what's good," Miriam stated with fierce loyalty.

"And Cousin Rissa said she couldn't tell anyone apart," Theresa added. "And she's Tania's age! She reads a lot!"

"But your Cousin Prim, she *loved* it," Miriam stated stoutly, naming Theresa's favorite cousin, who worked after school at a bookshop.

I praised and commiserated, and after pointing out that tastes vary, was bombarded with teen theories and digressions about the characters' pasts and futures that seemed likely to go on for hours, until a staff member appeared.

The girls shut up. The gray-haired woman nodded respectfully to me, then said to the girls, "It's getting dark, and the storm is worsening. Time to go home, students. Quickly!"

The girls scampered off, leaving me free. The woman apparently felt obliged to stick to me, but I said, "I know you have to lock things down. I can find my way to the door."

She thanked me, I thanked her, and we both were free, she rushing off with a muted air of hurry to check windows and doors.

I went to hunt up Phaedra. She was nowhere in sight. Of course! We'd walked over. She had probably gone to get a car to take me back the mile or so to the palace. And the perimeter guards had to be relocating to cover if a storm was moving in.

The splash of wheels brought my attention up — Phaedra was already here: twin highlights turned the falling raindrops to lit crystal. The shape of the vehicle was wrong, too square. It pulled up, and instead of Phaedra, a vaguely familiar figure called, "Quick, your highness, jump in!"

I stared suspiciously, then in relief when I recognized that unibrow the color of cookie dough. "Sig? What are you doing here?"

"Picking up supplies, as usual," he shouted over the roar of the rain. I was already getting soaked just leaning into the jeep, which had a roof but no windows. "But the king collapsed, and they're all scrambling. I offered to pick you up, since you can't possibly walk in this storm."

"Collapsed? Milo? Is Alec there?"

"On his way, your highness."

"Can you take me there instead of the palace?"

"Of course!"

"Thank you!" I pulled open the door, then stared in dismay — the front seat was loaded with two baskets of ripening pears. With rain pouring down, I chucked Sting behind some boxes in the back so the wind wouldn't take it away, flung myself in, and pulled the baskets into my lap, trying not to jostle them so that they'd bruise. "Okay, I'm in!"

Sig took off with a roar.

"Do you know what happened?" I yelled over the sound of the engine and the rain.

"All I know is, the Council meeting with the print guild was going like hammer and tongs," he bellowed. "Then the king complained about his chest."

I knew that some of the statistics Alec had been reading the previous night had related to typesetters and associated jobs. The conflict was over what would happen to those jobs if booksellers—Dobrenica's tiny publishing world—brought in printing software from outside the country. The guild was dead set against it; a couple of wealthy booksellers and paper merchants stood to make a profit with a switch to computers, which would be hooked to phone lines via modem.

Most citizens didn't care, Alec had explained, as you could count the number of computers in Riev, and all were in the ritzy end of town. The printers were a very staid bunch. Typeset had been going on for centuries, and could go right on for more centuries; they felt computers would only benefit the already wealthy—at the cost of ordinary folks' generations of trained artisanry. Typesetting being a highly trained vocation.

"The arguing caused Milo to collapse?" I asked anxiously. "What were his symptoms?"

"That's all I heard."

"Alec will know what's going on," I said, more to myself than to Sig. I was aware of relief washing through me, though when I recognized it I felt guilty. I didn't want Milo to die for years and years. But...

Better not to finish that thought. I stared out the windshield, wishing I'd brought a coat. I hadn't expected to be bumping along in a windowless jeep. Getting spoiled by the princess life, eh, Murray? That mocking voice inside my head prodded me.

Lights from street lamps and windows winked through the downpour, darkness descending fast. Ruli could probably come out early, I thought morosely. Where was she, anyway?

For that matter, where were we? The Council building lay almost in an exact line between the cathedral and the palace, but wasn't that the opera house we'd just passed? Was he going around via St. Ladislas Street? No, the Vigilzhi Station lay straight ahead. Okay, that made sense.

I rubbed my arms up my sodden sleeves, peering ahead. Wait, wasn't that King Alexander Park—right before and the bridge over the Ejya River branch—

"Sig?" I shouted. "Where are we going?"

"A quick stop first," he shouted back. "Very quick, then I promise to get you back to Prince Alec."

"Can't you drop me off at the Council first?"

He was looking straight ahead, fingers gripped hard on the steering wheel. Wind tore at the jeep, making me wonder if we'd be blown away entirely except for the ton of things in the back, and on my lap.

"Glad to, Durchlaucht," he said again, but kept driving straight.

I didn't want to be rude. He was clearly fighting against the storm, and driving required all his attention. We weren't going fast at all—the wind was far too strong, vibrating through the vehicle in an alarming fashion.

"Like, now, please?" I said finally.

"Glad to, Durchlaucht," he said again. But kept driving straight.

"Don't you have to turn right before the bridge?"

"On the way back, Durchlaucht," he shouted, without looking my way.

"If you've got some pressing errand, I can walk from here," I said finally, though I wasn't at all sure I'd survive it. The night was now ink black, and I could hear as well as feel the jeep nosing through running water.

"Just a quick stop, for the angel to talk to the princess," Sig said in that same tone.

I was already cold, and wet, but at the word "angel" my spine turned to ice. "Angel?" I said, hyper-aware that Sting lay beyond my reach.

I began sliding my fingers toward the jeep's door handle.

"She said I'd be a baron again. Wouldn't Magda like to be a baroness? Angels help people. She promised to help *you...*" Still in that weird calm as he fought the vehicle into the tearing wind and rain.

The sound of the wheels changed abruptly: we were on the bridge. My fingers tensed, then froze: what if the river was rising past the other side? I wouldn't be able to see it until I was swept away in it.

"Sig," I tried again. "That 'angel' is messing with you. How can you be a baron again? Do you even want to?"

"Magda will be a baroness," Sig said, reasonable-sounding, but orthogonal to my questions. "I'll give her anything she wants. Every woman wants to be a baroness."

"Did *she* ever say she wants to be a baroness?" I tried a different tack—trying to get him to speak about the woman he was going to marry. Even if she turned out to be secretly ambitious to take over the duchy, the subject might lure him out of that dreamy detachment.

"Magda will be a baroness," he repeated. The dashboard glow underlit his face, blue light making it seem eerily calm. Like his voice. "I love her. I will do anything for her."

This semblance of Sig had completely bypassed rationality, going straight to the indefinable realm of emotion. Had to hand it to the demons, I thought bitterly. They twist beauty, of course they would distort their victim's good emotions, not just the Seven Deadlies. I ought to have seen this coming. And we'd thought ourselves so clever having planned for goon attacks.

Then go for emotions! "Sig, you're putting us both in danger."

But he simply replied, "There's no danger. A quick, quiet stop, for the angel to meet you, and help you. She will help us all."

We'd crossed the bridge, and now jolted over the top of the ridge on which were built the streets of the mansions. If I jumped out and stumbled into the darkness, would he run me down? He was under compulsion. Think! Think!

I tried to open the jeep door to take my chances, but a blast of wind slammed it shut, nearly on my hand. I wasn't going to make it five feet in that blast.

We'd already passed the ridge's crest on which von Mecklundburg House, Ysvorod House, and Ridotski House, etc., lay — nothing visible in that wildness. Then the jeep tilted downward, and I had missed my chance entirely — we were on the narrow road that wound down the ridge; somewhere, I'd learned from Ruli, between the waterfall and the cemetery lay a portal. We had to be heading there. If I leaped now, I was likely to go over the unseen cliff.

Lights flickered off to the side, half-hidden by lashing trees and the rain. What was that? Another car on the other side of the ridge — probably coming from Zorfal, the popular hangout of the Vigilzhi. But it might have been a thousand miles away — there was no chance to signal anyone, no cell phone, nothing.

My only option was to jump out the second I saw far enough ahead to make sure I wouldn't be tossing myself straight off a cliff.

When the jeep slowed, I peered out, trying to see beyond a few inches. Then the vehicle lurched to a stop, and two arms tightened around me.

"Sig?"

Silence, as with enormous strength, he dragged me out the

driver's side, one sandal catching on the gear shift and scraping over my foot.

THIRTY

RULI

I went to find Sasha first. He and his command were still patrolling Mt. Tanazca, though there was no longer anything to patrol for.

In retrospect I ought to have taken as a warning the Vigilzhis' earlier disbelief at my claim that I'd dispatched two and that I would remove the threat of the other pair.

"Sasha, I think the princess is in trouble."

"Where? What kind of trouble?"

I couldn't say that I'd sensed threat from a vampire, not with him looking at me in distrust and wariness, rain pouring off the brim of his hat.

His suspicion was fast sharpening to conviction. I knew then that it was unlikely I'd get any better of a response from the Vigilzhi in Riev, most of whom did not know about my transformation. Sasha did—someone I'd known since he was a small boy to my teen self—and yet he still looked at me warily.

I'd have to go elsewhere.

I said distinctly, "Just remember I warned you," and sped away with the intent to shift to the portal below the ridge, which was so close to von Mecklundburg House.

But as I entered the narrow crevasse into which the Tanazca portal had appeared and mentally projected the familiar site, my radar tripped, freezing me between steps. Presence. Lots of presence. Someone lurked in that portal. No, they were lying in wait—ambush? Who? I could detect inimasang entities, but not identity.

The most obvious answer seemed to be Elena's gang. They might be there to trap any leftovers of Maritza's rabble. Or they might be from elsewhere. Rather than deal with a pack of them, I used the Old Market portal, which was empty, and sped for my house.

It was interesting running through heavy rain—and tremendously taxing. The wind and rain resisted like running underwater, and I had to push hard. I felt the water whirling wildly behind me in a corkscrew wake before the wind snapped the rain into one direction again.

I was thoroughly soaked when I reached the house, though not cold—that lizard skin again. All the beating hearts were either in the dining room or the kitchen, household and servants. With the intent of avoiding my mother, I risked a peek into the kitchen, where I spotted Marie Murray, Kim's mother.

She was in the midst of sending one of the staid old servants off with a tray of something, then she turned and saw me, stopped, and began to wipe her hands on her apron. "Kimli—" Her eyes narrowed. "No. You must be Ruli, right?" That American accent was startling, coming from this semblance of my own mother's face.

Except my mother had never worn that easy smile—nor would she have hennaed her hair.

"Could you get my brother's attention?" I asked. "It's an emergency. I think…I think there might be some sort of trouble. For Kim."

She hesitated one second, gave a tiny nod very like Kim's when she reaches a decision, and whisked herself out. A few seconds later she was back with Tony in tow.

"This better be good," he started.

"I think Kim's in trouble. I couldn't get Sasha Trasyemova to listen to me."

"Sasha's been a tool ever since he put on that damn blue jacket," Tony retorted, and turned to Marie. "Where's Sig? We'll need a ride. Is he eating with the staff?"

"Sig?" Marie repeated. "I haven't seen him since he stopped in this morning."

"He's supposed to be here. He's always here early enough to avoid driving up the mountain in the dark. Earlier."

Marie's grin was very like Kim's. "He likes my food." Then her smile vanished. "Could he be mired in the storm?"

"Not Sig. He's the best driver we've got, and that jeep of

his would probably run at the bottom of the lake as long as he was at the wheel." Tony scowled at me, then back to her. "Is this related to why Alec's had Kim surrounded with half the country's bluecoats ever since their return?"

"You'd have to ask them," Marie said—an answer so prompt I suspect it was her standard reply when anyone in my family tried to use her as a wedge, or informer, into Alec's citadel.

Alec. And Kim…

It was then that I thought of that portal, and the crowd massed just inside it. Elena's coldly detached gloat. Sig missing. That portal, crowded. For an ambush? From Elena? No. Elena could shrug at Kim's death by Maritza's gang or by accident, but she wouldn't be the cause while the Thorn pact still held.

They had to be from the demons.

Tony snapped his fingers in my face. "Ruli! What is it?"

"I think I'd better find Alec," I said, and gave them both a fast explanation.

Tony cursed Vrajhus and everything to do with it, and I thought he was going to retreat to his unfinished meal. But then he seemed to have second thoughts, whether on Kim's behalf or more likely Sig's, and he said to Marie, "I'm going to take Murray's motorcycle."

It wasn't a request, but Marie said, "Go ahead. George certainly doesn't need it in Herculaneum."

Cursing again, Tony stalked out.

So much for getting him to go to the Vigilzhi station in my stead. I didn't want to send Marie out into that wild tempest, so I decided I'd have to go after all, though I knew the only one who might listen to me would be Dmitros—who was probably at home by now—or Phaedra, who would of course be with Kim. Good, I thought. At least whatever is going on with Kim, she's got a bodyguard with her.

But when I reached the Vigilzhi station and looked through a window into the command center, there was Phaedra, sitting by their telephone as she spoke to one of the other night duty bluecoats. I thought I caught, with my sharpened hearing, a few of the same Russian curses that Tony had been using.

Though there was a cluster of Vigilzhi at various tasks, I tapped at the window, and again. She finally looked up, her face tight with anger. When she saw me, her jaw dropped, and she bolted for the door and came outside regardless of the rain driving horizontally past the side of the building. At least the worst of it was hitting there. "Ruli! Do you know where Kim is?" she shouted. "Where would Sig Sigismund take her?"

"Sig?"

Phaedra sighed sharply. "Old Milo started feeling chest pains right before the rain came in. I came over here while Kim was surrounded by her patrol plus the entire cathedral staff, to fetch the car. Nobody was going to walk in that storm…no, I'm telling it backward."

She stared into the window as the phone rang inside, but one of the duty officers picked it up, and she continued. "I was here when the messenger came in shouting that the king was ill. Dmitros pulled in Kim's patrol, being closest, and the cathedral has a phone. They were to fetch Milo and get him to the hospital while Kim was still busy at the cathedral school. Dmitros stuck me on the phones here while he went to locate Alec, until Ilya got back. As soon as he arrived I raced over to the cathedral for Kim—but I'd just missed her. Picked up by Sig! But that wasn't our arrangement. Someone else must have given him orders, except where would he take her, if not here, or to the palace? Do *you* know what's going on?"

"I'm not quite sure why, yet, but think there's a good chance they're headed for the nearest portal, off the road to the cemetery."

She scowled, then muttered, "To hell with waiting for orders. Let's go get her."

She whirled and we ran to her Maserati, parked some paces away, the wheels half-covered in running water.

Sig had taught her to drive not just fast, but in hazardous conditions. The Maserati was too low and heavy to be flipped by the wind, but even so she had a tough time with it as the water ran nearly over the tops of the wheels.

"People converging ahead," I said, partly to distract her and partly to inform.

"People? What people?"

"Identity unknown. I…sense their heartbeats. But this is the busiest part of the city, and their spiked heartbeats could be just the storm."

"If their hearts are thundering anything like mine, I'm surprised they aren't hearing it in Praga," Phaedra retorted. And then, with an angry look, "Does that get your fangs dripping?"

"They don't drip."

"Drooling, then."

"They don't drool. But if you're asking without asking if I'm so excited that I'm about to sink my teeth into you, no. I'm not…hungry. But even if I were, I wouldn't."

"Oh?"

Though most of my attention was focused ahead, as I tried to identify two adrenaline-heightened people moving toward the portal out of the swarm around us, I suspected she was poised to take her anger and frustration out on me. Still concentrating before me, I said, "I remember when you used to crave cinnamon petitsa. Do you knock people right and left to gorge on an entire baker's worth when you smell it?"

"I'm…I still trying to get used to you. The new you," Phaedra muttered. "Not that the old you wasn't really annoying, because you were. Everything was always so perfect for you, but you whined anyway. Danilov and I and some of the staff used to watch your television when you were off in Paris or Switzerland, because Tante Sisi had made it clear that though we were family, as second cousins we were not to expect the privileges of the *first* family."

"And her expectations. Don't forget those."

"I would have argued about that. I did. A lot, actually. Before Percy told us that you were locked up in the Sky Tower."

"That was Tony, actually — his way of looking out for me, while also stashing me for her. So he was free to run his parallel plot. Did you ever watch *Buffy*?"

A massive slam of wind rocked the low-slung car. "The vampire slayer one?" She let out a crack of laughter as she wrestled the car back in line. "Of course we did."

"Really? I can't imagine Danilov having much patience for the silly fights. Even I could see that. I remember Tony watched about ten minutes of it, scoffed, and never looked again."

"That's because he didn't have an intense crush on Spike." Phaedra chuckled.

"Right. Spike. Just Danilov's type."

"We watched everything you had, when the weather was too rotten to go out. This would have been a fine night, for example. What brought that to mind? You can't be thinking that some blond vigilante is going to stake you."

"You thought my life was perfect, whereas I thought you were the perfect model for Buffy — blond, a natural athlete, and no boy ever gave you trouble. You used to shoot stakes at a target with a crossbow!"

"And I never got to stake a single bloodsucker. Until last

year, I'd only ever seen one outside of the Night of the Thorn, when Tony let me watch. Not that I saw much." Phaedra snorted. "As for that show, we all thought you were a blond Cordelia."

"I guess that's fair. Though I identified with Willow. Until they gave her the television equivalent of Vrajhus."

Phaedra barked another laugh. "You could be Buffy now. A badass." She used the English word. "Except you're a vampire. A bit of a twist, eh?"

"I'm also a slayer," I said, testing the word. The idea.

"I saw that. At the mines."

"I mean vampires. I recently took down four of Maritza's rabble. I hope the last of them."

Phaedra grunted approval, then tapped the brakes as the road dipped, and we plunged into a stream. And began to hydroplane. "Hang on!"

She maneuvered us out of it, then came the turn down the ridge road. "That should be the last of the surprise rivers. Killing the evil bloodsuckers, are you? I like that idea. A lot, actually. We'll have to invent a new term for you — what's that?"

Headlights from what seemed to be a thousand vehicles crisscrossed the bottom of the ridge, appearing and disappearing among the wildly bending trees as they raced in arcs, to encircle two human figures, one dragging the other toward the slab of slanted rock in which the portal lay.

As Phaedra expertly slid the Maserati to a stop so that its beams caught the two figures straight on, I banged the door open and leaped out — then stilled.

In the middle of the rain turned to crystal by crossing beams, Sig now stood motionless with his arms around Kim, who squirmed and struggled. Distracted, I noted she had one bare foot, caked with road mud.

I am fast, but I could not shift speed around all those Vigilzhi wearing charms. In normal circumstances, the charms are painful to endure, but at speed it would be like running straight into a firebomb of sun poison.

I'd just barely had time to distinguish this in when, over the roar of the rain, I heard the clack of weaponry chambering rounds. In the fractured light, I registered all three vehicles — an ancient truck, another somewhat converted jeep from the 1950s, and a dilapidated Soviet Emka. From each had piled out Vigilzhi, their uniforms now sodden and black in the torrent, weapons gripped in hands.

"No," Kim yelled, her voice high and thin—barely heard. "Don't shoot."

"Stay still, princess. We won't—" one shouted.

At that moment, with a roar and a spray of flying mud that hit the half-circle of Vigilzhi side on, Tony appeared on his borrowed motorcycle, sliding it expertly into a stop. He leaped off, unslinging the rifle that he'd strapped over his shoulder in one movement. Taking a bead on the highest ranking of the Vigilzhi, he shouted, "Shoot Sig and I'll hunt every one of you down."

This time Kim screeched. *"Nobody shoot anybody!"*

Everyone stilled except for the driving rain and the wind tearing at clothes and hair. I could probably dodge the charms and disarm two or three at speed before one of the others could fire on me, exposed by the high beams. Maybe it would even be Tony.

Phaedra seemed unsure whether to tackle Sig—in which case she'd have to go through Kim, tightly locked in his arms, her own arms pinioned to her sides. This seemed one of those typically Dobreni situations that teetered between farce and tragedy. Or were all dramas such, especially when both sides knew one another, had shared bread together, maybe more?

The growl of another engine caused every head to swerve back toward the road—except for Sig, I noted. His face was a rain-washed mask, his eyes pits as he stared into nothingness.

Then a palace car stopped, bumper nudging the flung-down motorcycle, and four doors slammed open: Dmitros Trasyemova, Ilya, Alec—and a wrath-thin figure with a long, pale face. Tania Waleska?

"We can get him," someone said to Alec.

"NO!" Kim cried. "Tania! Can you break the hold on Sig?"

The Vigilzhi barked questions at one another—"What did she say?" "Isn't *he* holding *her?*"— which everyone else ignored, as Tania ran out into the lit circle, then halted, something in her hands. My skin crawled, and my sight bleared at the edges: charmed crystal.

Tania murmured softly, cadenced words that sounded rather like Latin—a wink of blue light and suddenly Sig's arms flung out to either side. His face suffused with horror, and he dropped to his knees, covering his face with his hands.

"It's okay, Sig," Kim said loudly, glaring side-eye in every direction. "I know *it wasn't your fault.*" Her draggled appearance, braid drooping over one shoulder, and one foot bare, added strongly to the farce, especially as everyone began moving then, shedding tension by shouting at one another, converging around the resistless Sig, then dropping back as Kim glared at the weapons still in hand.

Her face eased when she saw Alec. This time it was she flinging her arms around him. "Tell them not to hurt Sig. It wasn't *him!*"

Farce and yet not. It was so typical of Kim. Exasperatingly so. Perfectly in line with her insistence on trudging through a schoolgirl manuscript that no doubt would be forgotten within a year, including by its author. Or encouraging the endless blather of a newly vampiric goth look-at-me as we trudged the streets of Los Angeles.

A new thought hovered at the edge of consciousness, but this wasn't the time. A few startled looks slanted my way, but they were all too busy shouting questions and snatches of "...feast down the hill to Zorfal..." and "The captain said..." and "How is the king?" to register the inimasang among them.

Why invite trouble? Kim was clearly safe. As for questions, my own would have to wait until she shed the entourage.

I stepped back, well out of the range of the headlights, back again, drew shadows about me, and then withdrew, racing against the wind to von Mecklundburg House.

I found that my things had been duly lugged back up to my room—a silent reminder to Maman who had the authority here—though left in packing boxes.

As I approached, intending to change out of my dripping, squeaking silks, I saw a piece of paper laid beside an open box of desk detritus. I recognized my pens and stationery, and a fistful of year-old invitations. On the back of one had been written in fraktur, "Paris."

Fraktur was the handwriting of our grandparents' day.

That had to be from Rose.

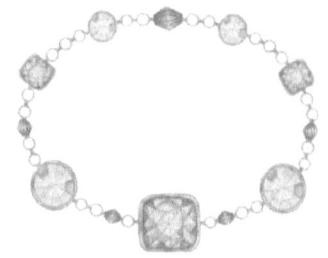

THIRTY-ONE

KIM

Suddenly I was shivering. Or maybe I had been, but only noticed it when I finally let go of Alec. Wow, two bear hugs in an hour, I thought with a weird thrill of hilarity that was probably closer to panic. Except Sig's had been sudden and unwanted, as if I were a bundle of slats of wood, engulfing me with the sharp smell of male adrenaline sweat.

Alec smelled like Alec—like safety, and enticement, as he put his arms around me far more gently than my instinctive, manic grip that had probably cut off his circulation. I began to decompress a little as he murmured, "If you can point out where it is, I'll send the boys to blow that bloody portal to hell. Preferably taking out whoever was lurking in it."

"I can't see anything. Not sure I could even if I tried looking into my prism—which I can't hold because my hands are numb."

"Then I'll get Ruli to—hullo, she's gone. Maybe just as well. Let's get you out of this rain and into the car."

I gave up on the portal—we had too many other worries. "Was that true, what Sig said, about Milo?"

"He was in the middle of yet another round of arguments from the typesetters when he said he felt dizzy. Short of breath. Then he admitted he'd been sleeping badly. Bad dreams."

Worry wormed its way through me. "Oh, not good. Not good."

"You think it was the demons?" He bent his head to look

anxiously into my face.

"Let's get home first."

He accepted that, and as we trod the last few glutinous steps, he began issuing orders. Sig was to go to the Vigilzhi HQ — and Tony stated shortly that he was going with him.

Someone else drove Sig's jeep, from which I retrieved Sting. Tony followed closely on Dad's motorcycle, bought just this spring, and in a long line we fought the wild, just-above-freezing storm back up the narrow road.

I sat in the back, squished between Alec and Tania. As he watched grimly through the windshield and behind, I turned to Tania. "How did you break their hold on him?"

"I could see the ribbon, your highness," Tania replied softly. "I was able to cut it because he was trying to escape it from his side."

Tania, I think I've said, was way ahead of me in our prism studies. Not just because she had more time, but her talent was beyond my reach; I still struggled to even perceive how interrelated refraction and resonance in crystals are. I'd even dug out my old college science texts, which my dad had shipped over earlier in spring, to read up on the matter. I could cite chapter and verse on how refraction is the bending of light as it passes through a medium, while resonance is the vibration of the crystal's structure when exposed to light of specific frequencies. The thing I struggled to get was how these two phenomena interacted to make a focus point for Vrajhus...energy.

It didn't help that even Tania had difficulty expressing in her home language what she perceived — and how.

Salfmatta Sarolta, I knew, had adapted a metaphor that Tania could use for her weird gift for perceiving...connections, call it, between people. Which included the occasional ghost. These latter even talked to her, or rather, talked at her. She'd reported that they seldom said anything useful. More like whatever had been in their minds before they died. Or else something they'd obsessed about, which had become so central to their lives that it persisted beyond.

"You've got to teach me to see those ribbons. Yesterday," I said, and to Alec, "*Thank* you for bringing her. That was the best idea ever."

Alec said somewhat bemusedly, "I wasn't going to, but she insisted. Kim, why did you get in that car with him? We had our plan — if Phaedra was gone, you were to wait." His tone wasn't accusing, which I have to admit would have set me off. He was worried.

And wow, did he have cause, but my ignoring the plan and getting into that jeep was only a side issue.

To ease his stress at least a bit, I kept my own tone calm. "He said Milo was on the way to the hospital with Phaedra. At that point, I figured Milo's needs would supersede mine. And none of us expected someone we knew to be demon-driven. Our plans were for resisting goons. Not a helpful ride offer from someone we know and trust."

"Right." Alec pressed the heel of his hand to his right eye.

I went on, giving him a chance to sort what had to be two wildly different worry lines, "And he was really nice. The entire time. Until I asked him to let me out. He agreed, but kept driving. It creeped me out a little, then a lot when he told me that Magda wanted to be a baroness, and the angels were going to help me and everybody. He'd gone from genuinely worried about Milo into the Bozo Zone."

"What?" Alec dropped his hand. "If Sig Sigismund ever harbored a secret hankering to get back a title from generations ago, I'd be very surprised."

I said, "I noticed that this was all for Magda, not really his wish."

"But if *she* ever had any lust for titles, she grew up among half a dozen single boys with genuine titles, free for the taking."

"I've never met her," I said, "but I'm willing to bet anything that the demons got at Sig through emotions. Love. Which doesn't have to be logical."

At that moment, we pulled up at Vigilzhi HQ.

"We're coming back to that," Alec promised grimly. "I've got to settle Sig first. Want to wait? No, you'd better come."

"Right," I said. "I'll also bet you anything they're gonna want to hang Sig out to dry for princess-napping. Because that's easier to deal with than the thought of some demon that might invade *their* dreams."

He smiled thinly. "I don't think I'd put it that way quite yet. Remember, there are only a few of us aware of the demon threat. This is not something we want a general panic about if we can help it."

I understood that. So far, the threat had been specifically mine. Or rather, the threat was against whoever had access to the necklace. If that was changing to a city-wide threat, he'd get the newspapers to print the facts that they knew—and a solution, or at least a defense.

Tania elected to stay, sitting there in the back seat absorbed in her crystal. Alec and I dashed inside, though we were soaked to the skin. The moment Alec spotted Dmitros Trasyemova, he said, "Milo?"

"Insisted on his own bed. And that he's fine. The physicians are present. The Queen sent the Queen's Companion to us." This was half a question.

Alec threw a glance my way, and I murmured, "Before you left to find us, I bet Tania asked Gran to send Salfmatta Mina, since this is a Vrajhus matter."

"We'll listen to whatever she has to say," Alec stated — it was an order. He turned his attention to the others. "Sig Sigismund is the victim of a Vrajhus attack. We're going to have to develop a strategy for dealing with it, but right now, I want him protected, not incarcerated."

They turned to stare at Sig, who sat in a chair, water dripping off him to pool on the floor. His head drooped, his big, strong hands loose — he looked the picture of misery.

Alec yanked a chair up next to him and sat. "Sig, what can you tell us?"

"I don't know anything, Durchlaucht. That is, I don't remember a lot..."

What followed was painful for everyone as he gave a disjointed account of days of bad dreams. Sometimes nightmares, except when the angel came and made the nightmares go away. Which he'd told no one, because manly men have to man up, not whine about a week or two of sleeplessness and weird dreams. Those weren't his words, but that was the gist.

He remembered everything clearly up to the time he offered to get me, and then he said that the next thing he really remembered was... He reddened to the ears, turning a thoroughly hang-dog look my way, then mumbled, "Holding the princess. I don't know how she got, ah, in my — why I was holding her. I don't!"

The Vigilzhi began a storm of questions, reactions, some scoffing. Only Phaedra remained silent, but I could see how very angry she was at having been blindsided.

Tony leaned against the wall, arms crossed, one hand still clutching his rifle, his long hair hanging all over like wet string. He watched narrowly, but didn't speak as Alec calmly fielded all the accusations about kidnapping, laws, and so forth.

The whole scene was depressing, as the true villains were

out of reach. All we were left with was the detritus of a close call, and a lot of justifiably angry and rattled people.

Then came fresh arrivals, two immaculately clad palace servants, one holding an umbrella over white-haired, diminutive Tante Mina.

She bowed quaintly to Alec, then to me, giving me a quick and tremulous smile. Then she said to me, "Your young secretary is a treasure."

I couldn't help gloating a bit at how this tiny, frail figure dominated all those beefy guys without making the slightest effort. Maybe it could only happen in this country. But not a one made a peep when she bowed again to Alec, and turned to Tony. She peered up at him—he was at least a foot and a half taller—and said, "With his highness's permission, your grace, I think you ought to take this young man to Dorike. To my house. The one with the old rose trees. The demons will not find him there, as you get a protection made for him. I doubt they will, but it's as well to be cautious." And to let the poor guy recover, I thought to myself.

Then she turned to sweep the Vigilzhi with her kindly, grave gaze. "You must all wear your charms waking and sleeping. It is not enough to have them in the windows and doorways. The demons cannot find you in the realm of dreams if you keep your charms touching you."

A few little signs of skepticism met this, but mostly it was relief. And no one argued, after Alec said, "We'll make it an order.".

There followed some logistical and bureaucratic nidgetry that I paid scant heed to, then we left.

When we got into the car to be driven to the palace— Phaedra glaring in all directions as though willing an attacker to put a toe out—Alec leaned across me to address Tania, "How did you know the demons were interfering?"

"I saw the ribbon," Tania explained. "When the steward reported that the princess had vanished, I found her, tied to another ribbon that was controlled from the unseen realm." She glanced briefly at Alec, then explained further, "Some see strings between people, or overlapping auras. I see ribbons. I have learned only this summer how to cut them. It can bring someone out of the grip of the dream world."

"It sure worked on Sig," I said. "He was like a robot at the end, when the guys surrounded us and he couldn't drag me to the portal. Then, bang! He seemed to realize he was choking me half to death in his grip and he couldn't let go fast enough. That had to be when Tania broke the demons' hold on him. He was so horrified that it was funny! Well, almost funny."

Alec did not comment on my 'humor'. "Kim, whatever you're paying Tania is not enough. Double it."

"Noted," I said, and laughed at how Tania blushed.

We were silent for the remainder of the drive (about three minutes max), but once we'd all gone to our rooms to change into dry clothes, we met again in our parlor, where hot food and drink soon came in, wafting delicious smells. Alec gestured for Tania to join us.

He was silent for a time. I'd been organizing my thoughts. When he began, it was easy enough, "We appear to have been too narrow in our expectation that if an attempt on you came it would be similar to what we dealt with in Vienna and Los Angeles."

"And was coming for us in Paris," I added.

"Right. But this is a very different, and far more insidious strategy."

He's coming around. But fighting it. I said, "I don't think it was real ambition that they distorted in Sig. I think the demons put the idea into his head about recovering his ancestral title, but they got to him by insinuating that this would benefit his fiancée. His motivation is love, more than a wish to retrieve a moldering castle and a wig, or whatever makes a baron. Which I find ten times sleazier than turning him into a raving fiend. They twisted his good feelings, and convinced him they are angels, and I bet they were just gorgeous in his dreams. How do we fight that?"

Tania nodded soberly.

"What disturbs me most? They attacked Milo just to provide a deflection so Sig could put the grab on me. But if it's true that charms can ward a further attack, at least that's one thing less to worry about." I added this last to east a little of the stress around Alec's eyes. It worked. A little.

"Salfmatta Mina will ensure his safety," Tania said with quiet conviction. "The king will now be invisible to them in the dream realm."

Okay, back to laying a logic trail toward what I had to do.

"But I'm not. Not anymore," I said to her.

"They now know your ribbon, or aura," Tania said. "The charms help to diffuse physical location, or so I am assured. But they have expended much effort to find you. The duke's steward should be safe now — he is no more use to them."

"This is what I hate," I said, taking another mental step toward that path. The one Alec was going to resist with everything he had. "They can mess with a guy like Sig to the point of nearly getting him blown away. I could see those guys with the rifles were not kidding. They were going to shoot him as soon as they had a clear shot. But to the demons he's just a handy thing to be used and forgotten."

Alec nodded soberly.

"And even though he didn't get shot, this will be a nightmare for him for the rest of his life. I hope his lady friend doesn't dump him over it."

Alec's smile flickered briefly. "Not Magda. She's…a lot like Natalie Miller. Practical, is what I mean. Knows what she wants. And what Magda wants is Sig. Far more likely she'd guffaw at the idea that anyone would think she'd want to be a baroness, when what she prides herself on most, besides her seven-layer hazelnut cake, is her chicken yard. She's insisted the secret for her family's superlative pastries is what they feed their hens."

"I'd like to meet her," I said.

"You will like her."

This was a new voice — we all jumped like crows on a phone wire as Ruli emerged from the shadows beyond the door. "And she'll like you." Then she crossed her arms. "Why are you looking at me like that? You left all the doors to this wing wide open."

"You're going to have to learn to clomp louder. Or, at all," I said, looking down at her fancy high heels. I don't know anything about fancy shoes — I'm the type who buys one pair of sandals, wears them until the soles are gone, then picks another pair just like the last. But I have to say, her shoes always look like what you'd wear to Buckingham Palace to attend a coronation. She always wears them with crackerjack style, never a wobble or a stork-walk. "And considering those heels, it's doubly amazing that you're as silent as a cat."

She gave me a thin smile, and perched elegantly on the edge of a table so that she could see the three of us.

"We're reassessing demon strategy," I said. "This is what scares me, that it could be anyone next. Anyone who doesn't wear charms. It could have been those kids I felt perfectly safe with earlier today. I hate that the demons attacked Milo just to get Sig in place."

Alec's expression had cooled to the remote one, and I knew that he was beginning to suspect what was next. Maybe I was a little too obvious — whenever anyone starts assuring everybody else of what they knew perfectly well, it's a good idea to be bracing for what's coming. Sure to be a stinker.

"You can't," he said to me, low, but definite.

Yeah. He knew.

"I think I have to," I replied.

And there it was, the silence of...I was going to say doom, but it hurt too much to joke even inside my head. It was the silence of total impasse.

And both of us were right.

THIRTY-TWO

RULI

The two of them locked gazes. Tania, I noticed, looked from Kim to Alec, her shoulders tight with stress, reflected in her elevated heartbeat.

Alec finally said, "Give me a plan that brings you back alive and unharmed, and I'll step out of the way. Can you honestly do that?"

"We all want a solution," I interposed, mostly to break the deadlock. "But expecting omniscience seems unreasonable."

Alec lamped me with that icy look he'd perfected when he was about twelve, and which I'd loathed because I was too young to see it as the defense it was. Tony striking out with his fists was easier to understand.

Then Alec spoke. "If you don't have anything useful to say, sod off."

"I have very useful things to say," I retorted. "Beginning with a reminder that I can do a little research in areas Kim cannot go."

Alec turned on me. "Why?" Then added, "I saw you there with Phaedra earlier. It almost looked like a handoff."

Sig was to hand Kim off to me? I guess I could see how it might have looked that way, especially if you didn't know about the vampires waiting just out of sight in the portal. I began to utter a protest.

He raised his hand, palm out. "I know you weren't. Because you vanished again. Suspicion, justified or not, is always going to come first because I don't understand who you are anymore. Your motivation."

English has blurred the difference between *you* the individual and the plural *you*, as in all inimasang.

"Who *are* you?" he asked, barely audible.

So, me as individual.

I was the now focus of his stress, a target he could at least see. I found it interesting, how clearly I understood that now, whereas all my life my perceptions had been murky, at best. Clouded partly by what I'd been taught conflicting with what I saw. I'd learned to blame myself for failing to comprehend the discrepancies.

It was also an interesting experiment, to test my own evolving sense of self against the perceptions of people I knew.

I said, "My understanding is that we become a hybrid, partly human and partly another life form. Some of us strive to keep our humanity intact. Some even go to strenuous effort to live like humans, and to walk among them. Get night jobs, even, to stay in human circles. There are those, I'm told, who get day jobs that might require them to endure a little sun, if it's indirect. But the cost is commensurate. Sunlight is poison."

Alec said, "I'm less interested in questions of identity than intention. Legally, you're dead. Circumstances — and Jerzy von Mecklundburg — contrived your replacement by Kim. You've been done out of everything you had, but you survived, in this form, which renders you a free agent. No obligations to anyone that I can see."

I wasn't completely free — not yet. Last spring I'd begun arranging ways to separate off my bank accounts from the family affairs, knowing that Maman would consider it her right to annex them. Probably intended to this winter, as she'd have to do it in person. But right now that was entirely irrelevant.

"I know what you want," I said. "Assurance that I'm not going to double-cross Kim in this matter with the demons. All you have is my word that I do not intend to."

"*I* believe you," Kim said promptly. "If you were going to pull a fast one, vamp-style, you had a zillion chances before this."

Alec considered that, then said, "I'll do anything to support an actual plan that has a hope of success. But I can't agree with Kim's going up against them alone."

Kim said fervently, "And I don't want to go up against them alone. All I'm saying is, I need to find a way to push back hard enough so that they go away. The necklace already protects me in ways we hadn't known about. I need to learn more. So I was thinking, my first step is to squeeze the Elders for every scrap they know, or think they know."

"I can't help with that," I said. "I feel very certain they would not speak to me but warily. However…there are other avenues of exploration."

Alec's expression eased a trifle, and Kim sent me a grateful look. I could see the sharp conflict between her habit of resolving matters her own way and whatever promises she had made when marrying him. That, I reminded myself, was a part of relationships. Maybe I was well out of any possibility of romance, for I no longer wanted to be answerable to anyone.

A palace page entered with a message that the queen desired an interview as soon as the princess had changed and was at liberty.

"Gran!" Kim jumped up. "She must have been out of her mind with worry about both Milo and me…"

I had come with the purpose of telling her about Rose's mysterious note, but decided that it could wait. It wasn't at all informative, after all. My 'avenues of exploration' would have to suffice.

Tania retired as Alec and Kim went off to call on Kim's grandmother. I retrieved my rain cloak from where I'd left it, considering how fastest to get to Paris — while avoiding portals. That much, I'd inferred from Rose's note.

Reaching Paris is easy enough if daylight isn't a problem. It's roughly a little over thirty-six of driving on good roads — which is a daunting prospect for anyone.

The first challenge is simply getting "off the mountain" — which is Dobreni shorthand for getting to civilization below our circle of mountains. There are several train stations, which in previous generations had been coaching inns. I don't like driving, but I can do it. The family had acquired some terrible old vehicles left behind when the Soviets vacated, repaired one by one with parts cannibalized from the wrecks that would never run again. I took one of these, having left word for my brother that I was doing so, and which station I intended to leave it at.

I had to find a place to hide for the day. At least October

brings shorter days. Once the sun was gone, I pieced together a train route, reaching Paris early the next morning.

My room was waiting in the Marais. No one except nosy Lya asked where I'd been. She wanted to know where the princess was and what she was doing. I disposed of that as briefly as possible, and retired.

The next evening, while I took the opportunity to bathe and dress, I contemplated where I was likely to find Rose.

During her short lifetime she had never actually been to Paris. I knew that she was drawn to the Nasdrafus's Paris from a century previous. Paris is always evolving and yet manages to retain its insouciantly charming distinctiveness. But she didn't like modernity—she found all the angular steel and plastic of modern architecture ugly. Which arrondissements would most evoke the atmosphere she liked best?

I decided to look for her in Montmartre, which retains traces of the golden days of the impressionist painters and their generation. Places like Le Rat Mort and so forth have largely become banks or suchlike in modern times, but a few of the old bistros still survive, and these I would try first, because Rose would never be anywhere alone if she could help it.

I spotted her gracefully framed in the window of the fifth bistro, a rundown place sporting only a weathered signboard of a blue fox. I knew within a step inside that it was full of vampires, with a few tipsy tourists near the leaded glass windows at the front. All oblivious to the dim wooden booths and alcoves beyond the tangle of potted pothos, from which no heartbeat was heard.

Rose sat at a tiny table next to the window, head bent toward a very tall, suave vampire dressed in charcoal gray slacks and an elegant black coat that only revealed a hint of white shirt sleeve at the wrists and neck. His features reminded me a little of the brother of a Persian friend I'd had at boarding school.

His appeared to be maybe eighteen or twenty, but the subtleties of his eye expressions were those of experience—a trait not uncommon among vampires. Framed in the leaded glass window, he and Rose had appeared a very elegant pair with a taste for vintage fashions.

His narrow gaze lifted toward me before Rose gestured prettily to a passing waiter, holding up three fingers. "And here she is. My dear, I was just wondering to Gervais here when we might see you." A winsome smile, then, "Have they caught up with your girl yet?"

"Your girl" undoubtedly meant Kim. The "they" had to be the demons. Her lack of interest was so obvious I did not trouble to answer, but decided on a riposte. "You've been paying court to them. Worth it?"

She turned to her companion. "Would you like to share your theory, my dear?"

The waiter returned with three tall, slim vessels of porcelain on a tray. From the heady, delectable smell they contained plasma, warmed to body temperature, and delivered in fine porcelain with narrow necks so there was little chance of drip or even sound. It came with different spices, for those with arcane tastes; ours had a savor of coffee, but a table away I smelled the tang of tobacco, and from farther away, apricot brandy.

"How much do you wish to hear?" Gervais asked.

"Everything," I said. "Beginning with this: have you met the demons currently presenting themselves as seraphim?"

"I have not met them, but I've observed them," Gervais said.

"No, no," Rose pouted. "Begin at the beginning."

"Which is?" He regarded her with an affectionate smile.

"You, of course."

"Me?" He gave a slight shrug, turning to me. "What do you wish to know?"

"Your background to begin with, perhaps?"

He complied with a courteous air. "I was born in the south, near Lyon, of a canut family. We'd been silk weavers for generations, but never quite made it to merchant status. I wanted badly to go to university, but there was no money. I had to work—we all did. The pay was abysmal, the hours long. I was part of a unsuccessful political uprising now all but forgotten. We were cornered, and starving, but we knew it was either death or Devil's Island for us. Then our leader made a pact with a third party, and we woke from hungry sleep like this." He turned out his hands. "The idea was to turn us into an army, but about half of us died within a short time, and the rest, having lost forever family, friends, lovers, dispersed. The lust for political reform had died with those connections. Me? I developed an interest in banking."

"Ah," I exclaimed.

"But my passion for knowledge never died. That is likely more than you wished to hear, so I will pass directly to my theory, at Rose's request. Beginning with the notion that in our world, life and death are part of a cycle," Gervais said, and paused, an inquisitive expression lifting his brows.

"The cycle of life and death," I repeated. "No argument so far. And so?"

"Humanity perhaps has off-balanced it with its numbers, as once the dinosaurs did. But humans are also very effective at thinning that number with its wars and plagues. My theory is that this past century's wars, pogroms, and the like were so effective they surrounded this world with an aura of death that attracted those who feed on the process of death."

"The demons," I said. "But the ones Kim met were around at the time of the French Revolution. Are you saying there are more of them?"

"So many more."

"'Demon' is so convenient a word it almost has no meaning. We're demons to many. So are ghosts. I know these particular ones feast on the dying. Are they akin to vampires?"

"Of a sort, except they were never human. Or alive, in the sense we mean."

"Are they a virus?"

"That I cannot say. The only thing I am sure of is that they are drawn to the worst in us, for they are creatures of chaos."

Still not really useful. I said, "At present my concern is their desire to control the door between the unseen world and the physical world."

"Even the word 'desire' might be misleading, with its human connotations," Gervais said mildly, as if this were a classroom discussion. "Their method of communication is here." He tapped his forehead. "As would be expected of entities with vaporous physical presence."

"Ah," I said. "The appearance of smoke. Their hair, their clothes, even those wings."

"Vapor," Gervais said. "Of a kind. They manifest in…what did you term the Unseen World, dear Rose?"

"Nasdrafus."

"A curious word. I would love to explore its semantic origins at another time. Nasdrafus. "They have to be sustained enormously by the chaos of death to cross to the physical world."

I remembered what Kim had said about them in Paris, clustered around Napoleon, whose chief desire was to outdo Alexander the Great. Who, in his short life, had excelled primarily at conquering. The demons had also clustered around Fouché, who preyed on hapless citizens by using whatever law was convenient. Between Napoleon and Fouché they had killed enough people to strengthen the demons so that they could fly through the physical world from battlefield to battlefield. "How do we get rid of them?"

"That, I wish I knew. Truly. One must be cautious, exploring in the Nasdrafus, for as you probably know, to expend curiosity is to risk creating a bond. And they are aware."

In the Nasdrafus, you thought about where and when you wanted to be. Whom you wished to meet. Mental energy was the stuff of the Nasdrafus, and to think vigorously about anything was to possibly connect to it. If the demons communicated mentally, and they actively listened in that way for anyone curious about them...

There was a little stir behind us.

Gervais laughed, dropped money on the table, and revealed his century-old origins in spite of his contemporary clothing by bowing to us both. "I came to meet one of my investors, and he waits. I do not wish to be rude when I am expected. I trust we shall met again." He went away to his group.

Rose and I left. "How did you meet him?"

"A poet I'm fond of debated him. He turned out to be knowledgeable in so many directions. Did you not find him informative?"

"Yes. And yet. It's a circle of frustration," I said as we walked downhill. "The only place safe to discuss the demons is here in the physical world, but humans don't know about them. They are known in the Nasdrafus, but to avoid them, one cannot think too much about them."

"And yet, here you persevere," Rose interjected with her winsome smile. "One foot firmly in the physical world. Most elegantly shod, I must add. You look better every time I see you."

"Tell me more about Gervais."

"Ah! You admire him? Excellent taste, dear. As I'd expect from a descendant of mine. He returns every ten years or so to tend to his affairs here in Paris, then he goes back to the Nasdrafus to study at the Sorbonne, and other such places. He loves those who gather there to debate the issues of their day. He mentioned the demons in a discussion of other forms of existence, and I immediately thought of you." She glanced over the rooftops as we started down a narrow alley I never would have ventured into at night when I was human. "Speaking of descendants. I confess myself a little surprised that the demons are not using Sisi."

"Since they apparently aren't human I don't want to try attributing motivations to them, but surely if they know anything of the interrelations of the Five Families, they'd be aware that Milo would love an excuse to escort her to the border."

"Mmm, he dares not, unless she outright breaks a law. I expect that that would cause more trouble than it's worth if he tried, as she does have her adherents. Half those old Romeos on the Council still hope she'll pick one of them and make him a duchess's consort." Rose laughed. "But the demons seem to want someone rather more forthright."

"Violent, you mean? Maman isn't violent. She does relish a battle of wits, and she will cheat, because that's just tactics."

"The emotional defense?" Rose asked, exchanging an elusive smile with a staring man passing us on the street. His heartrate leaped, but some instinct must have warned him off — or else he was raised right, for he passed on by after only a muttered *Bon soir*. "In our day, that's all women had."

I went on, "I won't defend anything Maman's done. But I will observe that she truly believes that she deserves the crown."

Rose said, "I know. Especially during the terrible decades after the war, when the Soviets replaced the Germans, as she grew up. Her mother was dead — so everyone believed. As did she. Her first husband died. The obvious solution, to her, was to marry Milo in order to retrieve her birthright. She was too young to be aware, but we had all seen how Milo raced across war-torn Europe in hopes my sister was still alive. Of course he refused to marry, until pressured — and then he made a political marriage, not even for love. How she hates him!"

"You say you watch over the family. You watched all this happen, but you never helped her."

"What could I have done? I would have liked to warn her, but she was so stubborn, and so *relentlessly* ambitious. I knew she would never listen. Also: there was the matter of my present state. She made her loathing quite plain. I even heard her telling Tony that if he just carefully placed his best sharpshooters on the Night of the Thorn, the problem would be solved forever."

"She had no idea what would have resulted," I said, and, reminded, turned the subject. "Elena dropped a hint that you're a…an observer among the demons. You could have told me, rather than pushing me to fling Kim to them as bait."

Rose lifted a shoulder. "But your thoughts would have betrayed you, darling, surely you see that! Come! Do not pout. So unattractive! How are things in Riev? When I was there, I overheard something or other about Milo collapsing. Isn't it about time for that righteous old bore to die?"

"Righteous old bore?" I repeated. I didn't pretend to know Milo, but he'd always been unfailingly courteous to us when we were small.

She didn't want me to pout but she was putting on a very fine pout herself. "I quite understand Sisi's determination to marry him. Father wanted me to marry him instead of Armandros after Lily ran off. Can you imagine the life I would have led?"

"To my understanding no one had a good life during World War II," I commented.

"So true, so very true." She gave a reminiscent little laugh. "But I confess it was rather exciting, once we discovered the Germans' odd government, to keep those Gestapo boys docile. So many of them fainting on the job, and no reason why!" She touched her fingers to her lips. "And all the extra shadows. They couldn't leave fast enough when their orders came from Berlin. I did show you how to hide the bite marks, did I not?"

"You did."

"Bon! You see, I always look out for the family. Now, introduce me to your new friends. For I noticed that you do not frequent Sisi's pied-à-terre."

The mortes-vivantes loved her, of course. Especially Lya, who was entranced to meet a actual born princess, one her own age. I wondered if next time I arrived, Lya would have swapped the goth look for vintage.

But leave I did, and without telling Rose, who was too much like a butterfly. So pretty, and charming, and sometimes when least expected showed a semblance of care, but I didn't trust her.

THIRTY-THREE

KIM

While I waited for Tania to contact Grandmother Ziglieri and any of the other Elders among the Salfmattas and Salfpatras who would meet me, Alec and I chipped at our impasse.

I knew that Alec was as aware as I was that he could speak half a dozen words and have me locked down in Riev. But we also knew that kind of high-handed action would whack our relationship, maybe irreparably. Likewise, I had to squash the lifelong habit of taking off to deal on my own. As I had been doing when we first met.

Because we were no longer twelve, we both knew that trust is easy to break, and really, really, really difficult to repair. If it's even possible. So we talked.

Oh, how we talked.

At least we had the chance to, because as he'd predicted, the Council pressures were easing off. Maybe because the weather was getting colder and rainier and no one on Council wanted to go out in the nasty weather if they didn't have to.

Dobrenica was slowly turning its mind toward the holidays. Those few of us who knew the threat turned our minds to…endless talk.

Three, four, five days passed. Mid-month, Aunt Sisi left for Paris — after being feted by half the nosebleed league. I'm sure that many were genuinely sorry to see her go. The others (like self) waved cheerful farewells. The only one in my own camp who seemed to miss her was Mom.

"She's so peculiar," Mom said over breakfast one morning with Gran and me. She had come over from Ysvorod House, empty with Dad still gone. "Dealing with her is like taming a tiger. And I am quite certain the others appreciate my drawing her fire."

"Even Robert?" I asked, shuddering.

"Oh, Robert is just a big old bear, once you get to know him," Mom said with a quirky smile. Was she actually fond of that guy? Well, come to think of it, he was her cousin to some degree — and she'd never had any relatives but Gran, growing up. "Get him on the subject of opera, which we both adore, and he's quite interesting. Did you know he studied voice at the music school? But his family considered going on stage degrading."

"He's got wandering hands when he's drunk," I said in disgust. Though I knew perfectly well that he'd been hearing a lot of lies about me — and of course I'd helped Tante Sisi along by lying like a rug when I first met the relatives. But!

Gran looked reproachful at this flagrant gossip, but Mom snickered. "He does have an eye for a pretty girl. And who can blame him, married to The Mummy from the Blue Lagoon?"

I tried not to spray tea through my nose, and Gran scolded, "Marie!" And for a moment, it was a lot like mornings in Los Angeles, when I was a teen.

"You know it's true, Maman," Mom said with a mischievous lift of her brows. "But I'm as good as gold when I'm over there. I listen to the gossip. Never spread it. Ah, speaking of mummies, George seems to be dividing his joys between his old bones and crypts and his new boytoy."

It was Gran's turn to sputter.

"Maman," Mom said with a gently chiding air. "I *told* you he bought something new and fast and shiny to race around all those hairpin turns down there."

I hadn't heard this; I'd received one scrawled postcard, with a seriously cool picture of one of the painted rooms recently uncovered at Herculaneum, and I assumed he was having a ball, so I hadn't asked further, what with everything else. I didn't even know if his new "boytoy" was another motorcycle or a racecar. As a kid, he'd done motocross up in the hills behind Malibu when he wasn't frowsting in his room, reading about Ancient Rome or building clocks. But he'd sold his bike and given up the sport when his newspaper went bankrupt and he was forced into retirement.

"Boys," Gran said on a sigh, and that ended breakfast; the church bell ringing in the distance meant she would be off to morning Mass.

Mom flitted off to scour the markets for the last of harvest foods, and I returned to prism resonance practice with Tania, who was ready, even eager, though there were marks of tiredness under her eyes.

"I'm determined to see your ribbons if I can. Sometimes I can al-l-l-l-most get it. I think. But not if you didn't get enough sleep. Are you okay?"

"I am well, thank you your highness."

That title always felt to me like the codfish of correction, to remember my place, that is, not to crowd her by being too pushy.

So we got to work—and as usual I had to fight against my own wayward gifts. It was far too easy to slide into those splinters of the past, and I had to consciously block those. Why couldn't I see what was around me in the here and now with the same ease?

The next day, Tania looked even more tired, the marks under her eyes like smudges of dark paint. As usual, she was dressed neatly, prism in hand, ready to work.

I eyed her uneasily. "Tania, I have never had an assistant before. You know that. So tell me, please, if I'm overstepping. But am I giving you too much to do? I can easily get someone else for the secretary stuff, to free you for Vrajhus studies."

"No!" Her eyes widened, then she blushed. "I like my job. My friends like it for me," she added a little quieter, and I suppressed a grin as I translated that mentally to *I like being known as the princess's assistant.* "Besides," she added candidly. "If I were to stop, no matter what I said, there are those who would think I had failed. Especially as I do not talk about matters of Vrajhus."

"Okay. But really, I can get someone else in for the princessy schedule stuff so you don't have to push yourself."

She thanked me gravely, insisted it was no trouble, and bent over her prism, making it clear the subject—for her—was over.

Two days later, she was still looking tired, but she said in her usual soft voice, "Salfmatta Sarolta summons us."

This meant a steep drive up old trails to the little house on the slope above Riev, hidden behind a daunting wall of hawthorn and holly, and backed by linden trees.

Here we met with Beka's tiny Great-Aunt Sarolta, a nun named Sister Franciscka, Grandmother Ziglieri, and a couple of other important elders.

And despite all this wealth of wisdom and experience, the meeting was frustrating more than enlightening. What had I expected? None of them had ever even seen the necklace protection. There was scarcely anything written down that had survived the nineteenth and especially the twentieth centuries. They told me all about the history of Navaratna necklaces, but about 90% of that I could have dug up from an Internet search elsewhere.

They did have a piece of advice: I needed to learn from the necklace itself.

I thanked everyone, for it was no small thing to bring Grandmother Ziglieri down the mountain in weather threatening the first snow, or drag a nun out of her retreat. I didn't know where the Salfpatras came from, but they couldn't all be Riev residents.

Learn from the necklace — how? Just more questions than ever. It sure didn't talk to me, and try as I might (both Tania and I had been trying) I couldn't see it in the prism. Did that mean schlepping up to Devil's Mountain in the worst weather of the year? Dead winter was far better, because at least then the sleighs came out, the reindeer came down, and travel wasn't bad as long as you kitted yourself out for deep cold. But near-freezing rain, with patches of ice just beginning, was a recipe for misery.

I rose, saying, "At least the charms keep the demons out of everyone's dreams, right?" I was going to add, *Maybe this is a project for after the holidays, if not next spring* when Grandmother Ziglieri gave Tania a sharp look.

"She does not know?" She fired the question — the demand — at Tania in Dobreni.

Up until then we'd been speaking German, for the sake of the nun, who was actually Romanian, and for one of the Salfpatras whose dialect in his far village was more Russian than the Dobreni spoken in Riev. But the old folk had all had to learn German during their young years.

Tania hung her head.

I looked from one to another. "Wait, wait," I said. "Are you afraid that those demons are going to escalate the attacks through dreams?"

"That is already happening," the eldest of the Salfpatras said.

Grandmother Ziglieri double-teamed by turning to Tania. "You did not tell her." It wasn't a question.

"There is already so very much stress for her," Tania said, with a quick, guilty glance my way. "I—we—have protected…"

I sat back down. "I've never yet given a real princess order, but I guess it's time to start. Tell me what I don't know."

Salfmatta Sarolta said, "You were not aware of the extent to which Tania and her circle have been protecting those around you day and night?"

"Does it happen often?" I asked, appalled. "I thought we spread the word to wear charms."

"But people will take them off to bathe, or to change their clothing. They set them aside to wash their hands, or to cook. They might even take them off in their sleep without knowing."

That was a serious level of attack. I turned to Tania. Her ashen face was half-hidden as she studied her feet.

Salfmatta Sarolta said quietly, "It is common for people to become forgetful, or merely careless, when charms have been so successful that they assume the threat is diminished."

I saw that for the deflection it was, but the fact remained that the attacks were constant, and Tania hadn't told me the extent of it. And here I was, thinking that oh, I'd wait until spring to go search for the necklace, when the slog to that valley between Devil's Mountain and the Dsaret mountain would be pleasant.

I thanked everyone once again, climbed into the cream-colored Pierce-Arrow princessmobile, and rode cocooned in my elaborate protective entourage. Tania sat beside me in silence, her gaze on her thin, tightly clasped hands. I looked at those white knuckles, and considered what to say. Like I said before, never been a boss. Never wanted to be, either—and because of moments like this. I'd been trying to finesse a comfortable way of communication between our two cultures, given our situations, boss and employee.

I'd also never had a sister. Out of the three Waleska sisters, Tania was the most sensitive, the one with the deepest layers; Anna was shy, but her identity was wrapped up in her husband and in the inn that she would inherit one day. Theresa was outgoing and passionate—what you see is what you get. Whereas Tania had spent her childhood regarded as an oddity for her penchant for making friends with cats and rats, not to mention talking to ghosts. Until she discovered that people thought she was lying to be interesting — after all, no one else could see those ghosts — after which she'd clammed up.

She was extraordinarily sensitive, with a fragile sense of self-esteem, and yet she was also passionately devoted to her studies. I was pretty sure that she had kept her lip buttoned because that had become her way of dealing with stress. But she was also not without ambition — the desire to save the world.

I finally said, "I get it, Tania. I totally get it. You've been hearing me moan and complain about the hassle of this demon mess coming right on top of the wedding and so forth. You can probably also hear the echo of our voices as Alec and I yak and argue and yak and argue. But that's our way of finding compromise. We have to talk it out. We're not mad at each other. Neither of us is going to order the Vigilzhi to start lopping off heads."

Her hands still gripped tightly — but at this last a tiny choke of laughter escaped her.

"I also get that you wanted to save us one more brick from the invisible pile on our shoulders. But we really need to be able to see all the bricks in order to decide which ones to hand off. Okay?"

"Your highness, I'm so sorry…"

"Tania, I'm not asking for apologies. Just for clarity. Your motives were the best, but we have to be able to talk all this out. Okay?"

"Okay," she whispered.

"So, that said, I think we'd better lay off the resonance studies, since I seem to be too thick, or too something, to get what you already see. Let's switch to trying to bring the necklace up in our prisms. I'd so much rather try that than have to try to find it in person. But if we can't by tomorrow, then off we go."

That's what we did, starting right at that moment. I figured there was no better anodyne for awkwardness than getting right back to work.

I remembered the necklace quite clearly from when Aurélie wore it, and I described it as clearly as I could. But it would not manifest in PrismVision. Not even for Tania.

I did catch scraps of crystals and gems that had been in the immediate vicinity over the recent and far past, which nearly made me dizzy before I had to put the energy into shutting them out.

Up front in that grand car, Phaedra never relaxed until we paraded through the palace gates and I was actually deposited, like a sack of mail, in the heirs' wing. She didn't say so, but I think she was boiling to face an enemy she could actually fight.

When we got back to the palace, I tried sketching the necklace for Tania. Then it was time for supper, and Alec was waiting—we were to dine with Milo, Gran, and Mom.

Milo was as fine as he ever was, but the doctors had put him on an even more strict diet than before—and he was not exactly a gourmand. But he ate his sensible, heart-healthy meal uncomplainingly; I noticed from the slight easing of his somber face that he rather liked being gently fussed over by Gran.

When we got back to our suite (early nights were also prescribed for Milo), I said to Tania, who's elected to eat in the suite, "Any luck?"

She shook her head somberly—and then I noticed that she was not alone.

"Ruli," I exclaimed, surprised. "I thought you were gone for good."

"Paris. I have some data," she said abruptly. "Third-hand, but you get what you get."

"Go on," Alec said.

"A source Rose found observed the demons in the Nasdrafus. He wasn't able to determine much beyond the fact that they are not human. He calls them chaos agents made of a kind of vapor."

"Vapor," I repeated. "Their hair was like smoke, that much I remember very vividly. Or fog. Their wings, too."

"Well, there you have it."

I said, "I spoke with the grandmothers today. They all think I need to actually visit the necklace. That it might have things to teach me. Since I can't reach it here—Tania and I really tried on the ride back, and she's been trying—I guess I have to go to Devil's Mountain."

"No," Alec exclaimed. 'It's full of —"

"Inimasang," Ruli finished.

"And bandits," Alec hedged, but we all knew what he'd really meant.

I jumped in before things got awkward: "I've been there before—you remember that, right? Last winter. In the middle of the vampire attack. Tony and I went to close Maritza's rift— which we thought was the entire Esplumoir."

"And vampires chased you all the way back," Alec said

tightly.

"But that was Maritza's vampires. We know that now. They're gone. Or most of them."

Ruli crossed her arms. "Leftovers from Maritza are easily dealt with."

Badass, I thought. Wow.

"Anyway, they rebuilt the ancient shrine, and below that, Tony had a monument raised to Armandros. Percy told me all about it—he designed it. My point being, that some of the mountain people make pilgrimages there. So it's not all *that* dangerous."

"Yes," Ruli said. "I've seen it."

"And I know Phaedra will go right in with me as well," I said. "She and my patrol can guard the trail. Though it's way too steep and narrow for anything more than a single-file slow-as-snail sort of attack. But…" I took his hands, gripping hard as I whispered, "I have to go."

I'd told him on our walk to the king's suite about the meeting earlier. He'd been as appalled as I was—he could easily imagine Milo absently taking off the ring they'd made for him for something as innocent as washing his hands. From Milo outward, all those innocent people…

I added, "We go up there, go to the shrine in the morning, come back right after. One day away. We. Not me alone. Whole team, outer and inner perimeter. Plus I'm sure Tony's people will be on the watch for any hint of vamp action."

What's the worst that can happen? I thought that but didn't say it, because I'd watched way too many movies in which those particular words were followed by the worst, plus ten. So I gave him a sickly, pleading grin anyway.

"All right." He commendably trying to hide his extreme reluctance, and I gave Phaedra a call to get things ready to hit the road first light the next day. I could hear from the lighter tone of her voice that she was champing at her bit.

THIRTY-FOUR

KIM

Next morning, after a few whispered words and a very hard kiss, Alec stepped away, watching me climb into the back of the waiting jeep, where Tania already sat, bearing a huge picnic basket and a couple of thermoses. No fancy princess-mobile. Most of this trip would be mountain roads. Phaedra got in front, sporting both rifle and sword. I had Sting with me— this time, laid across my lap.

The guards took up station around me, two vehicles in front and two behind. Our entourage headed out for the valley, and then the long, winding road up into Devil's Mountain, whose crown was already dusted with a light frosting of snow.

Shortly after noon, the top of the mountain vanished in mist, then gathering clouds. These towered, slate gray shading to blue, and it was clear a heavy storm was moving in, just in time for the last leg of our journey.

I yelled to Phaedra to outrun it if we could. She grinned, taking over the driving herself; I don't know who was up front, but they were the same sort of mountain-trained racer, for on a signal from the guy riding shotgun they punched the speed. This time they laid on the horns, no doubt to warn ox carters and the like to pull over, the way their ancestors had blown horns long ago.

We began spotting the Eyrie's towers when the first drops slapped the windshields. Sleet. Eccch. Just as the storm began to hitch up its slacks and spit on its hands for some serious work, there was the last twist before the Eyrie.

I'd hoped that Tony would be somewhere else, but I wasn't surprised to find him waiting at the gate when our mud-splattered cars rolled through, that long dark-colored duster he'd worn last winter flagging in the wind. I'd told Phaedra not to say anything about our uninvited arrival, and I'd trusted her to do that, but he'd winnowed it out anyway—either that, or more likely, someone in one of those isolated cottages over-looking the road out of Riev reported us, got word to him, and he raced the backways to get there first. Perhaps in sheer self-defense, the mountain people had their age-old ways of passing the word faster than anyone could drive up those narrow, hazardous roads sometimes scarcely wider than cow paths.

Anyway, we were clearly expected.

"Come in," he said. "We've got hot drinks. What brings you up here?"

I accepted tea gratefully, as we settled in the homey room off the Eyrie's smaller kitchen—Tony didn't bother trying to elbow us into one of the fancy (and ice cold) salons. They might keep the entire palace lit like a Christmas tree but they sure didn't heat it, I remembered from winter.

"I've a question for you before I answer yours," I said.

Tony lounged back. Handsome, curly-haired Niklos sat behind him, cleaning a pistol. I couldn't tell if that was a hint, or this was simply their nightly entertainment.

"Ask away," Tony said.

"Who were you going to shoot the other day, when Sig tried to drag me to that portal?"

"Are you expecting me to say it was you?"

"No, but I don't think you would have shot Sig. Anyway, you took aim at the patrol captain. Then I saw you looking around."

"For bloodsuckers."

"You were going to shoot Ruli?"

"No. She'd just alerted us. Sig was acting like someone was pulling the strings. I guessed it was vamps, though the blues seemed clueless. He had to be taking you somewhere. I was on the watch for who would appear for the handoff."

"Okay. The Vigilzhi were clueless because we've kept this matter tight," I said. "I'll fill you in if I don't have to listen to a lot of your usual arguing about how Vrajhus is all in the head, la la la."

Tony circled a hand in the air, his way of acknowledging

that he'd been totally wrong — and knew it.

I told him why my honeymoon had been cut short, and gave a quick rundown on the rest. I finished, "So I guess visiting Armandros's crash site is right out for today."

"Not unless you want to swim. In the dark."

"First thing in the morning, then."

He agreed with a gesture, and shortly after that, took off, murmuring to the hovering house steward to see to us.

I had no doubt that they had the space to host us. Sure enough, once I'd been offered and had turned down the "privy-lege" of resting my royal butt in the royal guest suite, which I suspected would be a refrigerated marble suite couple of miles away from everyone else, we were given a row of normal-sized rooms near Phaedra's.

Tania and I dumped our stuff, and sat down to see if we could find the necklace now that we were physically closer to it. Zip. I didn't know if it was because of the necklace just being really weird with all the charms loaded onto it, or if it was my lack of talent. I was still stinging from my total failure to make the leap in skill to that crystal resonance point that I knew existed but could never quite see.

Percy's lair was just around the corner. He was delighted to find us there, and happily joined us for dinner. Tony and Niklos, I was relieved to see, were absent; I wondered if they were with Sig, who probably wanted to avoid me. I didn't blame him. It would be awkward until time passed, then maybe we could laugh about it. I hoped, because that would mean the danger had been eradicated…

Yeah, a big if, there.

The food was hearty and delicious — plain fare of roasted meat, veg, and spuds, topped with gravy. I ate like a horse, figuring, might as well — who knew what tomorrow's jaunt would bring. Besides being wet. And cold.

After dinner, Percy gave me a personalized tour of the von Mecklundburg gallery, telling me stories about the various ancestors. Our ancestors. When I was at the Eyrie, it was difficult to forget that one of my grandfathers had been the Wicked Count Armandros — local hero.

We passed by the larger-than-life portrait of Pavel Dsaret, who had married the von Mecklundburg duke's daughter a couple of years before he died in the duel. It seemed odd to me that his brother — who had been a reigning king — might return here, of all places, to haunt, but when I asked, Percy said, "All the families were utterly furious after that duel, which was over something trivial. Said any more duels meant permanent exile. Everybody had loved Pavel. Especially his brother. It was believed that they talked mind to mind – including after Pavel died, though I suspect that much was just fancy."

He rocked back and forth from heels to toes as he spoke, hands clasped behind him. He, like Tony, wore his protective charm as a diamond in one ear, and it winked and sparkled. "The talent has always been strong in the Dsaret family, though few of them did anything about it. The demands of being king, I guess."

"Which is probably why it's died out in recent generations," I said, those refractions in his diamond a reminder of my repeated failures.

Percy turned to blink at me. "You really think you have no talent?"

"Oh, I'm thoroughly convinced I got something weird from my Scottish side, what used to be called Second Sight. Or just The Sight. The nasty habit of seeing bits of the past – which the Salfmattas says is totally bad, no good, don't do it. Which might be why my dad's relatives left the Borderlands to go all the way to California, as far from it as they could get."

Percy chuckled. "Doesn't work that way."

"And here's the evidence." I flung my arms out. "Figures, the one thing I can do effortlessly, I shouldn't. But Vrajhus matters? I seem to be a wild card at best. Mom can't do anything at all. Gran, either."

Percy mmmmed softly, then said, "The queen has a great pool of talent, of which she seems unaware."

"Gran?" I said, astonished. "She insists she has none. Wouldn't she know?"

"She might not recognize it – she had no training before she left. But Salfpatra Amiros told me her music is full of it. He said everyone in the palace hears it, and feels the emotion it carries."

I'd wondered idly once or twice how the palace managed to conduct the sound so far along those peaceful halls. I also remembered Gran's dreams of Queen Sofia while she was in the coma, and it occurred to me that Gran had been trying her best to convey all the complexities of her emotions through that music, but as I didn't know who she might have told besides me, I kept silent.

Talent or no, I was hyper-aware that on the morrow I'd be putting it to the test.

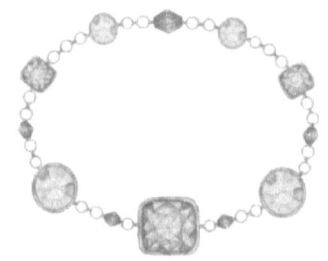

THIRTY-FIVE

KIM

We all retired early. Me to my cold, empty bed on my first night away from Alec. First and only, I vowed, unexpectedly maudlin. As soon as I recognized that ache in throat and heart I scoffed at myself. All my life I'd been perfectly content to be one to a bed. It was even great on hot nights not to have anyone's body heat adding to the sweat-factor, and I could starfish my limbs and be a bed hog as much as I wanted.

But I sure got used to sharing fast.

Anyway, I scolded myself. It's *one night!*

I wrapped my arms around a pillow, which I am here to say is not a sufficient substitute.

After uneasy sleep, with rain battering the windows midway through the night, I finally woke to watery light that resolved into patchy clouds.

Percy greeted us with a splendid breakfast, which included waffles with maple syrup. After I stuffed myself, we rose to go. Percy shambled to the courtyard with us, where we discovered Niklos at the head of a gang of toughs armed to the teeth. "Escort," he said briefly. "Hertsa'vos's orders."

Hertsa'vos being the equivalent of Durchlaucht — the liege-peoples' honorific for a duke. There was no use in arguing, not that I'd wanted to. I was just as happy to let them lead the way; though I'd found my way there by myself once, when I was still in ghost form, I wasn't sure the terrain would be the same two centuries later.

We climbed into our various vehicles then set out.

It was not as far as I remembered. When Tony and I had found the place in winter, we'd crossed horizontally over the face of Dsaret Mountain, coming from the other direction, so I still thought of the locale as being on Dsaret. In fact, the shrine was on a cliff above the great valley that was considered the border between Dsaret and Dhiavilyi. Though these mountains were not like volcanos, or pyramids, each with a distinct rise from ground to point. What I'm getting at is that, what with a couple of old paths having been cleared and widened, we didn't have to cross back and forth so much, and it only took a couple of hours to get there.

I sat up front with Phaedra, leaving Tania in the back seat with our lookout so that she could sweep the surroundings in her prism. I peered at the blue spruce and fir, and the wild tangle of leafless trees hunkered down for the coming winter, and said, "Ruli did promise to come along. But it's daylight."

"She'll turn up," Phaedra promised. "We'll probably find her waiting inside, well out of reach of the sunlight."

"What sunlight," I groused, giving the low, cloudy sky the hairy eyeball.

She snorted. "That's what she did when she went as you to tour those mines during summer."

Since I'd been out for the count, I kept forgetting that that had happened.

Presently Niklos way up front raised his fist in the air to signal a halt. The vehicles parked wherever they could. "From here, it's a single-file path," he called, slid his sword harness over his shoulder, gripped his rifle, and started on down the path, boots splashing in the mud.

I remembered that miserable climb. At least it wasn't thigh-deep in snow, though the mud was like soup, and my shoes were soon crusted, splooshing grittily onto my socks. I glanced enviously at Phaedra's sleek, elegant yet practical boots, then away. I could get some if I wanted them, I reminded myself. The days of a single pair of sandals were over.

Frost here and there promised ice soon, but at least there wasn't any now. The old monument to St. Xanpia had been restored, with a few dried posies laid before it. Above, a much plainer stone monument to Armandros, simply stating his name, birth, and death dates. The rusted detritus of the Russian plane had been cleared away — the metal, if I knew my Dobreni, repurposed.

I still hadn't told Tony about my weird conversation with Armandros's ghost moments after he crashed his plane into the Esplumoir in an effort to undo Maritza's plotting. But now that she was gone, and her rift as well, the ghost had vanished—at least from my view. Tania hadn't mentioned seeing him, either.

I realized I was standing there staring while everyone around me waited, their breath clouding.

"Okay, let's go," I said to Tania and Phaedra, and shot my mittened finger-gun toward the cliff with what I hope looked like confidence and leadership poise. But probably didn't.

The rest took up guard stations around us as we walked into the cave, which smelled like wet stone. Pending winter had not yet shifted the slow-moving air currents to icy. Phaedra had brought a lantern, which she lit. The match flared, throwing light around the striated stone, then the wick took the flame, giving us a warm golden glow that pushed some of the shadows back.

We ventured deeper in over the rough ground, and there was Ruli, perched on a stone slab, immaculate in silk and those stylish shoes. Her hands bare of gloves. "Thank you for coming. Don't you get cold?" I asked.

"Not really," she said. "Though I suspect if the temperature drops significantly past zero, I might have to put some energy toward avoiding getting sluggish."

"Hopefully we won't be around long enough for that," I said feelingly. I'd broken out my winter shoes and socks, but already my toes ached with cold, thanks to the mud I'd taken aboard on the hike down. "Okay. Here we are. The guys outside will keep any demon-driven goons at bay. Phaedra, you're the last line of defense. Ruli, I trust you to strongarm any and all vamp action. Can you?" It occurred to me belatedly that she might want help.

She gave me a funny, twisted smile. "That's why I'm here."

"Perfect. Tania, you're in charge of any sneaky Vrajhus stuff. As for me, I really have no idea what I'm doing, only instinct, but the Elders insist the necklace is here, and I'm the only one it'll talk to, so…here goes."

Here goes nothing, I almost said—but I'd dragged all these people out on this wild goose chase, so I didn't think they'd appreciate my total lack of confidence.

I took out my prism, held it before me, and looked down into it. Light flared, knocking me back a step or two. My balance lurched.

I shut my eyes. Okay, that was weird—especially as the others were looking puzzled. No, Phaedra looked puzzled. Tania's eyes had widened. She'd seen the light, too. But, judging by her silence, nothing else, or she'd have given me a shout-out. Ruli was still and wary.

I pocketed the prism and began to pace the chamber with my hands out. Where had I stood two hundred years ago when Aurélie gave me the thing? I couldn't remember. Not near a wall, I remembered that much...I walked in a small circle, hands swooping slowly through the air as if clearing spiderwebs. Nothing.

I widened my circle, still groping and feeling for that day in the past, and straining my eyes trying to see. Then it was there, just below the level of my nose, a circle in the air as if it lay on an invisible table. I plunged my hand through the loop as if the necklace might vanish on me again.

Color began to fluoresce up my arm, a slow crawl that I stared at in fascination. It didn't hurt. I froze, uncertain if I ought to wait or shake the necklace off, for now it hung from my wrist, swinging a little, lights twinkling and flashing off the facets. Reflecting from nowhere that I could see.

Then the colors reached past my shoulder to my neck—and I stood in space, or maybe floated. I was so overwhelmed by the sudden shift that it didn't occur to me to look down at my body, or even at the necklace.

The nearest I can come to what I saw? When I was about five, my dad gave me a box of Tinker Toys that he'd had as a kid, as my family couldn't afford Legos. I built spiky structures vaguely crystalline in shape, imagination clothing them as castles, bridges, doll apartment buildings (I achieved this by fitting cardboard floors onto the layers to make apartments that the dolls lay on) and the like.

My structures were more or less symmetrical because the little wooden bits only fit together that way, but this before me was mathematically perfect, endlessly so, a little bit like looking at the gentle curve of thousands of reflections between two mirrors, which I discovered when I ventured into an upscale restroom downtown LA, with walls of mirrored glass.

I remembered Aurélie's nightmares, made up of past experiences of necklace holders. In retrospect I think I might have been braced to endure that, only far more intense, for it wouldn't be thirdhand. But that was not my experience.

Perhaps the necklace gave her those to teach a child the consequences of actions? I don't know, only that this was my reality now, to float inside that ordered structure, absolutely captivated by the rainbow flash washing brilliantly around me as my wondering gaze shifted.

First all the shades of yellow through gold, which deepened to an infinity of green hues. Then the planes lost the yellow entirely, transmuting to such an intense blue I thought I'd shot into space. Maybe I had, except the crystal structure had come with me, and I finally grasped what I was seeing: here was that resonance point, all around me?

Then, as if in agreement, or as if a teacher with infinite patience had waited for me to absorb that, I became aware of sound. It was the piercing ring of crystal when struck, and each shade brought forth a different note, always harmonic. As if a vast choir of crystal sang.

I reveled in it until my ever-widening perceptions bumped me against shards of brokenness. After the beauty of the perfect structure, the shattered bits with jagged planes of color spinning aimlessly shocked me cold. Instinctively I nudged one of those shards into the jagged negative space that matched it in shape. Ting! It locked in, the broken line annealed to clarity and vanished with a crystalline ring.

Was that my task, then? Eagerly, I began matching shards together, then fitting them into place. Bing! Ting! When an entire wall was whole again, it added its note to the harmony. Elated, I moved faster, so much faster that my efforts, or energy, caused the randomly twirling pieces to spin faster, moving toward their proper spot as if magnetized. Tink! Bon-n-g-g-g! A deep bell-like reverberation shivered the air as a huge shard slid into place and locked in. Then the pieces spun and fit so fast that I withdrew to watch them rebuilding the broken crystal structure, adding depth and complexity to the sustained harmonic chord —

I got so involved in the infinitely satisfying phenomenon that I forgot everything else until an urgent voice penetrated my euphoria.

"...Kim. Kim!"

That was Ruli.

I had to make myself turn, and discovered with sick shock that I was once again in Paris. Not real Paris. For there were goblins cavorting madly across the courtyard between me and Notre Dame, which was dark and seemed empty — abandoned, even. I remembered: Nasdrafus, where you see what you want to see. I made an effort to see light, and there was candlelight, but weak.

Then I was confronted by the seraphs, taller than I remembered, their wings curving high over their heads. One had black hair and wings, one matte silver, the other ivory. Why the different colors? Was it important to differentiate them, or was that a deflection? Their robes and hair rippled in a wind I could not sense, as the silver one spoke this time. Uriel? *No, don't let them hijack the cultural baggage of those names, as they had a right to them* — as if the names really meant nothing. *The important thing is: they can't hurt me.*

"…your father," the silver one was saying.

My mind labored to catch up. I saw Ruli next to me, looking across the courtyard toward the Seine, except the river had been replaced by rocky, scrub-covered hills striped with vineyards and dotted with olive groves. The tops of the hills here sported marble pillars, and in the distance, the outline of Renaissance castle walls —

And there, on a narrow road, hair and beard flying in a fierce wind, raced my father atop a new motorcycle, a mad grin distorting his face so that he was almost unrecognizable. I had never seen that look on his face. But I had seen that look. On Sig Sigismund.

Was that even Dad? That was his old denim shirt rippling in the wind, and the ratty jeans he refused to get rid of…

"He will just keep going faster until we reach an agreement," the demon said smoothly. "Or he outruns the limits of speed…"

Goblin creatures danced around me, shrieking with laughter. Fury crackled through me, doused somewhat by sharp fear for Dad. Of course he was in danger! We *stupidly* hadn't thought that far. We'd thought the limits of the demons' reach was my proximity. But he was proximate in value, if not in distance. And though the demons were not human, they understood humans enough to use our emotional allegiance against us.

I wanted to use Sting to skewer them all. The swordstick was suddenly in hand — but I caught myself, remembering that they wanted rage. Rage was the easiest to turn to destruction and chaos, and chaos was their energy. And so I turned from the vision, struggling to remember that in the Nasdrafus you *saw what you wanted to.*

I reached mentally past those mock-angelic facades, striving to unsee them. *You are fakes. Show me what you really are.* I reached hard enough that the smoky drifts of hair and feathers melded and then I stared at a churning, roiling cloud. Lightning flared in its center, a nanosecond's image of wicked, glaring eyes.

Right. Here come the terror tactics.

I gritted my teeth and refused to see those.

The cloud swelled, a thousand voices whispering, *He will die on the next turn...we'll show you slowly as every bone breaks and tears...!* And similar horror. Accusations, secret worries, exposed to shrieking mockery. All my faults — especially those others saw in me. Yep, there was Aunt Sisi's cold hatred, and Cerisette's derisive contempt...

I wrenched my mind free of the noxious cascade. Ruli stood beside me, silent. I wondered if they were tormenting her as well.

How to break it? I had to see past what they wanted me to see! But it was so difficult to remember anything with those goblins screaming spittle-splattered invective in my face, and my mind bombarded by whispered exposure of all my fears, doubts, regrets. I retained enough sanity to fight to keep my thoughts away from home and my beloved ones, so that the demons would not have further fuel, but what could I do? What could I...

The necklace.

Still swinging on my arm, because they couldn't touch it. I had to surrender it then there would be peace —

Whose peace?

I caught myself on the verge of an emotion spiral of self-hatred for my ineffectiveness. This was all about the necklace, and what had it *just been teaching me?*

Yet how could I go back and finish repairing the mirror-crystals with Dad speeding faster and faster? I stared into that swelling, towering cloud of... vapor.

Vapor, Ruli had said.

Wasn't vapor part of the chemistry of crystallization? I teetered between fighting the onslaught and my memories of my battered college text, made a tremendous effort to gather my splintering thoughts, and remembered what the necklace had just demonstrated, what, a minute ago? Felt like a hundred years...

Another mighty mental effort. Cringing inside, I forced

myself to my hand — my focus — into the center of that cloud. I pulled out an oily, gritty handful of madly gyrating dirt and gravel and noise, and pinched out a smooth, shiny, obsidian plane. This was it, how crystal formed, wasn't it? Was it?

There!

Another.

It was as slow as an ice age, and more difficult than dragging a boulder by my fingernails, but once I had two planes aligned they notched together with a blue flare that sparked a shriek of metal-sheering roars of rage.

But once two planes had merged in a perfect ninety degree angle, here was a third, then — just as I'd learned in the cave — the stuff inexorably coalesced into orderly planes of glass-smooth ebony planes and snick! The snick became a ting, and as they fitted into crystal as blue as dawn, the ting became a bong. Bongs. Faster and faster, and here was that soundless, liminal resonance that shivered through me as a vast chord sung by an unseen choir. The bits of chaos coalesced faster and faster into a great wheel-like structure in three dimensions. No, more than three —

"…he's safe, Kim. Kim! He's…"

Ruli's voice was distant, fading, leaving profound relief that blended into the mounting joy as the wheel broadened into a measureless superstructure, gently turning. Around me I sensed the Esplumoir settling into place, the weakened frame now seamless, then I found myself spiraling into the growing crystal infinitely beautiful…

THIRTY-SIX

RULI

The gleefully cruel image of Kim's father's blank-eyed, grinning face faded as he regained control of himself — and his racing vehicle. Then the image vanished as the weird cloud of smoke slowly diminished to nothing.

That is, nothing that I could see. Kim saw something else entirely. That much had been evident from the moment she poked her hand into a wobbling bubble of glowing air and suddenly had a nine-stone, golden necklace dangling from her wrist.

She had appeared to be isolated from the tedious stream of human causation that the demons and their minions hurled at her. Its echoes lingered in my mind, a smear of aural trash — unsettling contrast to the bright, wide-eyed wonder in her face.

I reminded myself that this aspect of the Nasdrafus was no desire of mine. I turned to Kim. My experience with her had proved several times over that she did not find her fellow humans tedious at all. Irritating when they threatened her, but it was her nature to find the Lyas and the Waleskas of the world unique. Fascinating. To be cherished for merely being themselves.

These were matters to contemplate later. The Nasdrafus is timeless, but we who can visit in physical form retain a sense of time outside, if we concentrate. And here was Kim, who ought not to be here at all.

I took her wrist and consciously drew her back into that

pulsating rainbow of unearthly light. Which was already beginning to diminish. I did not know what it meant, but I didn't want to risk her getting caught in some "between" state.

It was only a matter of two or three steps. That, and my willing the shift from the unseen world to the seen. Once again we stood in the center of that weird bubble of glowing air, bright enough that I couldn't see beyond it. "Kim."

She did not react. I stepped in front of her, uneasy at that blank gaze, her pupils mere pinpoints. "Kim!"

Where were Tania and Phaedra? The latter could be counted on to snap Kim out, even if she had to shake her. The light was slowly fading, which increased my sense of alarm. I did not know what it was. Or why it was there—perhaps it had protected her living body while we were in the unseen world. But I was convinced that when it vanished, Kim's mind might very well vanish with it, and so I stepped close, and spoke her name distinctly. *"Kim."*

The light pool had dwindled to a spotlight around the two of us. I gave in to the instinct that I had been aware of ever since that night when I staked Jerzy, and there Kim was, coming to the rescue armed with…nothing but her desperate courage.

I had not let go of her wrist. I raised it unresisting to my lips. And bit her.

Only a nip.

She gasped, jerked, then she blinked awareness back into her eyes, and saw me. But even then there was no fear, and I heard the echo of that word, "trust." *Ruli, I trust you to strongarm any and all vamp action.* That was what she'd said.

Was that the true charm? How she created a connection with everyone by genuine interest, unprompted care, and most of all, trust? She simply didn't see the wary respect in the faces of Niklos and those mountain riders ever since she defended Sig, though he'd just tried to kidnap her.

"Whoa," she breathed. "Whoa. That. Was…amazing…"

"Kim?" Phaedra pounded toward us, heels ringing. "It was so murky we couldn't see you!"

I noticed that Tania did not agree with this, but remained silent, looking from me to Kim and back again. Did she see her "ribbons" connecting us? Connecting Kim and everyone she interacted with?

"We did it," Kim said, sounding frazzled. "We did it. The crystal…*thing* was what was needed. I mean, the necklace's charms needed someone to put it all together." She blinked at the golden chain hanging from her hand. "I'm pretty sure it's just a regular necklace now. Well, there might be a few really ancient spells or charms or whatever on it, but—here, Tania. You can have it."

"I couldn't," Tania said, backing away.

"Really, you worked as hard as I did. Also? The Salfmattas are going to want to give it the eagle eye, I'm sure. After they're done, stick it in your keepsake box, if you don't want to wear it. Alec once told me he inherited more jewelry than he knew what to do with, and he wasn't kidding. As his wife I've got enough rocks to sink a battleship, and—I'm babbling. Am I babbling? I'm babbling. I'm just so relieved it's over…" She started toward the entrance to the cave as the last of the light winked out behind us.

Phaedra paced at her shoulder, looking thunderous at being denied the chance to defend Kim against a horde of demon-sent goons.

I remained where I was. I could feel the sunlight, weak as it was, beyond the cave entrance. Besides, I had to consider what I had experienced. For though I had kept myself from drawing her blood, the fangs are sharper than a surgical blade, and I had tasted just a drop. Which was at the same time too little—the temptation was going to be exponentially worse, now—and so, too much. Partly because her blood had brought with it a powerful infusion of that light, and the strength it had imparted—which was far more powerful than the toxic energy burst from a dying vampire.

With that had come a glance into Kim's inner life force…and the two tiny sparks orbiting her like binary stars.

Thirty-seven

Kim

Nobody wanted to spend any more time at the refrigerator-like Eyrie than we had to, so we headed straight for the road. As all our gear was in our cars, that was easy.

Some of my enthusiasm for racing back at top speed waned when we were overtaken by rain, but at least that storm was as brief as it was violent. The sun was sliding behind the western peaks when we crossed the river. Briefly, golden rays shot horizontally across the entire bowl of the central valley, rendering an already beautiful scene so stunning that I, in my still-giddy relief, was taken by surprise as my eyes prickled and my throat tightened.

What's that all about? I have never been a crier. I guess I was just so glad to be done, to be going *home*. Leaving the worries behind me.

The sting was gone by the time we reached the outskirts of Riev. The streetlights had been lit, so that golden glows reflected in pools and puddles on the rain-washed streets. Here and there a wreath had appeared on a door; October 31st, coming soon, wasn't that big of a deal in Dobrenica, but All Saints Day right after it was: in Dobrenica it had become the harbinger of the holidays to come.

As we rolled passed the distinctive, charming buildings, taller ones with mansard roofs — I'd learned that one of Honoré de Vauban's French ancestors had brought that style to Dobrenica — smaller, round cottages in neighborhoods lower on the slope, I had come to love this city in all its variety. The sting in my eyelids was back. Homesick after one day? Wimp! Yet I waited impatiently until we rolled through the palace gates at last.

After we pulled up before the palace doors, I turned to face the patrol. "I know you have to wait for official orders, but I'm telling you now that there won't be any further need for you to shadow me. At least, not for this mess. Thank you!"

A few exchanged comments and jovial words, and they drove off, leaving the three of us to go inside.

Phaedra stalked at my right, grimly humorous. "That's really it? We're done?"

"You were expecting Armageddon, just so you could go up against them all?"

"I...just thought that was a reconnaissance run," she said.

"I thought it would be, too," I admitted. "On the other hand, I guess the actual reconnaissance run was two hundred years ago. We just didn't know it."

She grunted an acknowledgment then marched off with an air of *well, there's always tomorrow.* When I glanced at Tania, I thought I caught her trying to smother a smile.

Alec was waiting at the door to our suite — of course there would have been someone on the watch on the outskirts of Riev to let him know we were on the way.

I hurled myself into his arms as if I'd just returned from ten years in a gulag. And whoop, there was the sting in my eyes again.

"Are you all right?" he asked, after we'd sufficiently kissed each other's faces off.

"Of course I am! I'm just so happy it's over!"

"It's really over?" he asked. "As in, resolved?"

"Can you believe it? I wished I'd gone up there *weeks* ago. Although it might have taken longer," I amended, thinking it over. "I guess all that resonance practice turned out to be worth something, though at the time I never thought I was getting anywhere. But it must have trained something in my perceptions, because the necklace showed me what to do, and, well, I did it."

"Tell me everything."

"A lot of it I can't quite get into words yet," I said. "So much was so weird. But — other than the demons — good weird. Oh. They tried to get at my dad. Well, they did get at him. He was on his new motorcycle somewhere in Italy, and they were forcing him to race faster and faster. If he calls, he might need an explanation for what was going on, otherwise I'll fill him in when he gets back…Argh! I'm telling all backwards."

"Just this first. The demons?"

"Gone. They turned into…something entirely different. I suspect there was…something waiting in that necklace to be triggered off, and…call it the opposite of a bomb, because it was a sneak attack of…um, crystal structure. All it needed was to be put into place. The demons tried to stop me, but they really were entities of vapor, all terrifying bark—well, and slurping up death, let's not forget that—but they were unable to actually bite."

As I said the word *bite*, my wrist twinged. But those tiny marks were already fading.

He gave a nod, then said, "Milo and your family are waiting for us whenever you're ready."

"Okay, let me change, and we can go give them the good news."

I took a California shower—in, soap, rinse, out in record time—and as I dressed, I tried to sort out my still inchoate thoughts. My emotions were all over the place. To be expected! It was aftereffect relief, I thought happily. Sheer relief.

I pulled on a long-sleeved shirt, deciding not to tell Alec immediately that Ruli had bitten me, unless he asked outright. It had been startling, that glimpse of those fangs at my wrist, but I'd known immediately that she'd wakened me out of that glorious headspace. For which I would be endlessly grateful! As it was, I could so easily have tried to follow the newly formed ex-chaos as it floated out into space!

The dinner was full of questions, repeated questions, repeated answers, until everyone was satisfied that this threat truly had been dissolved.

Then he and I retired—neither of us had slept well, it turned out—and we made up for lost time.

After a profoundly good night's sleep, we lay slothfully in bed until the sun was well up, then decided to share the princely bathroom. Though it was ice cold with all that marble, once the gigantic tub was full of hot water it would be heavenly. Best of all, it easily fit two. I still didn't have a lady's maid to do chores that I can do myself, so I turned on the hot water then went into my own annex bathroom to deal with my usual morning stuff; I brushed my teeth, then reached for my birth control pill container. Urk! Which I'd completely forgotten to pack for yesterday's excursion. That was twice in a month!

I grimaced as I flipped it open, then really looked. And looked again. Yesterday ought to have begun Aunt Rose, as Hortense Beauharnais had told Aurélie so long ago. I'd scarcely paid any attention to what was going on down south of my navel when so much was going on up north in Brain Town.

I looked again, then shut my eyes and counted days. Even with the glitchy one, I was already supposed to be in day two...

A really weird feeling serried through my head, and I stared into the mirror to reassure myself it was still me. No one had ninjaed in to replace my head with a stuffed pumpkin.

Then I walked out. Alec was in his plain indigo dressing gown, (I made yet another mental note to get him one with a golden dragon embroidered on the back) watching the tub fill.

"Uh," I said.

He glanced up. "Problem?"

"May-y-y-be?" I tossed him the compact blue container — something Natalie got from the USA.

"I recognize this," he said very tentatively. "But what do you mean by giving it to me?"

"All my life I've been as regular as clockwork," I began and stopped, because the most extraordinary expression had bloomed in his face. I barely had a moment to recognize it as hope before he shuttered behind the familiar blank wall of politesse.

The clue bat finally hit me then. I'd assumed that the Forbidden Subject for him was yet another responsibility about which he was neutral, dispassionate, entirely rational. No, I'd told myself that, because I wasn't ready for him not to be neutral, dispassionate, entirely rational.

I thought I knew him, but I still had trouble understanding that the things he had the most trouble talking about where the ones he felt most deeply. Until this moment, I had not guessed that he wanted a family. Not merely an heir, another duty. A family. Of course there are a lot of ways to have a family. But...

"Welp," I finished uncertainly. "Looks like Gran's conversation is happening now."

"Gran's conversation?" he repeated.

"She cornered me the day after we got back. Heirs. An heir. She's majorly in favor, by the way, and dropped subtle hints like falling pianos that Milo is, too. But accepted that it's up to us."

"Ah." There was a little rise at the end of that exhale of

breath, not quite a question.

I took that as invitation to go on. "Though we're looking at a day and a half late. And considering everything else that's been going on, I suppose that things could be off-kilter… I'm babbling. I've been doing that a lot lately. Um, say something?"

But it seemed that Alec the articulate, who could talk down a rabble on the verge of becoming a mob, was trying to pick over his words.

Then he said, still polite, courteous, careful, "Do you want it to be true?"

Yep, there was my proof: he still was going to keep a lid on his own feelings until he was sure of mine.

Sooo, how *did* I feel?

"Um. Well. The truth is, I've been putting a lot of time and effort into *not* thinking about it. But Gran did say that the Council would be circling around you like vultures, probably sooner than later. Not that it's *any* of their business."

Alec didn't confirm or deny. We stood there, my bare toes curling on the cold marble as I worked my way slowly past the barricades that I had put up. "I love kids! I love babies. I just never thought that it would happen to me — that I ought to be really ready for something so…so mind-boggling. And when Gran reminded me that it's an expectation, a part of my job, I thought, wait till the demons were done for. Wait until we aren't newlyweds, and the country is all settled, and everything is quiet and orderly and we've made plans for every contingency and we're super ready…"

A rueful smile tugged at his lips, though it didn't quite reach his steady blue gaze. "I believed I warned you that there's always something going on. Always."

"Right. You did. Meanwhile, there's the fact that, while we're still young, I'm way past the traditional eighteen-year-old bride. For which I might add I'm incredibly grateful. Everything else aside, you would not have liked eighteen-year-old me."

"This is the first time I'm going to have to flat-out disagree with you." He smiled a little

"Oh, you have no idea. Obnoxious know-it-all, that was me at eighteen. I had the world all figured out, you see."

"I might interject here that that's SOP for being eighteen. But do go on."

"And I would offer my opinion, at length, whether you'd asked for it or not. It took a few more years before I realized I didn't know anything. The Kim you met was just beginning to puzzle that out when Gran got sick. You know the rest."

"And now?"

"And now...can I admit that I'm gob-smacked? Excited? But scared? Don't forget scared."

"But you are not alone," he said, so softly that there was that sting again. Was that hormones up on their hind legs and howling? I began to laugh, blinking against the threat of tears that I refused to let fall, then he took a step and closed his arms around me, and murmured into my neck, "Whatever you want to do. Know that you are not alone."

"Just promise you and Possible-Oven-Bun won't gang up on me."

He laughed, and then everything was okay. And there we were, talking about children. Names. What they might like. What they might hate. Schooling, not schooling, how happy Milo would be, the flood of talk flowing faster and faster.

I had never seen him so happy.

We took that bath—still what-iffing—because time was ticking, and he had to go up to the Vigilzhi to go over the rescheduling. By the time we were dressed and ready for the day, we'd decided not to say anything to anybody. A right couple of prats we'd look, he commented, if Aunt Rose arrived on the doorstep tomorrow.

As it turned out I didn't have much time for sitting around spinning my mental wheels. The sight of Tania ready for the day reminded me that we needed to hand off the necklace to Salfmatta Sarolta, and give them a report on what had happened.

By the time I (with Phaedra and Tania in tow, but not the posse of guards) got to the temple, Beka's great-aunt was waiting for us.

Since I didn't have to define everything, the conversation went pretty fast. Apparently the sensitive ones had detected a change right around the time the necklace's charms shoved me into the Nasdrafus to towel the vapor. Beka arrived, with the rabbi I'd met before, and the two listened intently as I described everything all over again.

At the end, Beka let out a slow breath. "It sounds as if the Esplumoir is sealed against passage of destructive forces, then. Which means, it, like the other two, is once more guarded. The question remains, by whom, exactly?"

Salfmatta Sarolta gave a sober nod. "I'll talk to Sister

Franciscka."

Beka turned to me. "Then we can continue to work with other Vrajhus studies, now that you are not constrained by the threat of demons."

It was on the tip of my tongue to point out that very soon my time might be filled with something radically different, but I looked at the slight marks under her eyes, and remembered her own emotional entanglements. Who knew what turmoil existed in her heart, hidden by that sober exterior? Would my babbling about my possible news hurt her? Too soon, too soon, insisted my inner voice, and so I only agreed about forming a new study schedule, and Tania and I left.

Outside the temple, I said to Tania, "You're the one who stayed up through nights. I'm ordering you to take some time off. Starting now. I'm also ordering you to fit having fun in, whatever else you choose to do."

Tania's sweet smile flared, and she walked off. In the direction of bookshop where her favorite cousin worked, I noted.

"Where to?" Phaedra asked. "Workout? I talked to my brother earlier. He said that Honoré will be at the salle."

"Okay, but first, let's stop by that bakery for one of those tarts I smell, and then I want to visit Nat for a minute."

Phaedra made no comment, and presently I left her lounging in the weak sunshine on Natalie's narrow, quiet street. She was munching a tart and watching the sky suspiciously as Natalie let me in.

"I have half an hour," she said. "What's up?"

I told her.

She let out a whistle. "What I told you was true, pregnancy is rare after a missed day. But it can happen. Either your eggs are really vigorous, or he's got some mighty determined swimmers. Either way, though early pregnancy tests are coming out back in the States, and parts west, I don't have any here. There is the regular test, which is messy—"

I waved a hand. "It can wait. I'm still trying to get used to the whole idea of a possible human life inside me—one I might mess up without meaning to."

"But you're not alone," Nat said, searching my eyes. "I'm not trying to talk you into anything. I'll do what you want. But if you want a sounding board, I'm here. Likewise, I can fill you in on the deets of what to expect."

"That can wait, too. I guess...you're right, of course. Any

kid I have is going to be surrounded by family, and a palace full of interested people. Yeesh, the kid might get spoiled rotten with privilege."

Nat grinned. "I don't think you'll have to worry about that. Might go in the opposite direction, if anything. Milo and Alec being prime cases of Duty Before Fun. But you've got your folks to counter that. And yourself. As for being surrounded by love, well, I'm a firm believer that there is never too much love. Unconditional love."

Unconditional love. For some reason my thoughts winged to Cerisette, who I strongly suspected had been hearing that toxic mom of hers warning her ever since she lost her two front teeth to *never* get fat, to behave like a princess-in-training...

"Right," I said, buoyant with that cloud of incipient worry lifting. Leaving me full of anticipation. Wonder. Even joy. I was *not* in this alone.

"As for what to do meantime: you live a healthy lifestyle, so keep on with it. The time of Victorian ladies retiring to their couches like broken birds is over, and halleluiah to that. If it's a strong implantation, it'll stick even if you have to go charging after demons once more. If it doesn't stick, you try again when you're ready."

I thanked her, we arranged a possible appointment for a month hence, and I went outside again, twirling Sting.

Phaedra straightened up expectantly.

"Let's go duel the boys," I said, laughing.

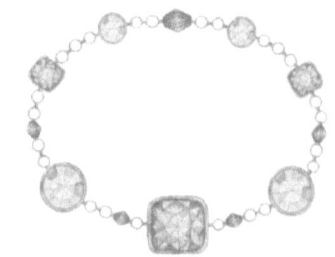

THIRTY-EIGHT

RULI

Kim was still somewhat dazed when they left the cave. I listened to their voices as they departed. Kim was clearly unaware of what I'd seen. I was not certain what to say. If anything at all.

Once darkness fell, the portal, now safe, enabled me to go to Paris, just because I now could. Paris was warmer than mountainous Dobrenica, the air humid, with a whiff of winter on the wind drifting along the Seine. I went to the Marais, where I found Noemi and Perrine preparing to venture out.

Marie-Benoîte hailed me with a smile of welcome. "When you return from roaming, there is an unusual adaptation of Corneille's *Le Cid* at the Théâtre du Marais. I've been longing to see if you think there is one of us behind it."

Intrigued, I promised to return in time for the curtain rising. We chased all the way back to the sewers a gang of young ruffians bent on purposeless mayhem, and shadowed some pairs of oblivious working women until they reached the Metro. It was good to be back.

The play was equally entertaining, though I saw nothing vampirish in the sharp wit of the adaptation. Yet I kept thinking, what would be vampirish? I could not quite characterize it, only that its absence seemed clear in an otherwise adept production.

We talked that over as we sat at the high little tables, drinking our hot chocolate. She saw it in the pessimistic wit, which I explained was common in contemporary theatre. I tried to formulate what I thought might hint at one of us behind a play, fascinated by the idea. "Something that reflects age?" I said.

She wrinkled her nose. "You mean archaic language?"

"Not that. Or only that. Archaic ideas, but presented as current? No, that's not it, either. A perspective that..." I was going to finish with *shows its age*, but stopped, because in my own ears that sounded merely vapid. And yet an idea was there, just out of reach.

We returned to find everyone gathered. Lya's latest obsession seemed to be the TV series *Les vacances de l'amour*, now that her French was improving enough for her to follow along. She seemed to be intrigued by idioms. I was tempted to retire early to avoid the inanities she clearly thought sophisticated, then stopped myself. Could I see in her what Kim saw?

I did see youth, and a forlorn desperation, a need to matter. Is that not true of us all? We are drawn to those to whom we matter. My understanding did not reach beyond that superficiality — and yet I discovered by impending dawn that her voice no longer irritated me.

I was also restless. No one had asked about my quest to my homeland. I needed to talk about what I'd seen. What I'd learned. Because my room in Paris was far more comfortable than the various hideys in Dobrenica, I spent the day there. At night I changed and returned to Riev, savoring the freedom from having to toil overland, always aware of the sun's position.

There is never much traffic in Riev, and when there is, more than half of it is horse, ox, or even goat-drawn carts or carriages — until winter, when the trained reindeer come down to pull the inkri sleighs. Nights when the weather begins to chill find few out. Thus Riev is quiet under its lovely street lamps.

I set out to make my old rounds. It felt as if years had passed instead of a few weeks. That seemed a very human realization.

Though there were changes. Gretl's house now had a different family inside. I hoped she had found contentment elsewhere; I did not care about him. In that house where once I had sensed fear and pain, I heard normal chatter, adult and child.

I went on to Lisi's. Ah, here was no change on the surface, and yet a subtle change in that again I smelled no fear, pain, or sorrow. Lisi and her man sat over dinner, and I saw her laughing. At least for now they had apparently found their way to whatever worked for them, though I know from experience the longing for alcohol can overcome the longing for affection, connection, even respect.

Above the now prettily decorated little spice shop on Prinz Karl-Rafael Street, there was still fear in Sareska, but much diminished. No pain. When I looked into the windows, it became clear that the sister now ruled the household. The wretch Sareska had married lumbered like a grumpy bear, but he was not drunk. Or raging. Not any sort of relationship I would have wanted to be part of, but those were their lives. Not mine.

That is, if I'd been alive in the proper sense of the word.

"I thought I might find you here," Rose said, tripping up to me, her fringed silk rippling about her slim ankles above her chic kitten heels. "Persistent, aren't you?"

"And so are you," I replied, indicating the street: after all, *she* had come to find *me*.

She smiled, and I said, "Are you ever going to speak to Lily?"

Rose regarded me with interest, her head in its cloche hat tilted. "Why do you care?"

"I like what I've seen of her," I said.

"You would." Rose made a moue with her lips. "Though you are one of us, there is a lot of the Dsaret duty in you."

I laughed at that. "Says Rose *Dsaret*."

"Ah, but I never had that dull sense of duty that made Lily so perfect. Always held up to me as an example of what I ought to be!"

"Did she do that?"

"Of course she did."

"Always, or did she stop?"

"Does it matter? If you must know, she stopped when we were, oh, ten or so, but she didn't have to nag. Her silence was a rebuke in itself. Perfect Lily! Everyone said so. And yet she was an utter failure."

"At sixteen," I said. "She's long past the choices she made then, in both age and experience."

A round shoulder came up. "And that is why I don't speak to her. We have nothing whatever to say to one another. Armandros was fun, and fun-loving, and he ought to have been mine. Milo was perfect for her—both more dutiful than the other. But she! She had to have *everything*. And look what it got her."

I could have pointed out that whatever had gone on between Armandros and Lily had been a two-way street, but that was well over half a century ago — even if Rose had married him, the Germans still would have come. And he still would have gone off to fight them, then the Soviets afterward…

As I looked into her smooth, seventeen-year-old face, for the first time I wondered what it had been like for her to live in the shadows and watch her old life trampled under German jackboots, family members rooted out and killed one by one unless they escaped to the hills, or out of the country altogether. She did fight back by preying on the Gestapo, but that did not restore the dead to life. Did one's emotional capacity truly halt at whatever physical age one was at when bitten? But then freezing at one emotional age was an entirely human trait — especially after extreme trauma.

She went on in that sweet, teenage voice, "There is no triumph in parading my youth before her now that she's old and hideous. One day soon she'll lie beside Father and Mother, Milo with them. She has no moral ascendance that I see."

"I doubt that she'd try to establish it, were you to speak to her. Or Kim would be quite different; Lily shared the raising of her. Maybe even the lion's share."

"Her?" Rose shrugged more sharply. "She's more duty-driven than any of them. Quite tedious, your heroic Kim."

I could see then that Rose was determinedly in a mood. She wanted entertainment, not whatever this conversation was. And yet she was not merely âme de boue. Butterfly, that had been my internal label for Rose. But there was no longer any disparagement. Butterflies are beautiful, they are what they are. And she does actually look out for us, in her butterfly way. Perhaps the only way she'd been able to, after the devastation of war and years of occupation. She could have gone to be elegant and carefree in any other place in the world — but she'd stayed here.

"She's a hero to them." I waved toward the quiet city. And, as I expected, she rewarded me with a little gesture meaning c'est la vie, and tripped away.

With Kim's image there before me, I decided to stop avoiding her and went to the palace, where I listened for her distinct heartbeat. To my surprise, I did not find it in the heirs' wing. No one was there.

I discovered Kim in the gallery, holding up a lantern as she studied the portrait of Queen Sofia. Remembering that she startled easily, I let her hear my heels ring on the floor.

She looked up, and there was that instant smile of welcome, completely unconscious. Uncalculated. "Slaymate!" she greeted me.

"Slay what?"

"Phaedra was the one who came up with it, actually. Like that TV show, *Buffy*? You're a vampire *and* a slayer. Or is it too on the nose?"

I laughed, a little flattered, in spite of myself, that she'd be thinking of me at all. "What are you doing in here?" I asked. "Isn't it cold for you?"

"Alec is hosting the Vigilzhi in thanks for all the extra hours they put in. No one says it, but I suspect they're a lot like Phaedra — disappointed not to have at least had a pitched battle of some sort. I could have gone, but it's all guys. And," her voice lowered slightly, "there'll be drinking."

That seemingly innocuous statement was very self-consciously said.

"Ah. You figured it out already?" I asked, relieved that the secret was in fact no longer a secret.

She looked over quickly. "Figured..."

"You're pregnant. I saw them quite clearly. As sparks," I hastened to add. "Nothing more than that."

"Them?" she repeated.

"Two. Identical sparks. At a guess, I'd say identical twins. But then those do run through the Dsaret line, don't they?"

"Two," she said softly. "Alec's already so happy, I guess I'll find out if utter happiness can double."

"Well, he always wanted a family," I observed. "Now he'll get one all at once. Very efficient of you!"

She turned to me, serious now. "So he admitted. Finally. I feel pretty stupid for not having figured it out. Or talked about it."

"Takes two to talk," I said. "And he's an expert at deflection."

"True. But I ought to have seen it. Or maybe I did and didn't want to see." She looked troubled.

"Accept half the responsibility for that silence, not all. You know he's very capable of stating what he wants or doesn't want. But this subject mattered to him — why do you think he was with us so much when we were small? Before Jerzy did away with my very nosy Aunt Eve, Phaedra's mother, I overheard her laughing about Alex with the other aunts. He'd told Milo that the only thing he wanted for Christmas was a brother. My mother volunteered to host him as often as Milo wished, which I strongly suspect he accepted partly to give Alec the family that he craved, and partly to foster peace."

"Alec told me about that last. But not about asking for a brother as a present."

"He might not remember. We were all pretty small. I can see now that when Maman realized she wasn't going to steer him—he was too much like Milo—she tried her best to put Tony and me forward, and thrust the cousins back so he wouldn't favor them some day. At the same time, undercutting him, especially with Tony, to prevent them from allying against her."

"That's pretty poisonous," Kim said, grimacing.

"Are you surprised?"

"Nope." She looked away, and up at the portrait as she blinked rapidly. "When we do tell everyone, Alec warned me that they're going to ring the bells. How embarrassing is that?"

"Welcome to living in the fishbowl," I said. "Speaking of. What brought you to want to contemplate our respected greats-grandmother again? Didn't you meet her in the flesh?"

"I've met her in the flesh, and as a ghost. I was wondering why she *was* a ghost. She had a long and satisfying life, if anyone did. Except that we were still in the Nasdrafus when she died. Margit insisted she always believed that Jaska was alive. I wondered if she wished herself there in dying, to find him. But that wouldn't explain her appearing to me in Vienna. Or to Gran."

She shivered suddenly, and turned away. "I guess it is getting cold. Anyway, I was looking at her, and thinking back over meeting her. And what happened in the Nasdrafus that time. Before and after I saw you. How little we knew about portals. Still a mystery, really."

"You can't go into the Nasdrafus now that the necklace has discharged its duty," I said.

"I know: instant Smrekar. Oh! Sorry. Private joke—and I know how obnoxious those are. Sorry again! But I like to understand. Elisheva found portals in her prism. I don't know if I could do that. Just to *learn*. The entire country seems to be full of them. LA, for all its size, only had a couple, right?"

"I didn't detect any beyond the ones Lya found. She's the portal expert," I said. "Just regard them as lightless mirrors: dangerous, bad, do not go."

Kim nodded soberly. "I'm not tempted to try that weird mirror at the Eyrie. I don't even want to go in that little alcove again. But...I wish I knew who guards the Esplumoir. There was an implication that somebody does. Or some *thing*. Right?"

"I was wondering that myself," I said. "Maybe the Elders will turn up some musty scrap about that, buried in some cave. I know they keep looking. Beka will surely know."

She nodded, shivered again, and we parted, she running back to her warm rooms and her happy life.

Life.

I thought I might as well return to Paris — either of them. There was the prospect of going to the Sorbonne in the Paris of the Nasdrafus, and finding Gervais, to discuss investing my funds. Who knows, he might turn out to be interesting on subjects beyond banking. Then there was the physical Paris, and the women in the Marais. I had work I enjoyed there.

Ah, choices! I was not nearly done with appreciating the restored ease of going back and forth between Paris, or any other place that caught my interest, and Dobrenica.

There was also my room at von Mecklundburg house, whose windows required blackout before I could rest there. But that was a lot of labor I was not in a mind to do now, so I returned to the Eyrie, intending to use its portal.

But I found Elena up on the ballroom balcony, waiting. The atmosphere in the icy, dark space was far colder than mere impending winter; the unlit chandeliers glimmered like ice crystals.

"You bit her," Elena said, with her rare smile. It had no humor in it whatsoever. "Was it good?"

"It was a bloodless bite."

"But you tasted it anyway." Her laugh was soundless — she wasn't going to trouble to draw in breath for me, unless she wanted it to be chilling. A flash of fangs only. "That old necklace left its traces in her. You could use that power."

"To do what?" I said.

"You could form your own family. You could rival me."

"Frankly? That sounds boring," I said — because it was tempting. If only to be rid of her and her posturing. But then what? Set myself up as some sort of vampire queen for someone else to challenge?

Her form was slight, shorter than I, but she exuded power. Usually it was a smoldering power, like a banked fire. Elena was an elemental, I sometimes thought. Ancient — very little trace of whatever humanity she'd had when bitten, full of fire. Fire is a dangerous but alluring element, and a useful one. Her harem of inimasang all circled that fire like an army of moths.

But the sense of power surrounding us was far colder, and I understood then that *he* was here: the one called Antonius Augustus, older still. I had no idea if that was his human name, a vampire cognomen, or a title. Whenever I sensed his presence, I always remembered that the tallest mountain in Dobrenica is Mt. Antonius.

"There is no human audience here for you to convince you are unchanged," Elena said, her voice thin and derisive. "Would you not like to draw in pure life essence? So very much more powerful. That's partly why I left Maritza's vermin to you, to teach you."

"You were testing me," I said. "But I'm just not interested in whatever you were testing for."

"Your allegiance to your humans is pathetic."

"I don't see how what I do, or think, matters to you," I returned.

"And so," a soft voice, cold as moonlight on steel, murmured next to me, "as they close ranks in mutual congratulation, they will still distrust you."

The light limned the splendid bone structure of eye socket and cheekbone, half hidden by long, silvery hair. He must have been old when bitten; the shape of that skull, the curl in the hair, reminded me of Greek statues.

I had never spoken to him before, nor had he spoken to me. I'd even been constrained from speaking about him. Though I thought about it, and pushed past that now as he continued, "My suggestion to you is to retire to the Nasdrafus and enjoy yourself. Don't come out for fifty years. They'll all be gone, and you will begin to gain perspective."

I thought of the promise I'd extracted from Kim, and the thought of never seeing her again, or Percy, or Phaedra with whom I'd fought side by side, even my exasperating brother, hurt deeply. I sucked in a breath, relishing this remnant of human action attended by emotion, painful as it was. In that moment I was alive again, or as near as I would ever come.

As if he read my mind—he probably did—he said, "Every time you see them again, you will be forced to begin anew."

Not with Kim, I thought. But I was not about to tempt this ancient being by bringing up her name. "Then I'll begin anew," I said.

"And yet again," the inexorable voice continued, amused, dispassionate. "*And* again, as you watch them wither toward old age and death."

Elena, the elemental sycophant, added her voice, "And afterward, with a new pet? And for what?"

"For love," I replied. "And maybe for honor, too. Both of which I discovered too late, or I might not be here now. But since I am, I will revel in my strength. I can relish their happiness."

"Transitory," Elena mocked, the glow in her eyes leaping brighter. "No one cares. No one will care."

I remembered my father consoling me once, when I'd run to him after Maman had been especially cruel. "'If I have not love, I am nothing. If I give away all I have, and if I deliver up my body to be burned, but have not love, I gain nothing,'" I quoted.

Elena uttered a growl of aversion. "You're still wet. We'll talk again in a century."

And she was gone, leaving me to remember my father's voice rising and falling: *Love is patient and kind... Love bears all things, believes all things, hopes all things, endures all things.*

Love never ends.

I was surprised that that shadowy figure was still waiting. So I spoke. "This is what I recently learned. Life is like a candle touched from wick to wick. Before one burns down, the fire can spread to two. And four. Love is the same way," I said, not unafraid, because I knew he had the power to extirpate me without moving his hand. But—belated—a little of the family penchant for risk had woken in me. "It might take some effort. But love never ends."

"Then guard them," he invited, and was gone.

ACKNOWLEDGMENTS

With grateful thanks to my eagle-eyed Patreon Readers.

About the Author

Sherwood Smith studied in Europe before earning a Master's degree in history. She worked as a governess, a bartender, an electrical supply verifier, and wore various hats in the film industry before turning to teaching for twenty years. To date she's published over fifty books, one of which was an Anne Lindbergh Honor Book; she's twice been a finalist for the Mythopoeic Fantasy Award and once a Nebula finalist. Her YA fantasy novel *Crown Duel* has been in print for over twenty years.

She reviews books at Goodreads and blogs intermittently at Dreamwidth.

Find her at Patreon: www.patreon.com/user?u=6632848

Visit her website, www.sherwoodsmith.net, and sign up for her newsletter at www.subscribepage.com/s5n1x6 to learn about new books!

About Book View Café

Book View Café is a professional authors' publishing co-operative offering DRM-free e-books in multiple formats to readers around the world. With authors in a variety of genres including mystery, romance, fantasy, and science fiction, Book View Café has something for everyone.

Book View Café is good for readers because you can enjoy high-quality DRM-free e-books from your favorite authors at a reasonable price.

Book View Café is good for writers because 90% of the proceeds goes directly to the book's author.

Book View Café authors include New York Times and USA Today bestsellers, Nebula, Hugo, Lambda, Chanticleer, National Reader's Choice, and Philip K. Dick Award winners, World Fantasy, Kirkus, and Rita Award nominees, and winners and nominees of many other publishing awards.

BOOK♨VIEWCAFE

bookviewcafe.com

www.ingramcontent.com/pod-product-compliance
Lightning Source LLC
Chambersburg PA
CBHW020602110726
47899CB00002B/331